Atlantis in the 21st Century

1st Chronicles

By

Keith Burnett

Forward

This series of books is written for tweens, teens and the young at heart of all ages. As I object to the "dumbing down" that seems to be going on these days, the vocabulary is advanced for tweens, and early teens. I have no apologies for asking them to stretch. My wife and I have ten grandchildren, and stretching is good for them – it's what dictionaries are for. They may need a dictionary as they read this, but that won't hurt them any – I promise.

This work is based on current events as well as events lost in the mists of time that could well have been true. This is a work of science fiction / fantasy … or … not. Let's take a look at some of the facts forming the foundation for this series of books:

1. In ancient Greek, Atlantic means "out where Atlantis is." The ancients called that ocean the "Atlantic Ocean" because they believed that was where Atlantis was.

2. In his book *Atlantis: The Antediluvian World*, Ignatius Donnelly assumed that Plato's description of Atlantis was an historical fact. You can read the text of that description in Wikipedia. While Plato's description certainly sounds factual, he was writing about events that he believed had occurred many thousands of years earlier. While it is entirely possible that Plato believed his account to be true, oral traditions going back that far are rarely accurate. All that can be said is that it is entirely possible that something happened. The question is what?

3. Approximately 10,000 years ago the rate at which human civilization was progressing seems to have accelerated. No one has adequately

explained why. This acceleration correlates with Plato's account of Atlantis. Could the two be related?

4. Language scholars have determined that the mythology of the Greek, Roman, Celtic, Norse, and Indus cultures had a common precursor. All of these mythologies sprang from a common source these scholars have called the Proto Indus European Mythology. This mythology first appeared about 10,000 years ago. Is this a coincidence?

5. If all of these ancient religious beliefs are related, how did a common belief get started across all of these diverse cultures?

6. Most of the mythologies that come down to us today could be explained by individuals from primitive civilizations witnessing advanced technology.

7. The legends of the Tuatha de Dana, which is Celtic Mythology, actually have a story about crafts that hover over the water and have lights shining forward to light their path at night. How does a primitive stone age Celt come up with something like that out of his imagination? Not even Jules Verne made such a leap.

8. The very earliest stories about the Norse God Thor who had a "hammer that could kill like a thunderclap" could have easily been a primitive attempt at an explanation of someone holding out a gun and firing the gun. Is this another coincidence?

9. The acceleration of the rate at which we were civilizing seems to be correlated with the appearance of the Proto – Indus – European Mythology, AND with legends of the appearance and subsequent disappearance of Atlantis. Maybe this is a coincidence. Maybe not.

10. Many of what are called UFO sightings have been de-bunked. Many is not that same as all. Some, have never been adequately explained. Could this be wrapped into all of the other coincidences?

11. Any way you want to slice it, this is a lot of coincidences. Is it possible that what comes down to us as mythology was actually an attempt by the people of that time to record and understand what they had actually seen?

These are all good questions. This is a work of fiction, but no one can prove that something like this did not happen and is not happening now. The names of individuals and companies in this book are all fictional and any resemblance to actual persons or companies is purely accidental. As for the rest ... all of our most cherished childhood legends came from somewhere. Where? Was it our imagination, or could it have been something else?

The first goal of _Atlantis in the 21st Century_ is to tell an entertaining story. But there is another goal. That goal is to incite curiosity in young people ... curiosity about science, the environment, the events of history that shape who we are today, and a body of literature known as "mythology." Could "mythology" actually be a primitive form of history? Could the people of those times have been attempting to record things they did not understand? No one knows the answer to that question but I believe that curiosity will be served.

Atlantis in the 21st Century

Release Schedule

- 2nd Chronicles – October 1st, 2013
- 3rd Chronicles – April 1st, 2014
- 4th Chronicles – October 1st, 2014
- 5th Chronicles – April 1st, 2015
- 6th Chronicles – October 1st, 2015
- 7th Chronicles – April 1st, 2016
- 8th Chronicles – October 1st, 2016

The League of Atlantis

Release Schedule

- 1st Chronicles – April 1st, 2017
- 2nd Chronicles – October 1st, 2017
- 3rd Chronicles – April 1st, 2018
- 4th Chronicles – October 1st, 2018

This book is dedicated to my wife Mary. After all of these years, and more miles and trials than anyone can count, I still wonder how this geeky awkward boy got so lucky.

Prolog

A tall elegant gentleman walked along the ridgeline path in the solitary silence of a misty mountain morning. The sun had barely risen in the east, bathing the peaks with the golden glow of warmth that would soon melt away the wisps of mist. It was a lovely morning but the man took little notice of the beauty that surrounded him. He absentmindedly fingered his belt as he walked the ridgeline deep in thought.

If asked for identification, he could have produced a Tennessee Driver's License stating his name as Herald Gordon, but that was not his name. That Driver's License would have shown a Knoxville, Tennessee address, and although the house at that address was real enough, it was not his home. To any casual observer the home appeared lived in on a seasonal basis, but no one actually lived there. To that same observer, the man on the ridgeline path would appear normal enough, but he was not normal.

His real name was Heraldon Glorfyndor, and he was a member of the High Council of Atlantis. He walked a ridgeline trail in the Smokey Mountain National Park lost in thought because there was trouble coming. Real trouble. The kind of trouble that would change everything. For thousands of years his people had remained hidden and that had worked out well, but the situation was about to get bumpier. There was no way to avoid it. At the rate at which the people of Earth were developing their technology, they would discover the people of Atlantis in another sixty-five years or so and that meant trouble was coming.

Over ten thousand years ago, when his people first arrived, there had been the necessary period of adaption to the pathogens and basic nature of the earth environment. He smiled as he thought of H.G. Wells' book *The War of the Worlds*. It was a great story and in the end the Earth's bacteria killed the invaders. Of course his people had known that would happen and were prepared for it. Any civilization with a technology capable of making the trip would have known how to deal with bacteria which was why he was smiling. That misunderstanding did not alter the excellence of the story.

Although the pathogens and ecosystems of earth were remarkably similar to that of his homeworld Atlantis, there were enough differences that assimilation took some time, almost a hundred years altogether. The hardest part was the genetics. Atlantan DNA turned out to be 99.97% similar to that of the people of Earth. But that .03% difference was significant. Atlantans were slightly more intelligent, slightly more creative, slightly more able to process spatial reasoning and the chains of facts that result in technology, and the decision had been made to virally adapt the earth people's genetics to precisely match the Atlantan variety.

Once that was accomplished, contact with the people of Earth was begun but the original inhabitants here had been immature. True civilization had only begun to develop and superstition ruled the day. The Earth people had been afraid of chariots that could fly … and strange lights in the sky. They did not understand the difference between magic and science, between supernatural power and the wonders of technology. Such distinctions were beyond their grasp. They had believed the Atlantans were gods, and either left them alone, or worshipped them. The only moral choice the people of Atlantis could make was to disappear.

Rather than build their civilization above ground as a beacon, they delved deep under the earth and built there. In time the thunder of the explosions excavating the underground cities stopped, the lights of the transport flitters carrying materials to and fro disappeared, and the chariots that could fly were seen no more. A rich literature of interesting but harmless mythology remained but that was all.

Although most of those ancient people had been afraid of the "Gods" and had largely left them alone, that had not been true in all cases. There had always been some venturesome souls whose curiosity overwhelmed them, but their encounters with the people of Atlantis had long since entered the realms of mythology as well.

Ten thousand years ago, most of the people of Earth had left alone the few Atlantans they came into contact with. Heraldon Glorfyndor knew that would not be the case in this day and age and that was the problem. What would happen when the presence of Atlantis was finally discovered by the people of earth, the planet his people, the people of Atlantis, had always known as Earthantis? When the authorities of Earthantis learned about the existence of Atlantis how would they react? Hard to tell, but one thing was certain ... the people of Earthantis would not leave the people of Atlantis alone, not in this day and age.

Heraldon Glorfyndor knew that his people had nothing to fear from the military arsenal of any nation on Earthantis. If necessary that could be dealt with easily enough, but he didn't think it would become necessary. Atlantis simply had too much to offer for military threats to make any sense, and if any arose they would be resolved in a matter of hours, but there were difficulties all the same … large ones. It was not just the technical gap, which was enormous. The cultural gap between his people and the people of Earthantis was nearly as wide and the wider these gaps when the discovery came, the harder this process was going to be. Was there a way to help the people of Earthantis grow? A way to make this gulf less wide? A way to make this transition easier? They had, perhaps, sixty, maybe sixty-five years. What could be done?

It was a difficult question worthy of a great mind.

He nodded slowly to himself as he walked and the glimmer of an idea began to form. He turned on his heel and headed back, a smile replaced the furrowed brow of concentration. There was work to be done. A lot of work.

Chapter One

The Selection

Paul Andrews sat at a battered old desk looking out a window of the Fourth Street Middle School in Calumet City, Illinois. He had no idea that his teacher was observing him ... or why. Oh, he knew that she would occasionally look in his direction, or ask him a question. All teachers did that, but he had no idea that she was paying special attention to him, recording nearly everything he did, and he certainly had no idea she was transmitting this information to a place he didn't even know existed. If he had, and if he had known what was at stake, he might not have been gazing out the window. Paul was trying not to look bored, but that was hard under the circumstances. His eighth grade English teacher, Ms. Merrill, was teaching the class how to diagram sentences. At the moment she was doing gerund-participle phrases, and Paul was hopelessly bored. He sat there wishing he was outside playing baseball ... or basketball ... or football ... or soccer ... or tennis ... or anything.

Diagramming sentences was bad enough, but Ms. Merrill was going over it for what seemed like the tenth time, and that was worse. Paul didn't know why she was so repetitious today. Normally her class wasn't boring. He supposed it had something to do with the Achievement Tests that were coming up.

Ms. Merrill had been his English teacher for two years now, and she had become his favorite teacher. That was not so much because he liked English, but because she was also his Science Fair advisor, and science was his favorite subject. He traced his fingers over the initials "B.J." that some other boy had carved in the desk. He was completely unaware that the reason Ms. Merrill was being so boring had nothing to do with achievement tests.

Ms. Merrill knew quite well that Paul wasn't paying attention, although he didn't know that she knew. She was far too well trained for that. She had learned a lot about him in two years. The boys and girls she selected had to meet some carefully developed criteria and there was one final test. Could this boy learn something truly boring, or was he only good at what he was interested in? That was the final test. If Paul was "selected" he was going to have to learn a whole lot of things, some interesting, some maybe not so much.

"Paul," she said without warning, "can you come to the board and diagram a gerund-participle phrase for the class please?"

Paul walked to the chalk board completely unaware of the effect this test would have on his life. He picked up a piece of chalk, diagrammed the sentence, it wasn't even hard, and walked back to his seat.

What Paul did not know was that the middle-aged teacher he knew as Ms. Merrill was not what she seemed to be. Not at all. In reality she was Carolicia Merilyndor, a citizen of Atlantis ... a "Selector" for the High Council and he, Paul Andrews, had come to her attention. Not only that, but as he whipped out the sentence diagram, more or less correctly, he passed her last test.

The bell rang, signaling the end of the school day, and the class broke. Carolicia Merilyndor walked to the window. A few minutes later the students began pouring out of the building, and as always she was watching.

Carolicia softly hummed the bars of the tune that would open the Comm Channel of her communicator. She wore a simple necklace around her neck that had several functions. One of them was a very sophisticated communication device. It responded to an audible signal, and would connect her to the Comm Center in Co-re-alis, the Atlantan City buried deep beneath the Smoky Mountains of eastern Tennessee. The channel opened and she gave her final report on Paul Andrews. Anyone watching would think she was muttering to herself.

Ψ

School had been out for a month. It was Wednesday morning and even though school was out, Paul was getting ready just like he was going to school. In a way he was. He had won the Eighth Grade Science Fair, and as one of the rewards, he and the other winners were going on a special behind the scenes tour of the Shedd Aquarium. Among other things, they would have scuba lessons and then get to swim with the Beluga Whales. He was really looking forward to both. He and his advisor, Ms. Merrill, got to go, and he was meeting her at the school. He finished combing his hair, kissed his Mom goodbye and set off.

Paul walked onto the parking lot and saw Ms. Merrill. She waved and as he walked toward her he noticed she was accompanied by another young woman … one he did not recognize.

"Hi, Paul," Ms. Merrill said, "This is Erinlicia Flyndor"

Paul shook hands with the lady noting the strangeness of her name.

"Here," Ms. Merrill said and handed him a wide belt woven of silver, gold, and blue metal strands. It had a large medallion made of a burnished metal he did not recognize with some sort of symbol on it. Paul figured it had something to do with the wetsuits they would have to wear at the aquarium. "Can you put this on?" she asked. "It won't go through your belt loops so just wrap it around."

"Sure," Paul answered, taking the belt and assuming she wanted to make sure it fit before they left for the aquarium. "Erinlicia, that's an unusual name," Paul commented pleasantly, as he wrapped the belt around his waist. "What's the belt for?"

"We'll get to that soon enough," Ms. Merrill answered, as the other lady smiled knowingly.

He brought the ends of the belt towards each other and much to his astonishment the two ends jumped together, buckled themselves all by themselves and then the belt shrank to fit his waist. He looked up with a startled question in his eyes.

"Paul," Ms. Merrill interrupted quickly taking one of his hands, "Watch the way I am tapping my fingers together?" She took the first three fingers of her left hand and tapped them with the thumb. "Can you do that?"

"Sure," answered Paul, still not realizing what was happening. He reached out and tapped his fingers as she had shown him, "but…"

"OK," she continued, not giving him a chance to ask the question. She pointed a ring on her hand at the belt buckle Paul was now wearing and said "Activate." A blue-green light came from the ring and the symbol in the center of the buckle changed colors.

Paul's eyes got even wider.

"Now, Paul," she went on quickly, "Get a mental picture of our classroom, and tap you fingers like I showed you."

"Why?" he asked.

"You'll see," she answered once again, "You'll see, Paul, I promise."

"OK," he said with a shrug. He visualized the classroom and tapped his fingers together as she had instructed. Suddenly he was in the center of a kaleidoscope of vivid colors dancing and swirling all around him. The swirling colors seemed to last only an instant, and then, just as suddenly they disappeared and he was standing in the middle of the classroom he had just visualized. Seconds later both of the women appeared.

"Whoa ... " Paul managed to say. It was difficult to believe the evidence of his own eyes. A second ago, he had been in the parking lot, and now he wasn't. He walked over to his desk and touched the initials "B.J." that had been carved there. They had the same feel and texture that they always did. He was in fact standing in the classroom. The question was how he got there. He turned and looked back at the two women.

They just smiled. "We'll start to answer your questions now, Paul," Ms. Merrill said, still smiling, "And by the way, my real name is not Carolyn Merrill. It is Carolicia Merilyndor." She took out the elastic that had contained her hair in an old-fashioned bun, and shook her head. Long light brown hair cascaded around her shoulders. The other woman took a small long tube from the belt she was wearing. It resembled Harry

Potter's wand. Suddenly a light shined out from the wand and on Ms. Merrill. The light was a pale blue color. Suddenly, as Paul watched, all of the signs of age melted away and instead of someone who was fifty-something, a much younger woman stood in front of him.

At first Paul was far too stunned to say anything at all. "What is going on?" he gulped and finally managed to ask.

"As I said, Paul," she continued after the transformation was complete, "My real name is Carolicia Merilyndor. This is going to be hard for you but, Erinlicia and I are from Atlantis."

"Atlantis?" Paul managed to say. For all practical purpose he was speechless.

"Why don't you sit down, Paul" the woman who had been introduced as Erinlicia said pointing to the front row of desks. Her voice was melodious and sweet, "And we'll explain all of this."

Paul walked over to one of the desks and began to sit down. He turned, realizing he still had the belt on. "Did this belt bring me here?" he asked.

"Yes," answered Erinlicia, "It is called a Transport Belt."

"And you guys are from Atlantis ... the Lost City of Atlantis?"

"Yes, Paul, we are," she answered with a grin and a toss of her head, "But it's not "Lost". We know exactly where it is."

Paul sat down. "We are not actually going to the Aquarium today are we?" he asked

"Well ... we can if that is what you want," she said with a smile. "But we have in mind a place you might find a lot more interesting."

"Where?" he asked.

"Atlantis. Why don't you hold all of your questions a minute and let us explain," Erinlicia Flyndor suggested with a broad grin. "It will be easier that way."

"OK," Paul agreed with a shrug of his shoulders.

"We are originally from a planet called Atlantis," the woman named Erinlicia Flyndor explained, "In a star system which we called Co-re-alis about four thousand light years from here. Atlantis was similar to your planet in almost all respects." She paused for a second. "Our sun was going to explode, and we had to abandon our world. Our Starship, named Atlantis after our home planet, arrived here over 10,000 years ago. The ship is the size of a small city. 50,000 Atlantans were aboard when it arrived, along with all of the materials and equipment needed for us to replicate our technology here on Earthantis."

"I though Atlantis was destroyed thousands of years ago," Paul interrupted, "Lost in an earthquake or a volcano or something."

"That is exactly what you're supposed to think," answered Carolicia. "Well ... not you so much as the people of that time. Atlantis is actually a thriving city of about 100,000 today. It lies beneath the sea about four hundred miles southwest of Bermuda."

"You're kidding?" he said with a disbelieving tone to his voice. In spite of the transformation of an older woman into a younger one and the trick with the Transporter Belt, this was all very hard to believe.

"No, Paul," she answered, "We're not kidding. Atlantis is still there ... really. In fact, we thought we'd take you out there today and let you see for yourself."

He continued to look at her in disbelief.

11

"Paul," she paused. "We're here for a reason. We'll get to that soon enough but that reason requires you to believe we are who we say we are. We want you to see this for yourself. We will take you to Atlantis and let you look around … we will answer your questions … all of them. Then we will bring you back. Or we'll go to the aquarium. It's your choice."

Paul shrugged his shoulders. The curiosity they had created was simply more than he could ignore. "OK. I'd like to go, but if it's in the middle of the Atlantic Ocean, how are we going to get out there and back in one day? My parents expect me home tonight at 5:00."

"You'll see," she promised with another brilliant smile and held out an 8 x 10 glossy picture of a mountain meadow. "Visualize this place, Paul. The Belt is tied into a microcomputer that recognizes the place you brain waves are indicating."

"It reads minds?" Paul asked.

"No. It recognizes certain brain wave patterns and connects them with images from a preprogrammed catalog. Tapping your fingers the way I showed you sends a bio-impulse that the belt recognizes as a desire to go to that place. A tiny wormhole through another dimension is created. That's what all of the colors are about. Go ahead. We will join you."

"OK." Paul said again and followed her instructions. Once again the kaleidoscope of colors surrounded him, but they lasted for a period of time that seemed a little longer. When the colors stopped he was standing in a meadow that looked exactly like the one in the picture. Seconds later the two women appeared.

"Where are we now?" Paul asked looking around at the meadow.

"In the Smokey Mountains," Ms. Flyndor answered as she reached for one of the tubes attached to her belt.

"The Smokey Mountains!" Paul exclaimed, "That's five hundred miles!"

"Yes," she agreed, "That's about the maximum range of the Belt. What you just did, we call "Jumping." She took another of the rods off of her belt. "Delta Wand … On," she said.

Just then Ms. Flyndor touched her ear as if she were listening to something. "Hikers are approaching the meadow," she said.

"Here, Paul, quickly," Ms. Merilyndor said holding up her left hand, "Watch. If you say "Cloak" and then tap you fingers like you did before, you will disappear."

"Really?" Paul asked in disbelief.

Ms. Flyndor said "Cloak," and then tapped her fingers and disappeared from sight.

"Do you want me to do that?" Paul asked.

"Yes. Until after the hikers have left the meadow."

He could hear her, but could not see her. "OK," Paul said and did as he had been instructed. Suddenly he could see Ms. Flyndor again. "It isn't working," Paul said.

"Yes it is," Ms. Merilyndor said with a smile. "When you are "Cloaked" you can see other people who are also "Cloaked". All of the three of us are invisible. Hush now," she said putting a finger to her lips. "We can't be seen but they can hear our voices."

The two hikers, a man and a woman, walked into the meadow, passed by very close to the three of them, and then walked on and out of

13

the meadow without incident.

"Uncloak" Ms. Flyndor said as Paul watched and tapped her fingers. Paul followed suit without being instructed. As far as he could tell nothing had changed. Well … one thing had changed. Two perfectly healthy adults had walked within 15 feet of them in broad daylight, and had not seen them at all, and he knew it. That had changed.

Ms. Flyndor took the tube in her hand, the one she had called a Delta Wand, and pointed it towards the center of the meadow. "Illuminate," she said and a soft green light shined out. Seconds later a craft that looked a lot like a flying saucer appeared.

Paul's eyes got wide. It seemed that this was going to be a day when he was suprised a lot.

"This is a called a "Flitter" Paul," Ms. Merilyndor said with a smile.

Paul got over his surprise and looked at the craft. It was about twenty feet in diameter and appeared to be eight feet thick in the center. It was constructed of a metal that was similar in appearance to the burnished metal of the Transport Belt Buckle. There was a border of colored lights around the bottom that were flashing on and off slowly.

"What's with the lights?"

"They indicate that the Gravitational Wave Generator is operating," Ms. Merlyndor answered. "A Gravitational Wave Generator is a device that creates or negates the effect of mass artificially. It generates gravity waves like an electrical generator generates electrical waves. In this case the gravity waves oppose the Earth's mass. It's how the Flitter floats there. Manipulating the gravitational wave output is also what makes it move."

Paul nodded. Erinlicia Flyndor walked over to the craft and said "Open." A doorway appeared in the underside of the Flitter and a ramp extended to the ground.

"Shall we go aboard?"

Paul walked over to the ramp and looked inside. He couldn't see much. He touched the side of the craft and it felt more like Teflon than metal, only harder. He followed the women up the ramp. They went around a curve, and into a space that looked quite comfortable. Although he hadn't noticed any windows from the outside, they had a 360-degree view around the Flitter from the inside. Apparently they had a form of metal that was transparent. There were six chairs arranged in two rows of three. Erinlicia Flyndor sat in the left-hand seat and an instrument panel came out of a wall and positioned itself in front of her. She began touching the controls and Paul realized that she was punching in some sort of map coordinates. He sat down between the two women and as he did so, the door closed, the Flitter rose in the air and headed up the mountainside. It rapidly gained altitude and speed, but Paul cold not feel any of the effects of speed. He could see the mountains moving by at a great rate, but he could not feel the acceleration of the flitter.

"So," he finally said, "For eight thousand years you have stayed hidden from us?"

"Well ... not exactly ... not hidden the whole time," Ms. Merilyndor continued, "You know all of that mythology I've had you studying for the last two years?"

"Yes," Paul answered. She had assigned him to read about Zeus,

15

Mt. Olympus and Greek mythology and the similarities to Roman mythology; then there had been Thor, Aasgard and Norse mythology; and after that even the Tuatha De Danann and Irish mythology. He had never realized that there was such a thing as Irish mythology, but there was and he had learned about it.

"Well," she continued, "Almost all of those stories are based on the first interactions between Atlantans and the people of Earthantis."

Earthantis?" Paul asked.

"Earthantis is our name for your planet," Ms. Flyndor replied.

"Wait a minute … are you saying those myths are true?" Paul asked, so full of questions that he was unsure of what to ask first.

"No … not true … exactly, but based on truth," Ms. Merilyndor tried to explain, "Do you remember that story from Irish Mythology … about the boat that flew through the water with a light on the front and no sails?"

"Yes," he answered. It was the first of the Irish stories he'd read and then it hit him. The resemblance of this craft to the one in Irish Mythology was uncanny … too uncanny to be an accident.

Carolicia saw the understanding dawn on Paul's face, "The Celts saw us using these flitters any number of times when we were building our city under Scotland and the myth grew from there."

Paul nodded his understanding, "I see," was all he managed to say. He pointed at the flitter surrounding him, "So you guys are behind the whole flying saucer thing?' he asked.

"Yes," she answered. "The technical progress you made as a result of the War you call World War II caught us by surprise. We've had

16

stealth technology for a very long time, way before we got to Earthantis in fact, but we hadn't bothered to fit out our Flitters with it. We were not prepared for the consequences of your rapid development of radar, and jet aircraft. Once you perfected those technologies, it took us almost fifteen years to get stealth technology on all of our equipment. Many of the early sightings of what you have called UFO's were actually sightings of us."

"And we are not being tracked now?" Paul asked.

"No. We're in a Stealth Bubble."

"Is that what happens with that "Cloaking" thing?"

"Yes. The Belt creates a Stealth Bubble around you. You're not exactly invisible. The bubble takes the light that hits one side and moves it around to the other side. You can Jump like that too. No one will see you when you get to your destination until you uncloak. What we have on Flitters is a lot more sophisticated. No currently available Earthantan technology can tell we are here. Look outside, ahead and to the left a little."

Paul did and saw that they were rapidly approaching a city. He recognized the dome of the U.S. Capital building. "Is that Washington? Already?"

"Yes." Ms. Flyndor answered. "We're traveling at six thousand miles an hour … and an altitude of ten thousand feet. Look at those planes out there," she said pointing at a spot ahead and a little off to the right. As it took shape Paul recognized a pair of F-22s. The jets were flying in the same general direction as the Flitter but they passed the pair of Air Force jets like they were standing still. The F-22s did not change course or give any indication that the pilots knew of their presence.

"Wow," Paul exclaimed, "They really can't see us! The Air Force would freak out if they knew we were up here."

"Freak out probably doesn't quite cover it," Ms. Merilyndor said with a laugh.

Paul drew in a deep breath. "So how many cities did you say you have?" Paul asked, as he looked out the window at the rapidly fading city behind them. He was still trying to get a grip on all of this.

"We have nine cities on Earthantis," she answered, "Including Atlantis itself plus two in space. The cities are all built under ground. Deep underground and all of them are shielded by stealth technology. Our two space stations are not in Earthantan orbit. We also have two undersea mining colonies, but they really aren't cities."

"Oh," Paul said. He was sitting in a Flitter high above the Earthantis, moving so fast that they were already out over the ocean. It was hard to believe. At the same time it was impossible not to believe what he was seeing with his own eyes.

"By the way," Ms. Merilyndor asked, "How do you think that the Atlantic Ocean got its name?"

Paul thought that over for a second. "I don't know."

"It's ancient Greek for "Out where Atlantis is," she answered.

After they had been out of sight of land for about three minutes, Ms. Flyndor entered more commands into the control panel and the Flitter began its descent.

As they approached the water Paul got alarmed, "Aren't we going to slow down?"

"No need," she replied. "Our understanding of gravity is a great deal more advanced than yours. The Flitter will remove the water from our path. We'll slow down before we reach Atlantis itself but until then, we will move in a bubble of air without touching the water."

As she finished her explanation the Flitter dove beneath the waves. Initially as the flitter dove you could see the light of the surface, but the deeper they went, the darker blue the surrounding water got. After what seemed like less than a minute, there was no discernible light outside the flitter at all. It was far blacker than any night Paul had ever seen. Then Paul saw some dim light in front of them which began to grow and take shape as they approached.

Ms. Flyndor entered more commands and the Flitter slowed. As Paul looked out he saw a large transparent dome beneath him. It was well lit and seemed to be about a half mile across. A little farther away was a smaller dome. He looked up to try and gage how far beneath the surface they were. All he could see above him was blackness.

"How deep are we?" he asked

"About 6,000 feet," answered the woman he now knew as Ms. Merilyndor. "When we originally sank our starship, it was in water about three hundred feet deep, but the hull is two hundred feet thick, so the top of the dome over there was only about eighty feet below the surface. At the time, that was sufficient, and there is a lot of sea life you could see from the domes. Where we were at that time was in the center of what became known as the Bermuda Triangle. The hull causes magnetic abnormalities that threw off the compasses of early sailing vessels which is what is at the bottom of the rumors about the Bermuda Triangle."

"Oh," Paul said simply. There was no way to express his

astonishment.

"Anyway," she continued, "We decided to move it in the late 1700's."

"So that's how come you haven't been discovered." Paul commented as he watched the lights get closer.

"Well," Ms. Flyndor, answered, "Your modern submarines dive this deep regularly and have very sophisticated monitoring equipment by Earthantis standards, so Atlantis has a Stealth Bubble too," she answered. "We are inside of that Bubble. No one outside of it can see us. The way things were before, occasionally people came upon us. The magnetic abnormalities caused people to investigate the phenomenon. That hasn't happened since we moved the ship."

"Oh," was all Paul could come up with. "I see the light of those two domes but where is Atlantis itself?" he finally asked.

"You're looking at it," she answered, "The dome is only a small part of the top section of the ship. The seabed you see all around the dome is sediment that has built up on the hull over the last hundred years or so."

"I can see lots of buildings in the large dome. What is in that smaller dome?"

"At one time it was our Command Bridge. We don't use it that way anymore. It's been converted to gardens. It's a peaceful place … almost like a park."

As they approached the large dome their speed dropped even further. Paul could see a few strange looking multi-colored fish swimming, but very little else. Inside the dome, buildings were becoming clearly visible. On the side they were coming towards there was a semicircular tube leaving the dome. Suddenly it opened and another Flitter left. It passed them quickly, and Erinlicia guided their Flitter into the opening. The door shut automatically behind them and moments later the water had drained and Carolicia opened the ramp. Paul stepped out and followed her down a passage towards the entrance to the dome. There was a light that seemed to come from nowhere and everywhere all at once. When they reached the end of the tunnel and she said "Open". A door obeyed her command and they walked into the dome itself.

Paul looked around and whistled. The light was not blinding, but everything was clearly lit. As they walked along the dome's edge, he realized this was not a visual trick. He actually was in a domed city on the ocean floor, and inside the dome itself was a world beyond his imagination. There were trees everywhere he looked and all of the streets had medians planted with flowers. There were shops and restaurants and gathering places of all descriptions. The people they passed seemed friendly, laughing and talking among themselves but they did not stop to speak. Some of them had small winged creatures about the size of large squirrels riding around on their shoulders. Paul presumed they were sort of like pets but they were unlike any he had ever seen. For one thing they were all wearing clothes.

"Those look like ..." Paul began.

"Fairies?" Ms. Merilyndor asked with a gentle laugh.

"Well, yes," Paul stammered, "The females look like Tinkerbell only a little bigger."

"We call them Pixies." she answered. "Where do you think stories like that come from anyway?"

Before Paul could answer, two very small people walked by hand in hand. They were about four feet tall, perfectly proportioned other than they had pointy ears, and obviously adults as the man had a full beard.

"Surely not Elves?" he asked incredulously.

The two women simply nodded with a smile as they walked on.

He walked over to look at one of the shop buildings. "Stone?" he said curiously as he ran his hand over the blocks the building was built with.

"Yes." Ms. Merilyndor answered matter-of-factly, "We like natural materials. Are you ready for some lunch?"

"Yeah. I'm famished," Paul replied.

They went into a restaurant and selected a table. Screens with menus popped up out of the table at each of their places. An object shaped like a tray only thicker flew up and hovered motionlessly. It had slowly flashing lights around the bottom that reminded him of the ones on the flitter. "Are you ready to order, sir?" it asked and Paul's mouth dropped open in astonishment.

"It's a server droid, Paul," Ms. Merilyndor explained, "Just tell it what you'd like for lunch."

"Anything?"

"Anything on the menu screen."

Paul selected a double meat cheeseburger, onion rings and a Pepsi. He was surprised to find products with names he recognized and even more surprised when the Pepsi tasted like a Pepsi. Both women ordered Philly steak sandwiches and moments later the tray floated back and delivered their order. Although Paul could see the flashing lights clearly, he could not see or even hear any moving parts.

The hamburger was delicious, and Paul enjoyed his lunch.

"We have to head back now," Carolicia Merilyndor said as they finished. "We want to have you home before your parents get there."

"Right," Paul said. It took them a half-hour to make their way back to the Flitter and not long after that they broke the surface of the water.

He looked at them and shook his head. Mythology, the legends of Atlantis, UFOs … Fairies … well … Pixies actually, but it all added up once you put it all together. "OK, look" he finally managed to ask "Why did you bring me here?"

She paused and Paul noticed that the eastern coastline was coming up. "How much longer do you think we will be able to remain hidden?"

"With your stealth technology … probably forever," Paul answered.

She shook her head. "I'm afraid not. At the rate your technology is developing, no more than another fifty years or so. What do you think will happen when that occurs?"

Paul whistled softly, "I have no idea. A lot of things could happen."

"Do you think it will be easy?"

"No," Paul answered without hesitation.

"Neither do we," Erinlicia agreed and looked at Paul carefully. "It could be a difficult transition, so we have recruited a group of your young people to help. It is called the League of Atlantis. The League engages in missions of various kinds to help this transition to be as smooth as possible

... pave the way so to speak. We have schools where we train young people like you to join the League and engage in these missions. We'd like to offer you the opportunity to be trained at one of those schools and upon passing qualification exams, to join the League of Atlantis."

Chapter Two
Uniforms

Paul Andrews boarded the silver Amtrak train just before it left Chicago. He carefully checked his watch. It was almost time. According to what his parents had been told, a bus from the Hawk's Nest Science and Math Academy would meet the train in Cincinnati. It was supposed to take students to the school located about ten miles outside of Hawk's Nest, Tennessee, but that was not what was going to happen. No bus would be necessary.

Paul had thought over the offer carefully. Since the trip out to Atlantis, his entire perception of the world had changed. There were aliens living on Earthantis. Or were they really aliens? They did not look like aliens. They did not act like aliens. Aliens were supposed to be weird looking, or different and these people were not weird looking or different. But they'd been born on a planet a thousand light years away, so if they weren't aliens what where they? That was a good question and he didn't have a good answer.

They had been living here for eight thousand years. How could people who had been here that long still be alien? There had to come a point when they weren't alien anymore ... didn't there? That was also a good question, but there was no book with the answer. He had to answer it for himself, and his answer was ... yes ... there had to be a point where these people were as much of Earthantis as he was. That wasn't the only question he had to wrestle with. This decision would change the course of his life. Did he want to join the League of Atlantis or not? One thing was certain. If he joined, nothing in his life would ever be normal again. If he didn't join, the women had explained, his memory would be gently wiped and he'd have no memory of his trip. He really was given a free choice, and he appreciated that. In the end, the prospect was simply too tantalizing to walk away.

Once he had agreed to come, he was surprised at how easily the Atlantans handled his parents. He had felt that they would have to be told the whole story in order to let him go, but Carolicia and Erinlicia had just smiled and told him to let them take care of it. A man named Arnold Johnson, and Erinlicia Flyndor who was introduced to his parents as Erin Flynn had come to his home that night and informed his parents that he had been selected for a scholarship to the Hawk's Nest Science and Math Academy. Paul's grades were extremely good, and he displayed a high aptitude for Science and Math, so his parents were not completely surprised. They were however completely proud.

Mr. Johnson and Ms. Flynn displayed the school's credentials, and showed his parents all that the school had to offer. Their presentation was impressive … the school's credentials were impeccable and the advantages that it offered its graduates were on a level no parent could refuse. Once the presentation was complete, his parents' willingness to send him was not ever an issue. His Mom and Dad were willing. They wanted whatever was best for him. The school itself was the only issue. Were the credentials real? Was this school actually as good as it looked? His parents wanted to check out the school.

They did.

His parents were thorough people, particularly when the issue touched their children. They visited the school with Paul. They checked out the school in every way they could and were impressed. They thought it over, talked it over, slept on it and then discussed it all over again. The process took two weeks but there was no way for his parents to avoid the conclusion. This was an opportunity for Paul that was simply too good to pass up. In the end they decided to let Paul decide.

He already had.

Once the decision was made, he had two weeks before he was to travel to the school for Summer Orientation. Ms. Flyndor had explained that during the summer, the school transformed into something that appeared normal. This was also done on parent visit weekends. The school Paul was now travelling too would not have more than a surface resemblance to the one he visited with his parents.

The period of Summer Orientation was one month long and began the first of August. Paul could hardly wait. The Atlantans stressed the importance of keeping this secret. He could tell his friends he was going to the Hawk's Nest Science and Math Academy, but other than that he was not to tell anyone anything. The true nature of where he was headed simply could not leak out. Those two weeks stretched on and on. It seemed like they would never end, but then finally it was time to go. His two trunks of clothes and other personal belongs had been shipped, and his parents had taken him to the train station. The instructions from the school were to bring one small suitcase with him and to ship everything else.

As his parents drove him to the station, neither of them was aware that he was wearing a Transporter Belt under his clothes.

They all said their good-byes, but this was not forever. His mother cried, of course. Mothers do that, but she knew he'd be back for Christmas, and they would get to visit twice during the term. His Mom and Dad would cope.

When the train had been underway for about fifteen minutes, Paul looked at his watch. It was 9:37 on Saturday morning. He was scheduled to "Transport" in at precisely 9:42 AM. Five minutes. It was time to head for one of the train's bathrooms. He picked up his suitcase, rose from his seat, and began making his way there. He shut the door, and set the suitcase between his legs. He retrieved the picture of his destination from his pocket, used it to form a mental picture, checked his watch and tapped his fingers. Once again the kaleidoscope of colors danced around him. When it stopped he found himself standing in the middle of the room in the picture. He looked around. There were two other students already in the room, a boy and a girl. The room was about thirty feet by fifty feet. Three of the walls had windows, but there were none in the front wall. Paul noticed that there were about thirty desks and that the light seemed to flow evenly from the ceiling almost as if the ceiling itself were the source of the light.

One of the kids, the girl, was walking over to him, "Hi," she said holding out her hand, "My name is Jennifer Thompson."

Paul shook her hand, "Hi," he said, "I'm Paul Andrews."

By that time the boy had joined them, "Did you say your name was Paul Andrews?' he asked.

"Yes," Paul answered.

28

"Hi," the boy responded, "I'm Jim Hawkins. We're supposed to be roommates."

"Right," Paul said recognizing the name; "They gave me your name too. We are in Suite #5."

"You guys are in #5?" Jennifer asked.

"Yeah," Paul answered while Jim nodded.

"I'm in #6," Jennifer said, "We'll probably be next door neighbors, and we'd better move out of the way." She pointed at a holographic message that was hanging out in the air about a foot away from the front wall. The letters glowed softly as they hung in the air. The message said:

Locate your roommate. Begin getting to know one another and please stay out of the center of the room. Incoming students will be arriving periodically.

There was no projector or any way to discover where the message originated. The letters were just hanging there in space. Paul walked over to the message and ran his hand through the air. It passed right through the letters without disturbing them in the least. Paul picked up his suitcase and headed over towards where the other two had put their things. He was just in time. A girl materialized where he had been standing.

The girl left her suitcase and quickly walked over to where the three of them were standing. "Hi," she said holding her hand out to Jennifer, "My name is Betsy Saunders."

"Betsy?" Jennifer said as Paul shook her hand, "Oh, good. I was wondering when you would get here. I'm Jennifer. We're rooming together."

"You're Jennifer Thompson?" Betsy asked.

Jennifer nodded, "Yes. It's real nice to meet you. We're in #6, right next to them. They are in #5."

"Oh, good," the newest girl said, "Paul and Jim, right?"

Paul and Jim nodded. "How did you know that?" Jim asked.

"It was on the rooming list," Betsy replied, "Didn't you get one?"

"Yes, "Jim answered, "but I didn't memorize it."

"My stuff is over there," Jennifer interrupted, pointing at where her suitcase was sitting. "Let's get yours out of the way."

"Oh, sure," Betsy said and walked over and retrieved her suitcase.

As she was walking back, Jim said under his breath so only Paul could hear, "Did you memorize the list?"

"No," Paul answered quietly. "I didn't know we were supposed too."

"Me neither."

Another new student arrived, followed closely by another. They also turned out to be roommates. "It looks like they have us coming in roommate pairs," Jennifer said as the four of them walked over to where they had piled their suitcases.

"Where are you from, Jim?" Paul asked.

"A suburb north of Detroit. It's called Royal Oak," he responded, "How about you?"

"Calumet City," Paul answered. "That's a suburb of Chicago." He looked at Jennifer.

"I'm from Philadelphia," she said before he could ask.

"And I'm from Colorado Springs," Betsy offered as another person appeared in the room.

A woman dressed in a tight fitting silver-white jumpsuit with blue and gold trim walked in. She was wearing what Paul immediately recognized as a Transporter Belt around her waist and one of the pixies he had seen in Atlantis was sitting on her right shoulder. A five-foot long floating cart followed her into the room. It was a good deal larger than the server droid Paul had seen in Atlantis, but it had slowly flashing lights underneath and seemed to operate in the same way. Paul noted that the cart just seemed to know where it was going and floated there. It was rounded at each end and made of an alloy that resembled stainless steel, only a little darker. There was mahogany trim around the edges, and it contained a variety of snacks.

"Students," the lady said loudly to get everyone's attention, "My name is Altracia Galvyndor. You may call me Professor Galvyndor. I am one of your teachers. I teach a course called The Science and Technology of Atlantis. We'll have all of the new freshmen here in another forty-five minutes. In the meanwhile these snacks are for you. Feel free to help yourselves," she said as she smiled with a bit of amusement. "As you will discover, there is plenty for everyone. When all of the new students have arrived, we will begin your Orientation. That includes a tour of the grounds, and then there will be a Presentation and Acceptance Ceremony." After her brief speech the professor left the room.

"She seems nice enough," Betsy offered.

"Yes," Paul agreed.

"I wonder what this Presentation and Acceptance Ceremony is," Jennifer wondered out loud as the four of them made their way over to the cart,

"I wonder what kind of creature that was sitting on her shoulder?" Betsy said.

"It wasn't a bird but it has wings," Jim observed, "It has a face that's human - just smaller and it's wearing clothes."

"They look just like Tinkerbell," Betsy observed, "Do you think they're Fairies?"

"Come on," Jim said a little sarcastically, "aren't you a little old to believe in Fairies?"

"Yeah," Betsy answered defensively, "and I'm also too old to believe in floating carts, but there is one right over there," she said pointing to the cart.

"They're Pixies," Paul answered, "I saw several of them down in Atlantis, and Ms. Flyndor told me what they were."

"Really?" Jim exclaimed. "I didn't notice any when I was there."

Paul nodded and walked over to the cart and got down on his knees. He looked at the lights carefully but there was nothing remarkable about them. He studied the underside of the cart to see if he had missed something. He ran his hand back and forth trying to feel for any connection to the floor that he could not see, but there was nothing. The cart was just floating there in the air with its lights slowly flashing.

"Anything?" Jim asked.

"No … nothing. No heat, no air blowing … nothing! It must be powered like the Flitters."

"We'll find out more about those little creatures pretty soon I'll bet," Jennifer said as she reached out to pick up a chocolate truffle. There were snacks of many varieties on the cart but only one or two items of each. There were four different flavors of truffles, a half dozen assorted fruit filled tarts, two pieces of chocolate cake, and three slices of Boston Cream Pie. There were bananas, apples and grapes. There were candy bars but only one of two of each kind. There were bottled soft drinks of several different recognizable flavors, and bottled water. No sooner had Jennifer picked up the truffle than another one materialized in its place.

"Wow," exclaimed Paul, "Did you see that?" he asked snatching up the truffle to see if another one would replace it. In less than a second the spot the truffle had been sitting on turned translucent and another one appeared. He picked up a bottle of Mountain Dew and it was replaced as well.

"Oh ... YES!" Jennifer exclaimed and the others looked at her. She had taken a tentative bite of the truffle; "This ... is ... SOOO ... good!" She said with her eyes wide with delight as she quickly gobbled up the rest of the truffle.

Paul made no pretense at being dainty. He popped the whole truffle into his mouth, and his eyes widened in surprise. The taste was definitely chocolate, but it had a velvety smooth consistency, and a delicate flavor he was not used to. "Wow! This ... IS ... good," he said as he reached for another. Before long everyone in the room was reaching for snacks of different varieties. As the new students soon learned, they could not take them away so fast that the cart could not keep up.

Paul walked over to one of the windows and looked out at the grounds. About a hundred feet down a slight incline was a small lake. There were concrete pads with benches spaced out around the lake and a bridge that went out to a Gazebo. Otherwise there were no other structures in view. Way off in the distance he could see a wrought iron fence. He guessed it was the Boundary of the School's grounds. The grounds were well manicured and neat. Even farther, almost out of sight, were the smokestacks of some sort of factory. Jim came over and stood next to him and they were joined seconds later by Betsy and Jennifer.

"The School itself must be up that hill behind the front wall," he said pointing in the general direction that was blocked by the front wall. Whatever was behind the hill could not see from where they were.

"I wonder what this building is used for?" asked Betsy. Just then the four of them noticed the chairs. They had no legs but floated motionlessly in the air. Unlike the cart, there were no flashing lights. There were two rows of floating chairs that formed a sort of "U" and near the front was a table. At least the table had legs, Paul noticed, but there were no desks to go along with the floating chairs. They were just chairs, or seemed to be.

"Hard to say what they use this room for," answered Jim, as he looked underneath one of the chairs. "They could set it up for lots of things." He sat down on the chair gingerly. It dropped an inch or so and then adjusted to his weight. Immediately his eyes widened as the chair formed itself to his body and arm rests appeared from the back, "Whoa," he said jumping up quickly. "Did you guys see that?"

"Yeah, Jim," Paul suggested. "Sit down again and stay longer this time."

Jim sat down and the chair conformed to his body and the arm rests appeared again. Seconds later the right arm extruded a table that could easily be used for taking notes or any of the other activities that students might need in a classroom. It was at exactly the right height for Jim's body.

"Sweet!" Jim exclaimed.

"Totally!" Betsy agreed as she sat down in one of the chairs. It also sank an inch, adjusted, and then conformed itself to her body and extruded a desk at the proper height for her. Paul and Jennifer sat down and the process was repeated.

"They're all like this," Paul concluded.

Just then Professor Galvyndor re-entered the room. This time there were three floating carts following her. They were similar to the cart with the food except that all three were piled with packages. She turned her back to the students and raised her right arm to shoulder level. She swept her arm from left to right as a soft green light beamed out from a ring on her hand. Immediately two sections of the wall recessed about three inches. They were shaped the size of doors. She turned back to the students.

"Attention, please," she said politely as if the strange light from the ring and the recessing of the two doors would not have been sufficient to draw everyone's attention. "First of all, let me introduce myself again now that all of you are here. My name is Altracia Galvyndor. Please call me Professor Galvyndor. I will be one of your teachers and I teach the Science and Technology of Atlantis. On behalf of our Headmaster, Professor Heraldon Glorfyndor, and the rest of the faculty, let me welcome you to the Hawk's Nest Science and Math Academy, which, as you all know by now, is a lot more than a regular school. Today's activities consist of two parts. First is your Orientation, and after that comes your Presentation and Acceptance Ceremony." She looked around momentarily. "In our culture all significant agreements are accompanied by a Ceremony."

She paused and looked over the room again. "We will begin with your Orientation. On these carts are your uniform and equipment packages. They are a gift from the people of Atlantis." She stopped and the first cart began to send out smaller floating objects. Paul noted that they resembled the server droids he had seen in Atlantis complete with the slowly flashing lights. Each of the small objects flew up to an individual student, and on each was a ring. She held up her right hand so that everyone could see the ring she wore there. "This is called a Power Ring. You will spend four years learning all of its uses. For now, you just need to know two things. You use it to open Atlantan packages. Just run the ring along any edge and the package will open. The other thing about a Power Ring is that it will act as a key for any lock. The doors to the school are all locked 24/7 with Earthantan style locks, primarily for cosmetic purposes, but we have had parents check; so the Key function of the Ring is important. It is how you get in and out of the school. Just point your Ring at the lock and say "open." This will work for any lock operated with a key."

Jim looked over at Paul, "Any lock ... interesting."

"Now ... moving on. All you have to do to get an Atlantan door to open is say "open." The door will recognize your voice, and it knows

36

whether you are allowed in that room or not. If you are, the door will open. If you aren't ... " she paused and smiled broadly, "Well ... let's just say you'll never get it open. On these other two carts are your Uniform packages. Your equipment is all identical, but for obvious reasons the girls' uniforms are a little different from the boys. Girls' packages are on the front cart, and boys' on the back. One size fits all; so don't worry about size. Once you have opened your packages you will find four Power Wands, an Atlantan uniform, and a set of instructions for the uniform. Each Power Wand is known by a letter of the Greek alphabet. They are called Alpha, Beta, Delta and Epsilon Wands. Power Wands are like the Power Rings, you will spend four years learning all of the things they do, just don't be too surprised when you un-wrap your package and take them out. Once you have your Uniform package you can change in the bathrooms. Boys on the left ... girls on the right. When you are dressed properly you may assemble back out here." With that Professor Galvyndor left the room a second time.

"See you girls later," Paul said picking up his suitcase and walking over to the cart in the back. He picked up one of the packages, and looked over at Jim, "Ready?"

"Yep," Jim said and they walked over to the door on the left. They had not consciously intended to get there first, but that was the way it worked out.

Paul looked at the door carefully. "Open," he said and the door immediately obeyed.

Both boys walked through together, and the door closed behind them. It opened seconds later to admit several of their classmates. The first thing Paul noticed was that there were benches that floated in the air much like the chairs. He and Jim sat down on one. It adjusted to their weight but did not change in any other way. Paul gave Jim a quizzical look. Jim shrugged and ran his Power Ring along the edge of his Uniform package. It opened easily. Jim pulled out a small cylindrical object. It was about five inches long, a half-inch in diameter and made from some sort of burnished metal. "This must be one of the Power Wands." he said and set it down on the bench. Immediately tiny lights began to flash and the wand floated up into the air, over to one of the vertical metal pieces on his Transporter Belt and attached itself with a click. "Whoa," he exclaimed, "Did you see that?"

Paul nodded speechlessly.

Jim grasped the wand and started to tug, but that was not necessary. Once his hand made contact, the wand came right off the belt. He set the wand back down on the bench. As they watched, it floated up into the air, back over to his transport belt and clicked on again.

"O ...K ... I guess they can make this floating stuff as small as they want," Jim said and looked into the package again.

"Yeah, and it doesn't look like they want us to lose these wands either!"

"Yeah," Jim agreed. As he reached back towards the Uniform package, he accidentally ran his Power Ring along the top of his transport belt. A pouch opened up. "Look! There are pouches," he exclaimed.

Paul looked at what Jim was doing. Sure enough if you ran your and across the top of the transport belt either immediately to the right or the left of the medallion, a pocket opened up.

38

Both of the boys experimented with the wands and the way they attached to the transport belts. As soon as they would let go of a wand, the tiny lights would begin to flash. It would rise into the air and float over to one of the receptacles on the belt and attach itself. There were a total of four different wands, and four receptacles on each belt. After a little bit of playing around, they discovered that each wand always went back to the same receptacle and clicked securely into place. They could be removed easily by hand, but could not be shaken off of the belt.

"I think you're right." Jim said as he watched his last wand click onto the belt. "It'd be pretty hard to lose one of these things.

The only things left in the package were a plastic sheet of instructions and a piece of silver-white material about eight inches wide and two feet long. It was the same color as Professor Galvyndor's outfit. Paul removed both and looked at the instructions. "It says to remove all of our clothes except our underwear, including our transport belts, and be sure to take off our shoes and socks." He noticed that Jim had already read his instructions and was taking off his shirt. Paul followed and soon both boys were standing there in their underwear.

"It says to wrap the cloth around your waist," Jim said picking up the cloth, "But it isn't long enough."

"Remember how the transport belts fasten?" Paul asked as he examined his own piece of material.

As Jim brought the ends around from his back they suddenly grew in length and joined together, forming a seamless joint in the front, and then shrunk to fit the size of his waist. Next it started to grow downwards, covering his buttocks, and abdomen, and then went down and began to cover his legs.

"It says that once your buttocks are covered to sit down," Paul called out hurriedly.

Jim sat down quickly and the material continued to grow down his legs. It ended up by forming a cushioned shoe-like affair on the soles of his feet. Once that was complete, it started growing up, covering his chest, and then growing out each of his arms, ending in a nice cuff at his hands.

"Far out," Jim said standing up. "I can see why they wanted you to sit down. They wanted your feet off of the floor so it could make the shoes."

"Look," Paul said pointing at Jim's left wrist. "The cuff has a wristwatch that tells time."

Jim looked down at his wrist and sure enough, there were digital numbers telling the time.

Paul went through the same process and a few seconds later, both boys were standing looking at each other in uniforms that resembled the jumpsuit the Professor was wearing. He reached down and picked up the instructions noticing how easy it was to move. "It says here that if you want gloves, you simply say "glove", and if you want a hood, you just say "hood. If you want them to go away you just say "un-glove" or "un-hood."

"Glove," Jim said and the uniform immediately grew out over his hands. "Un-glove," he said and the material covering his hands and fingers disappeared.

"Hood," Paul said and felt the material grow up the back of his neck, and then around covering all of his face. Neither his eyesight nor hearing were affected. He craned his neck around, and found that the hood did restrict his movement somewhat, but the only really uncomfortable thing was the sensation of having his face all wrapped up in the material. That was more than a little disconcerting and would take some getting used to.

Jim started to laugh out loud, "You should see yourself, dude," he said, "You look like an alien. Big round dark eyes and everything."

"Hood," Jim said and a moment later, he was also hooded. The silver-white material completely covered his head and face. Paul could tell where his ears, mouth, and nose were but the uniform made them blend together. Where his eyes were there were dark round oblong lenses.

"So that is where the alien thing comes from," Paul said looking at Jim. Anyone who saw Jim would think they were looking at an alien. "Un-hood," he said and a few seconds later the hood had retracted into the uniform collar. They looked down at the instructions again. "It says here that these uniforms will keep you warm in winter, cool in summer and can't be cut by a knife. There is a filtering device in the hood for breathing contaminated air."

"The whole uniform including the lenses is bullet proof!" Jim exclaimed as he continued to read. "What's up with that?"

Paul looked over at his roommate. "This is going to be an adventure, Jim ... the real deal."

Chapter Three

The Adventure Begins

John Moriarty sat at the large mahogany desk in his even larger office. He was the General Manager of the Hawk's Nest Division of the Apex Paper Company and his office was impressive. It was ornately furnished, and contained trophies from his hunting expeditions around the world. On the wall to the right of his desk were the heads of a Bighorn Ram, an Elk and a Moose. He had fond memories of the hunts in Montana when he had shot those trophies. To the left of the desk was the Predator Wall. There was a Grizzly Bear he had shot in Yellowstone National Park and a Bengal Tiger he had shot in India. The tiger was on the endangered list and it was illegal to hunt them, but there were ways to get around almost anything for the right price. There was also a Lion from Tanzania's Masi Mara.

As he looked at the trophy of the tiger, he remembered the thick morning fog by the watering hole and the way the tiger slowly majestically walked through the mist as he made his way down for a drink. When Moriarty had finally squeezed the trigger, the animal had been less than a hundred feet away. It had been an easy shot. The only hard thing had been the bribes he had to pay to get there. The grizzly bear had been even easier. The guide had baited the base of a tree with the carcass of a dead animal. That was illegal, but it was the only way to know a bear would come. He had waited safely in a tree about twenty yards away. The bribes required to hunt grizzlies in Yellowstone were the largest he'd ever paid, but it was worth it. He had gotten what he paid for, but there was room on his Predator Wall for one more. Next winter he hoped there would be another trophy hanging there. He very much wanted an African Cheetah and Jaguar, and he had arranged to hunt them right after the first of the year.

"Enough daydreaming," he said to himself as he rose and made his way towards the elevator. It was time to meet Ben Johnson for a progress report. Ben Johnson was the Operations Manager, and handled the day-to-day operation of the Mill itself. The Mill was profitable ... very profitable ... and Moriarty had plans to make it even more profitable. Ben Johnson was the key to those plans. The more profits there were, the more bonus money there would be, and it was the bonus money that made hunting trips to places like India and Africa possible. He walked out of the elevator and into the walkway connecting the office portion of the mill to the mill itself. As he expected, Ben Johnson was waiting in an open area just past the door.

"Hi, Ben," John Moriarty said pleasantly.

"Hello, yourself," Ben replied, reaching out to shake his bosses hand.

"How's everything?"

"Everything is on schedule, John," Ben Johnson replied just loud enough so that he could be heard over the noise. That was not the same as "Good" and Ben knew it. John Moriarty had insisted they switch from using sodium hydroxide to hydrazine. A strong base like sodium hydroxide was used to break down the wood chips into the pulp from which paper could be made. The sodium hydroxide worked well, and was economical. Especially since they had been illegally releasing it into the exhaust steam instead of paying to have it properly processed. Not paying for waste disposal was the key to Moriarty's profits. It was also the key to the bonuses. His competitors paid for disposal. He did not, and the money saved went right to the bottom line. He had gotten away with it for many years but now he wanted more. Hydrazine was much more dangerous than sodium hydroxide but it also had the advantage of breaking the wood down faster, almost twice as fast in fact, but that extra efficiency was normally offset by the extra cost to process the highly toxic hydrazine waste. Moriarty's plan was to use the hydrazine for the speed, and then release it into the exhaust steam like they had been doing with the sodium hydroxide. It was a good idea from a profit standpoint, but not from an environmental one. The environmental consequences would be much worse but it would take a long time for anyone to notice. He'd be retired and long gone by then.

"The first load of hydrazine arrived yesterday. We switch over on Monday," Ben Johnson reported.

"Monday!" John Moriarty exclaimed, "Really! That's great. You're a week ahead of schedule."

"I always am," Johnson replied.

"And we know why," Moriarty said with a grin and punched Ben playfully on the arm. Ben Johnson received an envelope from him every month ... an envelope that contained cash ... lots of it.

As Moriarty walked away, Ben Johnson knew there was a time coming when he would not be able to do this anymore. This part of the operation was beginning to make him sick. He'd quit but he couldn't. He needed the job. With the economy like it was he might have a hard time find another one. He had bills to pay and a wife and family to support, but it might be time to start thinking about finding another job.

Ψ

Paul sat next to Jim in the Transport Flitter as it wound its way up the hill. It was constructed of materials similar to those Paul had seen in the other Flitter, but it was oblong in shape, more like a sausage than a saucer, and big enough for all of them as a group, sort of like a bus, only one with no wheels.

Just before the flitter reached the crest of the hill, Paul turned and looked back. He could see the factory across the fall line of the valley. It was spewing out smoke from its stacks in the distance. "Steam," he said to himself. The white smoke that was billowing out of the plant was steam – water vapor. He knew that from a report he'd done for school. As he watched however, subtle shades of yellow appeared briefly mixed in with the steam. Paul did not think it was a trick of the light. That factory was releasing something other than steam, Paul realized. Just then they crested the hill and he got his first glimpse of the Hawk's Nest Science and Math Academy.

Paul looked down the hill at the school. It was larger than he had imagined. There were three connected sections built of hewn granite, and heavy wooden beams in a style that Paul recognized as English Tudor.

45

According to the pamphlets it had been the estate of a wealthy man named Cirrus Spaulding. He had died without heirs and donated both the estate and his fortune for the founding of a school – The Hawk's Nest Science and Math Academy. The stated Mission was to teach gifted youth regardless of their family's ability to pay. The grounds themselves were over three thousand acres, including a two hundred-acre lake.

As they continued down towards the school, Professor Galvyndor explained to the group that there never had been a Cirrus Spaulding. The house had been built as a school from the groundbreaking, but all of the formalities had to be observed. Every "I" had been dotted, and every "T" crossed, she explained. The new students looked down into a pleasant valley. Nestled on a ridge about half way down was the school. Past the school was another lake. Paul could see a boathouse with sailboats, but it was too far away to see what kind they were.

"As you will remember from your visit with your parents, the section in the center," began Professor Galvyndor, "contains Fellowship Hall, the Dining Hall, the Auditorium, the game rooms, and the Library. The wing to the right is the dormitory. There are four floors, one for each year of students. You will be occupying the third floor for your entire stay here. The students who were there last year have graduated. The left wing contains the classrooms. Farther to the left you will see the Greenhouse, and the Field House."

The Flitter pulled in under a portico and stopped gently. Paul noticed that the lurch you usually got when a school bus braked to a stop was completely absent. The Professor led the students inside and after they passed through the entry atrium, Paul looked around to see if anything had changed from his visit. Nothing noticeable had changed, at least not in this room. They had entered a large room, approximately forty feet square, and three stories tall. Around the edges of the room on the second and third floors were wide balconies with dark oaken railings. He didn't know if the room had a name or not, but it had a warm comfortable feeling in spite of its size. The center of the ceiling was a dome with a large symbol ... the same symbol as the one on the Transporter Belt. On opposite sides of the room were large flagstone fireplaces with intricately carved mantle pieces. As his eyes wandered around the room, he noticed that each of the three floors had two of the fireplaces. No fires were burning, but then it was the middle of summer.

"Hmmm," Paul hummed softly to himself. Why would anyone with a technology as advanced as the Atlantans be interested in fireplaces? That was a question with no answer at the moment. He would just have to wait and see.

On the ground level there were several pieces of furniture arranged around each of the fireplaces in what looked like places to gather and talk. It was difficult to see past the oaken railings that surrounded the balconies of the two upper floors, but Paul guessed there were more such areas up there.

"Students," Professor Galvyndor called. The pixie he had seen earlier was still sitting on her shoulder and it leaned over and appeared to whisper something in the Professor's ear and the Professor smiled. That had happened several times.

Paul leaned over to Betsy, "It seems that pixies can talk," he said pleasantly.

"Students," Professor Galvyndor continued, "This room is called Fellowship Hall. Our Library is through that doorway," she said pointing to her right. Paul looked through the arched doorway, bordered with the same dark oak trim that the railings were made of, and could see several stacks of books beyond. "Fellowship Hall," the Professor continued, "is frequently used for studying, particularly the areas on the balconies. There are plenty of places to get together and chat or read or whatever. The doorway on the other side, over there," she said pointing to a doorway opposite of the Library, "leads to a game room. This doorway behind me leads into a long hallway. If you go to the right, you will come first to a doorway leading into the Dining Hall. If you keep going you will come to a passageway leading you to your Dormitory. If you went left, you'd first come to the auditorium, and then to the passageway leading to the Classroom Building."

"Now, before we go on, there are several other things to tell you. When we came to Earthantis we brought several intelligent species with us. In the Presentation and Acceptance Ceremony you will be introduced to the faculty. It is important to tell you that some of the faculty at this school are elves. You may have noticed the little people when you visited Atlantis. They are elves. They are wonderfully talented musicians, as well as excellent artisans and craftsmen."

Just then the little creature whispered something else into the Professor's ear and she smiled and nodded. "Now, before we have the Presentation and Acceptance Ceremony, we have a special treat for you."

With those words the creature on the Professors shoulder flew up off of her shoulder and up to a height of about ten feet. The creature was

48

wearing a shimmering translucent skirt and costume that was similar to that of a ballerina. The creature, whatever it was, could not be mistaken for anything other than female. She held her arms out wide and said in a sweet childlike voice, "A very special treat."

"Look at that," exclaimed Betsy.

"This is Lucinda," Professor Galvyndor said by way of explanation, "She is a Pixie. The males are called Pixs, and the females are Pixies. If several are together the group is called pixies regardless of gender. It's easy to tell the difference. The females wear skirts ... the males don't. You have all heard the legends of Pixies, and Fairies ... you know ... Tinkerbell ... the Tooth Fairy ... Fairy God Mothers and that sort of thing? Well ... Pixies like Lucinda are where those legends about Fairies and Pixies come from. Like the elves, they came here with us."

Paul looked carefully at the Pixie. She was about nine inches tall, and had wings that enabled her to fly. She had long brightly colored orange hair, and seemed to hover effortlessly in the air.

"Now," the Professor continued, "Pixies have little talent for math or science. They won't be able to help you with your classes, in fact they are not allowed into the classroom section at all. They are too busy laughing and playing and having fun to put up with your classes anyway. There are easily amused, insatiably curious, incredibly loyal, normally kind hearted and frequently mischievous. The Pixs like to fly up and give you a high five. The Pixies like to come up and rub noses with you. The Pixs do that too but only on special occasions, or times when they think you really need a lift. Almost all Atlantans have been adopted by a Pix or a Pixie."

"That's right," Lucinda announced in a high pitched clear voice with an emphatic nod as she continued to hover.

"Before we go any farther, I need to explain about that," their teacher continued. "I want to make sure all of you heard me correctly. Pixies adopt us not the other way around. When a Pixie adopts you they are agreeing to be interested in what you are interested in, involved in what you are involved with, cheer you when you win, comfort you when you don't. They have a level of loyalty that few of you will ever have experienced, but they have to commit to it first. Once they do they're in … all in. When a Pixie has committed to you, they have "adopted" your ideas; they have "adopted" your interests, in effect they have adopted some of your personality traits, so this process is called being adopted."

One of the boys raised his hand. "Yes," Professor Galvyndor acknowledged with a nod and a smile as if she knew exactly what was coming next.

"What if you don't want to be adopted?" the boy asked hesitatingly.

She smiled, "You are under no obligation, but Pixies are fun."

Lucinda flew up to the boy and held her arms out wide, "Great fun," she said in her high little voice, and then flew over and whispered something in the boy's ear. He smiled too, and just nodded to the Professor.

"So …," she continued, "We are about to be joined by a lot of Pixies."

Lucinda spoke up again, "A whole … whole lot of Pixies," she announced, "They are all very nice Pixies and they are wanting to adopt you."

"Yes they are," the Professor said with a chuckle, "Nothing is ever boring around Pixies, I can tell you. They really are quite fun, although you never really know what they will do or say next. They will be a fun-loving, loyal companion throughout your entire life. Lucinda adopted me when I was twelve. We've been companions ever since."

"That's right," Lucinda announced with a nod, "Ever since." The Pixie flew down in front of the Professor's face, reached out with her tiny hands and touched her on the cheeks and rubbed noses. When the Pixie was finished she flew around and plopped herself down on the Professor's shoulder.

"How sweet,' Becky said quietly so that only Jennifer, Paul and Jim could hear.

Just then a Pix flew into the room. He had yellow hair and was wearing yellow pants. He was followed by a Pixie, and a large group immediately followed the first two. They flocked around for a few seconds and then spread out through the room. The Pix with yellow hair flew up to Paul. "Are you Paul?" he asked in a voice that was just as childlike as the one Lucinda had used, only with a more masculine tone.

"Yes," Paul answered, "my name is Paul." He had no idea how the little Pix knew his name was Paul.

"Oh, good. I was looking for you. My name is Ornith," he said as he hovered in the air, "Do you think you will like Pixies?"

"Why ... yes," Paul answered, caught off guard by the question. It wasn't as if it were an issue, it was just that he hadn't thought about the question.

"Good. I think so too." The little fellow paused for a second as if thinking things over and then continued, "OK, then. I will adopt you." Ornith smiled broadly. "We have to go over to Professor Galvyndor and register. I will ride on your shoulder if that's OK."

"Sure," Paul replied, "What does this adopting mean to you?" he asked as they walked over to the table where the professor was sitting.

"It means we are very special friends," Ornith answered. "Pixies are friends with anyone that wants to be friendly, but we only have one very special human friend."

Professor Galvyndor saw Ornith and Paul. There was a computer screen hovering in the air in front of the Professor. Paul had no idea where it came from or how it operated.

Are you adopting Paul, Ornith?" she asked.

"Yes," the little yellow haired pix answered, "I am."

"Record," she said to the computer, "Ornith has adopted Paul."

"Just like that?" Paul asked.

"Yes. That's all. You are officially adopted by Ornith," she answered.

"Oh! OK," Paul answered with a shrug and moved out of the way so the girl behind him could register.

"Um … Paul," the Pix asked, "When are we going to go and see our room?"

"What?" Paul said in surprise.

Ornith flew off of Paul's shoulder and around to face him. He began to ask the question more slowly this time, swinging his arms back and forth in time with the words, "When … are … we … going … to …

go ... see ... our ... room? It's where we are going to live and I would like to see it."

"I ... I don't know," Paul answered. He was still trying to adjust to talking with a Pix. "They haven't told us about that yet. I ... I don't know."

"Oh," Ornith responded, "OK. I'm sorry. It ... must ... be ... after ... lunch ... then. Did I do better that time?"

"Do better? Do better at what?"

"Well, they told us that we would have to speak "slowly" and "distinctly" at first until you got used to us, so I was wondering if I did better that time."

Paul raised his eyes and looked at Ornith, "You have to speak ... "slowly" ... and ... "distinctly," he said with a laugh in his voice.

"Yes," Ornith answered solemnly swinging his little arms, "Slowly ... and ... distinctly."

"Well, Ornith, you're doing fine."

"Oh ... good," the little Pix said and flew around and plopped back onto Paul's shoulder.

The weight of the Pix was nearly nothing. As he looked over towards Ornith, he noticed that there was a blue-haired Pix on Jim's shoulder and a red-haired Pixie on Jennifer's as well. Ornith leaned over to his ear. "Your friend Jim's Pix is named Aurileol, and Jennifer's Pixie is named Renalee."

"You know that Jim is my friend? You know Jennifer?"

"Of course,"

"How?"

"We have been studying up on you guys for weeks and days. You were all divvied up before you even got here." Ornith paused for a few seconds and seemed to be looking around, "Uh…Oh," he said finally, his voice dropping in concern..

"Uh…Oh, what?" Paul asked quickly.

"Gwenivere is missing," Ornith said solemnly.

"Gwenivere? Who is Gwenivere?" Paul asked.

Ornith flew around to look at Paul and said swinging his short little arms in time with the words, "Gwenivere … is … the … one … who … is … missing," Ornith answered seriously, as if this amount of information fully answered the question.

Paul looked around. There was no Pixie on Betsy's shoulder and Paul could see that tears were beginning to form in her eyes.

After a few seconds Ornith continued, "Gwenivere is also my girlfriend."

"Pixs have girlfriends?" Paul asked as he tried to figure out what to do about Betsy.

"Of course," answered Ornith. "But she is missing. But don't worry, she will turn up soon," Ornith paused and looked around again. "I think Betsy is sad though."

Paul looked over at Betsy and noticed that she had sat down. Ornith was right. She did look sad. He walked over to Betsy, "What's the matter?" he asked.

"Oh, Paul," she said dejectedly, "I spent all of my life wishing that Fairies were real, and now it turns out that they are. They're just called Pixies and I really wanted one to adopt me. They're so cute. Look at yours," she reached up and touched Ornith on the cheek. Ornith smiled at her but said nothing. "I really wanted one to adopt me … but … but … none of them wanted me." She sat down again and put her head in her hands. Paul could tell that she was about to burst into tears.

Just then an orange-haired Pixie came shooting into the room from the hallway that led to the Dining Hall. Professor Galvyndor had bent over and was straightening back up. The Pixie's feet bumped into the Professor's shoulder as she flew past and she went somersaulting topsy-turvy through the air into the center of the room. She finally came to a stop and was hovering in the middle with her hair going in twenty different directions.

"Well … at least Gwenivere is no longer missing," announced Ornith with a sigh.

"Is that Gwenivere?" Paul asked laughing, as he watched the little creature straightening out her hair as she hovered in the middle of the room.

"Yes," Ornith replied, "But she is not always this clumsy … just sometimes ... you'll see."

Gwenivere spied Aurileol and stuck out a little pink tongue and gave him a nasty look and then she saw Betsy sitting in a chair. She flew right up to her, "Are you Betsy?"

"Yes," Betsy answered, standing up.

"Why are you sad, Betsy?" the tiny creature asked.

"Because no Pixie wanted to adopt me?" Betsy answered truthfully.

"So … you really like pixies?" Gwenivere asked.

"Oh, yes," Betsy answered, "I really do."

"OK, I'm Gwenivere," the Pixie announced, "And I will adopt you."

"Really?" Betsy asked. "But … haven't you already adopted someone else?"

"No, I haven't. I was late. I will adopt you," Gwenivere said, and flew down, touched Betsy on the cheeks and rubbed noses with her. "I'm sorry I was late," Gwenivere said, "And that you felt bad, but it was Aurileol's fault." She pointed at Jim's Pix accusingly, "He played a trick. He told me we were to meet you in the Dining Hall and so I was waiting there for you." Aurileol had flown down off of Jim's shoulder, landed on one of the tables and was on his back laughing rolling back and forth and slapping his knees. Gwenivere turned and stuck out her tongue again and blew a raspberry at Aurileol, "But we'll get him back, you'll see. Do you feel better now?"

"Yes, lots," Betsy answered, drawing in a breath.

Paul leaned a little toward Ornith. "How did you know you wanted to adopt me, and how did Gwenivere know she wanted to adopt Betsy?" Paul asked.

"We read your files," Ornith answered matter of factly.

"Pixies can read?" he asked.

"Of course," the little yellow-haired Pix answered, "but we like little books. Big books pages are a pain to turn."

"Students," Professor Galvyndor called out, ringing a small bell for their attention, "Before we move into the Auditorium for the Presentation and Acceptance Ceremony, there are three final things we need to go over as part of this orientation. First … the dorm rooms are programmed not to allow you into each other's rooms. This is not just about boys in girl's rooms and vice versa, although that should go without saying, but boys are not allowed in other boy's room either. You and your roommate are only allowed in your own room. Your individual rooms are a place of refuge for you and your roommate, not for social gatherings. On each floor there is a nice Common Area for socializing, and you can also do that here in here in Fellowship Hall."

"Second … on the wall to your right you will see a list that shows which Quadro you and your roommate belong to. Before we go any farther, let me explain about Quadros. A Quadro consists of four people … a pair of male roommates and a pair of female roommates. Together your Quadro competes as a unit in the school's annual contest. We call it the Quadro Bowl. Each class competes separately. You don't compete against upperclassmen. We call it the Quadro Bowl because, well, if you win, each member of the Quadro gets a small trophy that looks like a silver bowl, and your names are permanently engraved on a much larger bowl that sits in the entry annex to the Field House. This is an annual competition, but at various times there are rewards for the teams that are leading. For example: In a few weeks we will begin to let you go down to Co-re-alis. That is the name of the Atlantan city directly beneath us. All of you are not allowed down there at once. Not at first anyway. You get to go down for your first visit based on your Quadro's standing in the competition, and this is quite a treat. These contests are important. Competition hones skills and helps you learn difficult material more quickly. It plays an important role in your training. You can gain or lose points in a lot of different ways and that will be explained later. For right now you just need to see who you and your roommate are paired with."

An immediate buzz went over the room as a holographic list of lightly glowing names appeared out in front of the wall and the students began to search. Paul and Jim were in Quadro #3 with Jennifer and Betsy. He saw the two of them walking over to them. Betsy smiled, "We're glad it's you guys."

"Yes," Jim said immediately, turning to Paul, "We're glad too."

"Now students! We come to the last thing before the Ceremony," the Professor continued, "Sponsors! As part of the ceremony, each of you will be introduced to an Atlantan family. They are your sponsors in our society and they will become a surrogate family for you. This is not to diminish the value of your parents, or replace them in any way. They will be a lot like Aunts and Uncles, and they will give you the ties you need to function in our society. You will find out more of what these ties mean as you go forward. Some of what you need to learn of our society, you will learn in school, but some of it you will learn from them. They will be a source of information, a point of connection, and they will treat you as a part of their own family. Their acceptance of you into their family is an important part of the Ceremony."

She paused and looked everyone over, "There is one final point. In the Presentation and Acceptance Ceremony you will be asked specifically if you will promise to keep our secrets. That is the only commitment we will ask of you at this time. Once you have agreed, you will be "presented" to your sponsors. They will "accept" you. Once you have been formally "presented" and "accepted", you are a member of an

Atlantan family, as well as the Society of Atlantis. You are awarded your own Seal." She tapped the emblem on the right sleeve of her uniform. "Visually yours will be just like this one, but each contains a great deal of information about you. Once you've received your seal, it will forever appear on your uniform."

She stopped and looked at the group seriously. "We do not teach our secrets to people who are not a part of our society so this is an important ceremony. In this ceremony, you are not joining the League of Atlantis. You have to pass your Senior Qualification Exams for that, but in this ceremony you are being formally accepted into the Society of Atlantis. That makes you one of us.

The Society of Atlantis is more than just a "society" in the common definition. It is also our government which is organized around the principals of a Republic. Our capital is at Atlantis.

Once you have been "accepted", you will exit the stage with your sponsors and take a seat in the Auditorium. At that time the Faculty of the school will be introduced. When everything is concluded, you will go with your sponsors to the Dining Hall where lunch will be served. After that they will take you to the dormitory, and help you get settled into your rooms. So ..." the Professor said, "It is now time for you to be "presented". Please follow me."

The part about the Ceremony brought Paul's feeling of uneasiness back more strongly than ever. He had never liked ceremonies, but there was nothing he could see to do about it.

Professor Galvyndor led them through the arched doorway at the back of Fellowship Hall, and turned to the left. About thirty feet down there was a smaller hallway to the right, and she turned down that hallway. When Paul got to the turn he looked on down the main hall. Thirty feet farther there was another doorway. Several groups of people were entering there.

As Paul followed the group down the smaller hallway leading to the front of the auditorium, he felt an unsettled feeling. He was about to be "presented" to people he had never met before. They were going to "accept" him into their family. "What if they don't like me?" he asked himself. These people would be of central importance to his relationship with Atlantis, yet he had never met them and they had never met him. Strangely enough, the presence of Ornith on his shoulder was comforting. Ornith had a choice and Ornith had chosen him. The group of new students gathered in a small room at the back of the stage.

"OK ... First ... all of you Pixies ... you know that you can't go out there with your new friends. Please rejoin them once they have been "accepted" and have found their way back to their seats ... Students," the Professor instructed, "When your name is called, simply go out to the center of the stage to the podium. The man calling your names will be Professor Heraldon Glorfyndor, our Headmaster. Your Sponsors will be standing there with him."

Ornith flew up off of Paul's shoulder and around to face him. "It will be alright, Paul," he said almost as if he could sense how uneasy Paul was, "You'll see. I'll wait with Gwenivere and the others, OK?"

"Sure," Paul answered, even though he was still quite unsure about all of this. He was going to have to participate in a ceremony he knew nothing about, make promises he knew little about to people he knew even less about. The truth was that there had been so much information presented so fast that it was all a little un-settling.

In the small room behind the stage it was difficult to hear exactly what was going on out on the stage itself, but they could hear someone calling for order, and beginning the Ceremony.

Paul's name was the third one called. He walked out on the stage and looked out at the auditorium. It resembled a normal theater in most respects. He noticed a man and a woman standing at a podium with a man he assumed was Professor Glorfyndor. It was easy to tell who the Professor was because he had a gold ribbon flowing from the front of his neck across his shoulders and down his back. Other than the ribbon, his uniform was the same as Professor Galvyndor's.

"Baralicia and Georaldon Erlyndor, may I present Paul Andrews," he began. "Paul, this is Baralicia and Georaldon Erlyndor."

The woman immediately extended both her hands towards Paul, and as he extended his right hand towards her, she reached out and took his hand with both of hers, shook them warmly, and smiled, "It is so nice to meet you at last, Paul," she said. "I've been looking forward to this for a very long time." Her words were sincere. Her smile was bright enough to light up a very dark night. It was obvious that the lady wanted this very much.

The man extended one hand, and Paul turned to him. He also shook hands warmly. He looked Paul directly in the eyes with a calm, even look. There was a glistening mirth in his eyes that made Paul feel that this "acceptance" was something that he wanted as well as his wife. "WE ... have been looking forward to this for some time Paul. It is very nice to meet you," he said with the same warmth and sincerity Paul had felt from the woman.

In his life, Paul had never been as warmly welcomed by anyone, and it caught him off guard, "Th ... th ... thank you," he managed to stammer, "Th ... thank you both. It's nice to meet you, too."

"Baralicia and Georaldon Erlyndor," the Professor intoned in a formal voice, "Will you accept Paul Andrews into your family with all of the privileges of any other member of your family?"

"Yes," Both of them answered in unison.

"Will you sponsor him into Atlantan society at large?" the Professor asked just as formally.

"Yes," Both of them answered in unison.

As Paul watched the ceremony unfolding around him he suddenly realized that this was a great deal more important to the Atlantans than he had realized. He had approached the event as if it were just another of the endless school programs he'd suffered through in Calumet City, but this was different, a lot different. These people were making a real commitment, and it was not something they did often or lightly.

"Very well," the Professor concluded and turned to Paul, "Now, Paul," he began, "after you have been trained in our ways, and given to understand the nature of the commitment you will make, there will come a day when we ask you to commit to the causes and goals of the Society of Atlantis. At this moment you do not know enough about those causes and goals to be asked to make such a commitment. What we ask today is two things: first, that you agree to keep our secrets, and second, we ask for your best efforts to learn." He stopped and looked at the young man standing before him. "Paul," he continued, "Will you make those commitments?"

Suddenly several things became clear for Paul. His uncertainties seemed to vanish. What they were asking was fair. They were not asking him to commit blindly to a code he knew nothing about, only to agree to study it and then decide. While you were learning, they asked you to keep their secrets. That was all. That was very fair ... in fact ... everything about these people seemed to be fair. That settled it. He was in. Fully in.

"Yes, Sir" Paul answered. His voice clear and firm.

"Good," the Professor answered, "Welcome to the Society of Atlantis, Paul," the Professor said, extending his Power Ring. A golden colored light poured from it first towards the right shoulder of Paul's uniform, and he could feel the sensation of something changing with the uniform in some way, and then seconds later the light shifted to his left shoulder. He reached out his hand and shook Paul's. The Erlyndors started to move towards the stairway at one side of the stage leading down to the first row of chairs and Paul followed.

As he walked down the stairway, he looked over at his right shoulder and saw the seal of Atlantis was there. There was one on his left as well. Moments later, as he was taking a seat in the sixth row of the theater and feeling the chair adjust to him; Ornith flew up quietly and settled onto his shoulder. At the same time that Ornith was settling in, two other Pixies were greeting each of the Erlyndors and settling onto their shoulders as well.

When all of the acceptances were complete, Professor Glorfyndor began to introduce the rest of the faculty, starting with Erinlicia Flyndor and Altracia Galvyndor.   Before long the music department was introduced. All four of its faculty members were Elves, headed by an elf named Professor Barnard Nimrodel. The elves were about half the size of Atlantans, had pointy noses, pointy ears and wore pointed floppy hats. It was hard to see from his seat in the sixth row, but it looked like they had pointy ears to go along with their pointy noses. Their clothing was little different from the Atlantans, perhaps more colorful, but otherwise it looked a lot the same.

After the faculty was introduced, the entire Assembly was dismissed, and people began filtering out of the Assembly Hall towards the Dining Hall. He and the Erlyndors made their way out to the Hall when he felt a tap on his shoulder. It was Georaldon, "Just a second Paul, we have something important to do."

Paul stopped and turned to his sponsors.

The Pixie on Baralicia's shoulder flew up, "That's right," she announced as she was joined by the Georaldon's Pix.

"This is Felinda," Baralicia said.

"And this is Ardant," Georaldon said, "They are a part of your life, now, too."

The Pix and Pixie flew over to Paul, "Welcome," they both said. Ardant flew up and raised his little arm in what was an un-mistakable high five gesture. Paul reached out his hand, not wanting to slap too hard, but Ardant flew up and gave Paul a gentle tap. Felinda flew up and placed both of her little hands on Paul's cheek and rubbed noses. Paul had never rubbed noses with anyone before and noticed a pleasant sensation spread through his whole body. Afterwards they went over to Ornith and

64

exchanged high fives and rubbed noses with him too. All three of them were smiling and laughing as if they knew one another well. Paul made a mental note to ask Ornith about that later.

The Dining Hall was a large room, fully three stories tall, with ornately carved wood, paintings, banners and other decorations. There were four double rows of tables set out across the room with a head table at the front, only they were not like any tables Paul had ever seen. They floated motionless in the air just like the chairs that surrounded them. Each table would seat twelve, and had two oblong cutouts in the center. Paul sat down with the Erlyndors and introduced his roommate, Jim. His roommate's surrogate parents were surnamed Lectosor, and they seemed as excited about this prospect as the Erlyndors. He saw Betsy and Jennifer at a different table with their Atlantan sponsors and decided that there would be plenty of time to meet them later.

In the center of the main table there was a much smaller floating table, complete with tiny floating chairs. Paul realized that it had to be for the pixies. "See you soon, Paul," Ornith said and flew off to join other Pixies at the small table.

Floating carts similar to the one that had served the snacks appeared with lights flashing slowly and settled into the cutouts. Smaller ones went over to the tables for the Pixies.

"Well," Paul said to himself, "I guess that answers how I'm going to feed him." Paul was watching all of this when he heard a bell sounding from the head table. Professor Glorfyndor had stood up, and was signaling for attention, "Students … let me show you how this works," he said as the room grew quiet, "On the cart on any given day there will be eight entrée selections. They change from day to day. Select a plate of food that you find appealing, point your Power Ring at that plate, and say the word "Acquire". You can say it as softly as you like. The Power Ring will respond and that dish will come to you, along with the side dishes it is programmed to offer you. If someone else has also selected it, don't worry, another will appear. All of our noon and evening meals are four courses, appetizer, salad, main course, and dessert. We know these meals are nutritious, but we believe you will find them tasty as well."

"Paul," Georaldon said pointing at a dish that looked like Barbequed Spare Ribs, "Try those. They're especially good."

Paul raised his Ring and the light shot out. He moved his hand until the light rested on the Ribs, and said, "Acquire," exactly as the Professor had. The plate had tiny lights that started flashing and it rose up from the cart and came over towards him, settling onto the place mat in front of him. Seconds later a smaller dish of mashed potatoes came over and immediately after that a dish full of Green Peas rose up and started over.

"Stop," Georaldon said holding out his own Ring toward the Peas. Golden light shot out and the dish of peas halted in mid-air. "Do you like peas, Paul?" he asked quickly.

"Well … No," Paul answered honestly. "I can't stand them if I have a choice, but I can choke them down if I have too."

"OK," Georaldon nodded, "You do have a choice," he explained, "What you do if the cart starts sending something you don't want is tell it to "Stop", and then tell it what you want instead. If you don't want anything at all, just say "Go."

"Even if you want something that isn't on the cart?" Paul inquired.

"Within reason," Baralicia answered, "you can get whatever vegetables you want."

"Neat," Paul said aloud. He looked at the peas, held out his ring and said "corn on the cob." The same gold light shot out of his ring and he maneuvered it to shine on the cart. Immediately the peas went back to the cart, a plate with corn on the cob appeared and came over to his place and settled down next to the mashed potatoes.

As the aroma of the ribs reached his nose, Paul realized exactly how hungry he was. He looked around politely and everyone else was starting to eat, so he dug into his meal. After a few minutes, Ornith flew up from the small table and came over towards Paul. He was holding out his hand in a clear signal that he wanted to give Paul a high five so Paul held out his hand and the little Pix flew up and slapped it lightly. "Those ribs were good, weren't they?"

"Yeah," Paul answered, "They were delicious. You can eat ribs?"

"Of course," Ornith answered.

"How did you handle the bones? The bigger ones are almost as big as you are."

"Well," Ornith answered with a sly little look on his face, "That depends on if we have to be polite. If we don't, we just grab hold, tear it off and snorf it down, same as you. The problem is the sauce." He shrugged and added, "Gwenivere can be a problem too sometimes."

"What's the problem with the sauce?" Paul asked.

"It gets everywhere," Ornith answered.

"Everywhere?" Paul asked with a laugh as he raised his eyebrows.

"Well … no. Not there, but just about everywhere else, wings are a particular problem."

"What if you have to be polite?"

"The Pix at the head of the table carves the meat off for everyone," Ornith answered. "That's what happened today."

"Oh. That seems reasonable. What is the deal with Gwenivere?"

"Well she hates it when I go into snorf mode. But you know, sometimes you just can't help it."

Paul laughed out loud.

"Paul," Ornith continued eagerly, "When can we go see our room?" Both of the Erlyndors smiled.

"Look, Ornith," Paul answered matter-of-factly, "I just now found out how I was going to feed you. I don't know when yet."

"Oh, I'm sorry," Ornith said sincerely, "I didn't know you were worried about me. It will be OK. We can go see our room any time."

"Pixies are not known for their patience," Baralicia said with a laugh. "Would you like to go to see your room now?"

"Well …yes," Paul answered, "If it's OK with you guys."

"Georaldon?" she asked.

"Let's go for a walk first," he answered, "I need to stretch out a little bit."

They left the Dining Hall, and made their way to the connecting passage. In addition to the passageway itself, there were doors leading outside. Paul walked quietly with the Erlyndors for a few minutes and then Georaldon stopped short. "Can you smell that, Honey?" he asked his wife.

68

"Yes," she answered with a small wince, "I can. I don't remember that odor though. Do you?"

"No," he answered, "I haven't smelled that odor up here before. What about you Paul?" he asked.

Paul sniffed the air. There was a faint tingle in his nostrils. "I smell something that seems to be a little acidic," Paul answered, "Is that what you are talking about?"

"Yes, it is," Georaldon answered, as he reached around to the rear power wand on the right side of his belt and pulled it off. "This is the Beta Wand ... it's the back wand ... right hand side," he told Paul and then turned his attention to the wand. "Beta Wand On ... Air Sample Analysis," he instructed and then waved it through the air. When he was finished he looked at it and then showed it first to his wife, and then to Paul. Words had appeared on the surface of the wand. They said "Sodium Hydroxide = 90 ppm." Paul was not quite sure what that meant.

"Sodium hydroxide is way over the limits; I wonder where it is coming from?" Baralicia asked.

"I'll bet it's that mill," Paul answered, glad that he hadn't had to ask what sodium hydroxide was. It explained about the twinges of yellow he had seen in with the steam.

"What mill?" Georaldon asked.

"Here, I'll show you," Paul answered and led them around to the other side of the school. "There," he said pointing at the paper mill in the distance, "I don't see any yellow though ... not right now anyway."

"Beta Wand ... Binoculars," Georaldon instructed and let go of the wand. Any normal object would have fallen to the ground, but the

69

wand hovered there and transformed itself into a set of binoculars. He smiled at Paul and plucked them out of the air, "They'll be showing you what all of this stuff is soon enough ... in the second semester you'll start a course called Basic Power Wands." He brought the field glasses to his eyes and studied the plant for a minute. "No Paul, I think you are right. I don't see any yellow either, but let's see." He held the binoculars towards Paul, "See these buttons here on the top?"

Paul looked at the top of the binoculars. There were five buttons. Two on the left, two on the right and one in the middle.

"These two on the left zoom it in and out," Georaldon explained, "The two on the right adjust the focus. The one in the center takes a picture." Georaldon focused on the smoke again, and pressed the button in the center. When he was finished he made no attempt to replace the power wand. Instead he simply said "Beta Wand Off," and let go of it. It hovered motionless while it resumed its original shape and then floated back to its position on his belt and clicked on all by itself. Georaldon removed the wand in front of the one he had just had. "This is the Alpha Wand ... it's the front one on the right hand side," he said to Paul. He released the wand and said, "Alpha Wand On ... computer." As it floated there it first extended horizontally to a length of about sixteen inches. Seconds later it expanded vertically another sixteen inches forming a flat screen.

"View Last Picture," he said to the computer as it floated in the air. Almost instantly a view of the smoke billowing out of the smokestacks appeared. "Spectrographic analysis," he instructed. In a little box at the lower right a small box appeared but Paul was not in a position to read it. "Nothing but water vapor," he reported. "Alpha Wand Off," he said. Paul watched carefully. Again, Georaldon made no effort to replace the wand on his belt. In less than two seconds the wand transformed back into a five-inch long, half-inch diameter cylinder and attached itself to the number one position on Georaldon's belt.

"Nothing but steam," Baralicia observed, "They must have just recently finished venting the sodium hydroxide. We must have just caught the last a minute ago."

"Right," Georaldon said in a tone that Paul clearly understood was one of frustration.

"What are the other wands for?" Paul asked.

"Well," Georaldon answered, "That's a long story. Each has many uses. The Delta Wand contains a cloaking device. You can activate it verbally and attach it to something you want to hide while you go away. Whatever you have attached it too will be invisible until you return. It also has other uses."

"I see a bit of yellow in the steam coming from one of those stacks now," Baralicia interrupted, "Just one though."

Georaldon and Paul looked quickly. They could see it too. Georaldon just shook his head.

"You aren't going to do anything about it, are you?" Paul asked.

"No, Paul. We would but we can't. For us to interfere with something thing like this is against the laws set down by our High Council," Georaldon answered, putting his hand gently on Paul's shoulder.

"Fixing this sort of thing is what I'm here for isn't it?" Paul asked.

"Yes," he answered slowly, "Ultimately. Right now you're here to learn what you need to know to join the League of Atlantis. Fixing this sort of thing is one of the functions of the League. It's not the only thing … but … it … is … one of the things and fixing them will be your job one day." Paul noticed that he answered the question with the same sort of firm, encouraging resolve that his own father might have employed.

"But this needs to be fixed now," Paul said as he looked of at the yellow twinges in the steam.

"True," was all that Georaldon said in reply.

"But I don't know how yet," Paul protested.

"Of course not," Baralicia said, "But don't worry … you will. All you really need to do for now is tell Professor Glorfyndor. He will inform the League." She was protective, much like his own mother would have been, and Paul noticed that too. The Atlantans might have developed their technology and their culture to fabulous levels, but at heart, Paul was beginning to realize, they were not that much different.

Chapter Four

Palacrosse

Paul awoke on Sunday morning from one of the most restful sleeps he could ever remember. The chairs were not the only Atlantan things to fit themselves to you. The beds did that as well, and it was like sleeping in a warm comfortable cloud. Saturday afternoon had been spent getting settled into his room. He hadn't known how difficult that would be, but there were many items of Atlantan technology in the rooms that needed to be programmed to recognize his voice and biosigns. Neither he nor Jim would have ever figured it all out, but their sponsors had everything up and operational before dinnertime.

He thought back to the pace of the previous day's events. The things they had learned in the morning were huge but that was only the beginning. The "room" he shared with Jim was a lot more than a room. It was really a suite. At the back end were two bedrooms separated by a bathroom. The bedrooms had disappearing closets, chests and even mirrors. You spoke the name of what you wanted, and it became visible. When you wanted the mirror you said "mirror on" and it appeared. When you were finished you said "mirror off" and it disappeared. If you forgot to say "Mirror off," and walked away, after a few minutes it would disappear by itself.

There was a hamper that automatically took dirty clothes to the laundry. It vanished into the wall when you didn't need it. There was a laundry delivery port where the clean clothes were returned. Turnaround time was about two hours, he had learned. When you weren't getting clothes from the Laundry Delivery Port, it disappeared too. The two bedrooms and the bathroom opened out into the main room. Along one wall were two reclining chairs. On opposite wall were two desks with bookcases and chairs along with an entertainment center, but you couldn't see it. All you could see was a painting hanging on the wall. If either Jim or Paul spoke the word "video", the painting vanished and a video screen became visible. They could get any normal Earthantis cable TV Channel, they could get Atlantan TV channels, and there were a great many movies available. If they said "music" all they had to do was tell the wall what they wanted to listen to, and it would be piped in through invisible speakers … only it wasn't like speakers. The music didn't seem to come from anywhere. It was as if the entire room was full of sound coming from everywhere.

The lights went up and down in intensity on voice command, so did the thermostat, but the neatest thing, both of the boys had agreed, was the snack dispenser. If either of them spoke the word "snack" an area of the wall retracted and a recessed area was formed. All you did then was tell it what sort of snack you wanted, and a few seconds later it appeared in the recess along with a floating plate that would bring the snack right to you.

"It's a transporter receptacle," Georaldon Erlyndor had explained, "The food or beverage you want is prepared in the kitchen and transported to the receptacle. The floating plates that bring the food over to you are called null plates. You can get candy bars and other snacks … soft drinks

74

... even a light meal ... whatever you want."

"Who prepares the snacks?" Paul remembered asking.

"This sort of thing is all done automatically by robotic machines," Baralicia answered, "in the school's kitchen. Same with the meals they serve in the Dining Hall. Most of these functions are performed robotically."

"You don't have to pay?" Paul had asked.

Georaldon had smiled at that. "There are many things that are different about Atlantan Society from what you are used to. Cash is obsolete among us. None of us carry "cash", but "money" and "cash" are not the same thing. "Money" is not obsolete among us, but a single monthly fee pays for all of your basic needs. Our technology allows us to produce those things at a very low cost. It works a little like a phone bill, but it covers all of your basic necessities, including food. As a member of this school, you receive an allowance that is more than the fee. After the fee is paid, there is money left over in your bank account ... so ... yes ... you do have to pay for the snacks ... but it is done automatically. The central computer recognizes your voice print and automatically deducts the amount from your account ... so ... no ... you don't have to carry or use any cash. None of us do, not when we're dealing with the things of Atlantis ... the things of Earthantis are another matter. When any of us are traveling on the surface, we carry American money. Whenever need any cash, all you have to do is ask the snack dispenser. It also works as an ATM. It will give you an envelope with the cash you need in US Dollars up to the amount you have in your account. But the amount is enough to cover most things"

"As long as it's reasonable," interjected Baralicia.

"Right," Georaldon continued, "but there is a contingency fund for emergencies. You won't have any "Atlantan" emergencies that are not covered by your monthly fee. This fund is for emergencies relating to Earthantis. The standard amount of the emergency contingency fund is $2,500 per semester. If you need more than that, you have to explain to us what it is for."

"So the snack dispenser is also an ATM. With everything covered by that fee, what will I need cash for?" he had asked.

Baralica had smiled a sweet smile, and shared a knowing look with Georaldon before answering. "There are ... girls ... here, Paul. You might want to go on a date sometime."

"We're allowed to date?" Paul asked. He hadn't had time to consider that. He'd been to parties, but he'd never been on a date.

"Of course," Baralicia answered with as small a smile as she could manage.

"Also for when you go into Hawk's Nest," Georaldon continued with a grin on his own face, "whether you have a date or not."

Paul lay in his bed thinking about all of the things he had seen yesterday. It had been the biggest day of his life. He looked around the bedroom and shook his head at the wonder of it all. Just then he noticed something stirring under the covers, and a few seconds later Ornith popped out. "Good Morning, Paul," the Pix said pleasantly. "Are we first in the shower or is it Jim and Aurileol?" the little Pix asked.

"Do you take showers with me?" Paul asked in disbelief.

"Of course not," answered Ornith, "All the spraying water doesn't work very well with wings, but there is a little tub in there and I will take my bath while you take your shower."

"Oh," was all Paul could think of to say.

Ψ

An hour later they were seated in the dining hall. At the head table were several teachers. Professor Galvyndor rose to her feet and rang a bell. "Students," she began, "let me have your attention. Morning announcements are always given at this time. First ... today is a day off for you. We hope you will explore the school ... the grounds ... and make yourselves familiar with the rules. Each of you will find a copy of the rules in the bookcase in your suites. Tomorrow, after breakfast, you will be introduced to an Atlantan sport called "Palacrosse." In the afternoon you will be introduced to a game called "Chorda." I believe you will find them to be fun. You will find information on both Palacrosse and Chorda in your bookcases and you should review the information today. These are the only announcements we have this morning. Have a nice day."

After breakfast, Paul and Jim started towards Fellowship Hall and turned a corner in the hallway.

"BAMM!!!"

A loud noise along and an intense green light went off behind Jim's shoulder. The concussion knocked Aurileol somersaulting forward through the air. The little blue-haired Pix tumbled end over end five or six times and just managed to get control of himself before he smacked into the ground. As he hovered there with his hair flying in all direction,

77

Gwenivere and Renalee popped into view. Both of them were laughing and slapping their knees.

"Got you back, Aurileol," Gwenivere said blowing a raspberry at Aurileol before flying off.

"What was that?" Paul asked.

"A flashblaster," Ornith answered. "It's kind of like a firecracker for Pixies."

"Pixies have firecrackers?"

"Of course," Ornith answered. "That particular one is called a Green Weenie. It has a smaller bang than the rest of them.

"Aren't they dangerous?" Jim asked shaking his head. His ears were still ringing.

"Nope," Ornith answered as Aurileol straightened himself and flew back over to them. Paul noticed that Aurileol was laughing.

"They … aren't … dangerous … or … anything." Ornith said swinging his arms to and fro for emphasis. "Even if they go off in your hand. Here. See." Ornith reached into a little pouch at his side and pulled out a tiny ball about a millimeter in diameter.

"Close your eyes, Paul," he said scrunching up his own. Paul closed his eyes and Ornith said, "Bang in two."

Two seconds later … BAMM!!!

This one was louder and even through closed eyes, Paul could tell the light was a bright blue. He opened his eyes and the little ball was still there and there was no damage to Ornith's hand.

"That one is called a Blue Banger. They come in all different colors. We have Red Rockers, Orange Crushers, Silver Slammers … all colors. If you are looking at the light it will blind you for a couple of minutes though. It is why I said for you to close your eyes."

Paul and Jim wandered through Fellowship Hall, and investigated the Library. It was far more extensive than they had originally thought. It turned out that there were over one hundred thousand volumes contained there. After lunch, Paul and Jim walked off the elevator onto their floor of the Dorm section and into the Common Area. They saw Betsy and Jennifer in one of the sitting areas. It looked as though they were waiting for them.

"Say," Betsy asked, "Would you guys want to go into Hawk's Nest and look around? Some of the shops may not be open but we could see what the town is like. There's a bus that comes by the front gate."

Jim looked at Betsy, "Before we get into that, are Gwenivere and Aurileol going to get along?"

"Of course," Ornith answered. "They are good friends. Aurileol got a trick on her, and now she got one back on him … happens all the time."

Jim shrugged, "OK, then. Sure. We'll go," he said looking at Paul. "Is there anything special we have to do if we leave the grounds? I haven't gotten all of the way through the rule book yet."

"Yes," Jennifer answered with a smile that indicated that she had read it all, and Betsy nodded in agreement, "But there's nothing to it. We have to check out with the Librarian and freshmen have to be back before six. If the Pixies want to come, they have to stay out of sight. That's all."

Paul turned his head towards Ornith, who was perched on his right shoulder. "Do you want to come?"

"Of course," Ornith answered.

"Absolutely," Aurileol agreed with a nod, "We haven't ever been into Hawk's Nest before."

"Do you think they have pigeon's there?" Ornith asked.

"Probably," Paul answered with a grin, "There are pigeons almost everywhere."

"Oh, goody!" Aurileol exclaimed.

"How do you stay out of sight?" Jim asked.

"We just Cloak," Ornith answered. "No one can see us. It's how Gwenivere snuck up on Aurileol."

"Really?"

"Yep," Ornith replied and launched himself off his perch on Paul's shoulder. "See," he said after he had flown around where Paul could see him. He was pointing to the belt he was wearing. It was just like Paul's only a whole lot smaller. "We have transport belts just like you."

"OK, then," Jennifer said with a nod, "This is good."

The four members of Q3 made their way back down to Fellowship Hall and checked out with the Librarian. It was a twenty minute bus ride into town. As they walked around, Paul noticed that Hawk's Nest was an old town, but a pleasant one. There was a square with a Courthouse in the center and shops of various descriptions on the surrounding streets. The buildings were built of stone and many of the shops had apartments over them.

"How quaint," Betsy commented as they walked past a bookstore. The books were new, but the store had been there for a very long time. They turned down an alley to go over by the courthouse.

"Look," Ornith shouted suddenly, "pigeons!"

Sure enough there was a small flock of pigeons in the alley.

"Jim, go to the end and see if anyone's coming" Paul suggested. Jim walked to the end and signaled that there was no one there.

"You guys can un-cloak and go see them if you want," Paul said, "Just don't get too close. They might try and peck you." The four Pixies immediately became visible and flew down with the pigeons. The birds clucked and squawked and flapped around for a minute trying to figure out what manner of creature the Pixies were. The four Pixies clucked, squawked and flapped back and the birds decided they were no threat and went back to searching for bits of food ... all except for one. The largest bird started chasing after Ornith. Ornith laughed and flew up about a foot and the pigeon flew after him. Ornith dodged around for a few seconds and the bird landed and went back to looking for food. Ornith flew down near the bird and it went after him again, but Ornith dodged away easily. Ornith looked over at Paul and laughed. Paul noticed that the little Pix's laughter sounded like the tinkling of a silver bell. Ornith landed near the bird again, and once again the bird gave chase. Soon all of the Pixies were teasing the birds into chasing them and their laughter brought smiles to the group.

"Someone's coming down the street." Jim called. The Pixies all cloaked and Paul, Betsy and Jennifer joined Jim.

"Let's go get some ice cream from that shop on the other side of the courthouse," Betsy suggested.

"Good idea," Jennifer agreed. They walked out of the ally and onto the sidewalk and found three boys approaching from the opposite

81

direction. The one in front had sandy blond hair and a mean look to his ice blue eyes. He was not particularly big, but the two boys with him were huge.

"Well … well," the blond boy said with a sneer, "What have we here?" He began walking in Paul's direction. "You must be one of those geeks from that science school."

One of the bigger boys sniggered, "You get 'em Joe."

Paul knew a bully when he saw one. "Excuse me," he said and quickly moved towards the street and walked around them. Jim and the girls followed Paul's lead and the four of them kept walking.

"Come back here," the blond boy demanded, "I wasn't through with you."

"Just keep walking," Paul said quietly. "Don't say anything, just keep walking. Maybe they won't chase us down." The three bullies stood there watching as the four members of Q3 kept on walking.

When they were out of earshot, Jim spoke up, "I hope there aren't a lot of guys around like that." They wandered through the town for another thirty minutes before heading back to the school.

The girls had gone back to their room to read up on Palacrosse and Chorda. Jim looked at Paul, "It's 3:00 o'clock. What do you want to do now?"

"Well, reading up on those games shouldn't take as long as the girls think. My guess is that thirty or forty minutes will be plenty," Paul answered, "We could walk up that trail to the ridgeline."

"Yeah," Jim agreed, "Maybe we can get a better look at that mill."

"Yeah. That's what I was thinking. Do you want to go too?" Paul

82

asked Ornith.

"Of course," the yellow-haired Pix answered.

"Me too," Aurileol chimed in, "I want to go too. We haven't ever been up there either. Please ... please, I want to come too."

"OK ... OK," Jim said, "You can come too. I don't think there will be any pigeon's up there though."

"That's OK," Ornith said.

Paul smiled, "We've got plenty of time before dinner."

They walked down the flagstone path from the rear of the school, past the greenhouse, and out to an iron gate at the rear of the property. Paul pointed his Power Ring at the lock and said "Open." The lock unfastened and they opened the gate. The path itself part way down. It petered out and was replaced by a dirt trail that led down into a gully and then up the other side. After about forty minutes they were up on the ridgeline, and both Paul and Jim were a little out of breath. Walking down the hillside was one thing, but walking back up was something else entirely.

They looked back at the school below them. "It's nice up here," Jim said as they looked around.

"There is that mill," Paul said pointing to the south. The mill was about fifteen miles away and they had a much better view from their vantage point on the ridgeline.

"Is it releasing anything?"

"I can't tell ... let's watch for a while."

"Good idea," Paul agreed and took the Beta Power Wand off of his belt. "I think I know how to use this thing ...Beta Wand On ...

binoculars," he said exactly as Georaldon had done. As both boys watched, the wand transformed into a pair of binoculars. Paul placed his fingers on the zoom buttons and held the binoculars to his eyes. As he adjusted first the zoom and then the focus to get a good look at the top of the stack he noticed yellow twinges in the steam.

"They're doing it again Jim," he said as he pressed the button in the center of the binocular and snapped a picture. He looked over at his roommate. Jim had copied Paul's moves and was looking at the mill with his own binoculars.

"They sure are. I can see the yellow streaks in the steam too. We ought to see if we can take a sample." Jim suggested.

Paul released the binoculars and they just floated there as if they were waiting for something. "Beta Wand Off," he said and the binoculars transformed back into their original shape floated over and reattached to Paul's belt. Paul took the Alpha Wand off of his belt. "Alpha Wand On ... computer," he said. In a matter of seconds the computer had extruded a screen, turned itself on and was floating there.

"Awesome," Jim said and Paul realized Jim hadn't seen this happen before.

"View Last Picture," Paul said to the computer screen and the picture he had just taken appeared. "Spectrographic analysis," he instructed. In a little box at the lower right a small box appeared *Water vapor... sodium hydroxide = 690 ppm ... trace metallic contaminants.*"

"690 parts per million!" Paul exclaimed.

"Isn't that more than before?" Jim asked.

"I don't know. The only sample Georaldon took was 90 ppm, but that was of the air down by the school. By the time he got the computer and binoculars out they had stopped releasing. This analysis is of the steam coming straight out of the stack."

"So it could have been diluted by the time it drifted over."

"Right," agreed Paul.

"Well," Jim said, "Now we've got a record, at least."

"Ummm … Paul," Ornith said with concern in his voice, "you should look back over in that other direction." The little Pix was pointing to the East. Thunderclouds were building and moving rapidly toward the ridgeline. As Paul watched he saw two large bolts of lightning flash across the sky.

"Nuts! Alpha Wand Off," Paul instructed.

"Can we make it back to the school before that storm hits?" Jim asked.

"I doubt it," Paul answered, "But we can't for sure if we don't get started." The boys put their gear away and hurried down the hillside. When they were almost at the bottom the storm caught them and they found themselves in a torrential downpour. From the thunder they knew that there was lightening not far behind the rain.

"We're still almost a mile away," Jim announced breathlessly as they got to the bottom, "and the rest is all uphill."

"Right," Paul agreed, "Let's go." They started jogging up the hillside.

Sheets of cold mountain rain washed over them. A bolt of lightning struck a tree about a mile from where they were standing. They found the end of the path and headed up towards the school and a few seconds later lightning struck again, closer this time.

"Things are getting a little exciting, Paul," Jim called out as he wiped rainwater from his eyes. "Maybe we should just find an open spot out of these trees and wait until this passes. We can put our hoods up and stay dry enough."

"I've got another idea," Paul shouted over the rain. "Let's visualize that spot in front of the portico by Fellowship Hall and just Jump there instead of trying to run all the way back."

"That's a good idea," Jim agreed as lightning struck close by again.

Paul closed his eyes, visualized his destination and tapped his fingers. He was instantly surrounded by the kaleidoscope of colors. When they stopped Paul was standing in front of the portico, and Jim appeared about two seconds later. Both boys hurried in out of the driving rain. All four of them were wringing wet from their necks up, but their uniforms had kept them dry underneath. Paul watched as Aurileol fluttered his wings to get the water off of them, and felt Ornith doing the same thing.

Ornith flew around and high five'd Paul. "That was great fun!" he said with his high pitched little laugh.

"Pixies like thunderstorms?" Paul asked.

"Of course," Ornith answered, "It was an adventure. Pixies love adventures and I've never been in a storm before."

"Or seen lightning," Aurileol added.

"Really?"

"Really!" Ornith answered with an emphatic nod of his little head. "It doesn't rain down in Co-re-alis and on our trips up here the weather was always nice. I liked watching the lightening. It was an adventure."

Later, as they sat down in the dining hall, Ornith flew up to Gwenivere who was sitting on Betsy's shoulder, "We went for a hike, Gwenivere. It was great! We got rained on and lightning 'ed at and everything."

"You were lightning 'ed at?" Gwenivere asked in wide eyed wonder.

"Yeah," Ornith answered, "It was great!" He flew over to the Pix's table followed immediately by Gwenivere. His hair was still wet from the storm.

Paul pointed his Ring at a plate of Greek Chicken. "Acquire," he said and the dish's lights started flashing and it floated up off of the cart and over to his place at the table. Seconds later some scalloped potatoes floated up and started over. Paul liked those so he let them come. After that some Brussels sprouts started over. "Stop," Paul commanded, "Green bean casserole," Paul said. The Brussels sprouts went back, and a plate appeared with the casserole on it and came over.

"So what were you guys doing out in that storm?" Betsy asked.

"Well," Paul replied, "we didn't plan on getting caught in it. When we left the weather was fine."

"Besides," Jim added, "We weren't out in it long."

"Some of the lightning bolts hit pretty close," Ornith yelled over from the Pixies table. "It is very loud and crackly when it's close … really neat."

"Lightning hitting close is neat?" Betsy asked as if she couldn't believe her ears.

87

"Yep," Ornith announced with a mouthful of food. He was eating Rock Cornish Game Hen, a tasty little bird similar to chicken only smaller and more flavorful. He had a drumstick in one hand. The drumstick of a Cornish Game Hen to a Pix was about like a large Turkey drumstick to a human. "This is good," he said to Aurileol, who immediately selected his own drumstick.

Paul looked at Betsy and shrugged, "They like adventures."

Betsy looked the two Pixs wet stringy hair and shook her head. "Honestly! You guys are as bad as … as … well … boys!"

"Of course," Ornith answered with a laugh, as he tore off another mouthful from his drumstick.

"Maybe even worse," agreed Aurileol taking a chomp out of his own. He was also laughing.

Ψ

The next morning Professor Galvyndor began again with announcements. First was the general schedule for the next few days including another announcement about Palacrosse instruction. "And," she concluded, "we have one last announcement … Professor Glorfyndor needs to see Paul Andrews immediately after breakfast."

Suddenly all of the students were staring at Paul with curious looks on their faces. He looked down at his plate and saw a piece of bacon. He picked it up and ate it washing it down with apple juice, trying not to fidget under all of the stares. A few seconds later everyone went back to their breakfasts.

"Boys!" Jennifer said shaking her head in mock disbelief.

"What's that all about?" Betsy asked with arched eyebrows, "Are you in trouble … already." Her tone indicated she wouldn't be surprised.

"No," Jim said supportively, "Paul's not in trouble."

"I'll bet," Betsy said with a tone of disapproval.

"You're a boy," Jennifer responded and looked at Betsy, "Have you ever known a boy who couldn't get into trouble?"

"Nope," Betsy answered, "I just hope you haven't cost us points,"

"No," Jim argued and looked over at Paul, "He's not in trouble. It's probably about the air sample. Didn't the Erlyndors tell you that you'd need to speak to him?"

"Yes, they did," Paul answered and then looked at Betsy, "I can't think of anything I've done to get into trouble."

"What air sample are you talking about?" Betsy asked as she gulped down her apple juice.

Paul told them about the yellow tinges he'd seen in the steam the first day, and the test Georaldon had performed. He finished up with the tests he and Jim had done before the storm hit the day before.

"High levels of sodium hydroxide," Jennifer mused, "This is …not … good."

"Wow," Betsy said enthusiastically, "We've only been here one day and we're already onto something."

"Not so fast," Jim said quickly, "No one's told us we can do anything about any of this stuff yet."

"But no one has said we can't either," Betsy countered.

"But Betsy," Jennifer objected, "We don't even know what to do."

"But we could find out," Betsy went on. "Look what Paul and Jim have already learned. And once we did …"

"Wait a second Betsy," Paul interjected, "Let's not get ahead of ourselves. Let me go see the Professor and find out what this is all about, and then we'll know more."

Ψ

Professor Flyndor had shown Paul the way to Professor Glorfyndor's office. As he stood there waiting for the Headmaster to arrive, Paul noticed that the office was not ostentatious but appeared well used and comfortable. It was paneled in dark oak, contained several bookshelves full of books, and a large desk in the center. Paul was looking at the books when the Professor entered.

"Sit down, Paul," the Headmaster said with a smile pointing at one of the two chairs in front of the desk, "Sit down. I suppose you're wondering why we Atlantans use books. Especially after all of the things you saw yesterday."

"Well, yes," Paul answered, wanting to be polite. It really was not the question he had in his mind at all, "Now that you mention it, don't you have Kindle's or things like that?" he asked quickly.

"Of course we do, but there is no technology that replaces the pleasant feel of a good book in your own hands," the Professor said, "We have everything on computers, but reading from a computer screen just doesn't provide the same sensation as turning the pages of a book does. Most of us like to pick up a book and just read it. Holding a book and thumbing through the pages as you read is not a sensation that is improved on by technology so many of us read the old fashioned way for the pleasure of it. There are a lot of things like that. Metal is not always superior to wood for example. It depends on what you want to use it for. The grain and texture of wood often add an artistic value ... anyway ... that is not why you're here, now is it young man?"

"No, Sir," Paul answered, "I don't think so."

Paul eased back into his chair. It was obvious from the Headmaster's demeanor that he was not in trouble, or at least did not seem to be.

"So," the Professor said taking his own seat, "Tell me about the sodium hydroxide."

Paul explained everything in detail.

"Hmmm ..." Professor Glorfyndor said in response as he looked at the display screen on Paul's computer. He studied it for a moment and then looked at Paul closely as if measuring him. Paul might have been shown how to set up the computer and binoculars by his sponsors, but only once. Paul had caught on quickly, and then used what he had learned and that was promising. One of the great challenges of teaching young people was to keep some semblance of control, but an even greater challenge was knowing when to let the reins out. As far as he could tell, there would be no harm in letting this go a little farther.

"Do you know what is going on, Paul?" he asked. Clearly the Headmaster did know. He was trying to determine if Paul knew.

"Yes, Sir," Paul answered, "At least I think I do. I had to do a report on it for ..." he paused and smiled at the Headmaster, "I get it, Sir.

I had to do the report for Ms. Merrill ... Carolicia Merilyndor is her Atlantan name. She was grooming me even then, wasn't she?"

Professor Glorfyndor simply nodded.

"OK," Paul continued taking in a deep breath, "They use a strong base like sodium hydroxide to break down the wood fibers in the process of making paper. Every now and then the paper mill is probably releasing some of the used up chemicals into the exhaust steam."

"Exactly," the Professor agreed with a nod, "Very good, by the way. Why would they do that?"

"Well," Paul answered, "It probably costs a lot of money to treat it. Whatever they release they don't have to pay for."

"Right again," the Professor agreed.

"May I ask a question, Sir?"

"Certainly," Professor Glorfyndor answered.

"Do all paper mills behave this way?"

"No, in fact most of them don't" the Professor answered slowly, "Not for a long time now anyway. When the people of Earthantis began adopting legislation prohibiting this sort of thing, most of the companies changed their policies and obeyed the law, but some didn't. They bribe politicians; they falsify their records and use whatever devious methods they can find to keep from spending the money. They have no concern for the environment, and they will break the law to increase their profits. Our studies suggest that only about fifteen percent behave this way, but the fifteen percent causes a great deal more problems than most people realize."

"What will happen?" Paul asked.

92

"Well, that mill has been doing this for a long time," Professor Glorfyndor answered, as he thought back to the first time he'd noticed the pollution. "If you look at the health of the forest surrounding the mill for twenty miles or so, and compare it to a healthy forest, you'll find all sorts of effects, but it just isn't the forest that's the issue. There will be a much higher incidence of respiratory illness in humans ... pneumonia and bronchitis for example, but also lung cancer. Somewhere between six and ten more people will die of lung cancer every year in Hawk's Nest than the national average for a town that size. This is one of the under reported facts of life on Earthantis. It never makes the news because there is no way to tell which ones would have died anyway and which ones were killed by the pollution, but air pollution actually kills people."

"Six to ten people dying every year," Paul said softly as he thought for a moment and then continued seriously, "Professor ... something ought to be done. Can't the League of Atlantis do something about this?"

"Yes," the professor answered, "And in time we will. The problem is that the League has a great deal more projects like this than there are people to handle them. Priorities are placed, and the larger projects have to be handled first. Besides, as close as this is to the school, the League would probably expect us to handle it as a senior training C-Op anyway."

"That would work," Paul said, "Aren't there some seniors who could take this as a C-Op?"

"No, Paul," Professor Glorfyndor answered, "All of our seniors are working on C-Op projects they developed last year. As part of your Junior Year, you see, each Quadro is expected to develop and plan its own

93

project. This planning is based on leads you research in your sophomore year. We don't assign the senior C-Ops, only approve and supervise. We do assign sophomores a series of research projects to develop leads. The best I can do is get this on that list for the sophomores."

"Hmmm ..." Paul said seriously, "I see. That means that nothing can happen for two years. What if ..." Paul began to ask but then his voice trailed off.

Professor Glorfyndor smiled as he rose from his desk and walked over to one of the bookshelves and pulled out two books. "The Rules of this school specifically prohibit students working on ... "school sponsored" ... operations of this kind until their senior year, and only then with close faculty supervision. What this means, as far as you are concerned, is that the faculty cannot help you. It also prohibits using school facilities, but most rules have two sides. The other side of that rule is this: what you and your friends do on your free time is up to you as long as you do not use school resources, break the local laws or violate *The Code of Atlantis*. As far as using school resources is concerned that means "use" as in use up. You do not have the right to use up what you can't replace without permission. Having said that, there is nothing in any of our rules that says that you cannot look into this on your own if you wish." He extended the books to Paul, "You already have a copy of the book on top, but this particular copy is highlighted. Reading the highlighted sections will help you grapple with this issue if you choose too. In the event you do, there is information in the second book that you may find useful. It is a textbook for juniors."

Paul took the books and looked at them, "Juniors?" he said with a question mark in his voice. The book on top was titled *The Code Of Atlantis*. The second one was titled *Corrective Operations*.

"Yes. That is when we begin to introduce you to the specifics of Correctional Operations … C-Ops as they are called. We begin teaching you the specific techniques for your Senior C-Op in your junior year. I want to stress the importance of not breaking the principals set down in *The Code Of Atlantis*." The Professor looked searchingly at Paul for another moment and then continued with a pleasant smile, "Now, I believe you have your first Palacrosse lesson."

ψ

Paul stood with Jim, Betsy and Jennifer as Coach Albeitron Conflyndor explained the rules of Palacrosse.

"First," he began, "This is a co-ed sport. Each team has four members, two males and two females. Each of your Quadros forms a complete Palacrosse team, and in the spring you will compete for the championship of your class. We have a school team that competes against the best players of the other schools. Freshmen are not allowed to try out for the school team, and it is extremely rare for a sophomore to make it. You'll get more on that later. For now all you really need to know is that you get three points in the Quadro Bowl for winning a match."

"Palacrosse is like a combination of soccer and tennis, played in a special 3-D field. There are several pieces of equipment. The first is the Wobble. The object of the game is to get this "Wobble" through your opponent's goal. You get one point each time you do. This is a

95

"Wobble," he said holing up a ball about the size of a racquetball. "It's the ball you use to play this game. It is slightly off center. If you hit it with insufficient spin, it will wobble as it travels which is where it gets its name. If you get enough spin on it, the Wobble will fly true, but it curves as it flies. You strike the Wobble with the Wobble Paddle." He help up a paddle that looked a lot like a Ping-Pong paddle only bigger, and it had holes in it. Around the edge was soft rubber padding.

"Next," the coach continued, "Let's look at a Null Harness." He held up a harness that consisted of a belt with flashing lights and straps that went up over the shoulder. "This harness," the coach continued, "nullifies the effects of gravity. That is all it does. A single touch on the buckle turns it on and a double touch turns it off. Don't do that until you're a foot or two from the ground."

"Now," the coach went on, "Palacrosse is played in a special "field". A Palacrosse Field Generator is required to play this game, at least the way we play it today." He paused and said clearly, "Palacrosse Field Generator ... On." Immediately a dark blue mesh in the shape of a large sausage lit up. It was about sixty yards long and twenty in diameter. About five yards from each end was a six foot red ring.

"That must be the goal," Paul said quietly to his teammates.

"Right," Betsy agreed.

In front of the Goal Ring was another mesh, like the blue one of the field itself, only red. It formed a 20-foot diameter ball around the goal.

"Now the best way to explain how all of this works is to demonstrate." The coach touched the belt once, turning it on and pushed off from the ground. He sailed up inside of the blue mesh. There was

96

nothing to stop him so he continued sailing upwards. When he got to the topside of the field, he somersaulted over, bunched his feet up under him and jumped off the mesh as if it was solid. The mesh acted like a trampoline and he flew away in the direction that had jumped. He flew in that direction until he reached the field's limit in the other direction, spun around, and pushed off again. Each time he reached the edge of the field he pushed again.

"Sweet," Jim said looking at Paul.

"Totally," Paul agreed and looked back at Jim, knowing that he was really going to like this game.

"Jumping off of the sides is called Bounding," the coach told them, and then threw the wobble. It came to the edge of the Palacrosse Field and bounced just as if the field was solid and traveled away until it hit the wall again. It bounced around back and forth like a billiard ball on a pool table only in three dimensions. The coach expertly judged the ricochet point of the wobble, adjusted his launch angle from the field's side, pushed off and intercepted the wobble. He struck it with the paddle, throwing his wrist over the top of the wobble giving it top spin and sent it towards one of the goals. The wobble curved from the spin a little like a baseball as it flew, and went straight through the middle of the goal. A gong went off, and the number "1" lit up at the other end of the Field.

"Totally sweet," Jennifer said and looked first at Betsy and then at Paul and Jim. The other three just nodded.

The coach jumped off the edge of the field and intercepted the wobble. This time he hit it very softly, breaking its momentum. "You are allowed to hit the ball twice, before someone else hits it," the coach

97

instructed, "but not more than that. Two hits are all you get. After that, you've got to let someone else hit it. It makes no difference if that is an opponent or a teammate. You can't use your hands to hit the ball, or throw it. You have to use the paddle. Any rule violation results in the opposing team getting a penalty shot. That is an unimpeded shot from twenty feet away. Also, the field you see around the goal is the Exclusion Zone. That mesh will let wobbles pass, but not you. You can bound off of it though, just like the field wall."

"OK," Coach Conflyndor said pointing to a cart of equipment that was floating out of a doorway at one end, and moving towards the group of students, "There are null harnesses and wobble paddles there for everyone. Just get into one end of one of these four fields with your Quadro and start to get a feel for the game."

Paul grabbed a null harness and a paddle as quickly as he could. He picked up a wobble that was lying there. Jim was already into a harness and picking up a paddle, and the girls were ready just as quickly so they walked over to the field that was closest to them. "Ready?" Paul asked.

"Ready," they all answered and touched their buckles and jumped into the field and kept on going. Somersaulting was easy, but timing it so that you could bound off of the other side was not, and there was no way to stop until you reached the field wall. It took practice and more than once they flew into the wall, but when that happened they just bounced off of it very much like bouncing off of a trampoline.

"Paul," Jim called out after a bit, "throw the wobble."

Paul tried to pass the Wobble to Jim, but the off center nature of the wobble took it towards Jennifer instead. She drew back her paddle, and managed to hit it, but not very hard, and she didn't throw her wrist over the wobble to give it spin. It took off in the general direction that she'd hit it but the flight was erratic. The others tried to intercept it, but this was harder than it looked. Finally Jim got into position and got a harder hit, but no spin. The result was a faster flight, but just as erratic. Then Paul managed to get into position. He knew how to hit a tennis ball with topspin. He made good contact, with good spin, and this time the Wobble flew true, curving a little at first and more as it traveled, but it went nowhere near the goal. It was obvious to Paul that this was going to take a lot of work, but it was also fun.

The coach blew a whistle. "OK, it's an hour until lunch time. I want you to take an hour break. After lunch you have your first History of Atlantis class. After that you will have your first Chorda lesson. Tomorrow these four fields will be up all day. You'll be able to practice as much as you want."

ψ

After lunch, Q3 made their way to the Classroom Building. They found the correct room and took their seats. No sooner had they sat down in a chair than a desk grew out of the right side and maneuvered into the proper position to take notes.

"They don't seem to have any shortage of these desks," Jennifer noted.

Professor Galvyndor walked in and took up her position at the front of the class. "OK," she began, "Welcome to your first class on the History of Atlantis. I am a science teacher but there is a reason why I deliver this particular history lecture. That reason will become obvious soon enough."

"Before we begin your first History class … let's talk about the League of Atlantis for a moment. Professor Heraldon Glorfyndor founded the League for the purpose of making it possible for the current societies of Earthantis and Atlantan society to merge together as smoothly as possible when this becomes necessary. The League's missions fall into two broad categories. The first, but not necessarily the simplest are "Technology Transfer" operations … called T-Ops for short. This is where we arrange for your scientists and engineers to make "breakthrough" discoveries. The people of Earthantis are doing quite well in this regard when compared to the pace at which we developed, but when compared with where they need to be for a smooth merge, that pace must be speeded up. Right now the gap is too great, so part of what the League does is to arrange for certain "ideas" to be suggested to scientists or ever more often, engineers, who are operating in that field. Often all that is needed is pointing a person in the right direction and asking "What if?" … amazing question … "What if?" but you'll learn a lot more about that later. That is not all there is to a T-Op, because often in Earthantan business circles, "new" ideas are resisted, and sometimes even fought, so we help with the resistance if that develops, and if the business interests that stand to benefit if things remain the same decide to fight the new development … well … let me just say that T-Ops can get very interesting."

"A good example of a highly successful T-Op is the Stem Cell research now going on," she continued. "The uses of Stem Cells are vast, and Earthantan scientists are going along quite nicely now, but something had to get them started. That something was the first T-Op conducted by the League of Atlantis."

"The other type of mission is called a "Correctional Operation" ... or C-Op for short. They are a lot harder because they can be dangerous. At this time there are many aspects of Earthantan society that are moving in good directions, but the progress is slowed or even stopped by a small number of individuals. Most frequently these individuals are motivated by greed and their actions are against the law. In some cases they are corrupt businessmen or politicians. In others they are outright criminals. In either case they can be ruthless and dangerous people. The numbers of such persons in the societies of Earthantis today is relatively small on a percentage basis, but the damage they do is vast. In many cases the nature of the criminal operation makes it impossible for the local authorities to do anything. That is where the League and C-Op missions come in. The object of a C-Op is to stop an illegal or corrupt operation, and that is what can make the mission dangerous. These people are willing to break the law to do these things which means they will break the law to keep from being stopped. Our technology gives us a great many advantages, and we've never lost a League Member but we have had close calls quite a few times. Catching the mobster Whitey Bulger was a C-Op, and the catching of a man like that is not the hard part. The hard part was that he had been protected by elements within the FBI. The FBI is, on the whole, a very good organization, but corruption has crept in, even there, now and then. Bringing that corruption into the light was the hardest part of the C-Op."

She paused and looked around the room. "So ... those are the sorts of things the League of Atlantis does. In order to join the League you must pass your Senior Qualification Exams. These exams are also known as Quals. Once you have graduated from this school and passed your Quals, you may join the League as an Associate Member. The first League assignment is always the same for everyone. Attend College! During your college years you will also learn how to conduct T-Ops. Other than general theories and practices, you won't get into them here. When you graduate from college you have to pass you Fellow Qualification exams, known as Fellow Quals. Once you do, you are awarded the title of "Fellow" of the League of Atlantis. Associate Members are involved in League Ops, both C-Ops and T-Ops during their college years but are not allowed to vote or sit on governing committees. A "Fellow" of the League of Atlantis votes on League matters and is involved in directing its operations."

"So much for the League," she smiled and looked around the class, "for now. Let's move on to what you will be doing here for the next four years. Your studies here are split into two sections. As a member of the League of Atlantis, you will be operating in the societies of Earthantis. In many cases having attended a prestigious college is the only way to get access to the people you need, especially for T-Ops. This is why Associate Members always attend a well-regarded mainstream college. In order to prepare you for college, three periods per day will be devoted to a group of classes that we call Earthantan Studies. If you want to know why the pace around here is so rigorous, it's because we fit an entire high school education into three hours per day instead of the normal seven. The second section is a group of four periods of classes we call Atlantan Studies. This is where we teach you about our culture, the principals of Atlantis, and what you need to conduct operations for the League. When you put all of this together, you are going to be working very hard, but we never told you it would be easy."

She picked up a textbook. "So ... let's begin. During the school year you will go through this history text in detail, but we don't do that during Summer Orientation. What we will do over the next few weeks is try to give you an overview to help you to feel more comfortable. We understand that this is all new, and that makes it all a little unreal. This is normal. We have found it helps to have some background, a point of connection so to speak, and that is the purpose of Summer Orientation. Some of you received pieces of this information in the process of your recruitment. Some may not have, so please bear with any repetition."

She paused and looked around the room. Paul noticed that she had everyone's complete attention. "First, all of you ... are now ... Atlantans. You are citizens of Atlantis the same as I am. I am old enough to vote, and you are not yet old enough. But other than that, I have no rights that you do not have. This is what the Presentation and Acceptance Ceremony was all about. When we speak of Atlantans, that group includes you. Now I have a news flash for you. Those of us who are native to the planet Atlantis do not have a significantly higher mental capacity than the people native to Earthantis, not now. Those disparities that existed when we arrived were small and taken care of not long after we arrived."

Once again she paused for emphasis. "In other words ... we are not smarter than you. We've just been at this a lot longer. 15,000 years ago, on Atlantis, our level of technology was at about the same level as that of Earthantis is now. We were beginning to explore our Solar System. We had sent unmanned probes to the planets in that system. We had one moon; and we had sent manned spacecraft to explore it. We had begun to explore the resources on the floors of our oceans and had discovered that this is actually harder than going to the moon, just as the engineers of Earthantis have. We had mapped our genetic structure. Our life spans were in the same range that Earthantans are now. Our technology was undergoing the same sort of explosive growth that Earthantan technology is now. There are a great many parallels. It was then that our scientists discovered our Sun would explode in a Super Nova in approximately 5,000 years."

She looked around the room and smiled. "You don't have to worry. There is nothing wrong with your sun. It has several billion years left in its life cycle. We were not so fortunate."

"Anyway," she said as she continued, "For some time very little was done about the coming explosion. 5,000 years is a very long time when a person's life span is about a hundred years. The first thing that happened was the research into our genetic structures began extending our lives. It was a little bit here and little bit there at first. Cures for major diseases like cancer and most forms of heart disease were found. Our life span went from an average of eighty or so to a hundred and twenty or so."

She looked around to make sure that all her students had kept up so far and then continued. "Then a big breakthrough occurred. From our research into stem cells and embryology we learned how to grow replacement organs. In the very beginning of this research, we used embryonic Stem Cells, but it was not long before we learned how to take adult cells and cause them to revert to an embryonic state. We learned to grow tissue, any tissue. Organs produced that way are a complete genetic match. If a person needed a new heart, a new one could be grown from the cells of their own body. Same with livers, kidneys, lungs, etc. This had the almost immediate result of greatly extending our life spans. No one would die from kidney failure, liver failure, heart failure, and diabetes … things like that. This made a huge difference in life spans. The benefits of that research continued to pay off and we learned how to continually replenish muscle and skin tissue. We learned how to regenerate damaged nerve tissue. We learned how to do the same thing with brain cells." She shrugged. "Within about forty years, our medical science increased our projected life spans from about a hundred and twenty years to … well … we actually don't know. No one has died from anything other than an accident for a very long time now. We have individuals living here today who are over fourteen thousand years old. I myself was born 11,478 years ago."

There was a stunned silence. No one in the room said a word. The woman standing before them looked to be in her late twenties.

She continued. "Since the success of our medical science meant that a great many Atlantans were going to be alive when our sun exploded, that event took on an entirely different perspective. This explosion was not some catastrophe that was going to happen to someone else in the far distant future. It was going to happen to us. We were going to live long enough to die in it. We began looking into star travel seriously. How could we evacuate Atlantis? How could we save our own lives? You have many TV shows that depict interstellar travel … Star Trek and Star Wars for example. We had TV shows like that too. It turns out that the sort of interstellar travel envisioned by those shows is not practical. We have developed a theory of essentially "surfing" on a space warp, but nothing we have learned about the laws of Physics allowed us develop the power to make it work. A warp drive, or a hyperspace drive like you read about in science fiction requires a level of power we simply do not know how to produce. We have a theory of a space warp drive but we do not have a theory of how to develop the power it would take to do it. It would have been nice, and believe me we tried, but we were not able to develop a practical way to travel back and forth at speeds faster than light."

She walked over to the wall and said, "Snack … Ice Water." A recess appeared, and a glass of water appeared. No one in the class had known that there were snack dispensers in the classrooms, but there it was, big as life. Professor Galvyndor took a long drink and set the glass down on the desk. "Finally," she continued, "We worked out the math and physics for a stable wormhole. A wormhole is a shortcut through another dimension. You aren't traveling faster than light. That's the key. The distance between the two points is just a lot shorter when you go through a different dimension. That is what a wormhole is – a short cut through another dimension. The energy requirements are still so vast that it is difficult to describe, but they were barely … just barely … within the theoretical limits of what we thought we could do. The problem "was" and "is" that the energy requirements are so vast that they cannot be generated with portable equipment. The equipment needed to produce the energy to maintain a stable wormhole is way too big to pass through it.

That equipment has to remain behind. What we eventually developed is called a Wormhole Generator. It allows an inter-dimensional wormhole to be created. A space ship can travel through it, but the equipment that generates the Wormhole remains behind. It's like a slingshot. Unless you construct a new Wormhole Generator at your destination, there is no way to get back."

"There was another problem too. The exit end of a large wormhole can have destabilizing gravitational effects on the star system. Releasing more than one or two large ships over a short period into any one star system could destroy the system, so we could only safely send one ship to each system. We would have preferred to send everyone to the same planet, but the laws of physics would not allow that."

"So we worked with what we had. We began to build city-sized starships. Each one contained 50,000 of us, along with Pixies, elves, and other life forms and everything needed to re-create our technology in a new star system. Almost 11,000 years ago, we began dispersing our people throughout the galaxy ... one ship to each star system that contained an inhabitable planet. We were the last ship to leave and we almost didn't make it out. Our sun actually exploded seconds before we got away but the concussion hadn't reached us. I was the individual who piloted our ship through the wormhole and to this planet. We arrived a little over 10,000 years ago."

Chapter Five
Chorda

The last thing Professor Galvyndor said as she left the room was that they would have an hour break before their first Chorda class in Room 203. The four members of Q3 walked back to their common area along the well-worn cobblestone path that wound around to their dorm. They walked quietly, contemplating the morning's lesson.

Jennifer pointed to one of the conversation areas surrounding the central fireplace; "We could sit over there." The common area in their dorm was far nicer than Paul had expected. It consisted of a large room with a circular flagstone fireplace in the center. Four separate conversation areas were built around the fireplace. Low stone walls separated them from one another and Jennifer was pointing to one of them.

"That's a good spot," Jim agreed and the four of them walked over and sat down.

"So," Betsy jumped right in, "what did Professor Glorfyndor say?"

"Well, first," Paul began, "he gave me these two books." He placed both of them on the table.

Jennifer picked up *Correctional Operations* and gave it a questioning look.

"That one is a textbook for juniors," Paul explained. "I guess they don't start teaching the specifics of C-Ops until then. I leafed through it a little bit. It's about specific techniques to fix a problem once one is discovered."

"Really," Betsy said eagerly. "What's the other one?"

Jim had already picked it up, "It's *The Code of Atlantis*," he answered, "don't we already have that?"

"Yeah," Paul answered, "But the Professor said there were highlighted sections in this one that would be useful."

"What else did he say?" Jennifer asked.

"A lot of things. For one, he said that between six and ten people will die each year as a result of the pollution from that mill," Paul answered.

"Really?" Jim asked.

"Yeah. And he said it was against the school's policy to conduct "school sponsored" C-Ops until our senior year. Even then we're supposed to have close faculty supervision. The C-Ops the seniors are doing this year are the ones they developed and planned last year. The juniors are developing plans for next year based on potential leads they looked into in their sophomore year."

Betsy whistled softly. "So nothing can happen for a couple of years?"

Paul nodded.

"Do we do those C-Ops as a class or as individual Quadros?" Jennifer asked.

"Quadros," Paul answered, and then went on, "He also said that it was against the rules to use school facilities. "Use" as in use up. He was quite specific. The strange thing was that afterwards he went on and told me what we did on our own time was our own business as long as we didn't "use up" school facilities, and did not violate any of the local laws or the *Code of Atlantis.*"

Betsy looked first at Jim and then back to Paul. "So we can do something if we want?"

"Yes," answered Paul, "So long as we don't use up school facilities. And if he actually disapproved, I don't think he'd have given me the second book."

"Right," Betsy agreed, "Why would he?"

"What's there to "use up", anyway?" Jennifer asked.

"Nothing that I can see," Jim answered.

Just then all four of their Pixies came flying into the common room. Ornith flew up to Paul and high five'd him. "Where have you guys been?" Paul asked, "We missed you at lunch."

"We've been off playing and forgot the time."

"Off playing. Playing what?" Paul asked.

"Playing Pix games," Ornith answered.

"Pix Games?"

"Yes," he answered swinging his arms in time with his words, "We ... just ...got ... busy ... and ... missed ... the ... lunch ... time. Will you get us a snack from your snack dispenser, please?"

"Please ... please," Aurileol chimed in, "We are just about starved to death."

Gwenivere and Renalee were about to join the chorus.

Paul held up his hand in a stop sign. "OK, OK," he answered and looked back at his friends, "Back in a second guys, got to tend to the Pixies."

All of them smiled as Paul walked off towards their room followed closely by four flying Pixies. Betsy looked at the other two and shook her head, "I still can't get used to how neat all of this all is."

"Yeah," Jim agreed with a nod, "Me either."

"I think it's all going to take a while," Jennifer agreed wistfully and then picked up the copy of *Correctional Operations*. "What are we going to do about this paper mill?"

"That's a good question," Jim replied. "This sort of thing is what we're here for. This looks like a legitimate C-Op to me."

"We could wait, and do this as our Senior C-Op," Jennifer suggested.

Jim nodded thoughtfully.

"The problem with that is the people who die as a result of the pollution," Betsy.

"Yeah," Jim agreed, "But how real is that anyway?"

"Seriously real," both Jennifer and Betsy answered in unison.

"I had to do a report on it," Betsy explained.

"Me too," Jennifer added. "It's the accumulated effect of small doses of the stuff over time that does the damage. It doesn't affect everyone, just a small percentage, the elderly are particularly susceptible. All of the studies I researched said that while the affects lasted for a period afterwards, the sooner the source was eliminated, the sooner those affects stopped."

"So stopping it sooner as opposed to later will save people's lives?" Jim asked.

"Yeah," Betsy answered with a nod.

Paul walked back into the area. "Well … the Pixies are chowing down on cheese, crackers and summer sausage."

Betsy rolled her eyes at him.

"Look, Betsy," he said defensively, "I tried to get them to eat a vegetable but the only one available until 4:00 PM is Brussels sprouts."

"So?"

"So … Ornith flew up and informed me that I wasn't mean enough to try and make him eat Brussels sprouts, and then Gwenivere flew right up next to him, crossed her little arms and said "That's right! You can't make us eat them.""

Jim laughed right out loud, and Jennifer put a hand over her mouth to try and keep from it. She wasn't very successful.

"Oh," was all Betsy said looking over at her roommate.

"Anyway," Paul continued, "What's up?"

"We're still talking about what to do about the paper mill," Jim began.

"Any conclusions?"

"Just that this sort of thing is what we're here for," Jim replied. "And that stopping this mill sooner as opposed to later will save lives. I think this qualifies as a legitimate C-Op."

"The Mill is operating against the law," Jennifer observed. "The data you guys got proves that."

"And they are in this out of the way back-woods place that makes it really hard to catch them," Betsy continued. "That's the category of law-breakers C-Ops seem to be about."

"True," Paul agreed, "but the problem is that we aren't ready."

112

"Not ready?" Betsy exclaimed.

"Right," Paul continued, "We don't know what most of this stuff on the belts even does, or how it can be used. We don't know what other tools we have. They normally spend three years training us before we get to do a closely supervised C-Op."

"All good points," Betsy agreed with a sigh, "but what if we could do something? My grandfather died of pneumonia aggravated by air pollution from the steel mill we lived near when I was little. We won't ever know the people we save, but some of those people will be somebody's grandparents. What if we could figure something out?"

"Also a good point," Paul noted and began to understand Betsy's interest. He looked at the two girls.

Jennifer shrugged. "It can't hurt to look into it."

"Yes it can," Jim said firmly. "There are seven other Quadros in our class. We need to get along with these kids. If they think we're out here trying to …"

"So you're afraid of peer pressure?" Betsy asked.

"No," Jim answered, "Not really. I just think it's important not to get caught."

"Ahhh," Betsy said with a smile. "So you do want to do something?"

"Yes," Jim answered and looked at Paul. "What do you think?"

"I think we need to be careful. Study every move." Paul answered nodding slowly. He had made his decision while sitting in the Professor's office. "Something should be done. I don't know what yet, but we can't do anything if we don't try. I think we should study these materials carefully," he said tapping on the books the Professor gave him, "so that we all understand them. Particularly the book on C-Ops. Let's start there. After that there is a whole Library full of books. Some of them are going to cover how all of this equipment works. We might not get it in class for a while, but that does not mean we can't learn about it."

Jennifer looked at Betsy who nodded, "We're in."

ψ

Paul sat at a table in Room 203 looking around. There were sixteen tables each with two chairs opposite each other, only the tables were like none he had ever seen. They had no legs; they just floated in the air. He selected one and sat down as Professor Erinlicia Flyndor walked in.

"OK. I hope all of you enjoyed your first Palacrosse lesson. Let's move on to another Atlantan game … Chorda," she said looking around the class to make certain she had everyone's attention. "For each regularly scheduled Chorda match you win, your Quadro is awarded one point." She paused and smiled. "Why are we introducing you to Palacrosse and Chorda? Why do we place such a large emphasis on them? What do these have to do with your Qual's? They are games after all, so what is the big deal? Before we get into the rules of Chorda, I'd like to explain why this is important. You are going to have to expand your minds a great deal in order to absorb all of the science and technology that we are going to throw at you over the next four years. Your mind is like your muscles in some respects. The more you exercise it the stronger it gets. Both

114

Palacrosse and Chorda are games of highly complex, rapidly evolving strategies."

The Professor looked around the room at her students. "Both of these games are fun. Yes," she said with an emphatic nod, "I really do think you will agree, and having fun is important, but there's more to it than fun. Together they will serve to improve the speed at which your mind works, and I think you will find that useful. Yes," she said again as if to answer a question that had not been asked, "I really do." She paused again and looked around the class. "So, at 7:30 PM every evening during this summer session you will play a member of a different Quadro in a regularly scheduled Chorda match. As I mentioned earlier, whoever wins gets a point for their Quadro."

She turned to the wall behind her and a display of a board a lot like a chessboard appeared. Paul counted the spaces quickly. The board was eleven spaces by eleven spaces. On one side were two digital timers separated by what appeared to be a light. Each timer faced one of the one players. Beneath each was a button. On the other side were two trays. Paul guessed that was for captured pieces.

"This," she said pointing to the board behind her, "Is a Chorda board. There are twenty-two pieces for each player. Each is named for a rank in the Armed Forces. The object of the game is to take your opponent's General. It is important to understand how each piece moves." With that she began explaining how each piece moved.

As she was explaining how the major moved, Betsy passed Paul a note. *Correctional Operations has a Basic Plan. I think it might work. Let's meet tonight after dinner.*

Paul realized that she had brought the book with her to the Chorda class. Paul looked up quickly to see if the Professor had noticed Betsy passing the note. As far as he could tell, she had not, but there was no way to be sure. Paul scrawled quickly on the bottom of the note *OK! Pay Attention!* He tried not to draw any attention as he passed the note back.

"Now that we've been through the pieces and how they move," Professor Flyndor continued and eyed Paul a little suspiciously, "It is important to understand the object of the game. This is not a game of points. The entire object is to capture your opponent's general."

Betsy passed the note back. She'd added *I'll tell Jennifer. You tell Jim.*

Paul nodded as imperceptibly as he could. He wrote: *OK! Stop this. We are going to get caught,* on the bottom and passed it back as carefully as he could.

"So, Paul," the Professor asked suddenly, "How does the colonel move?"

"Just like a queen in chess," Paul answered quickly hoping that Professor Flyndor hadn't caught them.

"Right," she answered with a knowing smile and turned her attention to Betsy, "Now, Betsy. How does the 1st lieutenant move?" Paul held his breath hoping that Betsy knew the answer.

"It's probably the most difficult. It can move in two different patterns," Betsy answered and proceeded to describe the two movements.

"Correct," the Professor announced, and Paul breathed a sigh of relief.

Paul sat across the small table playing Chorda with a classmate from Quadro #5 named Anne Chastain. He was getting beaten … pretty badly too. This girl was really smart. She moved her Sergeant two spaces diagonally, and touched the timer. Her move put him in a difficult spot. He now had to defend his Colonel or lose it. If he did, she was going to take one of his 1st Lieutenants with the Sergeant. He noticed that the light had gone yellow. That meant he had ten seconds left. It was time to make a move. He defended his Colonel, and touched the button below his timer. His timer went blank and the yellow light went off and Anne's came on. She didn't hesitate, but immediately took his 1st Lieutenant, and touched the timer again.

The game developed over the next hour and gradually, Anne gained the upper hand, and in the end, she captured his General.

"Nuts," Paul said.

Anne smiled pleasantly for a second. "So, how do you like the kids in your Quadro?" she asked.

"Fine," Paul answered, "We seem to be getting along really well. How about you?"

"We're good," she announced matter-of-factly, "I think we're going to be really good at Palacrosse. We have two tennis players in our group."

"Really?" he asked.

"Yeah," she answered, "That seems to help a lot. Tennis players already know how to hit spin on the ball and make it go in the right general direction."

John Moriarty took the bank bag from the courier, and the man left. In the bag were two envelopes. Each was stuffed full of one hundred dollar bills. It was their under the table bonus money … unreported and untraceable. The way the envelopes came from corporate, there was an equal amount of cash in each. Moriarty reached into one of them and removed half of the money and put it in the other envelope. He left the fatter envelope in the bank bag and placed it in his lowest desk drawer. He took the smaller one and put it in his suit coat pocket. The fat one would go home with him this evening. He rose from his desk and headed for the mill floor.

Ben Johnson, like most good plant managers, would be found out on the mill floor. That was the way Moriarty wanted it anyway. The mill was noisy, and he never wanted witnesses for any of the conversations he had with Ben. No witnesses was his main rule. It had been that way for over fifteen years now. Even so, Morairty had to trust Ben. Someone had to actually do the dirty work so he had no real choice. Even so, John Moriarty knew that he could only trust Ben so far. If Ben had witnesses, Ben could implicate him. There were no witnesses. Moriarty made certain of that.

He walked out to the floor, found Ben, made sure no one was watching and gave him his envelope. Ben knew better than to count it there, but he also knew that when he got home that evening there would be five thousand dollars in one hundred dollar bills. He got the same amount each and every month. As he watched Moriarty walk back towards the office, he had no idea that John Moriarty was skimming half of it. Their deal had been to split the money 50 / 50 and as far as he knew that was what happened. He did not know that in Moriarty's envelope there was now fifteen thousand dollars. But there was one thing he did know. Whatever amount of money the company was sending their way, it was a small amount compared with what they saved by not paying for the proper disposal of their toxic waste.

ψ

Paul hurried into the Dining Hall. It was Friday evening and he was a little late. He barely beat the serving carts. He noticed a plate that held roast beef, and extended his Power Ring, said "Acquire" and began to eat.

"So," Jennifer asked, "How did you do, Paul?"

"I lost," he admitted.

"Beaten by a girl," Jim said with a smile and an edge of gloat in his voice. Both Jennifer and Betsy gave him the high eye-brow, "I can't believe you just said that" look.

"I guess you won," Paul asked.

"Yep," Jim answered.

"Well," Jennifer announced with a toss of her head and a superior tone, "I ... beat a ... boy. So there."

"Yeah," Betsy added, "But I didn't."

119

Just then Gwenivere left the Pix's table and flew up to Betsy and rubbed noses with her. "It's OK, Betsy," she said, "You'll do better next time." Ornith flew up to Paul and gave him a high five and then they both went back to their little table and resumed their supper.

Paul looked at Betsy and shrugged, "You know, it really is nice having them around."

"Yes, it is," Betsy agreed.

"So we're two for two," Jennifer concluded, trying to get everyone back on the subject. "That's not bad. Q5 went three and one, but they were the only ones who did. Q2 went one and three. Everybody else split."

"So we're right in the middle," Paul said.

"Yeah," Jim said, "But that's not the best place to be. We do want to win this thing. Right?"

Everyone nodded.

"OK," Paul said, "Then we need to get to that Palacrosse field early in the morning."

They finished dinner and walked back to their dorm with the rest of their classmates. There would be more Chorda matches later that evening, but they weren't to start for another hour.

"Let's go over there and talk," Betsy suggested, pointing at the area by the central fireplace. She had *Correctional Operations* in her hand. Paul had the professor's copy of *The Code of Atlantis* in his.

Betsy wanted to start, but Paul held up his hand, "Betsy," he said, "there are some things in this other book we ought to talk about first. Let's end up with that one."

"OK," she said with a shrug.

"All of those underlined words are specifically defined at the end of the Code," he informed them. Paul turned to the first highlighted passage and read aloud:

When faced with something that is clearly <u>Wrong</u>, Atlantans are expected to <u>Act</u> to correct the Wrong. Failure to <u>Act</u> is the same as consenting to the <u>Wrong</u>. Consenting to the <u>Wrong</u> is not philosophically different from doing it yourself.

Jim had already read that section but the girls hadn't. Both Betsy and Jennifer gave out a low whistle.

"Based on *The Code* I think we have to try and do something, if we can. I really do," Jim began.

They all nodded in agreement.

"I agree," Paul announced, "The question is … what?"

"That is the question," Jim agreed.

"The first thing,' Betsy suggested, "Is to make a good plan. That's where this book comes in," she said tapping the book *Correctional Operations.*

"Right," Jim nodded.

"We all need to read that book," Jennifer observed.

"Right," Jim nodded again.

"Good," Paul said. "So we've agreed that we'll all read the book, but there is something else we can do in the meanwhile."

"What's that?" Jim asked looking at his roommate.

"Well, if we are able to do anything at all, whatever we end up doing is going to have to be planned," Paul said slowly, "Betsy's quite right about that. You and I got a better look at that mill from the ridgeline, but we will need to get a much closer look at the layout to make a good plan and all of us should be there. We've got tomorrow off. We can hike up there and just see what we can see."

"Reconnoiter the territory," Jim said with a nod of agreement.

"Yeah," Jennifer agreed quickly, "We can just ... go for a walk ... in the woods. Check it out. That's a good idea."

"Shall we leave right after breakfast?" Betsy asked.

"No," Paul answered, "Why don't we wait until after lunch."

"But it's a long way over there." Betsy noted, "Will we have time?"

"I've got an idea about that," Paul answered. He pulled the wand off of the back right side of his belt. "Beta Wand On ... binoculars," he said and Jim followed suit.

As the both of the boy's wands transformed into binoculars, both of the girl's eyes got a little wider. "Who showed you how to do that?" Jennifer asked.

"Georaldon," Paul answered as Jim smiled. A moment later all four had binoculars in their hands.

"Sweet!" Betsy exclaimed.

"Totally," Jennifer agreed.

"Now ... remember when Jim and I got caught in that thunderstorm. We Jumped from down in the ravine up to the portico. That's how we got out of the storm. One of us can get a good look at a position three or four hundred yards away, and then use the transport belt. The rest of us can get a look at where he," he smiled at the girls, "Or she … is … and then transport there. We can cover the distance a lot faster than walking."

Both girls looked at each other and then back at the boys. "Awesome," they said in unison.

They decided they would go after lunch, and the girls went off to their room.

Paul walked towards the doorway to their room with Ornith riding comfortably on his shoulder. It had taken him a little time to get used to the idea that Ornith might be up there at any time, and a little more time to get used to the idea that the little Pix was quite capable of riding along and that he didn't have to worry about him falling off. They were followed closely by Jim and Aurileol.

"Open," Paul said and the door slid soundlessly into the wall to allow then to enter. They walked in and Ornith jumped off of Paul's shoulder and flew around the room looking things over. Like most boys' rooms, there were things scattered about here and there.

"Paul, are you going to adopt a bear?" Ornith asked.

"Am I going to do what?" Paul asked.

Ornith began swinging his little arms back and forth in time with his question, "Are … you … going … to … adopt … a … bear?" he repeated in the fashion that Paul had come to recognize as Ornith trying to speak … "slowly" … and … "distinctly".

"I don't know anything about adopting bears," Paul answered as Jim settled into one of the chairs. "There is no way we can take care of a bear in this room anyway."

"Oh, yes there is," Ornith answered, "They are small enough, and they are house broken."

"House broken!" Paul exclaimed.

"Of course," Ornith answered, "They don't make messes, they are very neat, and you really need one."

"I don't know," Paul said with hesitation.

"Well, you should," the little Pix continued.

"Why, Ornith? Why on earth would we want to have a bear, even if we could?"

"Oh," Ornith said as if he had forgotten something, "That's right. I forgot. You don't know about bears yet. Well, they are very useful for keeping things clean and neat, and you can adopt one if you want." He made a little nod of finality and then flew around and settled back on Paul's shoulder as Paul settled into the other chair.

"Wait a minute? Did you say that they help keep things neat?"

"Yes, and we really need one," Ornith said emphatically.

"Well," Paul answered, "I don't know about that."

"Well … nothing!" Ornith replied flying up where Paul could see him, "We … need … one. Just … look … at … this … place," he swept his arm across the room at the things the boys had left out, "It's … a … mess. You'll need to ask the Erlyndors though."

"Ask the Erlyndors what?"

"About getting us a bear. This mess will be much easier to manage if you get one. The bear will manage it for us. It's what they like to do."

"OK, Ornith, OK," Paul finally agreed, "I'll ask the Erlyndors about it."

Note: The complete rules of Chorda and Palacrosse are contained at the end.

Chapter Six

A Walk in the Woods

The next morning dawned clear and refreshingly cool. It was one of the nice things about the Smoky Mountains, even in summer the mornings were cool. The foursome went to the Field House right after finishing breakfast. They were the first ones there, but everyone else followed shortly after.

Betsy looked at Paul as they got into their null harnesses. "You're the only one of us who has played much tennis. What should we do?"

Paul looked at the other members of his Quadro and noticed that all three were nodding in agreement. It was clear everyone wanted him to take the lead. "OK," he began, "Our first match is next weekend, and we have to have a strategy. This game is hard, and takes a lot of practice so we need one we can execute in a week. Before we jump in, let's agree on a strategy."

"Right," Jennifer answered, as confidently as she could manage, but there was a tone of hesitation in her voice.

Paul looked at her. Some girls in Calumet City had always been more confident about playing sports with boys than other girls. At home, the girls who didn't want to play sports with the boys … just didn't. That wasn't an option here, and it had not occurred to him that Jennifer would be uncomfortable. Nothing like that had ever made a difference before, but it did now, and the Atlantan reasoning behind the Quadro concept

126

became crystal clear. Jennifer needed to try whether she was comfortable or not, and the rest of them needed to find ways to help her. "We won't go too fast, Jenn," he said gently, "one step at a time."

"OK," she agreed.

Paul laid out a simple plan to play Palacrosse a lot like hockey, only in three dimensions. Short passes would be the key, and they decided to concentrate their practice on that aspect first.

As they jumped into the field, none of them noticed that Professor Glorfyndor was watching from the stands. He saw that Q3 was the first group into the Field House, and he also noticed that they were the last ones to jump into a field. They had taken time to get organized before they did anything. That was a good indicator. He nodded and smiled to himself as he left the Field House stands, glad that his original estimate of Paul appeared to be correct, and not for Paul alone, but for the rest of his Quadro as well. It wasn't too late to pull the reins in on them, but it did not look like it would be necessary. Not yet anyway.

ψ

Q3 practiced Palacrosse all morning. In particular they worked on close-in accuracy. They arrayed themselves in a semi-circle about ten feet outside of the exclusion zone, and worked on hitting the wobble through the goal. They would all hit a wobble at the goal, and chase it down as it ricocheted around the field. Once they had collected the wobbles, they would gather outside of the exclusion zone, and try and hit it through again. By the end of practice they were getting pretty good at getting it through, at least most of the time. At lunchtime, they broke away. "OK," Paul said, "Let's go see if this "Jump" idea will work."

The Pixies were ready and together they all walked down the path that led off of the school property and into the National Forest that was behind the school. Paul walked to the wrought iron gate and opened it with his Ring.

They went through the gate and walked down the path but instead of taking the fork that led down into the valley and up onto the ridge line, they took a fork that appeared to wander more in the direction of the mill.

"OK," Paul said as he reached for the Beta Wand on his belt. "Let's see where we should Jump first." The four of them activated their wands and produced the binoculars. He looked from the ridge they were on across to the next one. As the crow flew it was about six hundred yards.

"Paul," Ornith said seriously, "Do you see that big rock near the two trees growing from the same spot?

Paul could see an outcropping of a boulder by a pair of ponderosa pine trees. "Yes, but how can you see that?'

"With binoculars same as you," he answered.

Paul looked over at the little Pix perched on his shoulder. Ornith had a tiny pair of binoculars held up to his eyes. "You have binoculars?"

"Of course," Ornith answered, "Do you see the spot?"

"Well, Yes."

"OK," Ornith answered, "Is that a good place?"

"Yeah, it looks fine," Paul answered.

"Why are we waiting here then?" Ornith asked impatiently.

"No particular reason," Paul answered with a chuckle. "Did you guys see the spot?" he asked.

"Yeah," Betsy answered. "Are we all going to Jump there together?"

"No, why don't I go, and then you guys can see where I am for sure."

"That's good," Jennifer agreed. "No confusion that way." Jim and Betsy nodded.

Paul released the binoculars which transformed back into a wand and reattached to his belt. He visualized the spot he wanted to transport to and tapped his fingers. The kaleidoscope of swirling colors surrounded him and then stopped. He was standing between the boulder and the tree. Ornith was still on his shoulder. One of the things Paul had learned was that if Ornith was anywhere within three feet of him when he Jumped, Ornith would be transported too. He moved a few feet away, and stood there so that his friends could get a good look at where he was with their own binoculars, and a few seconds later they began appearing one by one.

"This is a lot easier than hiking," Jim said as they scouted out the next Jump.

"Faster too," Jennifer commented with an emphatic nod, "This is good."

Paul was already studying the terrain ahead, and had found what he was looking for. "Do you guys see that big outcropping a little to the left? Let's go there."

"Why there?" Betsy asked.

"There's something I want to try out," Paul answered. He had been thinking of the mill, particularly the picture he had taken of the top of the smoke stack and already had a glimmer of an idea in mind.

"What?" she asked, her curiosity aroused.

"I'll show you when we get there," he replied.

In a matter of a few seconds, all four of them were standing just below the outcropping. Paul walked around looking it over, and found a way to scramble to the top. Once he was up there, he was about ten feet above the others. He looked at a spot about twenty feet away from them, visualized it and Jumped off the rock. As he was falling, he tapped his fingers. When the colors stopped swirling, he was standing in the place he had visualized. The important thing was the momentum of his fall hadn't carried over across the Jump. He landed as softly as if he'd stepped off of a curb.

"All right!" he exclaimed.

The others saw where he was and came running over. "What is this all about?" Jim asked, "What in the world are you doing?"

"I wanted to see what happened if you Jumped while you were falling," he answered.

"Oh, I get it," Betsy said excitedly, "So if we slip or fall or something, we can tap our fingers and Jump someplace, and it will break our fall."

"Right," Paul replied with a nod.

"I'm going to try that," Jim said and walked back over to the outcropping.

After it worked for him too, both of the girls tried it.

"Well," Betsy concluded, "There's one more thing we've learned about how all this stuff works."

They took turns being first, and after about an hour they found themselves on a hilltop looking down on the paper mill complex.

"I didn't realize it was so big," Jennifer said as they took in the scope of the operation. It covered at least five acres altogether, and comprised several large brick buildings. The smokestacks themselves were also constructed of brick, and there was a road leading up to the mill that forked into three sections. The center one led to the main gate with a security shack and on to what appeared to be an office building. It was a two-story brick affair with a parking lot out front. There were no cars in the office lot.

The road forking off to the right led around to an area for unloading logs, and there were a large number stacked in piles underneath a crane. As they watched, the crane swung around, snatched up a bundle of logs, turned and deposited them in a chute that went into the building. Adjacent to the log receiving area was another parking lot. This one contained a number of cars and pickup trucks.

"Apparently they work Sundays." Betsy observed.

Paul's eyes followed the other road, the one that branched off to the left. It led around the side of the facility to the back and up to a truck dock area. "That's going to be the chemical processing area," he said pointing to the section of building in front of the stacks.

"How do you know that?" Jennifer asked.

"Because," Betsy answered, "The first thing they do to the logs is grind them into chips. That part of the plant will be directly next to where they bring the logs in. Over there." She pointed to where they had seen the crane operating. "The next thing is to break down the chips to pulp. That's a process requiring chemicals and heat, and it will be located next to the chip grinding section. Steam is what they use to supply the heat, so that's where the stacks are. Once they've got the pulp, they don't need steam for anything."

"How do you know all that?" Jennifer asked.

"I looked it up on the computer last night," Betsy answered, "That's what I was doing while you were going over the C-Ops book."

"Oh," Jennifer replied.

"There's a chain link fence all the way around this place," Paul noted, "And the only roads in and out have gates and guard shacks."

"Over there," Betsy pointed to some small buildings just inside of the fence on the backside by the log unloading section; "Those are kennels."

"Guard Dogs!" Jennifer exclaimed with a shiver, "They've got guard dogs!"

"Yeah, and they're mean," Ornith announced.

"How do you know that?" Paul asked quickly. It amazed him that Pixies would know about such things.

"We just do," all four of the Pixies answered in a chorus.

Paul shrugged, and the four members of Q3 studied the facility quietly for several minutes. "This may not be so easy," Paul said, "We need to get a look at the backside of this mill, as close to those stacks as we can get."

"Do you see that large clearing?" Jim asked. "There is a lot of brush around it that would give us cover. We could Jump there, check it

132

out, and decide if we need to get any closer."

"Yeah," Paul answered, "That looks like a good spot." He turned to the girls; "Do you guys want to wait here?"

The girls looked at each other, saying nothing and nodded to each other, "No," they answered in unison. Jennifer disappeared first followed by Betsy a second later.

Paul looked at Jim and then over to the clearing. He could barely see the girls standing there. "I guess they really don't want to wait here, and we are going to have to stop underestimating them." Seconds later the foursome was gathered in the small clearing on the backside of the mill. It was about twenty feet across and located in the middle of a small copse of trees about a hundred feet outside of the perimeter fence and up a sloping hillside. They walked quickly forward and knelt down behind some brush at the clearing. As they looked, they saw two guards walking along inside of the fence. They both had large dogs on leashes.

"That's a Rottweiler," Jennifer noted.

"Great," Jim said almost under his breath, "And Ornith says they are mean."

Aurileol flew off of Jim's shoulder and went around so he could see him, "Don't worry, Jim," he said, "We can handle the doggies if they find us."

"Really?" Betsy asked in disbelief.

Gwenivere flew around too, "Really," she answered with an emphatic nod.

"How do you know that?" Paul asked.

Ornith flew around as well, "From … the … Pix Games," he said swinging his arms.

"From the Pix Games?" Paul asked.

"Yep," he answered, "We like to play a game called Chase the Doggies!"

"For real?" Paul responded.

"For real" all of the Pixies said in unison, and then flew back and resumed their shoulder perches.

"Oh," Paul said with a shrug as he looked at Jennifer and Betsy. "They like to play "Chase the Doggies.""

"Who knew?" Betsy said with another shrug.

"It doesn't really make any difference," Jim said as he watched the guards with the Rottweilers. They walked the fence line with the dogs sniffing just about everything as they went along. "We're not going to get close enough to worry about them. Not this time anyway."

"Do you guys see that door?" Paul asked, "The one in between the two stacks?"

"Yes," everyone answered. Halfway in between the stacks was a metal door leading out of the building to a small porch. The porch had a metal railing around it and steps leading down to ground level.

"If we need to get in there, that will be the way," Paul noted. "Someone needs to draw a map."

"I'll do it," Jennifer volunteered.

"I wonder if they keep that door locked." Jim asked.

"It doesn't make any difference," Betsy said quietly, "Remember, we've got Power Rings. We can unlock the door if we have to."

"Not if it's dead bolted," Jim interjected, "If it's just locked, yeah, you're right, but not if it's dead bolted from the inside."

Just then a man opened the door and walked out onto the porch. Betsy quickly whipped her binoculars around and studied the backside of the door. "There is no bolt on the door, just a regular lock," she announced. "It won't be a problem for a Power Ring."

"This is good," Jennifer said making a note on her map.

Paul studied the situation. He focused his binoculars on the ladder winding around the smokestacks and noticed a small platform at the top. He turned his head slightly so that Ornith could hear; "I'm going in. Ornith, are you coming with me?"

"Of course," Ornith answered simply. "It will be an adventure." Paul could tell that the little Pix had thought it over already and had decided to come along, and there wasn't any point in trying to talk him out of it.

"You're going to do what?" Betsy asked.

"We need a look inside. This is too good a chance to pass up," he announced and focused on the small porch, "Cloak," he said clearly and tapped his fingers. Before any of his friends could object, Paul disappeared.

"Wait, Paul," Betsy started to say but Paul was already gone. "What's this "Cloak" business?" Becky asked.

Gwenivere flew around to answer her, "Betsy, if you say "Cloak" before you transport, nobody can see you when you get where you are going," she explained. "If you say "Cloak" and tap just one of your forefinger and thumb, you disappear, but you don't go anywhere, but once you "Cloak" if you want to transport somewhere else, you can do it and you are invisible when you get there. The guard will not be able to see him."

"Oh," Betsy replied, "How did Paul know about that?"

"I don't know the answer to that question," Gwenivere answered, "You'll have to ask Ornith, but disappearing is part of what we do when we play "Chase the Doggies.""

Paul materialized on the porch exactly as he had planned. He waited a second or two to see if he would be discovered. He was ready to tap his fingers and transport back to his friends instantly if the man had given any indication that he was aware of anything strange.

The man didn't react at all.

Paul looked around for a minute to get his bearings. The man was on the other side of him. The door was between them. If he moved towards the door before the man did he could slip inside without bumping into him. The one thing he didn't want was to be trying to go through the door at the same time the man was going through. He didn't think the Cloak function would keep someone from knowing that they had bumped into you.

"It's not working," Jennifer announced. She was looking at the porch through her binoculars. "I can see Paul. That guy is looking away right now but he'll see him any second now."

"What do you mean, it's not working?" Jim asked. "I can't see him."

"It's 'cause she is using the binoculars and you aren't," Aurileol explained. "The binoculars let you see "Cloaked" people."

"Oh," Jim said with a shrug.

"Paul's going inside," Jennifer announced.

Once Paul was inside he moved far enough beyond the doorway so that he didn't have to worry about the man bumping into him. The room was large, and at either end there were rounded sections corresponding to the position of the smokestacks. In the back were large double doors. They were closed, but Paul guessed they were for bringing things into the room.

Just then the man on the porch came back into the room and closed the door. He walked over to a small desk against the wall and sat down. Paul was in his direct line of sight, but the man took no notice.

Paul looked around the room some more. At each end of the room there were two large vessels on four wheels with "H.Z." stenciled on them in large red letters.

"What are those things?" Ornith asked in a whisper.

"They look like chemical containers of some kind," Paul whispered back. On the top of each vessel were pressure gages. He lifted his binoculars and took a picture as Georaldon had showed him, and then went closer to one of them and took another picture of the gages. About eight feet off of the floor there was some sort of steel access hatch to each of the smokestacks. Directly above the hatch was a steel I Beam with a chain hoist on it. Paul snapped a couple more pictures, and then visualized the platform at the top of the smokestack. "Hold tight, Ornith," he instructed, "It may be windy where we are going."

"OK, Paul."

Paul tapped his fingers and this time when the colors stopped they were on the platform at the top of the South smokestack, and true to Paul's prediction it was very windy that high up. Paul immediately crouched down to get out of the wind. The platform itself was no wider than the metal stairs leading up to it. But what interested Paul was how wide the stack itself was. The bricks themselves were four layers thick on edge, slightly over two and a half feet total. It was barely wide enough to walk on. Paul quickly took some more pictures.

"OK, Ornith," he asked "Are you ready to go back?"

"Yes," Ornith answered, "I don't like it up here."

Paul tapped his fingers again and as soon as the colors stopped swirling, he was back with his friends.

"Oh, Paul," Betsy said as she saw him with a relieved tone in her voice, "There you are. Good. Don't do that again."

"Yeah," both Jennifer and Jim agreed in unison, "We're doing this together, remember?"

"Yes, I remember, but listen," Paul explained. "I didn't know how long that guy was going to keep the door open. We can't just Jump in there if none of us has ever seen what the inside looks like."

"Yeah," Betsy said, "But we could use the Power Rings and unlock the door."

"What if someone is inside," Paul asked, "What would they think if the door mysteriously and magically opened itself up?"

Jim chuckled, "They'd probably think it was a ghost."

"Yeah," Jennifer agreed, "It … would … be better if we could Jump in Cloaked."

"Right!" Paul said, "And to do that we have to know what it looks like in there. I didn't know how long a chance we would have. It turned

138

out not to be too long."

"True," Jim agreed.

"Well, OK. What did you see in there?" Betsy asked.

"Vessels for one thing," Paul answered, "Large ones for chemicals of some kind. They're on wheels so they can move them around. I've got pictures. I also got a look at the ledge on the top of the smokestacks. It is only about two and a half feet wide."

"You went up there!" Betsy asked.

"Yeah," Paul replied, "I got pictures of that too." Paul drew in a deep breath to help him relax. "I've got everything we need." Paul took one look on Betsy's face and put both of his hands up, "OK ... OK, Betsy," Paul agreed. "I'm sorry. I won't do it again. I promise."

"Whoops," Jennifer exclaimed suddenly, "Those guards have spotted us."

The other three turned immediately to see what Jennifer had noticed. Sure enough the guards were angrily shouting at them, demanding that they come down to the gate.

"Are any of you guys interested in going down there?" Jim asked.

"Nope," Jennifer announced, "Let's get under cover."

"Right," Paul agreed and the four of them ran over to the brush line at the edge of the meadow and knelt down. They watched as the two guards rushed over to the nearest gate and opened it. Both guards knelt down to their dogs and removed the leashes and the dogs went charging up towards the meadow.

"Let's get out of here," Betsy said quickly, "Let's Jump back to the gate."

"Right," Jim said disappeared. He was immediately followed by Betsy and Jennifer. Paul visualized the spot by the gate and tapped his fingers but nothing happened. A bong went off that seemed to come from inside his head, followed by a voice he did not recognize.

"*Warning,*" it said, "*You have exceeded the allowed energy draw. It will be fifteen minutes before the belt is sufficiently recharged for you to Transport or Cloak.*"

"We're on our own Ornith," Paul said quietly as the dogs got closer and closer, "the belt needs fifteen minutes to recharge before I can transport or cloak. Your belt will still work. You should get out of here while you can."

Ornith flew up off of Paul's shoulder, "I'm not going anywhere, but don't worry, Paul. I know what to do." he smiled a mischievous little smile. "I've got flashblasters. Plenty of 'em." He said as the dogs got to within ten yards of them. Paul could see their black and tan markings quite clearly now. Suddenly Ornith flew straight towards the dogs. That startled them and they stopped in their tracks. Ornith flew to within feet of their mouths and then broke to the right and circled around behind them. Both dogs forgot all about Paul and began trying to chase Ornith but he was much more agile. He dodged first around one tree, and then another. The dogs tried to follow but couldn't catch him. Ornith darted around a tree and threw a flashblaster towards one of the dogs and darted away.

BAMM!!! A red rocker went off with a bright red light. The dog yelped, sat down on his haunches and began pawing at his eyes.

"Paul," he heard Jim say and felt a tap on his shoulder, "What's the matter."

140

"Stay Cloaked, Jim," Paul said quickly. "I've exceeded the allowed energy draw of the belt and can't Jump or Cloak for fifteen minutes."

"Oh," Jim said. "I didn't know that could be a problem."

"Me neither, but watch Ornith," Paul said pointing in Ornith's direction, "This is amazing. "Shut your eyes right after he tosses the flashblaster."

As Paul and Jim watched, Ornith flew off with the second dog in hot pursuit. Ornith dodged around a tree, and got behind the second dog. As the second dog tried to turn, Ornith tossed another flashblaster and darted away.

BAMM!!! A blue banger went off with a bright blue light. This dog yelped just like the first one. It sat down on its haunches and began pawing at his eyes too. At that moment the first dog eyes must have cleared up because he jumped up and began looking around. He didn't see Ornith, but he did see Paul, and went after him again. Ornith immediately flew straight at him. He drew the dog away from Paul, and set off another flashblaster with the same result. Before long both of dogs gave up and went back to the mill.

"Jim," Paul said, "We'll be OK now. Why don't you Jump back to the girls and tell them what is going on."

"Sure," Jim replied.

Ornith flew back to Paul. He was breathing hard. "Here Ornith," Paul said holding out his hand, "Sit here and rest." The Pix landed on his hand. "That was very brave," Paul said sincerely, "Thank you."

"You're welcome," Ornith replied with a smile.

"It that what you mean by Chasing the Doggies? Is that the game you play?"

"Yep," Ornith answered with a firm nod, "That's it."

Paul looked at the Pix resting on his hand. He wondered what he could say, and suddenly it came to him. "Well," Paul said emphasizing his words and swinging his arms the way Ornith did; "I … am … very … glad … you … adopted … me."

Ornith smiled broadly, "Me too," he said as his breathing returned to normal.

They sat down in the meadow, out of sight of the guards and waited quietly. After a little while, Ornith spoke up, "It's been about fifteen minutes. We can probably Jump now."

Paul visualized the gate and seconds later they materialized there.

"Paul!" Betsy exclaimed, "Are you OK?"

"Yes," Paul answered with a wide grin. "Thanks to Ornith."

"And the flashblasters," the little Pix added.

"Yeah," Jim agreed, "But you girls should have seen it. Ornith was awesome." He looked at Aurileol, "Can you do that?"

Aurileol nodded, "Yes, Gwenivere and Renalee can too, but Ornith is the best."

142

Chapter Seven
A Revelation Worth the Wait

It had been an eventful afternoon. After dinner, the members of Q3 gathered to chat in one of the conversation areas around the central fireplace of their common area. They would have almost an hour and a half before the evening Chorda matches. "I think we need to go to the library again. But this time we should get one of those group study rooms," Betsy suggested. "We're going to start getting too many questions if we keep meeting in here."

"Good idea," Paul agreed and they set out for the Library.

"Good," Ornith said just loud enough for Paul to hear, "I like the library. Can I check out some books while we are there?"

"They have books for Pixies?"

"Of course. Can I get some?"

"Sure. Why do you have to ask me?"

"'Cause they are checked out to you. You have to make sure they get back, but don't worry. I won't lose them."

"Oh. Well, sure. How many do you want?"

"Six or four," Ornith answered.

They walked from the dorm through the connecting hall to the center building. They headed into the portico and could hear some of the video games being used. "Those study rooms are upstairs, aren't they?"

Jim asked.

"I think so," Jennifer answered.

The foursome made their way up one of the ornately carved oak stairways that led to the balcony encircling the Atrium. They stopped and looked out at the sight beneath them.

"You know," Betsy commented as she ran her hand along the wood of the stairway's banister, "Watching things like Star Trek, I would have never guessed that an advanced society would care so much about woodwork ... hand craftsmanship ... things like this room. I mean ... look the fine grain of this wood ... the carvings ... the tapestries ... those little sculptures sitting around here and there," she swept her arm across the expanse of the rooms. "Do you think that Co-re-alis will be like this too?"

"I don't know," Jim answered. "The small part of Atlantis I saw was pretty neat but a little different ... like this but ... not ... at the same time."

"I know," Jennifer said, "But I didn't really get to see that much."

"Me either," Betsy said.

"Professor Glorfyndor's Office is a lot like this," Paul added.

"Really?" Jennifer asked.

"Yeah," Paul replied, "I don't know if his book cases were hand carved or anything, but they are highly polished oak. So is his desk. Come on ... we've got some work to do." He walked quickly through the stacks of books to the rooms that were behind them.

"I'm going to go and pick out some books now," Ornith announced to Paul but in a voice loud enough for everyone to hear.

"You're getting books?" Gwenivere asked.

"Yes," Ornate nodded. "Paul said he would check them out for me."

Gwenivere looked at Betsy. "Can I get some books too … please … please?"

"What about me?" Aurileol asked Jim.

"Me too!" exclaimed Renalee. "I want to get some books too."

"OK … OK," Jennifer exclaimed, "Don't all talk at once. All of you can get books. You can go pick them out and meet us in that room over there." She pointed out the first of the group study rooms.

The Pixies flew off and the four of them walked into the room and sat down in chairs at one end of the table. Paul pulled the out the wand in the first position. "Alpha Wand On … computer," he said and released the wand. A moment later the screen was floating there an inch above the table.

Both girls looked at each other and this time they rolled their eyes and said nothing.

"Did your sponsor show you how to do that too?" Jennifer asked finally.

"Not specifically," Paul answered.

"But he watched as Georaldon did it," Jim explained as Paul took the binoculars of his belt and set them on the table next to the computer. It sat there with its screen blank. He looked at the screen but there were no instructions. No keyboard. No icons to select. No buttons to click. No mouse to do it with. There was nothing but the blank screen. Paul studied the screen for a few seconds. It occurred to him that since there were so many Atlantan things that were voice activated that maybe the computer responded to voice input.

"Display pictures," Paul said as distinctly as possible. Immediately the first picture displayed on the screen. Five seconds later the second one came up, and the rest followed at five second intervals.

"Can we go back to the first two?" Betsy asked.

"I don't know," answered Paul, "Let's see. Display first picture," he instructed. The first picture came right up on the screen. This time the computer did not scroll through the others.

"Sweet," Jim said,

"Totally," Jennifer agreed, "We learn more all the time."

"Look at those tanks over by that curved area," Betsy said. "Is that the stack?"

"Yeah," Paul answered.

"Look, at that beam sticking out," Jennifer pointing at the screen. "What is that hanging off?"

"It a chain hoist," Paul answered. "They can pick up the vessels with it."

"Do you think it's strong enough?" Jim asked, "Those are pretty big tanks."

"Yeah," Paul agreed, "I wonder how much they weigh full." Suddenly, in a pleasant feminine voice, the computer said, *"Which vessel?"*

All four of their mouths fell open in astonishment.

"Did you hear that?" Betsy exclaimed. "It responded to your voice, Paul."

Paul nodded and held up his hand in a stop motion, "The one on the left," he answered.

As Paul spoke a box formed around the vessel on the left and the computer answered, *"The indicated Vessel's volume equals 532.375 gallons. What is the Specific Gravity of the liquid you wish to compute?"*

What does specific gravity mean?" Paul asked the computer.

Betsy gave him a funny look. Paul shrugged, "I don't remember what it means."

"Specific gravity is the density relative to water. If it is exactly the same density as water, the specific gravity is 1.000." The computer answered.

"This is good," Jennifer exclaimed.

"Use the specific gravity of sodium hydroxide," Paul instructed, smiling at Betsy and Jennifer.

"How strong is the concentration?" the computer asked.

Paul wrinkled his nose and thought for a second. "The strongest commercially available grade," he instructed.

"The specific gravity of the strongest commercially available grade of sodium hydroxide on Earthantis equals 1.156. If the vessel is filled to complete capacity, the weight of liquid equals 5288.931 pounds. At a projected normal capacity of 500 gallons, the weight of liquid equals 4,970.816 pounds." The computer answered.

"Go to picture number five," Paul instructed. The picture of the I-beam and hoist appeared on the screen. "Move the center of the picture to the right 3 inches and down four," Paul said. The chain hoist was now in the center of the screen. "Zoom to 300 percent," he instructed again. The hoist filled the screen. Cast into the housing was the inscription CAP = 3

TONS.

"There we go," Betsy said, "Five thousand pounds is two and a half tons. That hoist is capable of picking up a filled tank. Can we go to that second picture?"

Paul nodded, "Go to picture number two," he said, and the second picture appeared on the computer screen.

"What do you suppose the "HZ" means," she asked.

"I don't know," Paul answered.

"Could it be "hydroxide zone" or something like that?" Jim asked.

"Maybe its German," Jennifer suggested.

"Yeah," Paul answered.

"The problem is we don't know," Betsy said.

"You're right, we don't. We can't find out either. At least not right now. It's almost time for the Chorda matches," Jennifer said, "We can't be late, people will ask questions."

As they left the room, the Pixies flew up. Each one had an armload of small books. They went to the front desk, checked out the books.

The members of Q3 walked from the library, down the curving stairs, across the portico and into the Chorda room. Most of the students were already there, everyone but Q6. Anne Chastain smiled smugly. Ornith leaned towards Paul's ear, "I think she has won all of her matches."

"Is that why she's smiling like that?" Paul asked.

"Yes," Ornith answered, "I think so."

Just then Q6 walked into the room followed closely by Professor Flyndor. She said, "Display this evening's matches." A holographic projection of the names of who was paired with whom appeared.

Jim nudged Paul with his elbow and pointed rather low on the list. Betsy was playing Anne Chastain. Paul leaned over to Betsy, "Good Luck."

Betsy turned back to Paul and smiled a nervous smile.

"OK, students," the Professor said loudly enough to be heard over the murmurs of the students, "Let's begin." When the matches were over, Jennifer was the only one of the four that had pulled out a win.

"We are going to have to work hard at Palacrosse tomorrow," Paul said to Jim as they approached their room. "Open," he said to the door, and it opened soundlessly. "If we don't win we are going to fall behind."

"Yeah," Jim answered and walked up to the Snack part of the wall, "Snack," he began, "Coke ... Cheese Pringles," he said and looked over at Paul who held up two fingers, "Coke ... Cheese Pringles," Jim said again. In less than five seconds the first order appeared and floated out on its plate to Jim and a few seconds later the second one appeared and came over to Paul. The boys sat down in their recliners and started a movie.

ψ

The members of Q3 arrived at the Field House early. After Palacrosse practice they were to have their first class in the History of Atlantis.

"What should we do today?" Jennifer asked.

"Well," Paul began, "First, I think we should continue to work on our accuracy for a while. We've made a lot of progress on passing, so I

149

think we should spend some time on accuracy."

"OK," Jim agreed, "What about afterwards?"

"Afterwards we should split into pairs and just spend the rest of the day passing it back and forth as we jump around like yesterday. We should work on that tomorrow too."

"Sort of groove those skills in?" Betsy asked.

"Yeah," Paul continued. "And later in the week, I think we should play "keep-away." We take turns. One pair has the wobble and tries to pass it back and forth, working it down the field, while the other pair tries to take it away. That sort of practice should make us as competitive as possible next Friday."

"This is good," Jennifer said with a nod. Her confidence was growing. None of them knew it, but that was the point.

Q3 worked on Paul's plan, and before practice was over, both pairs were effectively passing the wobble back and forth. "We made headway today," Betsy said encouragingly as they walked towards the classroom wing of the School.

"I think so too," Paul replied. "None of the other Quadros seem to be as organized about mastering the basic skills as we are. I think we'll pick up some points on Friday."

ψ

Professor Flyndor had not come into their Atlantan History class yet so Jim leaned towards the girls, "Have you guys heard about the bears?"

"Bears?" Jennifer asked.

"Yeah," Jim answered, "Ornith was telling us about Atlantan bears, so we looked them up on the computer. Paul's going to talk to his sponsors about getting one when we go down to Co-re-alis the first time."

"You did say a ... bear ... right?" Betsy asked. She looked over to Paul.

"Yeah," Paul agreed with a nod.

"What, are you guys going to do with a Bear?" Betsy asked in disbelief.

"Right ... there isn't room in the suites for a bear" Jennifer protested. "What ... what ... what if it isn't friendly?"

"Well," Paul answered, "According to Ornith, they are small bears ... about the size of a Koala bear, and they are supposed to be very friendly. Cuddly too."

"Oh," Jennifer responded.

"These bears don't go out much, they're housebroken and they can't fly," Jim said, "They can talk though ... and read. We'll have to get books for it."

"It's housebroken, it can talk ... it can read ... you have to get books for it?" Betsy asked shaking her head.

"Yep," he answered nodding his head, "But the bear cleans up after you."

"It does ... what?" the girls asked in unison.

"From what Ornith says, it seems that these bears like to clean things ... so it cleans up your room," Paul answered. The girls both rolled their eyes in disbelief. "That's what Ornith told us," Paul added

151

defensively. He could tell he was getting nowhere.

"I think Ornith is playing a joke on you," Betsy teased.

"I don't think so ... and anyway, it's in the computer too," Paul answered, "Besides, he didn't say that girls could have one."

"He said girls couldn't have one?" Jennifer asked.

"No. He just didn't say that you could," Jim teased.

"I'll bet we can have a bear too, if we want ... besides ... we don't need any help keeping our room clean," Jennifer said with a superior tone, and sharing one of those eye roll looks with Betsy.

Just then Professor Flyndor walked in accompanied by a portly gentleman. Something about him was vaguely familiar, but Paul could not quite place it. The professor took her normal position in front of the desk at the head of the class while the mysterious gentleman settled into the chair to her right.

"Class," began Professor Flyndor, "Today we have a special treat. Yes," she nodded as she answered the unasked question, "I really do think you will like this. We have a guest from the Atlantan city of Aasgard. Please welcome Mr. Nicholas von Klaus."

As the class clapped politely, Paul noticed Betsy looking at their guest with a perplexed expression as if she almost recognized him from somewhere but couldn't quite put her finger on it.

"Good Morning," he said in a deep pleasant voice as he rose from the chair and looked over the class for a second. Mr. von Klaus cleared his throat and began. "Over a thousand years ago, in the year 373, I graduated from St. Germain's seminary at Auxerre, France. France was called "Long Haired Gaul" by the Romans in those days, but it was often shortened to

152

Gaul. It's a part of France now but it was not called France until much later. Those of us who lived there at the time called it Gaul. The Roman Empire was slowly dying and the period of time known as "the Dark Ages" were coming. Although the Dark Ages would not reach Rome itself for another hundred years, they already had Gaul firmly in their grip."

"At that time," he continued, "If you were the eldest son of a nobleman, you would inherit your father's title. If you were not the eldest son, you either went into the military, or the priesthood. My father was the Baron von Klaus and I was his third son. Our lands were up in the north of Gaul in a section that ultimately became part of Denmark. Since I have no talent for military things, I decided to go into the priesthood, and my father sent me to St. Germain's seminary at Auxerre. At that time, most of the seminary graduates would go back to their hometowns and serve as a priest in a local church, but in every class the top two students were given the opportunity to go out into pagan lands to spread Christianity. A good friend of mine, named Patrick, was sent to spread Christianity in Ireland. He eventually became known as Saint Patrick. I was sent to do the same thing in Scandinavia." Again he paused.

Suddenly Betsy sat bolt upright in her chair. "Nicholas von Klaus!" she cried out, "That's it! Your first name is Nicholas. Your friend Patrick became Saint Patrick, and you became … Saint Nicholas!" she paused. "Saint Nicholas Klaus as in Santa … Claus?"

"Yes," he said beaming broadly, "I always wonder how long it will take before one of you figured it out. Well done young lady. You were very quick." The room was suddenly buzzing with questions.

"Where's your beard?" a student from the back asked.

153

He held up his hand in a stop signal. "Perhaps this will work better if you allow me to explain." He looked around the class. "These days I only grow the beard out for the winter time. It's too scratchy for summers. Anyway, back to Scandinavia. I was there to preach the gospel, but it never seemed fair to expect people to investigate your religion, if you weren't willing to investigate theirs. My first task on arriving in the northlands was to learn about their religious beliefs."

"As I expected, their beliefs were drawn from the Nordic myths. Now you must understand that I believed what I had been taught to believe ... that the myths of Thor and the Norse gods living at Aasgard were nothing more than superstitious legends. After learning what the Scandinavians of that time believed, I began preaching. I made little headway at first, but finally found an idea that was helping. At Christmas time, I would give the village children a toy, to emphasize the significance of the Christmas season. This idea drew a lot of attention, and I was making progress in the southern regions of Scandinavia. As I moved farther and farther north, I noticed that the legends grew stronger and more persistent," he paused and took a sip of milk, "and the stories of Aasgard became more specific."

"Some of these legends and myths had actually been written down along with places and dates as if they were an actual record of real events. The farther north I went, the more convinced the people were that the legends of Aasgard were true. I got fewer and fewer converts, but the gifts at Christmas time were helping. People had begun calling me Saint Nicholas in some cases; Saint Nick in others, but in the far north, it was more a sign of respect than faith."

"In the end, I decided to go in search of this place called Aasgard. I didn't go to prove it was there. I went to prove it was not. I traveled to the places mentioned in their ancient legends to prove them wrong ... that there was no such place as Aasgard." He paused and finished his glass of milk. "I wonder if you can imagine how surprised I was when I found it."

Again the classroom buzzed with questions, and he held up his hand for quiet. "I was wandering in the deep woods one summer, and suddenly saw two people. I didn't know anyone was around, but tried to approach them. Before I could, they illuminated what I now know is the Pole of Aasgard. Needless to say this amazed me and I called out to them. I was welcomed by the Atlantans. I began to learn of their culture, and they began to learn of me. The Atlantans of Aasgard were as anxious as I was to dispel the idea that there was anything real underlying the legends, and wanted to help me. The elves of Aasgard were especially impressed with my gift giving, and offered their aid. They are talented carvers and make lovely wooden toys. We would work through the year making toys, and on Christmas Eve, I would put on a transport belt, and make the rounds of the villages, distributing the gifts. I would Jump into a home, leave a toy by the fireplace, and then Jump to the next. So you see, the legend of Santa Claus began with true facts. Over the centuries these legends have grown and been embellished, but they began with real events. Most legends do. Over time the legends of Santa Claus grew and the Norse myths faded."

"Do you have reindeer?" Jim Hernandez asked.

"Yes, but it's not what you think," he replied and nodded to Professor Flyndor. A moment later a holograph appeared in the middle of

155

the classroom. It was a sleigh being pulled by two reindeer. "This video was produced about forty years ago. Until the introduction of the snowmobile, a sleigh pulled by a team of reindeer was the easiest way to get around during the long winters in the far northern parts of Scandinavia. In the 4th Century, it was the only way. Many of the villagers had seen me moving about with a team a lot like the one you see hear. The villagers all knew I was the one giving the gifts. This was not a secret, but they had no explanation for how I could get around so far and distribute so many. They had to tell their children something, so someone made up the story of magical reindeer pulling a sleigh that could fly. I did have reindeer … still do … but not to help deliver the gifts."

"With a transport belt you wouldn't have to go down a chimney. Did you carry a sack of toys?" Jim asked.

Saint Nick beamed broadly again. "I actually do carry a sack, but it's not full of toys. The sack has a portable portal, like that snack dispenser in the wall over there. It only takes a minute to set up, and one of the elves back in Aasgard transports the toys for that home through the portal."

"What about the lump of coal if you've been bad?" someone asked from the back.

"I would never do that." Saint Nick said shaking his head. "I would never humiliate a child that way. I have no idea where that idea came from, either. Sometimes these legends take on a life of their own. They begin with facts, but things get added that have no foundation in fact. That's a good example."

"What about the North Pole?" Jennifer asked.

Another broad smile broke out on Saint Nick's face. "Until about two hundred years ago, the Atlantans had not produced enough transport belts for everyone. The only way for most Atlantans to get in and out of their cities were the portals. A special "pole" marked each city's portal. There is one not very far from here, in fact. It's called the "Co-re-alis Pole." All of these "poles" have to remain invisible to anyone from Earthantis so they're Cloaked, but the Power Rings can home in on them and guide Atlantans to the portals. Once the ring is close enough, it can illuminate the pole. As I said earlier, watching some Atlantans illuminate Aasgard's pole is how I found Aasgard. Anyway, Aasgard is very far north. It is, by far, the most northern Atlantan city. Because it is so far north, the Pole of Aasgard became known as the North Pole." He paused and looked around the silent classroom. "So you see, there is a North Pole, a real one. It is not Earthantis's north ... "magnetic" ... pole, but it is every bit as real when you understand how the term originated."

"Who was Kris Kringle?" Anne Chastain asked.

"He ... is ... the chief elf of my workshop," Saint Nick answered with another of his smiles. "I really do have a workshop. The tradesmen who help me are real elves, and it really is at the "North Pole", the Pole of Aasgard. All of that was true ... all of it still is." The classroom got so quite Paul could have heard a pin drop. Saint Nick nodded slowly. "I still distribute gifts at Christmas. Atlantan medical science works as well on the people of Earthantis as it does on the people of Atlantis, you see, so for about three hundred years afterwards, I kept on with the Christmas gifts. As time went on, the people of Earthantis began to travel more and more. Ships from many other places were coming into Scandinavian ports. The legend of Santa Claus started to spread into other parts of the world and would have eventually been traced back to Aasgard. Earthantis society was not ready for that, so, although it broke my heart, I decided to phase out the giving of toys to the children of Earthantan people. Even so, each Christmas Eve, Kris and I distribute a toy to every Atlantan child, a fine wooden toy carved well by the elves of Aasgard."

Chapter Eight

You Win Some

That night after dinner there was a chill in the air. Mountains are like that even in summer and the warmth of a fire is welcome. Atlantans had no need of fireplaces for heat but the flagstone hearth of the Great Room provided more than heat. They added ambiance as well. Cheerful fires had been lit in each of the fireplaces and the flickering shadows cast by the dancing flames almost brought the room to life. The members of Q3 paused momentarily, almost unconsciously, to breathe in the ambience, and then continued on to the Library. There was work to do, and they had an hour before the evening's Chorda matches.

"OK," Paul began as they settled into the chairs in the room they selected.

"Did anyone get a chance to look through *Correctional Operations*?"

"I did," Betsy reported.

"That's right," Gwenivere added, flying around to the rest of the group, "She kept us up at least half the night."

"It wasn't half the night," Betsy protested.

"Was so," Gwenivere insisted.

"It was not," Betsy said and looked at the rest of her Quadro, "It was an hour ... maybe an hour and a half." She looked at Gwenivere, "Now, will you please hush?"

The little Pixie flew around to Betsy's shoulder and plopped down, crossing her arms over her chest.

"Do I get a nose rub?" Betsy asked.

"No," Gwenivere answered in a huff, "Not when you keep me up half the night."

Paul began to laugh, "I think they always get the last word."

Betsy just shook her head, and then pulled out her copy of the book. "I didn't get very far but here is what I learned. We are not allowed to act in place of the local authorities."

"We're not?" Jim asked. "How do we get anything done then?"

"I have just gotten to that part," Betsy explained, "So I don't know all about it yet, but we gather the sort of data that forces local authorities to act. The Atlantan idea is to let the local justice system work."

"Will it work?" Jim asked.

"*Correctional Operations* says that if things are handled properly it does, and so that is the policy. We gather conclusive information, and then get it to the authorities."

"So we are sort of like spies," Paul concluded.

"Sweet!" Jim exclaimed.

"Totally," Paul agreed with a nod.

Betsy looked at Jennifer and rolled her eyes, "There is a lot more to it than that. For example, we also have to decide what to do with the information we gather. They have some specific techniques for making sure that the people we pass it on to ... "have" ... to do something about it."

"But you don't know what those techniques are yet?" Jim asked.

"No, not yet," Betsy answered, "But one important point was that the data has to be transmitted in a form that does not betray the existence of Atlantis. Whatever instrumentation we use has to be available from normal Earthantan sources. We can't blow the cover of Atlantis itself."

"Well, that's more than we knew yesterday," Jim said with a nod. "Not all we need, but more than we had."

Paul took out his Alpha Wand and set up the computer. Soon he had the picture of the stack room up. "Let's review what we know. That beam and hoist can lift the "HZ" vessel. That door in the stack looks big enough to let it inside. The steam that is coming in has to be piped in from underneath. So the next question is: Can the vessel release the contents into the steam?"

"Yes," the computer answered although the question had not been specifically directed to it, *"An analysis of the equipment on the bottom of the vessel indicates the presence of a servo valve. An analysis of the equipment on the top of the vessel indicates the presence of a timer that is wired to the servo valve. The timer can be set with a time, and at the preset interval, the valve will open releasing the contents."*

"Well," Jim said into the silence that followed, "I guess that answers that."

"I guess so," agreed Jennifer.

"So we know how they are doing it,," Paul summarized. "The question remains: can we do anything about it?"

ψ

162

On Thursday evening, Paul sat across the Chorda board from Joe Hernandez, one of the members of Q5. Joe's Quadro was ahead by 5 points. There were three teams clustered behind Q5 and Q3 was one of them. Palacrosse practice was going well. Q3 had spent two practice sessions trying to play keep away and working the wobble down the field. It was harder to control the wobble than it looked but they kept at it and it was going a little better with each practice. All four of them were looking forward to the tomorrow's Palacrosse match. This would be their first match against a real opponent and if they won, the three points they would receive would ensure that they were in the first group to go down to Co-re-alis.

He brought his attention back to the Chorda game. Joe had made his opening move. The last two times he had played a member of Q5, he had lost, but this time Paul felt he was better prepared. Betsy had gone onto the Internet, which turned out to be accessible from Atlantan computers, and read up a little on chess strategy. Chorda was harder than chess, but she had felt that there might be some good suggestions there. She had picked up a good tip and passed it on to her Quadromates, and Paul intended to employ tonight.

The tip was pretty simple. Don't worry about a grand strategy. Choose a high-ranking piece of your opponent's and plot a strategy to take it. Be willing to sacrifice lower ranking pieces to take higher-ranking ones, and do this early on. The strategy was to create an advantage in piece maneuverability. You end up playing with an advantage.

So far it was working.

He had taken a lieutenant colonel, and both of Joe's majors. In the process, he had lost a chief, a 1st lieutenant, and a captain, but he definitely had an advantage now. He had maneuvered his colonel and lieutenant colonel into a position to trap Joe's colonel. He would lose a major but that trade was to his advantage.

ψ

"What happened?" Betsy asked Paul as they all left the Chorda room. He was the only one of them who had drawn someone from Q5.

"I won!"

"Yeah, couldn't you tell," Jim gloated, "He wiped that smug smile right off of Joe Hernandez's face."

"How'd you do?" Betsy asked Jim.

"I won too," he answered, "Thanks to you."

"Great," she said with a smile, "So did I."

"Me too," Jennifer interjected.

"Really!" Betsy exclaimed, "We won all four! We're in second place – four behind Q5 and two ahead of Q1 and Q6."

"Yeah," Jim agreed, "But a loss tomorrow could still knock us out of the trip to Co-re-alis. Three points are at stake in a Palacrosse match."

"That's right," Paul agreed, "But tomorrow's match can't be played until tomorrow. Let's go up to the library before we go back to our rooms." It had been three days since they had talked about the mill and it was time to take stock again.

Once everyone was settled into a seat, Paul spoke carefully, "Now," he began, "we've all had a chance to read *Correctional*

Operations at this point. I think we should review it together so that we all understand this stuff the same way."

The other three nodded and Paul continued, "First, these operations are split into two phases. One is the collection of the data. The first thing is to discover and document the truth. And they stress careful planning. If something goes wrong, rather than push it, you back off, re-plan and start again. Over and over that concept is stressed. If something gets dangerous we back off and start again. Do we all get that?"

Everyone nodded.

"The second phase is delivery," Paul continued, "We get the data into the hands of the right authorities in a way that leaves them no choice but to do something with it."

Betsy nodded. "The concept of simultaneously informing both the press and law enforcement is really neat," she observed. "Especially the part where you let law enforcement know that members of the press have been informed, but not who. There is no way for the police not to act if the press is going to break the story, and no way to block it if they don't know who has it."

"Exactly," Jennifer said quickly, "While you guys were concentrating on *Correctional Operations,* I've been working on this." She laid a copy of *Rules of The Hawk's Nest Science and Math Academy* on the table.

"Good," Paul said looking at the book, "Anything we need to know right off of the bat?"

"Yes," she answered, "Most of this has very little to do with what we are intending to do. Mostly it has to do with curfews, grades, mean tricks and things like that, but there are a couple of things. First ... our equipment is not considered "school property". It was given to us by the citizens of Atlantis not the school. Second, using school facilities ... like we are right now ... to talk about something we might or might not do, is not considered using "school facilities." That involves taking school property off of the school's premises."

"So," Jim asked, "We're not breaking any rules now?"

"No," she answered.

"OK," Paul said with a nod.

"Moving on," Jennifer continued, "What kind of data do we need? In order to know the answer, we've got to read up on the laws about air pollution. Who wants to get started on that?"

"I will," Paul said.

"Another thing we need," Jim said, "Is to know about the kinds of instrumentation that we can use to collect the kind of air pollution data with that we can give to the authorities. What we need ... where we can get it. That sort of thing. I can get started on that."

"Good," Betsy nodded and looked at Jennifer. "Jen and I could get started on researching the press and government agencies for phase two."

"Right," Paul agreed. "We are all on the same page then?"

Everyone nodded in agreement.

The four of them split up and Paul and Jim headed back to their room. "Open," Jim said and the door glided open. They walked in and Paul went over to the snack dispenser section of the wall, "Snack" he said and it recessed into the wall. It had taken the boys surprising little time getting used to the snack dispenser. "Milky Way Dark ... Mountain Dew." Jim held up two fingers indicating he'd like one also. "Two," Paul instructed the machine and walked over to his chair and sat down. Seconds later the orders were floating out to them.

"Can I have some, please?" Ornith asked.

"Sure," Paul answered and broke off a small piece of chocolate and handed to the Pix. He plopped into his chair. "You know," he mused thoughtfully, "I know we need to take this plan in steps, but it sure would be nice to know how to use the rest of the stuff on our belts."

"Yeth," Jim agreed, his mouth full of candy bar.

"It's all in da c'puter," Ornith announced, his mouth also full of chocolate.

"What do you mean?" Paul asked.

Ornith chewed up his bite of candy, flew up into the air and around where both boys could see him, "It ... is ... all ... on ... your ... computer," he said waving his arms back and forth.

"No joke?" Jim asked.

"No joke," Aurileol agreed. "Directions for everything are there."

ψ

Paul stood looking up at the Palacrosse field. They had drawn Q6, and he had butterflies in his stomach. He always did before a big game. The reward for being in the top four was a trip to Co-re-alis this weekend and that was their goal. If they won they would make the trip, but if they lost they could easily fall into fifth place. The whistle sounded, and they

167

all buckled their flying harnesses and jumped into the field. The coach tossed in the wobble, and the game was on.

A Q6'er got to it first and hit it towards the Q3 goal. Another Q6'er had bounded off of the wall and managed to intercept the wobble. She hit it as best she could but missed Q3's goal. It ricocheted off of the back wall passing near another of the Q6'ers. He hit the wobble at Q3's goal again, and missed low. He'd hit it with a lot of topspin and when it came off of the back, that spin acted to bring it up a bit and the wobble hit the left side of their goal from the back side and bounced through. Through from the front or through from the back, it counted either way.

Q6: 1, Q3: 0 Q6 had scored first.

Paul looked at his teammates. They all knew that this was a lucky break for Q6, and had little to do with skill, but sometimes lucky was better than good.

"Let's go guys," Paul called out encouragingly.

Jim bounded off of the wall, and managed to intercept the wobble as it ricocheted around the field. He hit it gently towards Betsy. One of the Q6'ers bounded towards Betsy, but before he could get there, she passed the wobble to Paul who deadened it so he could hit it accurately. He saw that Jennifer was about to bound off of the bottom, and would be in the clear at the top, so he hit it where he thought she would be and then bounded towards the Q6 goal. Jennifer made a nice pass to Jim, who got the wobble to Betsy. Betsy deadened the wobble and noticed that Paul was only one bound out of the range they had practiced. She made a nice pass to Paul and he hit the wobble through the goal.

Q6: 1, Q3: 1

The game seesawed back and forth through the rest of the first period, and all the way through the second. Each time one team got into a position for a shot, someone from the other team was in the way. Neither team got a good shot on their opponents' goal. Each time one team got close, the other one managed to disrupt the play. Sometimes this was done purposely, to good-effect, other times it was as much an accident as anything else. It turned out to be a whole lot harder to bound around with four members of another team present than anyone had counted on.

The bell for the third period break sounded.

Paul gathered his team at the goal they would defend in the third and final period. "OK," he announced, "The score is still one to one."

"Yeah," Jim said, "Lucky for them."

"No," Paul corrected, "Lucky for us. We have not been doing what we practiced. Every time we hit the wobble, we're trying too hard. It goes wild and everything is getting screwed up." He looked at his teammates. "I think we've got to slow this down, and try and get methodical, like we did when we scored that first time."

Betsy nodded in agreement, "What do you want us to do Paul?"

"Jim … you start out down near our goal. Jennifer, why don't you be more towards their goal. Betsy and I can take the middle. When the wobble comes in, we'll try and get to it. Whenever we do, don't hit it right off. Deaden it so we can be accurate. Find a teammate and pass it. Let's play like we practiced."

The bell sounded, and Q3 moved to the positions Paul had indicated.

Paul moved to the middle with Betsy, Jim moved towards their goal, and Jennifer moved towards Q6's goal. The coach threw in the wobble. For most of the period Q3 tried to get their play together but every time they got a little ways down, some Q6'er would manage to break it up. With about a minute left on the clock, Jim hit the wobble towards Paul but a Q6'er got into position to intercept. The girl took a shot on the Q3 goal from the middle on the court. She hit a nice shot with plenty of spin but her shot was way off the mark, and Jim was waiting. He intercepted it, deadened it, and passed it to Betsy, who passed it Paul. Paul also deadened it, allowing Jim time to move to the middle and Betsy time to move forward, and passed it back to Jim. Jim deadened it, and then passed it to Betsy, just barely getting it past a bounding Q6'er, but she got the wobble.

"Thirty seconds," Paul called out.

Betsy deadened the wobble and let the clock run down. A Q6'er bounded to intercept but before he could get there she passed it to Jennifer. Jennifer also deadened it.

"Ten seconds," Paul called.

Jennifer took careful aim and hit it directly through the center of the Goal.

The final score was Q3: 2, Q6: 1. They had won their first Palacrosse match.

"Way to go, Jen," Paul congratulated slapping Jenifer on the back as they walked back towards Fellowship Hall. Jim and Betsy joined in, and Paul realized that this was going to do a world of good for her confidence..

The members of Q3 had gathered in the upper balcony of Fellowship Hall. There was an hour left before dinner and they had discovered that the conversation areas of Fellowship Hall were more comfortable than the study rooms of the Library.

"So," Betsy asked, "how are you guys coming with your research?"

"Good," Jim answered. "I'm making progress and learned a lot. There are several different kinds of instruments that can analyze chemical samples. Three actually. One kind is called an infrared spectrometer. Another is called a magnetic resonance imager. The last is a gas chromatograph. Most colleges have the stuff, also most medical labs. Some of it is portable, some of it is not. I haven't gotten that far yet, but I have learned that the controls on all of them are computerized these days and easy to operate. We'll have to figure out exactly how to use whatever we select, but it shouldn't be all that hard."

"What about getting one? How much are they?" Betsy asked.

"One question at a time," Jim answered. "All of this stuff is readily available at laboratory supply houses. The only pricing I have is for gas chromatographs. Portable models run about $8,500. I don't know how expensive the other stuff is."

"$8,500 Dollars!" Jennifer exclaimed. "Where are we going to get that kind of money?"

"$8,500 is easy," Paul answered. "Georaldon told me that our allowances from Atlantis are convertible to Dollars. Each of us has a contingency fee. Between the four of us that's $10,000."

"OK, so that's how we'll pay for it," Betsy agreed and looked at her roommate.

"Who knew?" Jennifer said with a shrug.

"How are you coming on the Regs, Paul?" Betsy asked.

"I'm making progress too, but it's slow going. There are a million regulations. The main problem is that the information is scattered all over. It's here a little there a little. There are only a few places where it all collected together."

"Where are they?" Jennifer asked.

"Washington is one," Paul answered, "the EPA has a special section of the Library of Congress that has everything in one place. There are libraries in places like New York and Chicago. The Library of Congress is actually the closest one that has everything."

"Really?" Betsy said giving Jennifer an inquiring look.

"Yeah," Paul answered. "This would go a lot faster if I could spend a few hours there. I was beginning to think that this was going to end up taking months ... "

"Then I reminded him of how we got here," Jim interjected.

"Yeah," Paul agreed a little ruefully. "We know what the Library of Congress looks like so we can just jump there. I keep forgetting things like that."

"How are you guys coming?" Jim inquired.

"Good," Betsy answered. She looked at Jennifer who nodded. "Really good. We've found out where to go in Washington to get data to the EPA. We've found where to go in Knoxville for the field office of the

FBI that covers this area. We've found the name of a contact with the Washington Post. That's a major national newspaper not far from the offices of the EPA. We've located another press contact with the Hawk's Nest Examiner. It turns out to be in Knoxville."

"So you guys are basically done then," Jim said, "That's great."

"That's right," Gwenivere said with her arms crossed in front of her, "They had one of those … stay up half the night … nobody sleeps things."

"Well," Betsy said defensively, "We … "

"Well … nothing," Renalee interrupted. "Flying around takes a lot of energy and we need our rest."

Gwenivere just nodded in agreement, her little arms crossed over her chest.

Paul and Jim just shook their heads.

Jennifer looked over at Gwenivere and then over at Renalee. "OK … OK," she said, "We're sorry. We won't do it again."

"Do you promise?" Gwenivere asked.

"Yes," both Betsy and Jennifer promised. Gwenivere and Renalee flew down and rubbed noses and then settled back onto the girl's shoulders.

"Anyway," Betsy continued, "we're really not finished. Once we get the data, we still have to actually deliver it to the right people in all of these places. We don't know where their offices are and we don't think it will be a good idea to go wandering around Washington like little lost lambs with arm loads of computer printouts."

"That might raise questions," Paul agreed.

"We think so too," Betsy agreed. "We think we are actually going to have to go to these places and ... you know ... figure out what we need to do. I don't think we can do it from here, not easily anyway. We were thinking that we'd wait until we had the data and then do the scouting afterwards ... but ... if Paul needs ... "

"I see," Jim interjected, "If Paul could use some time in the Library of Congress, we could just go ahead with it now."

"Right," Betsy agreed.

"When?" Paul asked.

"Well, this weekend is out. How about next Saturday after the Palacrosse match?" Jennifer asked. "We could go then. How about that?"

"This is good," Paul and Jim agreed.

Chapter Nine

Co-re-alis

Paul stood with his Quadromates in the Greenhouse. After lunch, Professor Glorfyndor had given them a choice. They could wait until morning, or they could go ahead and transfer down before dinner. The vote of the students going down was unanimous, and the Professor had smiled knowingly as if he always gave students this choice, and going down early was what they always choose.

"I'll see to it that your sponsors are informed," he had said after reading the results of the vote. "Meet me in the Greenhouse in an hour."

Everyone had been a few minutes early. Q5 and Q2 joined them in the Greenhouse. The competition was still close, but none of that was on the minds of the kids going down to Co-re-alis. There was excitement in the air as Professor Glorfyndor walked into the Greenhouse.

"Before we transfer down," he began, "Let me explain a little about the layout of Co-re-alis." A holographic image appeared behind him and he turned to it and pointed at the middle. "This section in the middle," he said pointing to what looked for all practical purposes like the hub of a wheel surrounded by spokes, "is called the Central Core. It is a very large area ... four miles across ... with a domed ceiling. It contains shops of all descriptions, theaters, schools, restaurants, the library, our civic center, taverns and that sort of thing. It is the area where Atlantans go to do things together."

He pointed to one of the spokes proceeding out from the Central Core. "These are called Living Quarter Cores. There are a total of ten. Each is six stories tall, has its own park in the middle. There are individual apartments built around each of the ten Living Quarter Cores." He pointed farther out on the spokes. "This rim, out past the Living Quarter Cores, is the manufacturing area. It is called the Manufacturing Rim. This is where all of the things we manufacture are produced. Out past the Manufacturing Rim is an even larger rim," the professor said as he pointed to the outermost part of the hologram. "This is called the Ag Rim, and contains agricultural fields. Beyond that is the largest Rim. It's called the Wild Rim. This is where we preserve the species we brought with us from Atlantis. You'll learn more about it later, but for now all you need to know is that you have to have special clearance to enter that area. Some of these species are quire dangerous. So that is the layout. The place where we transfer down is the General Hall of the Civic Center.

He pointed his Power Ring at a vacant spot in the greenhouse and said, "Acquire portal." A greenish light came from his ring and a pole appeared. He trained the green light from his ring on the pole and said "Open Portal." A shimmering doorway appeared. "Transferring down is very simple," he said, "You just walk through that doorway. Your sponsors are waiting."

Paul said goodbye to his Quadromates, and with Ornith clutching his shoulder in anticipation, followed one of the Q5'ers through the shimmering doorway. Once again he felt the swirling kaleidoscope of lights, but this time he had formed no visualization of where he wanted to go. He just did as he had been told and walked into the portal. When the lights stopped moving, he was in the middle of a large hall. It looked as if it had been built of marble, but he couldn't sure. He kept on walking, not wanting to be in the way of the kids transferring down behind him. There were a group of people gathered ahead of him, and he recognized Baralicia waving.

"There they are," Ornith whispered excitedly.

"Yes, I see them too."

Seconds later Baralicia walked up and took both of Paul's hands in both of hers, "It is so good to see you, Paul. We are really glad that you were in the first group."

"That's right," Felinda said flying over and rubbing noses with Paul, followed immediately by Ardant who gave him a high five instead of a nose rub. After the Pixies had welcomed Paul they went over welcomed Ornith in much the same fashion. Again Paul noticed that there seemed to be some sort of special relationship between Ornith and Felinda and Ardant. This time he would try and remember and ask Ornith about it.

As all of this unfolded around Paul, he was struck again by how genuine Baralicia was, and then Georaldon had him by the hands as well. "Yes, Paul, welcome. Come; let's show you around a little."

The three of them walked out of the Civic Center into a large space.

Paul looked up and caught his breath. "This place is huge," he exclaimed. He couldn't tell how far it was to the ceiling of the Central Core but it had to be at least two hundred yards. Furthermore it looked like a light blue sky. A bright light that he supposed was to simulate the sun was nearly down and that made sense too. Up on the surface it was not long until sundown. If he hadn't known he was underground, he didn't think he would be able to tell. There were no signs of Co-re-alis having been carved out of solid rock at all.

"The Central Core is four miles across," Georaldon said proudly, "There are over eight-thousand acres in the Central Core alone." He pointed to an opening on the outer edge that was barely visible in the distance. "Those are Living Quarters Cores. We live in that one, LQC #7."

Paul looked at a building across a wide veranda. It looked as if it was constructed of marble. At the apex of the roofline was engraved the word "Library". Paul looked around. Although none of them were lit, he could see streetlights. They resembled an ornate Victorian style that had gone out of fashion in the United States early in the Twentieth Century. To the right of the Library there was what appeared to be a small amphitheater. An ensemble of elves was playing woodwind instruments for a group of people gathered there. Beyond the amphitheater was a building that appeared to be a restaurant with outdoor seating. Everywhere he looked there were trees, well-manicured bushes, and beds upon beds of colorful flowers. Ornate wrought iron decorations and sculptures of various descriptions appeared in nearly every direction he looked. The architectural style of the entire area within his view was Victorian, and very well done.

"This is amazing," was all Paul could manage to say as he looked around. "It's beautiful. Everything looks so ... antique ... almost old fashioned ... but not ... all at the same time."

Baralicia laughed lightly.

"Yes, Paul," Georaldon agreed with a nod and a smile, "That is a good way to put it. Does that surprise you?"

"Actually, yes," Paul answered and turned to look at the Erlyndors, "You know, we always thought that advanced civilizations would be different. I mean ... you have all of the technology we ever imagined ... more actually ... but you like wooden furniture, ornate stone columns and wrought iron. That is not what I expected. You like carved things ... flowers, and ... trees, and ... nature, and ... sculpture. It's everywhere. Now that I think about it, Atlantis was a lot like this too only in a different style. I never thought you would be like this."

"Why not?" Baralicia asked gently.

"Well, I don't know really. I thought you'd do away with the low tech, antique things and display your technology more."

"We used to," Georaldon explained, "Especially when it was newer for us. But we outgrew that long ago. We've learned that beauty is beauty, and we like to surround ourselves with it. We live a long time Paul. We can take our time with things, and its fun."

They began walking out towards the Living Quarters Core that Georaldon had pointed out. As they walked, they would pass people and all of them would nod pleasantly and speak to Georaldon and Baralicia by name.

"Does everyone know you?" Paul asked.

"Actually ... yes, pretty much everyone," Baralicia answered. "Over a period of time you do get to know everyone."

"Yes," Georaldon said with a nod of agreement, "Our sense of community is very important to us. Have you noticed all of the little amphitheaters and gathering places?"

"Yes," Paul said simply. They were everywhere. In the hundred yards they had walked, they had passed three, all in use. In one, a group was putting on a theatrical play of some kind. In the other two, music was being performed. In all three a collection of spectators had gathered. It would have been impossible not to notice.

"We get together and do things all the time," Baralicia continued, "Sometimes it is in very small groups, sometimes larger groups, and we have festivals frequently that involve everyone. All of us feel a connection to all of the rest of us. We take a great deal of pleasure from that. It takes effort too. We all work at these things, but the amount of pleasure you get back is much greater than the work you put into them."

As they continued walking, they stopped in some of the shops to let Paul look around. There were bakeries, delis, fruit and vegetable markets, bookstores, and clothing shops. There were restaurants of many different descriptions, and Chorda halls were people gathered to play Chorda and many other games.

As they walked on they passed a building labeled "Hospital."

"Paul," Georaldon said, "please pay very close attention for a minute. This is important. Get a good mental image of the entry to that hospital. If you or any of your friends are ever injured, this is where you come. There is no infirmary at the school. We see no reason to duplicate up there what we have so close at hand here. Be sure you get a good image of this in your mind so the transport belt can find it. I hope you never get hurt, but if you do, this is where you Jump. You don't have to use the portal. Don't worry about the school … or us … or anything …

just Jump straight here. The hospital staff will take care of you and let everyone know who needs to know."

Paul took a good long look at the entry to the hospital, memorizing its details. He wondered if Georaldon had figured out that something was up.

As they walked along Paul noticed a floating cart with slowly flashing lights rise from behind one of the shops and head out towards one of the Living Quarter Cores. He looked around and saw several other similar carts moving about. They flew at a level that carried them about fifteen feet above the rooftops. "I see those everywhere. What are those?" he asked, pointing at the cart.

"Oh," Georaldon answered, "Those are called del droids. They contain a standard gravitational nullification system and are programmed to deliver goods."

"So someone just bought something at that shop, and the floating cart is delivering it to their home?" Paul asked.

"That's right."

"They look a lot like the food carts at school."

"That's because they are a lot alike," Georaldon explained. "What you are calling a food cart is actually a del droid with a transport receptacle that allows the food that has been selected to be replaced from the kitchen automatically. Standard del droids like the one you just saw don't have that feature; otherwise they are pretty much the same. You know the floating platters that deliver your food orders off of the carts, and the ones that fly over and deliver your snack orders?"

"Yeah," Paul answered.

"Those are actually del droids too, just small ones."

"What's with the flashing lights?"

"That tells you what direction it is going. The lights flash red in the direction the del droid is traveling. Green means it is going directly away from you. If you see red flashing lights that means it is coming right at you. Blue means it is going to your right, and yellow means your left. The colors are primarily for safety."

When they were still a half a mile from outer edge of the Central Core, Paul noticed that there were corridors moving away from the Central Core that did not appear to be Living Quarters Cores.

"Do those go out to the outer Rims?" he asked.

"Yes," Georaldon answered. "We'll show them to you sometime, but probably not this trip. Too much else to do."

"I'm looking forward to showing you the one farthest out," Baralicia added.

"The one called the Wild Rim?" Paul asked, remembering the Professor's comments before transferring down.

"Exactly," Baralicia answered.

"Why would you want to leave that part wild?"

"Well, Paul," she began, "It's pretty complicated. Basically it's because the trees, plants and animals living there were native to our home world Atlantis. We brought them with us when we came. We didn't want them to become extinct so we brought them with us."

"Oh, yeah," Paul interjected, "Professor Galvyndor told us about that."

"Right," Baralicia continued, "We don't like to cage things more than necessary; so all of the individual animals in there are free to roam the entire area. It's about eighty thousand acres all together."

Paul whistled, "Eighty thousand acres. So it's a complete ecosystem?"

"Yes," Georaldon nodded, "The Wild Rim contains the flora and fauna from a continent on Atlantis that we called North Umber. Each of our cities has a distinctly different yet complete ecosystem in its outer rim, replicating and preserving the ecosystems of Atlantis."

"Right down to the predators," Baralicia said with a laugh.

"Predators?" Paul asked with a tone of alarm.

"Of course," Baralicia answered, "Predators are an important part of any ecosystem."

Georaldon smiled, "Baralicia is one of our leading naturalists, Paul."

Oh, Georaldon," Baralicia objected, "don't say "leading." I'm not a leading anything."

Georaldon smiled mischievously at Paul. "She's the Chief Naturalist, Paul. What would you call that?"

"Leading," Paul answered.

"Well, maybe," Baralicia said modestly, "In any event, you have to have predators for a complete ecosystem. They can be dangerous if they get out. It almost never happens, only once in the last hundred years, but it has happened."

"But don't worry about that Paul," Georaldon interjected and held out his hand. "Light." He said and a soft yet bright light poured out of his Power Ring   "The light from your power ring will handle them if you

184

ever need to."

"Are you saying that Light will scare off a predator?" Paul asked.

"Yep," Georaldon answered, "Any predator, large or small, Atlantan or native to Earthantis."

"Even something like a Lion?" Paul asked.

"Even a Lion," Baralicia answered with a tone that suggested she knew from firsthand experience.

As they walked on Paul saw a small shop with a sign saying "Bears". He turned quickly to Baralicia. "Could you explain what this bear business is all about?" He felt Ornith squirming with excitement on his shoulder.

"Certainly," Baralicia answered with a little laugh as if she suspected what was coming next. "Why do you ask?"

"Ornith says I need one."

Georaldon laughed out loud.

Baralicia smiled knowingly and answered sweetly, "When we came here, we brought several species along with us that are capable of speech. Five altogether. You've been adopted by a Pix, and you know about Elves. Those are two examples. Another one is the Atlantan Bear. They weigh about twenty pounds, are about two feet tall when they are standing on their hind feet, and they are very soft and furry. They are not dangerous, not in any way. In fact they are very gentle and kind. Bear food is delivered by any snack dispenser, and they are potty trained, so feeding and caring for them is no trouble. They are very friendly, and they like to keep things neat; so they are happy to pick up after you, clean floors, and things like that."

"Cleaning makes them happy?" Paul asked. That was what Ornith had said, but he wanted to be sure.

Baralicia smiled broadly. Atlantan boys of Paul's age were little different from the boys of Earthantis. Neither group was especially famous for keeping things neat and tidy.

"Atlantan Bears like to keep things neat and clean," she explained. "They are very talented at picking things up, putting them away, and doing general cleaning chores. They really like to do these things."

"OK," Paul said although it was hard for him to imagine how anything could like to clean. "Ornith says they can talk and like to read books too."

"That's right," Georaldon said, "Although most of them never progress much above a sixth grade reading level. They are lots of fun and Pixies like them a lot."

Paul thought this over for a few seconds, "I think I'd like one." He felt Ornith squirming. "I know Ornith would. Do you think it would be alright?"

"Yes," Baralicia said with a smile, "You can have one if you want, but we have one at home. Why don't you see if you like him and then decide?"

"You have a bear?" Paul asked.

"Oh, yes," she answered, "They are very common among Atlantans. His real name is Bill, but we usually call him Snazzy."

"Snazzy?"

"Yes," Georaldon answered with a smile, "He likes plaid pants with matching suspenders."

186

"He wears pants?" Paul asked in amazement.

"Well, yes," Georaldon answered, "All of them do. They are very modest animals."

"They're modest?"

"Yes, quite modest."

"What about shirts? Do they wear shirts?"

"Not unless it is a special occasion, or something that they want to dress up for. Mostly they just wear pants with suspenders," replied Georaldon. "Anyway, we're almost home and you can see for yourself."

"One thing I don't see are automobiles or busses," Paul noted.

"Everything you need is within walking distance," Baralicia answered, "Or you can just Jump where you want to go, so we really don't need them.

Paul walked with the Erlyndors through the tunnel that went under the outer rim of the central core to the living quarter's core. Ahead of them was an opening cut away from the central core. That opening was six stories high and a hundred feet wide and allowed a clear view of the park that was beyond. At the left side, half - way up was the numeral "7". As Paul looked into the living quarter's core he could see a succession of balconies separated by open-air elevators that moved freely between the balconies.

"Each balcony is connected above and below by the elevators." explained Georaldon. , "The quarters themselves are delved back into the rock."

"Six stories of them?" Paul asked, stunned by the magnitude of what he was looking at.

"Yes. There are 6,000 homes in this section alone, all built around the core's park. That's the section we are in now. It is what joins to the central core."

"And there are ten of these Living Quarter Cores?" Paul asked craning his neck to try and take it all in.

"Yes, that's right," he answered.

"So there are 60,000 homes?"

"Right," Georaldon answered. "They are not all lived in. In fact less than half of them are. We grow slowly, but we do grow. We have room for expansion as we do."

"All carved back into the rock? How big are they?"

"Let's go fix dinner boys," Baralicia said as she watched Paul's open-mouthed wonder with a grin, "And you can see for yourself."

They walked to the fourth bank of elevators on the left side of the core park. The elevator was constructed of ornately fabricated metals constructed to resemble wrought iron. Paul reached out to touch it and realized that it was not really wrought iron. It didn't have the same feel … it just looked like it. He didn't know what kind of metal it was but he knew that it was not iron. The metal was fabricated into a cage and was open to the air. They got on the elevator and Georaldon said the word "three". The elevator rose three floors and stopped. They got out and were standing on a private entry balcony. On the right was an entry to one home, and on the left was the entry to another. Both doors were made of intricately carved wood but each was unique. The one on the left reminded Paul of mahogany. The one on the right looked like oak. The Erlyndors moved toward the one on the right. Farther to the right was a bay window. In the window, sitting on the back of a couch looking out, was something that looked almost exactly like a teddy bear with light brown fur. Suddenly it sat up and waved at them and then hoped down off of the couch.

"I wish he wouldn't sleep up there," Baralicia complained with a sigh, "He gets hair all over the couch."

"But he cleans it up," protested Ardant.

"He always does," Felicia, added nodding her little head in support, "always."

"Yes, but not always right away," Baralicia said.

Georaldon looked at Paul and winked, "I think I'll stay out of this."

"You would," Baralicia said and then looked at the door, "Open," she said, and the beautifully carved oak door slid back into the wall. Waiting inside, dressed in red and green plaid pants with red and green matching suspenders, was the little bear.

"Hi, Snazzy," Baralicia said reaching her hand down and scratching the bear behind one of his ears, "Come meet Paul."

"Paul is here?" the bear asked in a rice resonant voice as he peered around Baralicia.

"Yes. Come in Paul and meet Bill … also known as Snazzy."

Paul walked forward, and then kneeled down on one knee, he was about to say hello when the bear extended his paw. Obviously he wanted to shake hands. "Hello," he said in the same deep, rich voice, "My name is Bill but everyone calls me Snazzy."

Paul took the bears paw and shook hands. "Hi. I'm Paul,"

noticing that Snazzy's paw was rough, yet soft at the same time.

"Nice to meet you," Snazzy said and then turned and went running on all fours into the living room.

Baralicia followed, and Georaldon held out his arm indicating that Paul should go next. Paul walked into the entry foyer and the first thing he noticed was the spacious feel to the living room beyond. It was not pretentiously large, but it was definitely comfortable. There were leather chairs, upholstered sofas, and other pieces of furniture. There was carpet on the floor, but there were also accent rugs in different places. Against one wall was a fireplace. There was no fire burning, but there were sufficient scorch marks to indicate that the fireplace was functional. Past the living room, Paul could see a room with a dining table. It had to be the dining room, and beyond that was a room that had to be the kitchen. To the right of the living room was a hallway. Paul guessed it went back to bedrooms. To the left of the fireplace were several small pieces of furniture. One of them was a small chair, and that was where Snazzy was sitting. From the chair the little bear could see everything that was going on in the living room. Next to the chair was what looked to Paul like a dog's bed. He inclined his head towards Ornith, "Do you suppose that is that where Snazzy sleeps?"

"Oh, yes," Ornith answered immediately, "He sleeps there sometimes."

Snazzy's ears perked up and he looked up at the Pix in recognition, "Oh, Hi Ornith. I didn't see you up there." The little bear looked at Georaldon as he jumped up, "Goody! Goody! Goody!" he said gleefully and started running around in circles. "Goody! Goody! Goody!"

"I think he's glad to see you Ornith," Georaldon said with a very broad smile.

"Hi, Snazzy," Ornith said and flew down and rubbed noses with the bear.

Baralicia had gone on into the kitchen so Paul turned to Georaldon, "They know each other?"

"Of course," Georaldon answered, "Didn't Ornith tell you?"

"Tell me what?"

Ornith flew up to Paul, "We have been very busy, Paul. Please don't be mad at me."

"Mad? Why would I be mad?"

"Because ... I ... didn't ... tell ... you?"

"Tell me what?"

"Felicia and Ardant are my Mom and Dad. I was raised here. Right here. I've known Snazzy all of my life."

"Oh," Paul said suddenly understanding the familiarity he had noticed. "It's OK, Ornith, totally OK."

"So that's why Snazzy was glad that you adopted me?" Paul said as it all began to come together.

"Come, Paul," Baralicia called, "Let me show you your room."

Paul followed Baralicia down the hallway to a doorway a little way down. He went down and looked in. The room was larger than the private room he had at the school. There was a comfortable chair in one corner, a double bed and a chest of drawers that looked both old and new at the same time. There was no sign of a closet.

"We already have some clothes for you Paul," she said, "Come and see." Paul walked over to where she was as she began pulling out drawers and they were full of clothes of various descriptions. "Open," she said and a door next to the chest of drawers opened up. It turned out to be a closet. It too was full of clothing. "You can take some of them back to school with you if you want."

"How did you know all of my sizes?" Paul asked as he picked out a shirt.

"Oh, we don't worry about sizes. Everything is one size fits all. Our clothes adapt themselves to you just like your uniforms. Here put it on. You'll see."

Paul took the shirt off of the hanger and put it on. It had a burnished blue color and the material had a silky feel to it. The shirt started out way too big, and there were no buttons. As he brought the two sides around towards each other they jumped together and formed an invisible seam. The sleeves, which started out too long, shrunk back to the right length and the collar, which was also too big, shrank to the proper size.

"Neat." Paul said.

"Mirror ON," Baralicia said and a full-length mirror took shape next to the closet door.

"Do you like it?" she asked.

"Yeah," Paul answered as he looked at the mirror, "Oh, yeah." He looked at Baralicia, "Thank you. You must have spent a lot of time getting all of this. Thank you very much."

Baralicia smiled, "Well, you're welcome." She looked at Georaldon who was also smiling, but not at Paul. He was smiling at his wife. "I'll go fix dinner," she said.

"This is quite an honor for us, you know," Georaldon said, "There are over 22,000 families here in Co-re-alis. Only a little over three hundred families have had the chance to be sponsors so far. Baralicia is as happy about all of this as I have ever seen her. Now, let me show you the rest of this room. "Laundry," he said and a place recessed in the wall. "You put anything dirty in there just like you do at school. It will go to the laundry and be cleaned and folded automatically. Snazzy will put them away for you; so you don't have to worry about that. There is a snack dispenser that works the same as the one in your room at the school. "Library," he said, and a different place recessed and then extruded a screen. "You can tell it the subject you want, or the author, or a keyword and a title list will appear. You use your voice to instruct it how you want to scroll through, just like you do with your computer at school. When you are ready, you make a selection simply by saying "select," and the book will appear in that cavity. A lot of us like to read in bed for a while before we drift off to sleep. "Reading light," he said, and a special light came out from the wall behind the head of the bed and came on. "You adjust the brightness the same way you do at school. Just tell it "light up" or "light down." Now, let's see. Yes, I think that covers it. Oh yes ... Snazzy. If Snazzy takes a liking to you, and I think he already has, he might want to crawl into bed and sleep with you. He often does that with us. Is that OK?"

"Sure," Paul answered.

"Well, I think that's about everything then. Let's go eat." He smiled broadly. "Baralicia is a really good cook."

"She cooks?" Paul asked.

"Well … yes." Georaldon answered, "but I often help her."

"I mean … well," Paul stammered, "All of our meals at school are prepared automatically. I thought … "

"You thought we didn't cook?"

"Well … yeah."

"We don't have to, but cooking is frequently fun. Plus, if you do it yourself, you can get things seasoned exactly the way you want. Baralicia and I don't always cook, but it is something we do together for the fun of it."

ψ

Dinner was gorgonzola crusted prime rib of beef with garlic-mashed potatoes and caramelized carrots. For desert there was a three layer devils' food cake with dark chocolate icing. It was one of the very best meals Paul had ever eaten. After dinner was over they all went into the living room. Paul sat down in one of the chairs, and it had barely adjusted to him when Snazzy came ambling over, "May I sit in your lap?" he asked.

Again, Paul noticed the deeply textured tones of the bear's voice, and grinned broadly. "Sure, Snazzy," he answered, and the bear jumped up onto his lap, and began the process of snuggling in. He squirmed around for a minute as the chair made some adjustments, and finally found a spot that was comfortable.

"There," the little bear said, "How's that?"

194

"Fine," Paul answered, and Georaldon set about finding a movie for them to watch.

"How about Robin Hood?" Baralicia called from the kitchen

"We have the one with Kevin Costner and the one with Russell Crowe," Georaldon added.

"How about the one with Kevin Costner," Paul replied. Snazzy sat comfortably in Paul's lap while they watched the movie. It was a pleasant evening, having a Pix on one shoulder and a bear in his lap watching the video. Snazzy was quite cuddly and no trouble at all. After a while Baralicia got up and made them all some popcorn, and the little bear sat there with Paul, enthralled with the movie and eating popcorn from a small bowl of his own. When it was time to go to bed, Snazzy hopped down and ran on all fours over to his own bed by the fireplace. He curled up there for a minute as Paul started towards his room, and then looked up. "Can I sleep with you tonight, Paul?"

Ornith flew off of Paul's shoulder and into eyeshot, "Yes, Paul … can … Snazzy … sleep … with … us … tonight … please … please …please?" the yellow-haired Pix begged, swinging his arms back and forth.

"OK," Paul answered quickly. "OK."

Georaldon walked up behind Baralicia and encircled her with his arms. He didn't have to see her face to know she was smiling as the threesome of Paul, Ornith, and Snazzy headed off for Paul's room. "Is this what you had in mind when you applied?" he asked.

"Yes," she answered and snuggled a little deeper into her husband's arms, "Exactly this."

195

Chapter Ten

A Bear

The next morning Paul was awakened by Snazzy, who was trying very hard to squirm out of the bed without waking Paul. "Oh, Good Morning, Snazzy," Paul said as he sat up and rubbed the sleep from his eyes. Ornith started rustling under the covers, crawled out and started getting his wings organized.

"Morning, Snazzy," the little Pix said pleasantly.

"I'm sorry to wake you," the bear said.

"Don't worry about that," Paul said, "What time is it anyway?"

"8:13 AM," came an automatic response from somewhere in the room.

"Well, see, we slept in anyway," Paul said as he started getting dressed.

At breakfast Georaldon asked, "How are you and Snazzy getting along?" The little bear was sitting in a high chair just right for him to reach the table, and he looked at Paul. So did Ornith who immediately flew over.

"Are ... you ... going ... to ... 'dopt ... a ... bear?" Ornith asked.

Paul looked at Snazzy and smiled and then turned to Georaldon, "We're getting along very well, thank you, and yes," he said turning to Ornith, "I'd like to adopt a bear."

"Oh good," Ornith said and flew back to his place and stabbed a small piece of sausage with his fork.

"Well," Baralicia said looking at Georaldon, "We can start picking one out right after breakfast."

By lunchtime they had been to three shops that had Atlantan Bears. The process of selecting a bear involved talking to them as well as petting and looking at them. It was more involved than picking out a puppy. By noon, Paul had spoken to bears with white fur, gray fur, even black and gray dappled fur, but the ones he liked best had the same sort of tawny brown fur that Snazzy had.

"OK," Georaldon announced, "There is only one shop left, I think. It's up around that corner just ahead. Don't forget, Paul, if you give a bear a name and don't take it home the bear will be heartbroken. Naming the bear is what lets it know that you are adopting it. Don't name one until you're sure you want that one." They walked past trees and flower boxes that formed a median in all of the streets. At the junctions there was a circle that contained something. In some cases it was a fountain, in others an amphitheater for music. Paul was looking at the circle ahead of them. It contained marble sculptures of three lions looking outward with a fountain in the center. Suddenly a question hit him.

"I know there are no cars," he said and looked at Georaldon, "but what about powered walkways?" They had met any number of pedestrians but at no time had Paul seen anyone going anywhere except by walking. Everyone seemed to walk wherever they were going. He looked around carefully. Indeed, the streets were not set up for powered transportation of any kind. They were not like any street in any American city.

"Well," Georaldon answered, "We design our cities so that there is no need. Anything you might want is a short walk from where you live. Anything you might need to carry is delivered by del droids right to your quarters. Our streets are far more beautiful without powered walkways. Look," he said sweeping his hand around at the flowered medians and sculptured circles. "Why have vehicles or other things that interfere with the beauty of these spaces?"

"We actually ... do ... have vehicles Paul," Baralicia added, "we just don't need them to get around in Co-re-alis. We need them to get to our other cities or if we want to go out to the moons. We need them for moving things that are too heavy for a transport belt."

"Oh," Paul said in understanding as it all came together, "that's what the flitters are about?"

"Yes, but they won't go out to the moons. We have null grav shuttles for that."

"That last shop is just ahead," Georaldon interrupted, pointing to a shop across from a wide place in the center median that contained a cascade of orchids.

Burt's Curios, Bears, & Knickknacks, the sign said.

Paul entered the shop first and looked around. Sure enough there were five or six bears sitting in chairs in various places and there were several more he could see through the rear window, romping around out back. Inside there were chairs nearby so that anyone who was interested could sit down and talk to one of the bears. Some of them were reading books, two of them were sitting at a small table playing cards, and one was watching a video screen. All of them but one perked up immediately. One of them, who had an especially large book in his paws, did look up but did not perk up as much as the others had. He was a tawny brown color like Snazzy. Paul walked over to him and sat down in the chair that was provided. "Hi," he said pleasantly.

"Hello," the bear said pleasantly in the rich resonant tones that Paul had learned to identify with a bear, but this one's voice seemed to contain a little sadness.

"You seem sad. What's the matter?" Paul asked.

The little bear marked his place and closed his book and looked up at Paul, "I don't think anyone wants me," he said, "I've been here the longest."

"Oh," Paul replied sympathetically, "How long have you been here?"

The bear reached around into his back pocket pulled out a little note pad and considered it carefully. "It's been almost three months," he said, "And it is very hard to stay excited when people come in and talk to you, scratch behind your ears and everything, and then leave with a different bear."

"My sponsors have a bear that looks a lot like you," Paul said, "He's great. He likes plaid pants though."

The little bear gave an involuntary shudder. "I don't care much for plaid pants. I'm very sorry, but I really don't."

"Hmmm ... " Paul said, "Me neither really. Do you like to have your ears scratched?"

"Oh, yes," the bear answered, "Very much."

Paul reached out and scratched behind his ears as the bear leaned a little closer. "Thank you," he said politely after a minute. "You can go talk to the other bears now. I understand. You have been very nice to me. I will be OK." The little bear's eyes were moist and he looked resigned to being disappointed again. He picked up his book and went back to reading.

Paul looked over at Ornith who had said very little up to this point. He liked this bear. The book in the bear's paws was *A Connecticut Yankee in King Arthur's Court,* by Mark Twain. It was one of the funniest books Paul had ever read, and harder to read than any book he had seen a bear attempting yet, other than Snazzy.

Suddenly the bear let out a belly laugh, and then looked up at Paul, and put a paw over his mouth in embarrassment. "I'm sorry. It is a very funny book. The Boss just blew up Merlin's tower."

"Yes, it is very funny," Paul agreed.

Ornith leaned over and whispered in Paul's ear, "I like this one. I think he will be a fine bear."

Paul nodded solemnly and looked at the little bear. "Me too." The bear noticed that Paul was about to say something and looked up from his book. "Well, OK," Paul said with a grin, "I can go talk to the other bears if you want, but if you'd like to come with me, I shall call you William."

"Really?" the bear said jumping up excitedly. "You want to adopt ... me?"

"Really, William," Paul answered with a nod, "I want to adopt ... you."

"Oh ... goody, goody, goody," William sang running around in circles exactly as Snazzy had done. "Goody, goody, goody."

Paul held out his hand. The bear reached up took Paul's hand and they turned to the Erlyndors. Baralicia was beaming and Georaldon was already over with the shopkeeper finalizing the sale.

ψ

On their return from Co-re-alis Sunday night, Freshman Summer Orientation was officially over. The entire student body was on the school premises. They had arrived over the weekend. As a result, the demands on the school facilities were a lot greater. To accommodate the upper classmen, freshman Chorda matches would only be held twice a week – Tuesdays and Thursdays - and the freshman Palacrosse matches would be held early Saturday mornings.

Sunday evening's dinner was also completely different. The dining hall was filled with students, all of whom were chattering, and eating and having a good time. It was segregated by class with four rows of tables, one for each class with the freshmen occupying the row farthest to the left. The number of students in the hall had gone up, but the availability of food hadn't changed, there were just a lot more del droids serving it. There was as much variety as ever, ordered items reappeared as quickly and the quality of the food hadn't changed. Paul decided that the extra students had not slowed the kitchen down at all, just raised the noise level in the hall.

ψ

Professor Galvyndor rose after breakfast Monday morning for several announcements. First, class schedules were distributed. Paul looked at his class sheet and noticed that the first three hours of each day were devoted to Atlantan Studies. Earthantan Studies came after lunch.

"Now," Professor Galvyndor continued, "You returning students are aware of the pace of these classes, however our freshmen are not. Everyone should note several things; first your classes will be in full swing in a matter of a day or two. We do not fool around for the first few weeks so you can get your feet on the ground. Unlike a normal high school on Earthantis, all of your instructors hold doctorates in their fields. We are real professors. Although the material is not as complicated as what you'll get in college, we treat you like college students. We ... do ... not ... dumb ... things ... down! We do not teach to the level of the slowest person in the class. We do not go over the same thing time and time again. We will present the material thoroughly and well ... once. We will answer questions thoroughly and well ... once, and then we will move on. If you need extra help, we are always available to help you after class, and there are no limits to our patience with students who are trying, but, just like in college, if you need extra help, you have to ask for it. The pace will be faster than anything you freshmen have experienced. The homework load is heavier ... much heavier ... also like college. The key is to get started early. Do not fall behind. It is extremely hard to catch up if you do."

She looked around the Dining Hall. "Now, once again primarily for the freshmen, but also as a reminder for everyone else, we have midterm grades, and semester end grades. Your grades add points in the Quadro Bowl. You get three points for each A, two for B's, one for C's, minus one for D's, and minus three for F's. Typically half of the points your Quadro will receive during the semester come from Chorda and Palacrosse, the other half come from your grades. OK, then," she concluded, "I'll see you in class."

Breakfast concluded, and the students made their way to their first class. Paul sat next to Betsy in the front row of their music class. He did not really like the front row, but Betsy did, and he didn't want to be rude so he sat with her. Jim and Jennifer were sitting right behind them. Q2, Q5, and Q8 were also part of the class. As soon as Paul had entered the music classroom he noticed a difference. Everything on the student side was the same as every other classroom. It wasn't the student's side that was different it was the teacher's. The desk was smaller ... the chair was much smaller. On the desk was a violin. That was the only thing that was normal size and then it hit him. One of the elves must be teaching the class. That would explain why everything for the teacher was smaller.

An elfin teacher walked in and took his place behind the desk. "My name is Professor Barnard Nimrodel," he began, "I am head of the music department." The professor was about four feet tall and slender. His ears were pointed and he had a neatly trimmed beard. He wore a green pointed hat that flopped over and had a tassel on the end. He had green pointed shoes with the ends curled up that matched his hat. In that moment Paul knew exactly where the elf legends came from. Professor Nimrodel looked like he had stepped out of one.

The elf reached over and picked up the violin. "First, a selection from an Earthantan composer named Amadeus Mozart." The Professor tucked the violin under his chin and began to play.

"That was a selection from Mozart's 38th Symphony. This instrument, when performing a piece like that from Mozart is called a "violin," Professor Nimrodel explained.

"Now," the Professor said as he finished with a gleam in his eye and the hint of a smile on his lips, "A selection from another Earthantan composer named Charlie Daniels," And with that he took the violin and launched into a spirited rendition of *The Devil Went Down to Georgia*. As the elf's fingers flew over the violin the room literally came alive. The entire class was patting their feet or tapping their hands to the rapid beat of the music. The professor finished the piece and set the violin down almost reverently. "The same instrument when performing something like Charlie Daniels is called a "fiddle." I have tried to demonstrate the range that can be found in just one instrument. Music is such a vast field that there are simply no words to describe it, but I will say this," he paused for emphasis and looked around the room to be sure he had everyone's attention.

"I love music. It is my life. I love what it can do to your spirit, how you can get lost in a well performed piece of music. You may not yet understand that music can do this. You may not yet appreciate this medium as I do. That is OK. It is my job to teach that appreciation to you, and not just appreciation, but also some skill with an instrument. In this semester's class we will begin by teaching you the basic mechanics of how all instruments are played. You will learn a little about each one. As the semester unfolds you will gradually discover an affinity for one of these instruments. It will happen naturally. You don't need to force it. Next semester we will concentrate on teaching you how to play that particular instrument. For now all you need to do is open your soul to the rhythm … feel the music ... let it resonate inside you. Your own soul will tell you where to go with it. There may be nothing you learn in this school that will give you more pleasure throughout your lives than what you begin to learn in this class."

ψ

"Now students," Professor Galvyndor said addressing her class on The Science and Technology of Atlantis. "Part of what we cover here is all of our various gadgets and how they fit into our lives and cultures. At times we will distribute the equipment we are discussing. That will be the case today. We will be discussing and distributing comm units."

Two del droids floated into the room. They were identical, as far as Paul could tell, to the ones that had delivered their uniforms. Both were piled high with packages.

"Girls," she said, "Get a package off of the del droid in front, Boys, get a package off of the one in back."

Paul opened his the same way he had the uniform package. He ran his finger along one edge and it opened. He looked inside. There was a golden necklace. He pulled it out and remembered seeing one similar to it around Georaldon's neck. It had a braided golden chain about a quarter of an inch thick, and a medallion hanging from the center. The medallion was a copy of the Seal of Atlantis. From the one that Paul could see in Betsy's hands there was only a little difference between the one for the boys and the one for the girls. The girls unit looked feminine, and the

206

boys unit was more masculine."

"Now students," the Professor instructed, "Put both your hands together in the back, and it will open automatically. Put it around your neck, and brings the ends together. It will refasten automatically."

Paul followed her instructions and immediately the unit refastened. He felt for a seam with both hands. There was no seam but it re-separated. He held the ends together and it refastened. He felt for a seam with one hand only and the unit did not separate but he could not find a seam.

"OK," the Professor continued, "With this comm unit you are connected at all times to anyone ... anywhere ... so long as that person is also wearing a comm unit. There are several ways to activate it, and you'll learn more about those ways in your 2nd year, but for now all you do is say "Comm ON" and then say the first and last name of the person you're calling. A light "bong" will go off in that person's ear and you will be able to have as clear a conversation with them as if they were in the same room. By the way, Pixies have comm units too so you can contact them as well."

The class spent the remainder of the class period contacting each other. Even in the midst of the din of everyone talking all at once, the words of the person you were talking to were crystal clear.

"No homework in this class either," Jim said quietly.

"For now," Paul agreed. "But that can change."

ψ

Their next professor was already standing at her desk when the members of Q3 walked into their Atlantan Culture class. For this class, Q3 was in with Q1, Q4 and Q6. By the time they arrived all of the seats on the front row were taken, so Betsy settled for a seat in the second row.

"Attention class," the Professor began as the last students took their seats, "My name is Professor Ristondor. You will have an assignment due next Monday. It is a profile of the accomplishments of a famous Atlantan. In your computers you will find a list of acceptable individuals. Please hand in a 5 page profile of one of the individuals on that list. There will be one such profile due each Monday from now until year's end."

"5 pages," Paul complained quietly under his breath so only Jim could hear, "a week ... every week."

"Shhh ... " Jim hissed, "We're not going to have much homework in music ... not to start anyway. We can't get off that easy on everything."

"Now, let's begin," the Professor said, "By this time at least some of you will have been down to Co-re-alis. Did you notice anything interesting down there?"

"Everything was interesting, Professor," Jennifer answered.

"Of course it was ... of course it was. I should be more specific, shouldn't I?" She stopped and took a sip of water from a glass on her desk. "Was there anything that struck you about the city of Co-re-alis itself that might be different from a city in North America?"

"No cars!" Anne Chastain said.

"Right! That's one. Any others?"

Jennifer held up her hand, and the Professor pointed at her.

"Flowers. You could smell their fragrance everywhere."

"Good. Did any of you notice how clean the air was?"

Betsy tapped Paul on the shoulder, "That's right," she said, "It … was … cleaner." There were other students murmuring in agreement throughout the class.

"Now let's talk about why that is. I know you think that the reason is because of our advanced technology. This is certainly true, but it was not always like that. Petroleum ran low on Atlantis a lot sooner than it has here on Earthlantis. We had no choice but to seek alternatives at an earlier stage than the people of Earthantis have. We had developed a technique to liquefy wood. It was an emulsification process using steam which resulted in a liquid hydrocarbon we could use as fuel. This process replaced petroleum for several decades before we invented the magnetic engines that provide our power today."

Jennifer held up her hand, and Professor Ristondor called on her. "Professor," Jennifer asked, "We have a lot of problems with lumber companies clear cutting our forests. Wouldn't that have stripped them bare?"

Yes," the Professor answered with an emphatic nod. "That was an issue we had to work through, but let me ask you a question, do you know how many trees fall down and die every year, just say in North America?"

"No, ma'am," Jennifer answered.

"There is enough energy in deadfall to provide about twenty times the energy currently consumed in North America," she answered.

"Really!" Jennifer exclaimed,

"Yes. What we had to do was outlaw clear cutting, and instead concentrate on collecting deadwood. It took a few years … well …

209

decades actually, to get all of this worked out, but once we did, the system we ended up with was far better than the petroleum one it replaced. Liquefied wood was a renewable and abundant source of energy for us on Atlantis, just like it would be here on Earthantis, but it required a lot of forest management. Our environmentalists wanted us to use less so there would be less interference with our forests. It took some time to resolve the political issues. We had many of the same sorts of squabbles that you are having today, but after a while we began to take a serious look into the cost benefits of conservation. Using less saves money if it is done correctly. The biggest key turned out to be the way we laid out our communities. You don't have to drive anywhere in order to go about your daily lives in our communities. Everything in Co-re-alis is within easy walking distance. Think of the fuel that saves. It was like that on Atlantis as well."

Joe Hernandez held up his hand.

"Yes Joe?"

"What about getting to work?"

"Excellent question, Joe. In our communities "Work" is located within walking distance of residential areas."

"What about shopping?" Anne Chastain asked.

"Same with shopping ... all within walking distance."

"What about larger communities?" Betsy asked. "Co-re-alis is about 60,000 people isn't' it? Did you have larger communities, or were they all small?"

"Another good question. An average community on Atlantis was about 300,000, a good deal larger than Co-re-alis. We had any number of cities a good deal larger than that. We stayed within the general idea of keeping things decentralized so you could still live close to the centers of work, shopping, entertainment, etc. but larger cities invariably meant that some of these things were going to be a very long walk at best, too long at worst. We developed a crisscrossing network of powered walkways, a lot like the people movers you see in airports. They were covered against the weather. You could get anywhere in a five mile radius in about thirty minutes. The way things were laid out, there was rarely an occasion to go any farther than that. In an American community of one hundred thousand adults, how many cars are there on average?"

No one answered.

"Over seventy-five thousand. Now, what is the value of all of those cars?" The Professor held up her hands. "Don't bother to figure it out ... the average value of those cars is about twelve thousand dollars apiece, which makes the total about nine hundred million dollars. What is the value of the roads in a community like that?"

Again there was silence.

"About 1.8 billion dollars," she answered. "A total of over 2.7 billion US dollars is invested in the cars and infrastructure to support them in a community of a hundred thousand adults. The larger the community, the worse this gets. Now," she continued, "Covered, powered walkways like we went to on Atlantis would cost about two hundred forty dollars a foot in US dollars. For a town of a hundred thousand adults, how many feet of walkways would be required?"

Once again the question was met with no hands. She smiled. "It's OK. I don't expect you to have answers to questions no one has ever asked you to consider before. The answer is about 5 million feet of walkways altogether, and that makes the total cost of a complete system of powered walkways 1.2 billion dollars. In other words, less than half that of the automotive system. It comes to an annual savings of over twelve hundred dollars per person per year."

Someone behind Paul whistled softly.

"The point is," Professor Ristondor continued, "that it is a lot cheaper to build covered powered walkways in a community than it is to buy that number of cars, and build the roads to support them. In the days when we were still using liquefied wood as fuel, a network of powered walkways crisscrossed all of our cities. Altogether it was remarkably more efficient than individually owned automobiles. We called towns like this "Operationally Integrated" communities."

"What about carrying packages and things?" Anne Chastain asked.

"Good question. Now we have del droids to do delivery, but back then everyone had portable carts for small stuff, and delivery people for larger loads. Any idea how much fuel was saved?"

Again there were no answers.

"The average transportation cost for a household of two adults is 40 dollars a week. For a town of a hundred thousand adults that comes to over a hundred million dollars a year. Now the power to run the system isn't free, but that cost comes to about 20 million dollars a year. The savings on average are over 800 dollars per person per year on the fuel cost side, two thousand dollars per person per year total."

Paul held up his hand.

"Yes, Paul."

"Wouldn't this isolate people in their communities ... you know ... cut one community off from all the others?"

"Well, it could I suppose, except what happened on Atlantis was that people had all this extra money to spend. One of the things they spent it on was traveling, and there were plenty of ways to do that. We had jets of course, busses, trains, rental cars. It was easy to get from community to community whenever you wanted to. What happened was we actually got around a lot more because we had "more money" to get around with, we just did it in a much more efficient manner. We became more connected, not less, and as a result, more concerned for each other's welfare, not less. There are a great many other benefits to better-planned and more fully integrated communities. Energy efficiency is just one of them."

The professor paused and looked slowly around the room. It had fallen silent. "I understand. Right now you are thinking about how hard it would be to change to a system of Operationally Integrated Communities. You'll hear this many times before you graduate. Nothing is possible until someone starts asking "What if?" What if a group of people got together and built an Operationally Integrated Community? The technology to do this exists on Earthantis right now. The cost savings for the residents of such a community would be very large, and their lives will be better as a result. That's how it started on Atlantis, in fact. A couple of developers with vision got backing from some philanthropists and built two of these communities from scratch. Things followed from there. Once people could see the benefits, the momentum of our society went in that direction. That's probably what would happen here too."

She walked over to the wall. "Snack ... Water," she said and a few seconds she took a sip of water. "If anyone is thirsty, help yourself." Several students went to the dispenser and got glasses of water.

When everyone was seated, the professor continued. "You guys have four years here, and then four years, at least, in college after that. When you are finished with your education, and your Fellow Quals, one of the things you might consider is developing a T-Op for an Operationally Integrated Community. If someone were to build one ... just one ... the benefits would become so apparent that in time it would take off on its own." She held up her hands, "Just a thought, let's continue. What is the most important thing we said here today?"

Again there was silence.

"Nothing is possible until someone starts asking "What if?" she answered as the bell ending the period rang. "Next Monday," the professor announced, "in addition to the profile paper, I require a ten page project paper on Operationally Integrated Communities."

"Gees," Jim said as they filed out, "Music may not have much homework but this teacher is going to make up for it all by herself."

"Interesting class, though," Paul commented as they looked at their schedule to see what was next.

"Yeah," Betsy agreed. "Do you suppose this was what Professor Galvyndor meant when she said they would move fast, like they do in college?"

"I hope so," Jennifer answered for all of them. "I don't know how I'll keep up if they go any faster than that."

ψ

Q3's last class of the day was self-defense. Their self-defense instructor was waiting in the auditorium and brought the class to order quickly. "Now, class," Professor Karlendor said earnestly, "We have to settle exactly why we are teaching you self-defense." He paused and looked over the class. "C-Ops can be dangerous. T-Ops under certain circumstances, depending on how hard the entrenched interests try and fight the introduction of something new, can be even more so. League Members have been called on to defend not only themselves, but also others any number of times. That all starts here."

"The first thing you must master is the art of "The Block," he continued, "If you can block well, your opponent cannot hurt you. Blocking is the first and ultimately most important part of self-defense. Blocks are divided into two categories, high blocks and low blocks. They are further divided into blocks that protect your left side, and those that protect your right. So, let me demonstrate how you block high punches."

At that point a mechanical device came floating into the room. It was about a foot in diameter, Paul noticed and about four feet tall. It floated vertically, and had two appendages, resembling arms hanging at its side, and two more resembling legs protruding from the bottom. There was a band of the slowly flashing lights that Paul had come to recognize as a G-N System.

"This is a practice android," Professor Karlendor explained. "Also known as "ANDY". This particular one is ANDY 206. It does very little good to practice blocks against thin air. Each of you will have an "ANDY" to practice with. It will throw punches ... and ... you will block them. Observe."

The Professor walked over to the android and assumed a stance similar to ones all of the students had seen in the movies. His weight was on his back foot, his arms in front with his elbows in and his hands brought up in front of his chest. His hands were not balled into fists but were open. Suddenly the android assumed a fighting stance as well. It looked like a mechanical boxer with no head. The Androids right appendage drew back and threw a punch at the Professor, who slapped it effortlessly aside. "Again," the Professor said, and ANDY 206 threw another punch. The professor blocked it easily.

"The keys to blocking are recognition and timing," he said, "and timing is the hardest part. Too quick, and you miss the block, too late and you might as well not have tried. The first thing is to recognize that a punch is being thrown at you. ANDY mimics the body mechanics of people preparing to throw a punch. When you can recognize that ANDY is preparing to throw a punch, you will also be able to recognize the same things in living people. Observe. Slow motion ANDY 206."

ANDY 206 stood there still for several seconds with his arms hanging at his sides, then slowly moved one leg forward and brought up its right arm. "Stop!" ANDY froze. "You saw the movements ANDY 206 made just prior to throwing the punch. There are only five basic patterns people use to prepare to throw a punch. The use of these ANDYs will train you to recognize all of them. So much for the recognition part - on to timing. The act of bringing your arm up so it contacts and deflects the punch is timing. It takes practice. That is also where the ANDYs come in. You can get a lot of practice with an ANDY in a short period of time.

Without warning, ANDY 206 brought his arm up and then threw another punch at the professor's head. With his left forearm, which was already in position, their instructor simply deflected the punch. He did it without even thinking, without even blinking. He smiled.

"Now, let me demonstrate that move again," he said, and repeated the procedure.

Before long thirty-two ANDY's came floating into the gym. "Now, students," the Professor instructed, "Today the androids will be throwing right handed punches at your head. Right-handed only, and at your head only. Today that is all you have to worry about. Tomorrow we will work on lefts."

Paul stood nervously facing ANDY 303. These androids looked like they punched hard. Paul assumed the position he had seen the professor use as closely as he could. Suddenly ANDY 303 threw a punch. Paul could see it begin to develop … things seemed to slow down … he saw the android draw back his fist … saw it start to move forward … and almost unconsciously … Paul reacted as the professor had taught and slapped it away. His motion was not so elegant as the Professor's but it was effective.

"Wow," he said quietly, "This works!" He remembered that the android had tried to hit the professor when he wasn't looking, so Paul decided not to gloat. Seconds later the same sequence was repeated. ANDY 303 threw a second punch. Paul saw it coming, just like he had the first time. He was in the stance that the Professor had demonstrated so his hands were already in position to deflect the punch, and he did it again … and again … and again.

217

After about six punches a light began flashing green on top of ANDY 303, and the professor walked over. "Ah ... doing well, I see," he said.

"How can you tell, sir," Paul asked.

"The ANDY's will flash two different colors under different conditions. Red means you're getting stomped and need some help. Your light is green," Professor Karlendor answered. "A green light means that the ANDY has analyzed your mechanics and determined that you are ready to demonstrate this for me. You are the first in the class. Well done."

"I have to demonstrate?" Paul asked and felt a knot develop in his stomach.

"Yes," the professor answered, "now, please."

ANDY 303 prepared to throw a punch so Paul demonstrated the techniques in spite of the knot in his stomach. When he finished, the professor nodded and then reprogrammed the android to vary the place from which it started the punch. Before long Paul had mastered that as well. All in all, he felt quite pleased with himself.

The bell rang. "Attention, students," Professor Karlendor called out loudly, "Next class I require ..." after what had happened in their last period, the entire class drew in its breath, "a good attitude," he concluded with a smile. "There is no homework in this class. Just bring a good attitude."

Chapter Eleven
More Scouting

Paul and Jim walked past the conversation areas and central fireplace of their dorm floor to the door of their suite. "Open," Paul said and the door responded automatically.

"How are we ever going to get all of this work done?" Jim asked.

"Good question," Paul answered as they walked in.

William was sitting in the little armchair that Georaldon had given them. Ornith was sitting beside the little bear and flew up to Paul. "William is very sad."

"He's sad?"

Ornith nodded solemnly as he hovered in front of Paul. "Very sad."

Paul looked over to the little bear who nodded but said nothing.

"Why are you sad, William?" Paul asked.

"You don't have any books for bears," he answered with a sniffle. "Only school books. I looked everywhere and you don't have any."

Paul walked over to the little chair, picked William up, sat down in his own chair and placed him on his lap. "William, I am really sorry. We got up here from Co-re-alis just last night, and I had to go to school today. How about if we go to the library and get you some books?"

William's facial features brightened up a bit but not much. "OK," he said with another sniffle. "When will you go?"

"How about if we go right now?" Paul answered.

The little bear's eyes got wide and his ears perked up. "Will you?" William asked with a lot more excitement. "Will you really go right now?"

"Yes," Paul answered with a reassuring nod. "There's enough time before dinner, I think."

"Goody," William said, "Would you get me *A Connecticut Yankee in King Arthur's Court*? I didn't get to finish it and it's very funny."

"Sure, but don't you want to come too and pick it out yourself?"

"Can I come too?" the little bear asked with even more excitement. "Can I really? No one ever let me do that before."

"Yes, you can come," Paul answered, "I checked. Georaldon said you were allowed to go to the library or to the greenhouse with me."

William jumped off of Paul's lap and began to run on all fours in circles around Paul's chair, "Goody ... goody ... goody," he sang as he ran around, "Goody ... goody ... goody."

Paul looked at the bear running around and singing and looked over at Jim who just smiled and shook his head. Paul looked over at Ornith, "Are you coming too?"

"Of course," Ornith answered, and flew up to Paul's shoulder.

Paul reached down and took William's paw and the three of them left and made their way to Fellowship Hall.

"The library's main floor is right through there," Paul said pointing at the ornately carved doorway, "We'll go in and ask the librarian where the books for bears are." Paul picked William up and walked into the library and up to the librarian's desk. He was about to ask where the books for bears were but the librarian saw the little bear in Paul's arms and answered before he could ask.

"Books for bears are in that second section over there," she said with a smile and pointing towards some stacks that were behind her and to the left. "There are eight rows of them all together."

"Eight rows!" William exclaimed, "How many are on a row?"

"Several thousand," the Librarian answered.

"That's a lot of books," Paul said.

"Yes. Bears like to read a lot," she answered. "You can only check out six at a time, but that should hold him for a couple weeks or so."

"Six," William said wistfully, "Six books. I never had more than one before." He looked at Paul. "Can I get six?"

"She said you could," Paul answered. "It's OK with me." They walked over and had hardly begun looking through the stacks when Paul came across *The Chronicles of Narnia* by C.S. Lewis. There were three books in the series. "William," Paul suggested as he remembered how much he had enjoyed reading them a few years before, "these are very good. We could get the whole series. Would you like that?"

"Oh very much," William replied.

Paul removed the books from the shelf.

"Now ... do you think we can find ... "

"I know," Paul laughed, "I know... you want the *Connecticut Yankee* book by Mark Twain."

"Yes, please. Would you mind trying to find that one?"

"No, William. I wouldn't mind at all." He walked back to the front of the first aisle and over to the row containing "T's" for Twain.

"I'm not sure if this will be in the Bear section." Paul said as he walked down the aisle. Sure enough, it wasn't there.

"Oh," William said sadly.

"It's OK, William.' Paul said. "I'm sure they have it. It's just not in this section especially for bears, that's all."

"You mean you will look in other sections too?" William asked.

Paul looked over at Ornith, "Of course," he said mimicking the Pix.

Ornith grinned broadly.

"There were a lot of bears in that shop where we got you, William," Paul explained, "and the shopkeeper had to care for them all, but you are the only bear I have, so you can expect a lot more attention now."

"Oh," William said happily, and looked over at Ornith, "I am going to like this."

Paul walked back to the librarian and asked her where to find the book. She was a little surprised that a bear would want that book, but her directions were quite clear and they went right to it. Once they were in the T section of the stacks finding *A Connecticut Yankee in King Arthur's Court* was easy. If you like Mark Twain," Paul said calmly with a barely suppressed grin, "you might like those two." He pointed to *Innocents Abroad,* and *Life on the Mississippi.* William nodded eagerly, so Paul picked the books up and they headed back toward the Librarian.

"OK," Paul said as he tried to juggle one bear and six books. "Are you ready?"

"Yes," William answered happily, and they went to check the

222

books out. "I didn't know there were that many books in the whole world."

As they walked out of the Library, Ornith whispered in Paul's ear, "This was very nice of you, Paul. I'm sure he feels much better now."

A few minutes later they were back up at the suite. Paul got William a bowl of bear food from the snack dispenser and set it down next to his little chair. William was already reading *A Connecticut Yankee in King Arthur's Court* and munching on his dinner. He could reach down and get a kernel of food without getting up.

William looked up at Paul as he placed the food bowl down and smiled the scrunched face smile that Atlantan bears use, "Thank you," he said, "Thank you very much."

"OK, William. You're welcome." Paul said, "We'll be back after dinner."

After dinner when Jim and Paul returned and opened the door to their suite, William jumped up out of his chair and ran over on all fours as fast as he could and jumped into Paul's arms.

"Whoa," Paul said. He barely managed to catch the little bear. William weighed twenty pounds, which was a lot to catch without warning.

William reached around Paul's neck and gave him a hug. "Hi, Paul."

"Hi, William," Paul looked at the little bear, "So it seems you are feeling better."

"Oh, yes," William answered, "Much better, thank you."

ψ

The first week of formal classes flew by. After dinner on Thursday, Jennifer sat waiting for her Quadromates on one of the couches in front of the central fireplace in their common area. The boys joined her and they waited for Betsy.

Ornith whispered in Paul's ear, "Now Betsy is missing. First Gwenivere ... now Betsy."

"Yeah, but Gwenivere showed up."

"So will Betsy," Ornith replied, "but ... she ... is ... still ... missing ... now."

After ten minutes, Jim spoke up; "Maybe she's already at the library."

"You guys wait here," Paul suggested, "and I'll go see. If I'm not back in five minutes, you'll know I found her."

"Good, idea," Jennifer agreed and Jim sat down next to her.

Paul headed for the Library and when he got to Fellowship Hall he noticed that Betsy was already sitting with a large pile of books at one of the study tables on the second floor balcony of Fellowship Hall. He walked around to the curving staircase and went up.

"Hi," he said. "Weren't you supposed to meet us in the common area?"

"Oh, nuts," she said hitting herself in the forehead, "That's right." She put her book down and looked at Paul, "I'm sorry, I just forgot that we were going to the Library and came straight here. It's all of this homework." She pointed at the books spread out around her on the table.

"You're forgiven. Jim and Jennifer will be along shortly."

"Good. Thanks, " she said pleasantly, "Oh, by the way, I have a bear now too. My sponsors helped me pick her out last weekend. Her name is Shirley and she's really sweet."

"Does she clean up after you?" Paul asked teasingly.

Betsy's chin came up and she arched her eyebrows, "She doesn't have to. Anyway, look at this."

Paul looked at the book in her hands. *The Wormhole Generator – A History.* "What's that for?"

"The profile paper we have to do for Atlantan Culture," she answered. "Look, there's a whole section devoted to Professor Heraldon Glorfyndor."

"No kidding?" Paul said and slid into the seat next to her. "You're profiling Professor Glorfyndor?"

"Yeah."

"I didn't know he was famous."

"Oh, yes … very famous," Betsy replied, "He was the Principal Engineer on the wormhole generator. He led the first team to travel through a wormhole to another system ... back when they were trying to figure out how to do it. There was a star system two light years away called En-roy-alis." She tapped the pages of the book. "They had a theory. The mathematicians and physicists had figured and figured, and it worked on paper. They had built some lab models, and they seemed to work; they built a small scale model and sent it to En-roy-alis. Two years later they began receiving transmissions from that equipment, but someone had to build a full size model and try it out with real human beings.

225

Professor Glorfyndor designed and built the first wormhole generator large enough for a team of people. He took a team of eight, and went to En-roy-alis. They took the parts they needed with them and built another launcher there so that they could get back to Atlantis. It took them six years."

"They took a wormhole generator with them?"

"Yeah. The parts anyway. They had to put it all together when they got to their destination." Betsy answered, "It was the only way. For the first two years no one knew whether they had made it through alive or not. Then the signals started coming from Professor Glorfyndor's team and they knew they could do it."

"Really?"

"Yeah. Someone had to do it. Someone had to go. Someone who could build another launcher in the En-roy-alis system to get back."

"And Professor Glorfyndor took a team and did that!" Paul said shaking his head, "No wonder he's famous."

"Who are you going to profile?" Betsy asked.

"Dr. Carolicia Erlyndor. She's my sponsor's great grandmother so I thought I would do her."

"What did she do?"

"Dr. Erlyndor was the one who figured out how to grow replacement organs."

"Wow," Betsy said in awe, "A woman did that?"

"Yeah, but that shouldn't surprise you."

"Why not?"

"Well," Paul answered a little surprised. "Haven't you noticed how their women are involved in everything?"

"It's all happening so fast I hadn't really noticed," Betsy admitted.

"Even Palacrosse is like that," Paul emphasized, "It's the only team sport they have talked about. It could be a men's sport, or a women's sport. It would still be a great game, but the way they play it is co-ed."

"Right," Betsy said thoughtfully, "That's right ... men and women play it together."

"Yeah. They may have other sports, but this is their big deal and the men and women do it together. Women are involved in everything here."

"I think it's nice," Betsy admitted.

ψ

As Paul was walking with his quadromates to their first class on Friday, he heard the "bong" of his communicator go off softly in his ear. "Hello," he answered with a little hesitation. It was a little disconcerting being in instant communication without a telephone or anything.

"Hi, Paul! Georaldon here."

"Oh ... Hi!" Paul replied.

"How's everything going?"

"Very well, thanks," Paul replied.

"Good ... good," Georaldon said. "Say, Baralicia and I were hoping you could come down on Sunday. How's your schedule? Do you think you could do that?"

"I don't know," Paul hesitated. Q3's scouting expedition was planned for the weekend, but on Saturday not Sunday. That was not the problem. It was all of the homework the professor's had piled on. "I've got a lot of school work," Paul answered.

"Well, bring it with you," Georaldon suggested. "That is actually what we wanted to talk to you about anyway."

"Really?" Paul asked.

"Yeah." Georaldon answered. "Making sure you are staying up on your classes is one of our responsibilities."

"Oh," Paul said. "Well sure. I'll come down right after breakfast. Do you want to meet me in that building?"

"No. You can Jump right in here. Right into our living room, now that you know where you're going."

"OK," Paul agreed. "I'll see you right after breakfast on Sunday."

"Great. See you then. Bring your books and assignments."

ψ

"OK," Jim said as they got ready to split up for their scouting trip, "ready?"

"Yep," Paul said confidently, "remember. It is extremely important that we do not draw attention to ourselves. It is unusual for people our age to be wandering around in these places without parents. We don't want adults asking us questions. We especially don't want anyone telling a security person that we look lost or something. We need to do everything we can to avoid that."

"If all else fails," Betsy reminded everyone, "pretend you have to go to the bathroom, and then Jump back here. We'll see you guys back in

Fellowship Hall before dinner."

"Right," Jennifer agreed, "Ready Jim?"

Jim nodded, "Are you Pixies ready?"

"Yes, we're ready," replied Renalee and Aurileol. "Cloak," both Jim and Jennifer said in unison, and disappeared.

"OK, Betsy, Ornith, Gwenivere … our turn. "Cloak," Paul said and tapped his fingers. The colors swirled around him for what seemed like a longer period of time, but then they were going a longer distance, and there was a mountain range between where they were, and where they were going. Then the colors stopped and he was looking at the Lincoln Memorial. There were a lot of people winding around in a line up to the statue. He looked around and found Betsy. They made eye contact and walked towards each other.

"How about over behind those trees," Betsy suggested.

"Still too many people," Paul said, "What about the rest rooms?"

"That would work," Betsy agreed, "We can de-cloak there and then meet over by the trees."

"Right." Paul walked over towards the men's rooms. As he was trying to edge his way in, he bumped into a man on his way out. Paul took two steps back immediately. The man looked around in wide-eyed alarm. Something had bumped into him … something that simply was not there. He felt the air and found nothing … felt it again … still nothing. After a moment, the man shrugged his shoulders and moved on. Paul found an empty stall, shut the door, and de-cloaked. He left the stall, washed his hands, and left for the stand of trees. Betsy was already waiting.

"What took you so long?"

"He bumped into someone," Ornith reported with glee. Although both he and Gwenivere had remained Cloaked, they could be heard plainly. "You should have seen it. The man felt the air and everything and look on his face was very funny."

"I'll bet," Betsy agreed.

"OK," Paul said, "What now?"

"We can take a cab to the EPA," Betsy suggested.

"That's a good idea," Paul agreed, "That way we don't really have to worry about how to find it." They walked over to one of several cab stands and the driver in front opened his door for them.

"EPA," Paul announced.

"Which building?" the cab driver asked.

"Ummm ..." Paul said and looked at Betsy.

"Investigations Division," she answered confidently.

The driver put the cab in gear and drove off. He wove in and out through traffic for what seemed like twenty minutes and then pulled up in front of a large multi-storied building. Engraved on a marble plaque out front was the name:

Environmental Protection Agency
Investigations Division

"Seems like we've got the right place," Paul said after he had paid the cab driver. "What are we looking for?"

"I'm not sure," Betsy answered.

"I thought you guys figured all of that out."

"Just how to get here and which building we needed," Betsy replied, "not everything."

"Well," Paul began, "We need to have a way to visualize where we want to go so we can Jump directly there."

"Right," Betsy agreed, "We need a name of someone in the Investigations Unit."

"Yeah, but which one?" Paul asked.

"I don't know, but I'll bet they have an information desk. We can ask them."

"Who do we ask for?" Paul continued."

"We can ask for the Enforcement Office covering Eastern Tennessee."

"Right," Paul agreed, "Let's try that and see what happens." They walked into the building and noticed an information desk right in front.

"We need the Enforcement Office for Eastern Tennessee," Betsy asked the guard as politely as she could.

"What is the nature of your business?" the guard asked.

Thinking quickly, Paul said, "We think we may have a violation to report."

"Air or Water?" the guard asked.

"Air," Betsy answered.

It turned out that they had no trouble at all. The guard looked through a directory for several minutes and then announced, "Air Pollution violations for Eastern Tennessee are handled in Room 1607. You go over to those elevators over there and take them to the 16th floor and follow the signs.

Moments later the elevator doors opened and they walked out on the 16th floor. On the wall in front of them was a sign:

1601 – 1605 >
1606 – 1609<

"To the left," Paul said pointing in the same direction as the sign, and they turned and walked down the hall.

They came to a door that said 1607 on it.

"We don't really need to talk to anyone," Paul suggested, "We just need to walk in and get a good look at the room. Engrave it in our minds so we can visualize it, and Jump back to it when we are ready."

"OK," Betsy said. "But I'll take a picture or two just in case. Let's go on in. If anyone asks, I'll just say I'm looking for my uncle. That will buy us a minute or so."

They opened the door and walked in. The room was a large one with many cubicles. Paul took note of one of them in particular. He noticed where the computer was, the sorts of personal items the occupant had on his walls, and other things like that. Betsy noticed where Paul was focusing his attention, and snapped a picture.

A lady was walking up to them, "He's not here, Paul," Betsy said loud enough for the lady to hear, "Maybe he said seventeen."

"OK," Paul said, "Let's go and see." They smiled at the lady, turned and walked out of the room.

"That was easy enough," Paul concluded, "On to the Washington Post."

The Washington Post turned out to be even easier than the EPA. The newsroom itself was not open to the public, but there was an observation room that was. It was vacant and they could speak freely.

The observation room looked down not just on the newsroom but also out on the pressroom with its large web printing presses and equipment for putting the paper together. The newsroom was a large room containing a great many cubicles arranged in rows. There were computers, printers, and people bustling about everywhere. "When we come back, we are going to have to do it at night," Betsy said. "There are too many people around."

"Or very early in the morning," Paul said. "There is probably a lot of activity until the paper is finished. Early mornings would probably be the best time. Even then there may be some people around."

"We can Jump here," Betsy suggested. "There won't be anyone in here then." She shrugged her shoulders, "If there isn't anyone here now, there won't be in the wee hours of the morning for sure. We can see the newsroom from here, pick where we want to Jump to and then just be in and out."

"That'll work," Paul agreed.

Betsy took some pictures of the observation room. "OK," she said, "Let's go find the Library of Congress."

"We can get another cab," Paul suggested. "The driver will know how to find it."

They walked out to the curb and hailed a taxi. The Library of Congress turned out to be easier to find than the EPA. It was right behind the Capital next to the Supreme Court. They walked up the marble steps and into the building and both of them immediately and involuntarily caught their breath.

"Have you ever seen anything so beautiful?" Betsy gasped as they looked out over a center court of Corinthian columns, marble balustrades and incredible works of art.

"I had no idea this was even here," Paul agreed in awe. "When my family toured Washington we did the Capitol, and the White House. We did all of the monuments and the Smithsonian but we missed this."

"We missed it too," Betsy added simply as she looked around.

They walked down a sweeping marble staircase and located an information desk. The Librarian there directed them to a room on the third floor.

"Back up again," Betsy noted as they made their way back up the staircase they had just descended. A few minutes later they had located the room and Paul walked up to a computer directory.

"This may be the key," he said.

"The key?"

"Yeah. The problem with these air quality Regs is that they are scattered all over."

"Do you think they do it on purpose just to make it difficult?"

Paul looked at Betsy. "I hadn't thought of that, but it is almost like they did it on purpose. What I really need is an index that tells me where to look. Ash … here we go," he said as the index he was looking for came up. He quickly jotted some numbers down on a pad provided for that purpose. "Everything we need is here, and none of it is checked out," Paul remarked as he looked over his list. "OK, Let's see if we can find these volumes." Thirty minutes later they had them all gathered into a pile on one of the tables.

"This saved weeks, maybe months" he said as he began pouring through the books. "Look," he said pointing to a section in a Federal Air Quality Manuel. "Here is the section that pertains to what the mill is doing," he said and slid the book over to Betsy.

She looked at the section Paul had indicated, "You're right." she agreed. "This is what we need. It's got the limits as they come out of the stack." She looked over to Paul. "It's 10 ppm."

"Yeah," Paul agreed with a disgusted look on his face, "A maximum of 10 ppm sodium hydroxide as it leaves the stack."

"You guys got 690 the other day, right?"

"Yes," Paul answered. "I'll make some notes so I can find these references back at the school."

They met Jim and Jennifer in Fellowship Hall before dinner as they had planned.

"Any problems?" Jennifer asked.

"We had a little confusion at first," Betsy reported, "But we got it worked out. We got what we needed. How about you?"

Jim shot a quick look at Jennifer, and started to say something. But Jennifer gave him an aggravated look and he thought better of it. "That about sums it up for us too."

"Great," Ornith interrupted, "I think they are going to have those Cornish chickens available tonight. Those little guys are good and I'm about starved to death. Can we go eat now?"

ψ

Right after breakfast on Sunday morning, Paul Jumped into the Erlyndor's living room. Ornith was sitting on his shoulder, and immediately flew off to greet his mom and dad.

"Hi, Paul," Snazzy said, "How do you like William? Is he settling in OK?"

"Oh, Hi Snazzy. He's settling in just fine, especially once we went to the library and got him some books. I like him a lot."

Baralicia walked into the living room from the kitchen as Paul set his books down in one of the chairs. She gave him a hug. "Hi, Paul."

Just then Georaldon walked in from their bedroom. "Oh, Hi Paul." He walked over and shook hands, "Nice to see you."

"Yeah ... you too."

"Are these your books?" Baralicia asked looking at the huge pile Paul had deposited on the table.

"Yeah. I've got lots of homework to do."

"Right." Georaldon said with a nod, "Well ... let's have a look. In most cases a student's grades are not so much a measure of intelligence, but whether the home work is being done. There is nothing being taught that is beyond your ability to learn. It is simply a question of doing the work required to master the material. Doing the work is the student's responsibility, but seeing to it that it is done and done well is a parental responsibility. Your parents aren't here, but we are," he said with a grin, "so the job of seeing to it that you're getting everything done falls to us."

Baralicia put some cinnamon rolls into the oven and brought a pitcher of freshly squeezed orange juice over to the table. "It is up to Georaldon and me to see to it that you are keeping up with all of this work," Baralicia agreed, "We'll be hearing from you. We'll be hearing from your professors as well."

Georaldon poured himself a glass of juice and then poured one for Paul. "Doing the homework is not optional," Paul. "At your old school, you might have been able to get by without doing all of it. That won't work here. At the end of each school year is a set of comprehensive finals, and you have to pass them. Students who do the work will learn the material and will pass. Students who don't, won't. It's all about doing the work. It really is just that simple."

Georaldon picked up a book out of Paul's stack and noticed it was about his own great-grandmother. He looked at Baralica and smiled and then at Paul. "You're doing your first profile on my great-grandmother?"

"Yes," Paul answered, "I saw her name on the list. They had a short bio and it looked interesting."

Baralicia looked at her the grin on her husband's face. "Is this what you had in mind, dear?" she asked sweetly.

Georaldon looked back. "Yes," he answered, "exactly this."

Paul gave them a puzzled look.

"It's one of those husband and wife things," Baralicia said as the oven timer buzzed and she got up to go get the cinnamon rolls.

Georaldon picked up Paul's first draft of the report on his grandmother and began to read. "Anyway, every week we will be getting together with you to see how you are coping. Sometimes it may be on a Sunday morning like this. Other times it might be on a Friday night, or even some other night depending on what is going on, but once a week we will get together to see how you are doing, more often if you're having problems. If you start to fall behind, we will be here to help. He continued reading the report. He looked over at Baralicia and raised his eyebrows a little, "This is good … very good."

Chapter Twelve

Instrumentation

John Moriarty took the bag from the courier. He knew what was inside. Once again it was payoff time. He thought for a while on what he would do with the money this month. The truth was that he didn't know what he would do with the money ... the important thing was that it was there. He opened the bag, withdrew the proper amount from Ben's envelope, placed what was left in his pocket and headed out for the shop floor.

He found Ben and gave him his portion. Once again, as always, there were no witnesses. Moriarty was under no illusions. They could get caught. If that happened, he had made sure that there were no trails leading to him. Ben was the one who had to sign the orders for the hydrazine and there were other EPA records that Ben had to falsify. If they ever got caught, everything pointed to Ben. There was no way around it and that was why Ben got a cut at all, and if they were ever caught, it was going to be Ben's problem not his.

ψ

All of the members of Q3 were up to their eyeballs in homework. They simply had to get their projects under control. Doing something about the mill was a priority for them, but it was a personal priority. They had all agreed that the homework had to come first. It took them three days of hard work to get on top of it all; but they finally managed it. They were meeting on the second floor balcony of Fellowship Hall. Paul looked at Betsy first, and then at each of the others. "We've got to get some pretty sophisticated data if we are going to be successful in doing anything about that plant. We need to have good information on specifically what chemicals are being released. What we think they are is not good enough. We have to get a positive ID. Not only that, we have to get the exact concentrations that they are releasing, and the exact duration's of the release. Under EPA rules they are allowed to release small amounts of pollutants."

"Why," Betsy interrupted, "would the EPA allow that?"

"Who knows," Paul continued, "but the point is, we have to prove that they are releasing more than the allowed amounts."

"How do we get data like that?" Jennifer asked.

"With a gas chromatograph," Jim answered with a smile; "My research has been coming along too. A portable gas chromatograph is what we need. I've studied it thoroughly."

"That's right," Aurileol interjected quickly, "Betsy isn't the only one keeping everyone up half the night. Paul and Jim are doing it too. Ornith and I haven't had a good night's sleep in weeks or days. We just don't complain about it." He blew a raspberry at Gwenivere.

Jim chuckled as he continued, "What we need is a portable gas chromatograph. The good news is that we can get all of the data Paul is talking about with that one instrument."

"OK," Betsy interjected, "but what exactly … is … a gas

chromatograph?"

"Well, that's kind of complicated," Jim answered. "A sample gets inserted into this special tubing filled with microscopic glass beads. Different chemicals take different times to get through; so, every different chemical component of the sample separates and comes out at a different time. The exact time of transit is precisely timed, and the computer tells you what it is. It is a precise method of documenting the nature of the sample."

"Oh," Jennifer said, "That's simple enough. I thought it was going to be hard."

"Anyway," Jim continued, "Most gas chromatographs have two methods of putting a sample through. One is manually. The other is to program it to automatically take a sample every fifteen seconds. There is a tube and you can place it into a gas stream for this purpose."

"Perfect," Betsy exclaimed, "Now the question is where do we get one?"

Just then Ornith flew into the middle of the group. "Guys," he said in his little voice, swinging his arms back and forth, "They ... have ... all ... this ... stuff ... in ... the ... Library."

"What?" Paul asked incredulously.

"The Library in Co-re-alis," Ornith continued with a nod, "and you can just check it out."

"That's right," Gwenivere chimed in.

"There is a section in the Library," Ornith went on, "for Earthantan technology. It has ... everything. It will have a gas chromat – o – whatever it is thing you want and you can just check it out. That

Library is not just for books. It's for stuff too. Baralicia gets stuff there all the time. If it gets broken you still have to pay for it, but that's where you can get one."

The four members of Q3 looked at each other.

"Well that settles that," Jim announced for everyone. "If we break it we pool resources to from our contingency fund pay for it." There were nods from everyone.

"So back to business. How do we document times and durations of release?" Jennifer asked.

"That'll be done by the computer," Jim said.

"Right," Jennifer noted, "But a printout does not establish where the release came from. We're going to have to document that too."

"True," Jim admitted.

"We could use a video camera," Paul suggested. "I'm sure we could set one up in the stack room. We can use that portable cloaker from the transport belts so no one would see it. It would be easy to set the field wide enough to prove the video came from that particular stack room."

"And the computer time function can correlate with the time and date function in the video cam," Jim said.

"Right," Paul agreed, "So what we can do is set up both pieces of equipment, and take the data. The time will be correlated. When they put in that vessel, the video will show it. When the gas chromatograph registers the impurities it can be traced directly back to the vessel's contents."

"That will work," Betsy agreed.

"How long should we collect data?" Jennifer asked.

Jim shrugged. "A month?"

"A month's good," Paul agreed and everyone nodded.

"So what we need now is a video camera," Jim concluded.

"We can get one this weekend," Paul suggested. "We can get one in Hawk's Nest on Saturday and then set everything up on Sunday."

"Everyone is forgetting one thing," reminded Jim.

"What's that?" The other three said in unison.

"We still have to go down to Co-re-alis and check out the gas chromatograph."

Betsy looked at Paul and shrugged.

"We could do it tomorrow after class?" Paul suggested.

"What are we going to do with it once we get it?" Jim asked, "It might not be a good idea to keep it here."

"We could take it to that spot where we practiced jumping off of that bolder and transporting before we hit the ground," Betsy answered.

"That's a pretty good place," Jennifer agreed. "There is a lot of underbrush around there and nothing to indicate any foot traffic. No one would bother it and it would be easy to hide."

"Do you think we just Jump there with it?" Paul asked.

"Why not?" Betsy asked.

"OK," Paul said. He looked at Jim and Jennifer, "Well, the two of us can handle it. We don't all need to go to the Library. You guys could just go straight to that boulder and find a place to hide it and get ready while Betsy and I go get the instrument," Paul suggested.

Jim, looked at Jennifer, "OK," they agreed.

ψ

In the next afternoon's self-defense class, Paul was once again pleased with his performance. He had been first with the rights … then he had been first with the lefts. This week they had been practicing against combinations of lefts and rights. Paul was the quickest to master the blocks required to counter the flurry of punches that the androids could throw.

After class the members of Q3 headed for the Great Room. Once they were alone in the passageway, Paul and Betsy visualized the entrance to Library in Co-re-alis, while Jim and Jennifer locked on the boulder, and all four of them tapped their fingers.

Paul and Betsy arrived at the Library. They went quickly up to the Librarian at the main desk.

"Where do we find items on Earthantan Technology?" Betsy asked quickly, almost nervously.

"On the 3rd Floor," the Librarian answered as if he were asked every day. "That section is in the East Wing."

Moments later they walked into a section of the Library. There were stacks, just like for books only bigger. All sorts of items of equipment were stored there. The went to the catalog computer and located the place where a gas chromatograph was stored. "There," Betsy said pointing at the instrument and the computer that went with it, "It's got a battery pack and everything."

Paul looked it over. There was a nameplate.

Portable Gas Chromatograph Model 2003
E. I. Lilly

"Right," Paul said, "Let's check this out, then and meet up with Jim and Jen."

Paul picked up the instrument itself, while Betsy picked up the laptop. They went to an unoccupied desk, and found that the procedure was all voice activated through a computer. Seconds later the computer indicated they were authorized to have the gas chromatograph in their possession for one month. If they needed it longer they had to notify the Library computer via voice comm. They could renew their checkout twice without returning it. They walked outside, nodded to each other and Jumped. Seconds later when the swirling lights stopped they were in the clearing in front of the boulder.

"Any problems?" Jim asked.

"None," Paul answered.

"OK," Betsy said, "OK. Let's hide this stuff and get back."

ψ

It turned out to be an average week for Q3. They gained another two points in Chorda, but lost their Palacrosse match for a net loss of one point. They were still in second place, which was not a bad place to be. After lunch they changed out of their uniforms into street clothes. They wore their Power Rings, and underneath everything they each had on their transporter belts.

As Paul was getting ready to walk out of their suite Ornith flew up, "Do you mind if we stay here this afternoon?" he asked.

"No," Paul answered, "Why?"

"We're having Pix games."

"Oh. OK." Paul answered, "We'll see you later. Good Luck."

"Thanks," Ornith said and flew off quickly with Aurileol when the door opened.

There was a bus stop near the school and they took a bus into downtown Hawk's Nest.

"I hope we don't run into those kids again," Jennifer said as they got off of the bus.

"We need to find an electronics store," Paul said as he looked around the square from the bus stop, "Does anyone see one?"

"Uh ... Oh," Jim said quietly.

"Uh ... Oh, what?" Paul asked.

"We've got trouble I think." Jim said and pointed down the street. There were the three boys walking rapidly towards them.

"Maybe they won't be trouble this time." Jennifer said hopefully.

"That's not the way to bet," Jim answered.

The leader swaggered up, "So what have we here? Oh ... it's the geeks who turned tail last time we tried to talk to you."

"Look," Paul answered, "We really didn't want any trouble with you then, and we don't now. Say, you don't know if there is an electronics store on this square do you?"

"Why would I answer a question of yours? You didn't answer me that last time. You are geeks from that school aren't you?" he demanded.

"So what if we are?' demanded Betsy, "and who says we're geeks?"

"I do," answered the boy leading the others.

"And who would you be?" Paul asked.

"You mean you don't know?"

"If I did I wouldn't have asked, now would I?" Paul responded as calmly as possible, and one of the two boys snickered.

The leader turned around and glared at him and the boy got quiet. "Joe Moriarty is my name. My father runs the mill."

"That explains a lot," Betsy said sarcastically, and Paul immediately turned and gave her a hard look.

"What do you mean by that?" Moriarty demanded clenching and unclenching his fists.

"Nothing," Paul answered quickly.

"Why are geeks like you with pretty girls like these anyway?" one of the two boys, the one who had not laughed asked in a menacing tone of voice.

"They're not geeks," Betsy snapped back.

"Really?" Moriarty said with a sneer, "I bet they don't know how to have fun ... not like we do. You should go off with us, we'll show you about fun."

"No way," Jennifer said with a resolve that could not be mistaken.

"Why don't you guys just leave us alone," Paul said quietly, adjusting his feet so that he could get his arms into a self-defense position quickly if he needed to.

"What did you say?" Moriarty demanded.

247

"I said you should leave us alone," Paul repeated. He saw the leader's fist clench. There was a punch coming and it was going to be a right. Paul felt sure about that, but good against ANDY 303 was one thing. Good against these guys might be a whole lot different. All he knew for sure was that he was about to find out.

Moriarty launched a right-handed punch at Paul's jaw. Paul moved quickly into the stance they had been taught and blocked the punch easily. Moriarty stood there with his arm hanging out in space. Paul had not yet been taught what to do next. He did not know how to punch so he decided it was better to just step back and do nothing. He took a step back, as Moriarty jerked his arm back.

"You can try again if you want," Paul said quietly from his stance. This guy was slower than ANDY 303, and his punch had turned out to be much easier to block. Moriarty threw another punch. Paul blocked it as well. Paul thought about punching him in the stomach. It would be easy to do, but there were three of them. The best thing seemed to be to see if this wouldn't just end up going away so he took another step back.

Just then one of the other boys took a step forward and threw a punch at Paul. Paul turned slightly and blocked that punch and as he did so, Moriarty threw a left, and Paul blocked that too.

"Is that all you can do?" Moriarty demanded as he pulled his arm back.

"As a matter of fact it is," Paul answered, "That's all they have taught us so far, but if you want," he continued, "We can come back next week and show you what they teach us next."

Both of the girls laughed involuntarily at that but then cut it off, realizing that laughing might only make things worse.

Moriarty spat on the sidewalk and turned on his heel and stalked off. The two boys with him followed.

Paul drew in a deep breath as he watched them leave and let it out slowly.

"That was great," Betsy said putting a hand on Paul's shoulder, while Jim slapped him on the back.

Jennifer was looking at the ground when her friends noticed she hadn't said anything. She looked up at her friends, "Why do people have to be so mean?"

Jim shrugged. "Who knows, Jenn," he answered softly, "but some people just are."

"I guess that's why they teach us martial arts," Betsy added, "and a good thing too."

The four of them walked to the corner and found an electronics store. They selected a camera, and Jennifer used her ATM card to make the purchase. "Do you guys really want to take that bus back to the school?" she asked.

"No, not really," Jim answered.

They found a deserted alley and Jumped to the clearing where they had stashed the gas chromatograph, and hid the video camera with it.

Betsy was getting set to Jump back when Paul interrupted, "Wait a second. There's something I want to checkout." Paul removed the Delta Wand from his belt and activated it. He placed it next to the video camera. "Cloak," he said. The wand disappeared but nothing else happened.

"Maybe you have to attach it first," Betsy suggested.

249

"How?" Paul asked.

"I don't know," she answered, "but everything else seems to be voice activated. Why don't you hold it against the camera and say "Attach" or something?"

"Good idea," Paul agreed. He placed the wand against the video. "Attach," he instructed as he held it in place. He let go and this time the wand stayed exactly where he had placed it. "Cloak," he said and this time both the wand and the camera disappeared from sight.

"What happens if you have the chromatograph touching the camera? Maybe they would both be invisible," Betsy wondered aloud.

"Good idea," Paul agreed, "Let's see. Un-cloak," he instructed the wand and the camera became visible. Paul scooted it over so that it was contacting the chromatograph. "Cloak," he said and this time both items disappeared. "OK. That's good to know."

"We could just leave it that way," Betsy suggested, "No chance anyone will find it if it's cloaked like that."

"Right," Paul agreed with a nod, "but then I have to leave the wand here. Someone might notice that I don't have all four."

"Right," Jennifer agreed, "but you could say you were using it to hide something from William."

"That'll work," Paul agreed with a nod and the foursome went back to school.

ψ

On Monday morning, as they walked towards the dining Hall

everyone discovered that mid-term grades were posted. The freshman class, used to the patterns of Earthantan schools, were surprised that the grades were posted on the holographic bulletin board outside the dining Hall for everyone to see.

"I wonder why they post them," Jennifer asked.

"Well," Jim answered, "They'd have to I guess, since they count in the points competition."

"It probably has more to do with accountability than the points competition," Betsy suggested. "If everyone knows how everyone else did, no one can hide.

"Let's see how we did," Paul suggested and they walked over and studied the Board.

"Looks like we're down a point on Q5," Jim concluded, "And up one on everyone else. Pretty good overall."

Chapter Thirteen

A Price to be Paid

Sunday morning dawned clear. There was a hint of Fall in the air, but the weather promised to be perfect for Q3's expedition.

"Ready, guys," Paul asked as they walked to the rear gate.

"Ready," each of them answered.

"OK, then," he said with a nod, "Ready Ornith?" Paul asked.

"Ready, Paul," Ornith answered.

Seconds later all four of them were standing a few yards away from the place where they had hidden the equipment.

"Un-cloak," Paul instructed, and immediately the camera and gas chromatograph appeared. "Delta Wand ... Release ... Off," he said. The wand detached from the camera, floated over and attached to his belt.

"Awesome," Jennifer said shaking her head. They collected the equipment and Jumped to the meadow they had used before, and brought their equipment up to a line of bushes bordering the meadow.

"No sign of activity," announced Betsy as she studied the Mill through her binoculars.

"Good," Jennifer said and looked at Paul. She and Paul were taking the chromatograph and computer to the top of the south stack to set them up. Betsy and Jim were setting up the video camera. "South stack. Everyone got that?"

"Right," Betsy said still looking at the door to the stack room.

She put away the binoculars and the members of Q3 looked at each other.

Jennifer looked at Paul, "Do you think we should have our hoods up?"

Paul though for a second, and then shook his head, "They're pretty restrictive, Jenn. I think we need to be as unencumbered as we can."

"OK," Jim said at last, "Let's do this thing." He nodded to Betsy and they disappeared with the video camera.

"Ornith," Paul said before they Jumped, "I know you don't like it up there. Renalee isn't going to like it either. You've already had this adventure. You guys can stay here if you want."

"No, Paul," Ornith said firmly, "I will go with you."

"What about Renalee?" Paul asked.

"I will go with Jennifer," the Pixie answered with a similar resolve.

"OK," Paul said the Jennifer, "I've got the chromatograph, you take the laptop. There isn't room on that platform for both of us so after I Jump, count to six first. I'll get out of your way."

Jennifer nodded, and Paul visualized the platform at the top of the stack, gathered up the gas chromatograph and tapped his fingers. When colors stopped and he was standing on top of the south stack. The wind was blowing pretty hard, so he knelt down to steady himself and moved off of the platform to make room for Jennifer.

Jim and Betsy had jumped into the stack room. It turned out to be occupied. There were four men in there working on a vessel. Jim and Betsy were Cloaked so none of the men saw them. With hand signs Betsy motioned Jim over to a platform at the rear of the room. It would provide a good view of the south stack, and they began setting up the video camera. As they did so, the men in the room began hoisting a vessel into position to load into the south stack.

"Uh … Oh," Jim said quietly, pointing at the activity.

"That won't bother us," Betsy whispered as she began fastening the camera to one of the handrails.

"But if they start releasing that acid right away," Jim observed, "It might be a problem for Paul and Jennifer up top."

"Oh … right," Betsy acknowledged.

"I'm going to call them," Jim decided.

"OK," she agreed, "speak quietly. I'm going to finish this." She tightened the mounting bracket and removed the Delta Wand from her belt. Seconds later the camera was invisible. No one inside the plant would ever know the camera was there.

"Comm On … Paul Andrews… Jennifer Thompson," he said as quietly as he could, hopping not to be heard by the men in the Room.

Paul heard a bong in his ear and looked quickly at Jennifer. She was busy booting up the laptop, and as he looked at her, she looked at him. They both heard Jim's voice as if he were standing there with them.

"They are loading a vessel into the south stack. I think they may start releasing stuff soon."

"OK," Jennifer said, "We hear you. I'm almost done - Paul's got another two or three minutes."

"Hurry up, Paul," Jim said.

"I will," Paul acknowledged, and bent back to the instrument he was working on.

Jennifer's computer came up, and she activated the necessary program. "Ready on this end," she said.

"Good," Paul answered. "Why don't you pass me the communication cable, cloak the computer and then Jump down."

She handed him the end of the computer cable that Paul would have to screw into the back of the gas chromatograph with the two built in screws that were common to Earthantis's computer systems. "Cloak," she said and the computer disappeared along with the cable. "Nuts," she said. "I didn't know the cable would get cloaked too."

"It's OK," Paul said immediately, "I can attach it by feel it think." He felt for the chromatograph's Comm Port, attached the cable and started tightening the screws. "It's OK ... I got it," he said as he felt then start to tighten up.

"I don't want to leave you alone up here," she said.

"It'll take me two more minutes to get the system up," Paul answered shaking his head negatively, "Besides, I'm not alone. Ornith is with me, and there's nothing else for you to do up here."

"You're sure?"

Paul was busy finishing with the screws, and nodded. "Yeah, I'm sure."

"OK, then," she said, "Just be careful." She tapped her fingers and disappeared.

"Paul," Jim said from the Stack room, "They have closed that hatch, and all four of them are leaving now. They act like they are in a hurry. That stuff is going to be released soon."

"OK," Paul answered, "Do you and Betsy have the video

running?"

"Yes."

"Good! Then go ahead and get out of there," Paul instructed. "I won't be long."

Two of the men who were loading the vessels had gone out on the porch to smoke a cigarette. Both of them saw the three students in the meadow and called security. The men with the dogs were on the other side of the mill but immediately headed around to the back.

Once Paul had the cable hooked up, it was possible to power up the instrument and he did so. He watched as a series of lights started to come on indicating that the machine was functioning.

"Are you OK, Ornith?" Paul asked.

"It would be better if it were not so windy," the Pix answered, "But I'm OK."

The last of the lights came on, indicating that the machine was functioning. Paul selected the auto sampling function. The machine would take a sample once each minute and send the results to the computer, which would record the analysis and time reference the data.

"Done," Paul said reaching for his Delta Wand. He attached the wand to the Chromatograph. "Cloak" he said and everything including the sampling tube disappeared but he still had the end in his hand. He couldn't see it but he didn't have to as long as he kept hold of it until he got it where he wanted it "OK, Ornith. Now all we've got to do is dangle this tube into the stack itself." This was actually the part he was most worried about most. He crawled along the top to a good place, flattened out into a prone position, secured the tube around a post and moved to the edge, dangling the tube into the stack. Suddenly he smelled a really nasty odor and held his breath. After a second or two he was satisfied that the tube was going to stay where he put it and he eased back from the edge.

"Ready Ornith?"

Ornith began to gasp and choke, "I ... can't ... breathe," he managed to say and then fell off of Paul's shoulder.

Ornith landed on the rim of the stack. Paul reached for him but a gust of wind pushed Ornith further away. Paul reached out farther trying to maintain his own balance, and Ornith reached out as best he could for Paul but another gust of the swirling wind pushed him over the edge of the stack."

"Ornith," Paul shouted and lunged but the Pix was out of reach and falling. Time stood still. He knew he could dive off of the stack after Ornith, and knew he could transport safely to the meadow once he caught him. Without hesitation he dove off of the stack after Ornith.

Paul saw the little Pix ahead of him. He was definitely gaining on Ornith, but the ground was gaining on both of them. It still looked like it was a long ways away, but there was no way for Paul to concentrate on catching Ornith, and watch the ground at the same time. He just concentrated on making the catch and hoped he would be in time. Paul caught up to Ornith and grabbed him. The ground was rushing up. He visualized the meadow, and tapped his fingers. Seconds later he was standing in the meadow with Ornith in his hands. He stood there for a second; glad to be alive, and realized that Ornith was trying to say something. He bent his ear as close to Ornith as he could.

"What happened?" Betsy asked as Gwenivere flew over to see.

Ornith's words were faint, "Thank you … Paul." After that he lost consciousness.

"I'm not sure," Paul answered. "One second everything was fine. The next, some of those fumes were released. They smell really bad. Ornith couldn't breathe and fell off the stack." Ornith's body lay almost lifeless in Paul's hands. The little Pix was breathing but barely.

Gwenivere settled onto Paul's arm. "He must have inhaled some very bad fumes," she said. She was crying. None of them had ever seen a Pixie cry before.

"What are you going to do?" Jim asked.

"I'm taking him to Co-re-alis," Paul answered. "Right now …comm unit ON … Georaldon Erlyndor," he said as he visualized the hospital in the underground city, "I'm coming in with Ornith … he's badly hurt – it's respiratory," Paul said. He didn't wait for an answer and tapped his fingers.

ψ

Paul materialized on the steps of the hospital, and a few seconds later was joined by Georaldon and a few seconds after that Baralicia appeared. Before Paul could say a word, someone from inside the hospital came running out with a tray sized bed. It was just the right size for a Pix. Obviously the hospital was prepared for medical emergencies involving Pixies.

"I told them you were coming," Baralicia said quickly. "This is Dr. Mondifort. She specializes in Pixies."

258

"What happened?" the Doctor asked as she whisked Ornith's limp form out of Paul's hands and onto the tray and attached what appeared to be a tiny O_2 mask. Ardant and Felinda flew over to him immediately and began hovering around.

"He's breathed some bad fumes, real bad ones. Sodium hydroxide fumes or something like that, I think. He choked, told me he couldn't breathe and fainted," Paul answered.

"He's barely breathing," the doctor said, "But he … is … breathing. If I need more information, will you still be here?"

"I'm not going anywhere," Paul said emphatically. "Is he going to be all right?" Paul sputtered before she could leave.

"I don't know. We've got to get him stabilized before I can tell," she answered, gently squeezing his arm, "There is a lot we can do. The first key is to get him stabilized. I'll let you know as soon as I can." She turned and headed inside with the little Pix.

"OK," Paul said and started after her.

"You'll need to wait in the waiting room." the doctor said over her shoulder and hurried through a door with the tray-sized bed that Ornith was laying on.

He was about to tell the Erlyndors what had happened when Betsy, Jim and Jennifer materialized on the hospital's porch.

Gwenivere flew over to Paul. "How is he, Paul?" the Pixie asked. There were tears streaming down her face. "Is he going to be OK?"

"We don't know Gwenivere. Not yet. All we know is that he is breathing."

The Erlyndors led Paul and the other Q3 members to a section of the hospital where all of the equipment seemed to be very small, and Paul assumed they were in a section devoted to Pixies.

"We'll have to wait out here," Baralicia said pointing at some chairs, "Pixies too."

Paul walked over to the chairs slowly, sat in one, and didn't even notice as the chair contoured itself to his body. He put his head in his hands and struggled not to cry. He had lost a pet before, and that was very hard, but the simple truth was that Ornith had become a lot more than a pet. Ornith was more like a little brother.

Georaldon sat down on one side of him, and Baralicia sat down on the other.

"The chemical was not sodium hydroxide," Paul said slowly. "This was different, nastier. I don't know what it was."

"Don't worry," Baralicia spoke as encouragingly as she could, "They'll find out. There is a lot they can do. A lot more than you know."

"Are you all right, Paul?" Georaldon asked, concerned for Paul as well as Ornith.

"I think so," Paul answered. "I just got a sniff. I knew I was almost done, and just didn't breathe."

"Take a deep breath for me?" Georaldon instructed. "As deep as you can."

Paul did as he was instructed. He coughed a couple of times but was able to take deep breaths, and fully exhale them.

"OK," Georaldon decided, "You're all right for now. We'll get you checked out later."

Doctor Mondifort walked briskly into the room and straight up to

Paul. "Could that compound have been hydrazine?"

"HZ." Paul exclaimed, and looked at his friends. "HZ. Those vessels said "HZ" on them. That could mean hydrazine"

"That's the only thing it could mean," doctor said gravely. "This is much worse than I thought," she turned quickly on her heal and ran from the room.

Paul looked at his friends, and then at Gwenivere. There were tears in his eyes. "I didn't know he would get hurt."

"Of course you didn't," Betsy said quickly.

"And you jumped off of that stack after him," Jim said, amazed that his friend had done something like that."

Gwenivere flew over to Paul; "It was the bravest thing I ever saw," and although there were tears running down her tiny cheeks, she reached out her hands, and rubbed noses with Paul.

"You did ... what ... Paul?" Baralicia asked.

Paul looked at his sponsors; and then down at the floor, "The wind was blowing in gusts down on the ground the first time we went over to scout the mill. I figured it would be even windier up there. I knew that you could Jump while you are falling and land as if you were standing still. We practiced it before we got there and that was why. We had all rehearsed in our minds what to would do if the wind blew one of us off of that stack. If I hadn't known what to do, I wouldn't have gone up there the first time."

Baralicia handed him a glass of something that looked like Mountain Dew and he took a sip. "When Ornith fell off of my shoulder, the wind carried him just out of my reach. I tried to get him and he reached back for me, but another gust carried him over the edge. I knew what to do if it was me. We already had it figured out. I knew I could go after him … I knew how … we'd practiced it … so I did. I dove off after him, caught him on the way down and Jumped to the meadow. The landing wasn't any harder than jumping off of a bed."

Georaldon whistled softly and draped his arm across Paul's shoulder, and all of them sat in the waiting room quietly. "That was an extremely brave thing to do, Paul."

"Ornith was the one who was brave," Paul replied, "He didn't like it up there. He came only because he didn't want me to be alone. He thought it all over and came anyway. I just reacted quickly. It isn't the same thing."

"Oh, yes it is," Betsy said and all of them, Georaldon and Baralicia included, nodded in agreement.

Just then the doctor returned, "We've made a little progress, but I need to ask you a couple of questions, Paul."

"Sure," Paul answered, "Anything."

"How long has it been since Ornith adopted you?"

"More than a month … six weeks I think."

"Not very long," the doctor observed and looked over at the Erlyndors and then back at Paul. "Are your feelings for him strong?"

"Yes," Paul answered.

"Extremely strong," Baralicia said simply. "Strong enough that he dove off of a two hundred foot smoke stack after him, doctor,"

"You did what?" she asked her eyes getting wider.

"He jumped off of a two hundred foot smoke stack to catch him,"

262

Georaldon repeated. "He risked his own life to save Ornith's."

"I guess that makes your feelings about as strong as they get!" the doctor exclaimed.

"Yes, ma'am," Paul answered. He didn't understand the direction that the conversation was taking. "Are you trying to prepare me for something, Doctor?" he asked her as directly as he knew how.

"No, Paul," she answered, "We have not gotten Ornith stable yet. Pixies feed off affection and love. We all do actually, but especially Pixies. If your bond with him is strong, you can help pull him through this to a place where we can stabilize him. Will you help?"

"Of course," Paul answered, "But I don't know what to do."

"Just come with me." The doctor answered, "I'll show you. It's not hard."

Paul followed the doctor to the room where they were keeping Ornith. He walked over to the table where the small bed was sitting. They had a plastic cover similar to an incubator for infants over the bed, and there were hoses hooked up to the cover. From one of his arms there were very small tubes leading away. Paul didn't know but he assumed the hose were for oxygen and the tubes were for intravenous fluids of some kind. He noticed that Ornith's skin tones were nearly grey, and realized that couldn't be a good sign.

"Take the cover off, Paul, and say "Hi" to him," the doctor instructed.

Paul did as he was told and once he had set the cover aside he said, "Hi, Ornith."

Ornith's eyes opened and he turned his head towards Paul.

263

"He can't talk to you Paul," the doctor said, "He doesn't have enough lung capacity left for it. Bend down and rub noses with him. It's more than a sign of affection for pixies. Under conditions of stress it releases their endorphins, which raises their metabolism."

Paul smiled at Ornith and saw a little smile in return. He bent over and rubbed his nose with Ornith's, and then straightened up. The smile on the little fellow's face seemed a little stronger.

Slowly Ornith lifted one of his hands a bit and held out two fingers.

Paul was puzzled for a second and then asked, "Do you want another nose rub, Ornith?"

There was a barely perceptible nod, and Paul bent over and rubbed noses with Ornith again, longer this time. It was not the sort of thing that any teenage Earthantan boy back in Calumet City would have ever done, but this was not Calumet City. None of the boys he had ever known would have willingly rubbed noses with anyone, but then none of those boys had ever been adopted by a pixie. When he finished Paul was sure the little fellow's color was better.

"We need to replace the cover now," the doctor said.

"Get well, Ornith," Paul pleaded, "Get well. You're a part of me now. I didn't really understand how true that was before, but I do now." He paused, and then continued, "I ... need ... you ... to ... get ... well," he said in the singsong voice that Ornith used when he wanted to emphasize something. They replaced the cover, but Ornith smiled a little and Paul was sure he saw the grey color of his skin become more of a pink.

"Very good, Paul ... that was very good," Doctor Mondifort

acknowledged with a positive nod. "We need to let him rest now while we try and get his vital signs to stabilize."

"OK," was all Paul could say. The doctor went to work and an assistant led him back to the waiting room.

A half-hour went by and there was no word ... then another half-hour ... still no word.

Ardant came over and sat on Paul's shoulder. "Waiting is hard," he said softly, "But the longer they take now the better. It means that they have not lost him. Time is now starting to be on our side."

"Would you like something to eat?" Baralicia asked.

"No thank you," Paul answered. "I couldn't possibly eat anything right now."

Another half-hour passed. Finally Doctor Mondifort walked in. She had a tired look on her face, but also a thin smile. "We've stabilized his vital signs," she announced. Paul did not know exactly what that meant, but the sighs of relief from Baralicia, Georaldon, and the Pixies were audible and Paul deduced that this was a good thing. She looked at Paul and explained, "I know you don't know much about Atlantan medicine yet, but we can fix almost anything if we can stabilize a patient. Ornith breathed in a large amount of hydrazine. That is particularly nasty stuff. It is probably fifty times more dangerous than sodium hydroxide, and a Pix's lungs are more sensitive to that sort of thing than ours. Ornith has lost 85% of his lung capacity. That's OK, because we can keep his bodily functions going in good order on the remaining 15% for the time we need. He'll have to be on a respirator most of the time until we get his new lungs grown, but he will be OK."

265

Paul heard the word OK, and heaved his own sigh of relief, "You're going to do a lung replacement?" he asked.

"Yes," the doctor answered, "Do you know what that is?"

"Yes," Paul answered, "I'm doing a report project on Dr. Carolicia Erlyndor."

"I see," Dr. Mondifort said with a smile and a nod towards Georaldon. "Well ... I already have Ornith's new lungs in process, and they will be ready in about ten days. The surgery he has to go through is trying, and he won't be up to full strength for another ten days after that, but in about three weeks your little friend should be fine."

Paul looked at the doctor thankfully, "He's a lot more than a little friend."

"I know, son," she replied gently and reaching out and squeezing his shoulder, "I know. But until you realize that yourself, we don't try to tell you. Some things you have to come to on your own. You were the deciding factor though I think. The technicians said his vital signs began to stabilize as soon as he realized you were there. They said the biggest boost though came from the words you spoke to him at the end."

"Can I see him now?"

"No," she answered, "We have him in a medically induced coma state. We need to keep him that way for at least twenty-four hours. We will be able to restore a portion of the lung capacity he lost in that time I think. You can come down tomorrow night and see him if you want."

"Is that OK?" Paul asked Georaldon.

"Yes, Paul," he answered, "That will be fine. It'll be good for Ornith too."

"OK, then," the doctor said, "I will see you tomorrow night."

"Thank you," Paul said as she left.

"Now," Georaldon began, "We need to talk more seriously for a few minutes." He drew in a deep breath as he considered what had brought Paul and Ornith down in the first place. "Do you guys plan on finishing this thing with the mill?"

Paul looked at his friends.

Gwenivere flew up to Georaldon and Baralicia, "If we don't," she said, "then all of this was for nothing. Ornith wouldn't want that."

"That's true, Georaldon," Baralicia agreed but she bit her lip as she said it.

Georaldon nodded, "OK. Do you know why this happened?"

"Not really," Paul answered.

"Your hoods have air filtering devices in them," Georaldon explained. "If you had gone up there with your hoods up, they would have protected you. If you don't put yours up, then the pixies aren't going to put theirs up either. The hoods will restrict your motion some, and aren't all that comfortable, but there is a reason why you have them. If you're going to finish this, you'll have to go back up there to get the data, so next time, use the hoods."

He looked at the four students. "You know the term, "Better safe than sorry"? I think you understand that better now. So I won't belabor the point. My advice, at this point anyway, is not to tell anyone at the school about what has happened. I'll do that, but I'll wait a few days. You haven't broken any school rules ... not any that I know of. You have not violated *The Code of Atlantis*. The only problem is that you have engaged in a C-Op without any authorization. That is not a violation, nevertheless, it is going to come out. There will be an inquiry. There is at the end of every C-Op. It isn't a disciplinary action. It's done so that whatever lessons need to be learned can be passed on to everyone. Since there was no prior authorization, and there was a serious injury, you will have to defend your actions. What will be most difficult to defend is the idea that you four should be allowed to continue with this project as young as you are. If you have already finished the task, completing it will not be an issue at the inquiry."

"Are you saying that we might not be allowed to finish it?" Paul asked.

"Yes," Georaldon answered, "Since this has already turned dangerous, there is that distinct possibility. You're too far into this for someone not to finish it; the only question will be whether you four are old enough and well enough trained to do so. If you don't want those questions asked, then you need to finish this before they are asked."

"But you aren't required to notify the school? What about the doctor?"

"Regarding Baralicia and I ... well ... we are not expected to report anything we don't want to, so as long as you promise to use the hoods next time, we won't," Georaldon explained, "As for the doctor, she is prohibited from releasing Ornith's records without his express permission. I don't think he will give it, do you?"

"No," Paul answered.

"OK, Paul," Georaldon said with a sigh, "I wish you had been coming down under better circumstances. I wish you could stay, but you guys had better get back up to the school before anyone misses you. We'll see you here tomorrow night."

Paul and his friends Jumped back to the grounds of the school. No one saw them walk in the front doors of Fellowship Hall; so no one asked where they had been. Paul and Jim approached the door to their suite. "Open," Jim said and the door opened. William came running out and jumped into Paul's arms. He stood there with the little bear in his arms and gave him a tighter hug than normal.

"Is something the matter?" William asked.

"Yes, William," Paul answered, "It's Ornith. He's been hurt. We took him down to Co-re-alis."

William buried his head in Paul's shoulder, and Paul understood that William was close to Ornith too. "Is he going to be all right?" the little bear asked.

"Yes, we think so," Paul answered. "The doctor has him stabilized."

Chapter Fourteen

Recovery

John Moriarty, father of the Joe Moriarty that had tried to pick a fight with Paul in Hawk's Nest, and Manager of the Apex Paper Mill, sat at his desk reading the reports from his Chief of Security. On two occasions students from *The Hawk's Nest Science and Math Academy* had been spotted in the meadow behind the plant. That meadow was not the property of the mill, it was a part of the Smokey Mountain National Park, but there were no trails or park facilities that brought any of its visitors into the region behind the Mill. He had always treated that area as if it were the property of the mill. In the past it had just been a matter of his own vanity, but lately, with the requirement to dispose of more and more hydrazine, it was becoming an important security issue.

That meadow and the adjoining forest was about the only place that someone could get close enough to the mill to actually smell what they were doing. By the time the fumes had drifted five or six miles, they were too diluted to smell. The only way they could be discovered was by someone back behind the mill. Two more years of bonuses and he would be independently wealthy. He had a vacation home on a golf course in Florida. In two years he intended to retire there, and he did not intend for students from that school to interfere with his plans.

They had to be stopped from coming to that meadow. "Sooner or later," he said aloud although there was no one in the office, "They are going to get a whiff of what is going on." He smiled to himself at the literal statement. One way or another those students had to be stopped from coming. The question was how?

He trapped his fingers on his desk, and looked out of the window. His standing orders to sic the dogs on anyone back there didn't seem to have worked. They had done that once. These were fully trained attack dogs and from the way the dogs were trained, he had anticipated that the guards would have to pull the dogs off of the students, and that hadn't happened. According to the report those kids had used firecrackers to scare the dogs and gotten away. Even so they should have been scared enough not to return.

Not ever.

But they had returned.

That was what really concerned him. Those students had come back. Of course there was no way to really know that they were the same students, but the best idea was to assume that they were. The second time, the students had left the meadow before the dogs had gotten there, and that was part of the answer. The response time when the dogs were around front was too long. Then there were the firecrackers. All he had to do was have the guards start setting of firecrackers around the dogs on a regular basis, and they wouldn't be afraid of them anymore. He'd done things like that before with hunting dogs. Get them used to the noise and they'd be effective, particularly if there were more of them working in a pack.

He drummed his fingers on the desk a little longer and came to a decision. He would move a kennel of four of the guard dogs up near that meadow, and have two of the guard's camp out up there with them. They could build a makeshift fence for the dogs and start the fireworks training. The guards could rotate staying up there, and since they would have no other duties, there would be no objections. In fact, he would probably get volunteers. If those students came back, they would be detected much faster because the guards would already be back there, and the dogs would be too close for them to get away.

"Eight," he said aloud, changing his mind. They had a total of twelve fully trained attack dogs. He could relocate eight of the dogs up by the meadow. They only really needed four on the mill property itself. The truth was that they didn't need that many, but they could keep up appearances with four. Especially if the back of the mill were being covered from that meadow. He would move eight of the dogs up there. He reached for his phone to give the necessary orders.

ψ

Paul had returned with his friends to the school but he found that he had a hard time concentrating. It was a good thing that their mid-semester exams were over and his homework was up to date. He could not wait to get down to Co-re-alis and see how Ornith was doing and studying was out of the question. He tried hard in Monday's classes to pay attention. He tried as hard as he could, but all he could think of was Ornith getting blown over the edge of the stack, and the sinking feeling he had felt in the pit of his stomach simply would not let him go. He knew his friends were taking good notes, and would help him catch up, but he had trouble thinking of anything else.

After dinner he was walking towards the greenhouse with the rest of Q3 when his comm unit bonged in his ear, "Yes," he answered.

"Paul, this is Georaldon."

"Hi," Paul responded, "Any word on Ornith?"

"Yes, Paul," Georaldon reported, "He's doing well. His signs remain stable and have improved remarkably. In fact, he's off of the critical list and they are bringing him out of sedation now. I think he'll be really glad to see you."

"Oh," Paul said slowly, "I thought you were going to tell me that I shouldn't come down tonight."

"No, not at all," Georaldon said, "But I don't think it's a good idea for you to come down via the greenhouse."

"Why not?"

"That way leaves a record. Questions will be asked why you're coming down without advance authorization from the school."

"I see," Paul interrupted, "Fewer questions if we just Jump down."

"Exactly. Make sure no one sees you."

"What about my teammates. They want to come too."

"That's probably not such a good idea. Betsy can come down with Gwenivere, but the other two should say up there."

"Fewer questions?" Paul asked.

"Yes. If your classmates see two of you around, they will assume that the other two are somewhere close by."

"OK, Betsy I will jump straight to the hospital."

"Good, wait about thirty minutes."

"OK. We'll walk out past the back gate. See you soon."

"How's Ornith?" Jim asked.

"He's doing much better. He's off the critical list. Georaldon thinks that we will draw too much attention drawn if we all go. He thinks it's a better idea for you and Jennifer to be seen in the common room up here," Paul answered.

Jim's face fell. So did Jennifer's.

"OK," Jennifer agreed slowly, "If he's sure that's best."

"I guess," Jim agreed with a lot of hesitation. "Would you tell Ornith that I asked about him?"

"Sure," Paul answered.

He and Betsy walked out off of the grounds, past that back gate into an open field just off of the pathway leading down into the ravine. They made sure that they had not been followed and Jumped down to the hospital.

Paul and Betsy materialized in front of the steps of the porch, where they had the day before. Georaldon and Baralicia were waiting, and escorted them inside immediately. Did anyone see you?" they asked.

"Not that we could tell," Paul answered.

"We were pretty far out in the field when we Jumped," explained Betsy.

"Good," Georaldon replied, "Ornith is over this way." He led them through several corridors and they came to what appeared to be a central nursing station. They were met by Dr. Mondifort.

"Hi, Paul," she greeted him warmly, "Who is your friend?"

"This is Betsy Saunders," answered Paul, "She was here yesterday."

Dr. Mondifort shook hands with Betsy and then turned her attention to the Pixie on Betsy's shoulder, "Hi, Gwenivere."

"Hi, Doctor Mondifort," Gwenivere answered, "Can we see Ornith now?" she asked impatiently.

"Yes," she answered, "He's right in here." She led them into one of the rooms surrounding the nursing station. On one of the small beds made especially for Pixies they could see Ornith propped up. He had a breathing apparatus over his mouth and nose.

"Ornith's lung capacity has recovered a little but not enough," the Doctor explained, "I didn't think it would. The damage from the hydrazine was too great. We have a new set of lungs growing in Organ Replacement. He has to wear the mask most of the time. We are giving him pure oxygen under a little pressure. That brings his lung capacity up to about 50%. That's not enough for him to fly or to move around a whole lot, but enough so he can talk. He shouldn't have the mask off for more than ten minutes. Plus he does not have too much air to speak with so you need to lean in close so that he doesn't have to try too hard."

"Taking it off and talking won't weaken him?" Paul asked.

"Not much," the doctor answered, "But talking to you and Gwenivere will more than make up for any of that." The doctor began fussing with the mask so she could take it off.

"OK," Paul said and bent over and rubbed noses with Ornith as he had the day before.

"Hi, Paul," Ornith said weakly but his smile was there.

"Hi, Ornith. How are you feeling?"

"Better than last time, but not so good as a few days ago."

Gwenivere flew down, rubbed noses and settled onto the bed next to Ornith. "Hi, Ornith," she said. "I've been worried about you. Everyone is."

"Me too," answered Ornith, "But I will be all right."

"I'm so glad," Paul said, "I didn't really understand how close we would get."

Ornith smiled even more broadly at that, "It's what is supposed to happen, Paul."

"So, I've learned," Paul replied.

Ornith looked at Gwenivere, "Do all of our friends know what Paul did?"

"Everyone," Gwenivere answered solemnly.

"Everyone knows?" Paul asked.

"Yes," Gwenivere answered.

"Good. Can I ask one favor?" Ornith interjected.

"Sure," Paul answered.

"When we go back up on that smoke stack can we make sure they aren't dumping that stuff while we are up there?"

Paul smiled, "You can count on that. Besides, we'll have our hoods up next time. You're sure you want to come?"

"We've … been … over … this … before," Ornith answered.

"Yes, we have," Paul laughed, glad that Ornith's sense of humor was intact.

"You must promise me not to go until I get well, Paul," Ornith said solemnly.

"Don't worry, we've got to get a month's data before we go back anyway" Paul promised.

"I'll be ready by then," Ornith said.

"OK," Paul agreed.

Just then the doctor walked in. "Times up."

Gwenivere rubbed noses with Ornith first, followed by Betsy, and then Paul. Afterwards the doctor refastened the oxygen mask.

"Can I come back tomorrow?" Paul asked.

"Don't you have Chorda matches tomorrow?" Baralicia asked.

Betsy nodded, "But we could miss them."

"That's not a good idea," Georaldon answered, "Not now. Why don't you both come down day after tomorrow. No one will really miss you that way."

"Is that OK, Ornith?" Paul asked, "I miss you."

Ornith couldn't answer because of the mask, but he nodded his head.

ψ

Paul and Betsy Jumped back into the same field they had left from.

Somewhere ahead of them a branch broke. "Paul, it's getting dark," Betsy said quietly.

"So?" he asked as they hurried towards the school.

"People may ask questions. We should have an answer," she said as Paul opened the door for her. Anne Chastain was sitting in one of the chairs and she had already seen them. Paul thought this over quickly. The more he or Betsy protested, the less anyone would believe them anyway. It would be better to confess to a minor thing and let that be believable, than to protest a major one and have everyone be sure that they were lying. He took Betsy's hand as if they had been holding hands before they reached the door.

"Ou - La – La," Anne said with a smile, "What have you two been up to?"

"We just went for a walk," Paul said as casually as possible, "That's all."

"A … walk … , or a … WALK … ?" Anne asked in that universal language that girls use with girls and boys never understand.

"A … WALK … ," Betsy answered with a smile, "We're going to go to the Thanksgiving Dance together."

"Oh you are!" Anne said excitedly looking at Paul as if she expected some sort of confirmation from him.

Paul knew he had to play along, "Yes, we are," he answered although he didn't have the faintest idea what Betsy was talking about.

"Great," Anne exclaimed, "That's great!" She closed her book and hurried off towards the dorm.

They walked into the hallway. Once they were out of earshot of Anne Chastain Paul spoke up, "First of all … what Thanksgiving Dance?" he asked, "And second of all, why is she is so excited?"

"They have a Thanksgiving Ball" Betsy explained. "It's a real big deal."

"They do?" Paul asked a little embarrassed that he didn't know about it. The only thing he remembered from their orientation was that

Freshmen and Sophomores were not allowed to take dates into Hawk's Nest.

"Yes, Paul. It was in the literature on the school. When we got here I checked. Freshman boys don't have to go unless they want to and freshman girls are not allowed to go with older boys but we can go with a freshman boy if we want to."

"Oh. OK. Why is Anne so excited?"

"Because she can let it get around that we are going so she will be able to get the guy she wants to go with to ask her." Betsy got very quiet and looked at Paul.

Paul looked back at Betsy and saw the expectation on her face. It was difficult for him to believe that a girl as nice looking as Betsy would want to go to a dance with him, but he decided to ask anyway. "Would … would … well … ," Paul stammered. He finally got it together and spit it out, "Would you actually like to go to the dance with me?"

"Yes," Betsy answered with a grin, "I would. Thank you. Nice of you to ask."

It turned out to be the best of weeks and the worst of weeks for Paul. Ornith continued to regain his strength and was going to be ready for his lung replacement surgery on schedule. Dr. Mondifort reassured Paul that what sounded difficult and dangerous to him, was routine to them. In self-defense class they had begun to learn a few simple upper cut punches into the stomach region and he continued to excel. His self-defense skills were no longer quite so one-dimensional, and he got to hit ANDY 303 and that helped him work out his frustration. He had a date for a dance that he didn't even know was coming up. Word about that spread at the speed of light, and their classmates interpreted the development to mean the he and Betsy were going together. That wasn't so bad, especially since Jim and Jennifer were cool with the idea. As soon as Jim found out, he asked Jennifer to the Dance, which pleased her no end, but his relationship with everyone else in the freshman class seemed to change overnight. The girls were nicer to him than they had ever been, and the guys rode him harder. They teased him so hard that he lost every single Chorda match – four in all. That was bad. He was so flustered by their constant heckling that by the time the Palacrosse match came around Saturday, he made a lot of mistakes and they lost that as well. By noontime on Saturday Q3 had dropped from second place in the Quadro Bowl to a tie for fourth. That was the worst.

ψ

"Let's go into town," Betsy suggested to Paul on Saturday afternoon. "There is a video arcade there and you need to chill out some."

"You think!" Paul agreed with a laugh.

Just then Jim and Jennifer walked up, and Betsy nudged Paul. Jim and Jennifer were holding hands. Jim shrugged, "It seems as if you started something, Paul. Almost every one of those guys that's been riding you all week has asked someone to the dance."

"Everyone, Paul! It was only a matter of time," agreed Jennifer with a pleasant smile.

"Yeah," Jim agreed, "So … maybe you can settle down now… Huh … Paul?"

"We're going into town," Betsy announced, "There is a video arcade there. You guys want to come?"

"OK," Jennifer said. After the ease with which they had Jumped back from their first trip to town, they had decided that anytime they wanted to go it would be best to just Jump back to that little clearing in the park rather than take the bus. It was an easy walk to the town square from there. They walked into the video arcade and bought their tokens and walked over towards the games.

"Uh … Oh," Jim said under his breath, "Look who's over on that race car game."

Paul recognized Joe Moriarty.

"Nuts," he said under his breath.

"Do you want to leave?" Betsy asked.

"No," Paul answered quickly. "Running from him will only make things worse. Let's just go over to the other side and hope he leaves us alone."

They walked over to some pinball machines. Paul looked at Jim and Jim nodded at the machine. Paul inserted a token while Jim took up a position where he could watch Paul play and at the same time watch anyone who might be walking up from behind. Jim was smooth about it, and the girls did not pick up on what was happening so Paul began playing the game. After two minutes, Jim cleared his throat. Paul got the signal, let the ball go and turned around.

Jim Moriarty walked up, and stood there smirking with his two buddies behind him, "What are you geeks doing here?" he demanded. Other kids began gathering around to watch.

281

"I thought we settled who ... "was" ... and who ... "was not" ... a geek the last time we met," Paul answered evenly.

"Maybe I just had a bad day," Moriarty said with a sneer.

"Maybe," Paul answered agreeably, "The question is: do you want another one?"

The kids who had gathered around snickered.

Moriarty looked around quickly and decided that he had drawn too much attention to do nothing. He threw a punch at Paul's head and Paul blocked it effortlessly. This time Paul knew exactly what to do next. He hit Moriarty with a single uppercut punch in the stomach.

Some things take time to go down. A tree, felled by a woodsman's axe gives up its grace and dignity slowly, it falls almost under protest. There was nothing stately about the fall of Joe Moriarty. He went down like a well-roped steer in a rodeo. Paul looked at Moriarty's two friends and knew he did not want to handle both of them at once. "Which one of you would like to be next?" he asked in a calm but loud voice, figuring that if he said "one" loud enough, the peer pressure of the group would prevent both of them from jumping on him at the same time.

They both held up their hands indicating that they were not going to fight, and helped Joe Moriarty out of the arcade.

"The best thing now," Jim said quickly, "is to just wait here."

"Why?" Jennifer asked.

"We'll explain later," Jim answered.

"How do you know that?" Betsy asked.

"It's a guy thing," Paul answered, "Let's just act natural and play some of these games." After an hour they were out of tokens and decided to leave. They walked out of the arcade and onto the street. As they turned to walk towards the park, a car pulled up to the curb ahead of them a little ways. None of them took any notice of the first two men who got out but when Joe Moriarty got out Jim nudged Paul. "Trouble?"

"Who knows?" Paul answered.

The last man out bore a resemblance to Moriarty. "That must be his father," Jennifer concluded.

"Let's just keep walking," Betsy suggested, "Maybe there won't be any trouble."

"Maybe," Paul said. He didn't sound too convinced.

"You there," the man who resembled Joe Moriarty said with a tone of command. "I want to know why you beat up my son?" he demanded in a menacing tone. The two men who had gotten out of the car first were right behind him.

"I didn't," Paul answered.

Joe Moriarty climbed out of the car. "That's a lie," he accused.

"No, it's not," Paul answered, "You took the first swing at me. I blocked it, punched you in the stomach … once. You went down in a heap. After that you're friends helped you out of the arcade."

"That's a lie, father," Joe Moriarty said, "I have witnesses."

"He has witnesses," his father said, "that's good enough for me. I don't appreciate you calling my son a liar."

"Then maybe he shouldn't be one," Betsy interjected defensively before either Jim, or Paul could stop her. "We have witnesses too. A whole arcade full."

John Moriarty glared at her. "Are you the kids who have come to that meadow behind my mill?" he demanded.

"Yes," Paul answered, "We are."

"I don't want you back there anymore."

"It's part of a national park," Betsy objected, "You have no right to tell us we can't go there if we want."

"I'll decide what rights I have and what rights I don't have, young lady," John Moriarty said with a sneer, and Paul realized where Joe's sneer came from. "And I think my boys here will just teach you a couple of lessons, one to stay out of that meadow, and two, to leave any place my son happens to be." The two men stepped around the Moriartys and advanced towards Paul.

Suddenly a person stepped out of an ally in between the two groups. "Is there a problem here?" the distinctive voice of Professor Altracia Galvyndor asked. She was dressed in street clothes.

"It's none of your business, lady," the older Moriarty growled.

"I'll decide what is and is not my business, thank you," she answered and held up what was obviously a Motorola hand held tape recorder, "Didn't you just say something like that a second ago?"

"I'll take that tape lady," Moriarty demanded.

"No," Professor Galvyndor said with a chuckle that bordered on an outright laugh, "I don't think you will."

One of the thugs approached and drew back his hand to slap her. Before he could she reached up and grabbed him by the windpipe with the thumb and forefinger of her right hand. "I don't want to hurt you," she said with a calm and even tone to her voice, "But I can, and if you insist on it, I will." She pushed back and the man fell to the ground clutching his throat. She turned to Moriarty, "The testimony of your son's friends may well be good enough for you, but it would not be good enough for any court, and it is not good enough for me. This young lady's point is a good one," she said indicating Betsy, "Why don't we go in and question the arcade's employees as to the facts?"

The younger Moriarty spoke up immediately, "They're just dweebs, father, working for half what you pay the janitors in the mill. Why would you believe them?"

"Why indeed?" the professor said addressing the younger Moriarty, "Perhaps it would be because they have no reason to lie."

"Come on, son." the elder Moriarty said. He knew quite well that his son was lying. He had known it all along. For him it was not an issue about truth; it was about power, and in his mind power issues always prevailed. "We'll let this rest for the time being." The four of them got in their car and drove away, but as they reached the car Mr. Moriarty whispered into his son's ear for a second, and the boy got a wicked grin on his face as he climbed in. None of the rest of them knew that he had just told his son about the attack dogs that were now in a kennel on the far side of the meadow.

Both Paul and Betsy noticed the exchange between the Moriartys, but were too far away to hear the words.

Paul turned to the professor and was about to ask a question but she held up her hand in a stop signal. "It is somewhat normal for there to be friction between the students who attend our school and the people of their same age in this town. You are part of a private school after all, and they are not. For this reason, there is always one faculty member aware of what is going on whenever any of our students might be here. There will come a time when you will be prepared to handle a group of men like that. This is what your self-defense classes are about, but that will take several years and in the intervening interval, it is best for us to be prepared."

"Aware?" Jim asked, "How?"

"We have monitors here and there." The Professor looked at Paul, "We have several in that arcade. We know you did not pick the fight, or throw the first punch, and we know you did not beat that boy up. We do not tolerate bullies and we know that none of you are. In fact, Paul, you did nothing more than what was necessary to defend yourself. Now, I think we can safely Jump back to the school from back in this alley here."

ψ

Georaldon sat at the dining room table looking over Paul's homework. "It looks like you are keeping up with your projects. I like the way you are knocking them off one at a time," he announced as he finished his inspection, "Well done!"

"Yes, Paul, very well done," Baralicia agreed. "Now we need to talk for a minute about something else."

"What's that?"

"Rules!" Georaldon answered with a nod and a smile.

"Rules?"

"Yes," Baralicia smiled, "Rules for dating girls."

"Rules for dating girls?" Paul exclaimed.

"You didn't think there wouldn't be any rules, did you?" Baralicia asked.

"Well … well … I hadn't thought about it," he stammered.

"What you mean is that you didn't know … we … knew," Baralicia laughed, and then reached out and touched Paul on the arm. "It's OK, Paul, it really is. Betsy has to select an evening gown. That takes time and help from her sponsors, so she told them you had asked her … which is what she is supposed to do … they told us which is what they're supposed to do … and that is how we know. It's perfectly natural to be interested in girls at your age."

"She has to get an evening gown?"

"Yes," Baralicia answered.

"Is that a big deal?"

"Yes," Baralicia answered again. Georaldon just smiled.

"I didn't know … " Paul said, his words trailing off.

"It's OK, Paul," Georaldon said, "There are very few things girls like to do more than shop for dresses like that."

"Oh," Paul said simply although he didn't understand. He didn't know that something as simple as a dance could be this complicated. "What about her sponsors?"

"There is nothing they would rather do either, or at least the women anyway," Baralicia assured him with a coy little smile tossed in Georaldon's direction.

"Why?" Paul asked.

"Have you ever seen a girl in an evening gown, Paul?" Baralicia asked giving Georaldon a knowing nod, "I don't mean on TV, but a real girl … one who likes you a lot … standing there right in front of you?"

"Well ... No ..."

"Right," Georaldon said quickly, "Believe me ... you will understand what all the trouble is about when you see Betsy. You really will. Now ... back to the rules. This is really pretty simple," he continued, "Betsy is considered an Atlantan girl. Just like you are considered an Atlantan boy, so the same rules that apply to children born down here apply to you as well. We make no distinctions, but we are very serious as to how Atlantan girls are treated."

"OK," Paul said as he realized that he was not in any trouble, and there was nothing wrong as far as either Baralicia or Georaldon were concerned.

"Here," Georaldon said handing Paul a plasticized card, "This will explain everything, but the principal thing for freshman and sophomores is that you are not allowed to go out on unsupervised dates. You can go to any school function. You can go to any community function. We have a teen park. You can go there. It has a teen dance club called Dazzle, a game arcade, several restaurants, and a few other things. You can go there anytime you want, but that's all. You just can't go out on your own by yourselves. Not as freshmen or sophomores. You'll get more flexibility as juniors and more yet as seniors. There's more. It's all on the card."

Paul looked at the card. Across the top it said:

Dating Rules for Teenagers

"We've found that everything is much simpler if all kids of the same age have the same rules," Georaldon explained. "One set of Atlantan parents does not have one set of rules while a different set has another. This way there are no debates. There are no challenges. There are no misunderstandings. The boundaries are the same for all of you. Believe me, it … is … better this way. Everything is all explained there."

"By the way," Baralicia said in an encouraging tone, "Weekend after next we have a Fall Music Festival down here. There is a lot of great music, and also a lot of dancing."

"Great food, too," Georaldon interjected.

"The dances are simple," Baralicia continued, "most of them anyway, and it's a lot of fun, especially if you have a date."

ψ

Thoraldon Flyndor stood before the class on The History of Atlantis. From time to time, guest lecturers were brought in to help bring the history they were studying alive. "We had these stocks of ancient weapons," he began, "Artifacts from the time when our technology was where Earthantis's is now. No one had used these weapons in a long time. I was fourteen and wanted to see if they would still work. It had been thousands of years since anyone had fired one, so I took one of the handguns and Jumped into a clearing in the middle of a forest. "I was young and arrogant," he smiled ruefully. "I thought the clearing would be vacant so I didn't bother to Cloak. I was wrong. There was a Viking religious ceremony in progress, and I found myself in the middle of it. I was attacked by a man who was less than ten feet away from me. He had a

289

war axe and could have easily killed me, uniform or not. The only thing I had to defend myself with was the handgun. Before I realized what I had done, I had raised the gun and shot this man. Another man standing about twenty feet away, placed an arrow in his bow and was preparing to shoot it at me. My uniform would have protected me from the arrow, but I didn't have time to think it through. Things were happening too fast for thinking. I shot him too. After that they all fell down on their knees and worshiped me as a God. I tried to get them to stop. I thumped my chest and said my name. I said I was from Aasgard. That is the name of our city in Scandinavia. All they understood was my name was Thor and that I was from a place called Aasgard."

He hung his head briefly before going on. "I wish I could tell you how much I regret that my arrogance cost the lives of those men, but there are no words to convey those feelings. Once it was done, there was no way to go back and do it over again." He paused again to collect himself, and then continued. "In any event, after they had got my name and Aasgard, a priest said something to me in a language I did not understand. So I repeated my name and that I was from Aasgard. They had no framework in which to understand a handgun. They equated the sound of the shot to the sound of a hammer striking an anvil. This is where the mythology of Thor and his hammer that could kill came from. The Nordic legends of Aasgard, the home of the Gods also grew from there."

Professor Flyndor stood then, and their visitor took a chair. "Now class," she said clearly, "The principal reason we study history is not to learn a bunch of facts and dates. There would not be much point in that. We learn history to understand the lessons of the past and that is a different thing entirely. Some of those lessons are positive, and we can learn what "to" do. Some of them are negative and we can learn what "not to" do. It is not sufficient to learn "what" happened, and "when" it happened. Far more important is to understand "why" it happened. I want a ten-page project paper from you on the "whys" of Thoraldon's situation, and what lessons you might learn that apply to your lives today. Yes," she said nodding and answering the unasked question, "that is what I want from you."

"Another project paper!" Betsy complained as they left class and returned to the dorm, "Another ten page project paper."

"Yeah," Jim said shaking his head, "And it isn't as if we don't have enough to do already. Open." he said and the door to their suite opened. "We'll see you girls at dinner."

William came running out and jumped up into Paul's arms. "Ornith is feeling a lot better, Paul," he said in excitement. "He's even been flying a little more than yesterday."

"Did he fly too much?" Paul asked quickly, a note of concern in his voice.

"I don't think so," William answered, "Just more than yesterday."

Paul walked quickly into his bedroom with the little bear still in his arms. Ornith's lung replacement operation had been a complete success. He was gaining strength quickly and Dr. Moriarty had said he could spend the last three days of his recuperation with Paul up at the school. "No flying for the first day, Paul," she had instructed, "For the second day, just a little. Limited flying on the third day, but very limited. After that he needs to work himself up to full strength. That should take about a week." Today was the third day. Paul looked at Ornith with concern that he had overdone it. Ornith was propped up in his bed against a pillow reading a small book.

"Hi, Paul," Ornith said, and started to get up.

"No, Ornith," Paul said quickly sitting on the bed, 'I'll come to you." He bent over and rubbed noses with the little Pix and felt the same sort of warming sensation that he had the first time. During the early days of Ornith's injury, there had been very little of that. Now it was becoming much more of a two-way thing again. "How are you doing?"

"Pretty good," Ornith answered, "I wish I were stronger."

"You will be … you will be," Paul encouraged, "You just need to be careful."

"I watch him pretty close," William said, hopping onto the bed next to Ornith and patting him gently on the top of his head. As bears went he was rather small, but he was he as a good deal larger than Ornith.

"Good," Paul said to William and then turned his attention back to Ornith, "Are you up to going to the dining hall for dinner tonight?" Paul asked. "I think those Cornish Game Hens you like so much will be available."

"Oh yes," Ornith said happily. "I'd like that." He knew that Dr. Mondifort had forbidden him to do that for the first two days, but after that she had said it would be up to Paul.

Once dinner was over and he had taken Ornith back to bed, Paul decided that he could not put off talking to Betsy any longer. He knew exactly where he to find her as he walked up the stairs to the second floor of the balcony overlooking Fellowship Hall. It was her favorite place to study. If he was going to ask her to the Fall Music Festival at all, he needed to go ahead and do it. He wondered if girls knew how hard it was to ask them out, and before he could answer his question he saw Betsy sitting at a table surrounded by books. He walked over and sat down, "How's it going?"

"Nuts … completely nuts … is how it is going," she complained, "I don't see how they expect us to do all of this work. The pace in Earthantan Studies is relentless and then there are all of these project papers on top of that. Aren't you going crazy too?"

"Not really," Paul answered with a shrug of his shoulders.

"How do you do it then?" Betsy asked. "I mean … your project papers are on time. The professors compliment you on them so I know you're doing a good job. How do you do all that without going crazy?"

"It's a couple tricks I learned from Georaldon," Paul replied. "Ten minutes a day spent organizing your work will save you at least an hour … get all the day to day stuff we get in Earthantan Studies out of the way first and then focus on one major project at a time. Just knock it out and then go on to the next one."

"That's what my sponsors said too," Betsy agreed sheepishly.

"So, aren't you doing it?"

"Well, it's just that all of this is a little intimidating. If a Professor assigns something and I'm not working it I feel … "

"Guilty?"

"Yeah."

"Don't Betsy," Paul said gently, "You don't need to feel guilty. I tried this "one major project at a time" idea and it works. It takes less time to concentrate on one thing and finish it and then move to the next, than it does just bouncing around. It's how I get my projects in on time. I don't feel guilty because I have a plan as to when I'm going to start on each project."

"Oh," she said. "Well ... OK. That makes sense. I'll give it a try."

"Good," Paul said and then hemmed and hawed around for a second. In spite of the fact that the whole school thought he had asked Betsy to the Thanksgiving Ball, it was really the other way around. He knew it and he knew she knew it. They'd had to do something about Anne Chastain, and the Dance was the natural thing. The question was: would she like him to ask her to something else? Or was that pushing his luck? That was the question, and he just did not know the answer.

Betsy watched him struggle, and had a good idea what the struggle was about. Every girl in school knew the Fall Music Festival was coming up, and that to go you were supposed to have a date, but none of the girls had been asked yet. None of them. They were all waiting and hoping, but no one had been asked. She wondered why it was so hard for boys to ask girls out.

Finally, Paul decided that waiting was not going to make it any easier and that he needed to just plunge ahead. "That's good. Because they are having a Fall Music Festival down in Co-re-alis this weekend. It sounds like a lot of fun. According to Baralicia, there is a lot of dancing and it's more fun if you have a date. She says the dances are easy to learn ... so ... maybe we could ... check it out ... together?"

"OK," Betsy answered with a smile. "Is this like a date?"

Paul looked at the expectant gleam in her eyes, and smiled. He didn't know much about girls but he was clearly on solid ground. "Yes." He answered.

"Good. I think it will be lots of fun." She looked at him coyly, like Baralicia did with Georaldon sometimes, "Does this mean that what they are saying about us is true?" she asked.

"Depends on what they are saying, I guess," Paul answered.

"You know … about us "going" together. Are we?"

"Oh …" Paul answered, "Well … I'd like that if you'd like it."

"I would," she answered, "I would like that very much."

ψ

Professor Galvyndor walked into class and tried not to notice the members of Q3 who were sitting together. It was quite natural for them to feel grateful right now, but gratitude had always made her feel uncomfortable. "OK, class," she began quickly, "You have all been up in a flitter. Is that correct?"

She looked around the room and no one was saying that they hadn't. "So let's examine what you know. You know that we have a device called a Gravitational Nullification System. It is what floats the del droids. We abbreviate that by calling it a G-N System, but what you know does not satisfactorily explain how the flitter or a del droid works. How does it rise? How does it get its forward momentum? Any ideas? Anne? What about you? Any ideas?"

"No, Professor," she admitted reluctantly.

"OK. Let me begin by explaining what a force vector is." Behind her a red glowing arrow appeared. It was pointed straight down. "Let us say that this arrow represents a force. Let us say further that the longer the arrow the greater the force is." Just then the arrow got longer. So the arrow now would represent a force greater than it did a moment ago. If you have an object that weighs ten kilograms, that means that the force of gravity that is attracting it is a ten-kilogram force. In order to make it float that force has to be opposed by a ten kilogram force in the opposite direction."

A second arrow appeared. It was of the same length as the first only it was pointed straight up and joined at the tail with the arrow pointed down. Where the two arrows met was a small ball to tell where one arrow stopped and the other started.

"These arrows represent two force vectors. The one pointing down we will call the gravitational force vector. The one pointing up we will call the opposing force vector. They are each acting in opposite directions," the Professor continued, "When perfectly balanced as we see here, an object will float." She looked around the class to see if everyone was following her.

"So. What will happen if the opposing force vector is increased?" The arrow pointing upwards grew longer all by itself in response to her voice. Betsy raised her hand and Professor Galvyndor pointed to her.

"It will go up."

"Correct. Now, let's angle this opposing force vector." The arrow pointing up leaned away from the professor. "What is going to happen now?"

Paul's hand shot up, and she pointed to him.

"It's going to move forward," he answered, "And it might move up too."

"Good, Paul, but how can you tell whether it will just move forward, or if it will also go up?"

No one raised a hand to answer.

Just then the opposing force vector began to pulse on and off and it was joined by two blue arrows. Both had their tails connected to the ball, but one went straight out and the other went straight up. "These blue arrows are called components. If you look carefully at the opposing force vector, you will notice that the amount that it leans forward is the same length that the horizontal arrow extends out. It is the horizontal component. Same with the vertical blue arrow. It extends upwards the same amount that the opposing force vector does. It is the vertical component. Notice please that the vertical component is the same length as the gravitational force vector. In this instance the object would float in the vertical plane and accelerate in the horizontal plane."

She looked around the room and saw that everyone was following her. "The length of the horizontal component determines how fast the object will accelerate. Both flitters and del droids have only one G-N System, but it can be varied in intensity, and angle."

Just then the opposing force vector angled over more and increased in length. The vertical component arrow remained the same, but the horizontal arrow was much longer. "In this configuration, the object will accelerate much faster. We create motion in any particular direction by altering the angle of the G-N System and increasing the intensity so the vertical component is still sufficient to oppose the force of gravity."

ψ

LeRoi Jackson sat across one of the Chorda tables from Paul. They were well into their match, and LeRoi was winning.

"So," he asked carefully, "Is it true about you and Betsy?"

"About us going together?" Paul asked as innocently as he could manage. "I thought it was all over the school."

"Well," LeRoi replied, "it is, but girls will say anything when it comes to things like that. That does not necessarily make it true. None of the guys have heard it from you."

"So," Paul answered as he saw an opportunity to take one of LeRoi's colonels and even up the game, "You thought you'd ask."

"Yeah," LeRoi nodded. "I'm not one for rumors."

"It's true," Paul said simply. "We're going together."

LeRoi looked at Paul even though it took time off of his clock. "Do you think it is OK? You know … with the Atlantans?"

"We're Atlantans too, LeRoi," Paul reminded his opponent, "Besides they have these rules for dating girls."

"They do?"

"Yeah. Have you seen your sponsors since you asked Beth to the Thanksgiving Ball?"

"No. I'm supposed to see them this Friday. We've been communicating by video comm, but I haven't been done since our first

298

trip."

"Well, they have these rule cards that tell you all about it. You get them from your sponsors. Jim got one from his and I'm sure you can get one from yours, but here, you can borrow mine," Paul said as he fumbled around and got it out of his pouch.

"Betsy and I have made no effort to hide anything, and we are staying within the rules for dating. No one has said anything to us and our sponsors are supportive."

"Good!" LeRoi responded as he looked at the card, "Because I plan on asking Beth today."

Chapter Fifteen

A Fall Festival

Paul and Betsy were walking hand in hand towards the portal in the greenhouse, but they were not the first ones there. Once again, they had broken the ice. About an hour after word had gotten around that the two of them were not only going down to the festival together, but were "going together" nearly everyone had a date. Jim had asked Jennifer almost immediately, and after that it had been like dominoes. There were four couples ahead of them at the portal. Asking first had nothing to do with going down first. The nice thing about the portal, they had learned, was that it let you go down together.

When it came their turn, they stepped into the portal and the colors swirled around both of them. They could see each other in the midst of it all, and when they found themselves in the middle of the civic building in Co-re-alis, still hand in hand, they just smiled and walked towards the exit.

"Sweet!" Paul said.

"Totally," Betsy agreed and seconds later they were out into Co-re-alis. Paul had figured that there would be signs to the festival, but he was mistaken. None were needed. Co-re-alis was decked out for a party in all directions as far as either of them could see. Ribbons had been draped from the Street lamps, and there were banners announcing different musical concerts almost everywhere you looked. They walked towards one of the amphitheaters and noticed a refreshment stand with punch and some sort of sausages.

"Would you like something?" Paul asked.

"Sure," Betsy answered, and they walked over to the refreshment stand.

"Ah," the man tending the stand said with an air of recognition, "Would you be the Paul Andrews I have heard so much about?" There was a faintly British accent to his words.

"You've been hearing about me?" Paul asked.

"Aye. That I have. There is a real quiet word out on you. Real quiet ... mind you. Not a lot of people know what you did, but a well-connected Innkeeper hears about most everything. Word is that you've got nerves of steel. Here, let me get you two some cider." He winked, "Of course I can't give you guys the hard stuff. Not at your age, but I actually prefer the non-alcoholic cider anyway." He took a wooden mug and ladled it full of cider from one of the two tubs and handed it to Betsy. He took another mug and filled it for Paul. "And who's the pretty lassie?" he asked.

"Betsy Saunders," she answered, extending her hand to shake his.

Instead he took her hand and brought it up slightly as he bent forward and kissed it lightly. "Well, Miss Betsy," he said, "It is my pleasure to meet you. Angus Mac Tavish is my name."

"Angus Mac Tavish?" Paul asked as he reached out to shake hands with the man. "That does not sound Atlantan."

"That's 'cause it's not. It's a Scottish name. I'm a Scotsman."

"You're a Scotsman?" both Betsy and Paul exclaimed.

"Aye ... that I am. Would you care for a banger to go with your cider?"

"A banger?" Paul asked.

"Aye ... you don't know about bangers, then, do you?"

"No. I never heard of a banger," Paul admitted.

"Well then, we shall have to do something about that now, won't we?" He reached over and picked up a wooden platter and a pair of tongs. He snatched one of the sausages off of the grill and placed it on a bun and handed the platter to Betsy. "Sorry there, my little lassie, but all the food at these festivals is finger food. Normally you'd eat bangers with mashed potatoes, but that means knives and forks so for now a bun will have to do." Several seconds later he had one in Paul's hands as well. "Bangers are the best sausages in the world if you ask me," Angus said, "'course they're Scottish and that would be why. If you'd like to try them the way I eat 'em, you won't be wanting any condiments. Lots of people put mustard on them like a hot dog, but some things aren't improved with all that stuff. Bangers 're one of 'em if you ask me."

Paul reached down, picked his up and took a bite like the Scotsman suggested, "Umm ... this is good," he exclaimed. He washed it down with a swallow of the cider. The banger was excellent but the cider was by far the best he'd ever tasted. "Betsy, you've got to try the cider."

Angus Mac Tavish beamed as he watched the two of them go from tasting the food tentatively to wolfing it down ravenously.

"So how did a Scotsman get here anyway?" Betsy asked, after she had finished.

"Now, there's a very long story," he answered. "As it happened ... a couple of hundred years ago, I was working my farm. North and a little west of Peterhead it was. Peterhead's on the East coast of Scotland, mind ya. I was building a rock wall to keep in the sheep, and well, I noticed some things that just didn't seem to add up. Little things. People strolling about that weren't from the clan ... that was one thing. Not much of that going on in Scotland back then, and there were strange lights in the sky now and then. Then one day I caught a glimpse of a flitter. Course I didn't know what it was, but it sure got my curiosity up. I had to know what was going on. I eventually tracked them to their portal pole. Took me the best part of two years, it did. The portal turned out to be out in the middle of a lake that bordered my farm. I accosted one of them on his way back in. He took me down, and I sort of got adopted. From Avalon, their city under Scotland, he was."

"Avalon?" Betsy exclaimed, "Isn't that where Merlin the magician was from?"

"Not ... was," Angus answered, "... Is! Merlin is a member of the High Council. You'll meet him one day."

Before either of them could react to that statement, several elves mounted the stage of the amphitheater and began tuning up their instruments. In front of the stage was an area that had been cleared in a circle.

"You'll be wanting to go over to that instruction booth over there, now," he said pointing at a booth that bordered the cleared circle, "That's the dance circle in the middle. They'll show you how to dance a proper jig in that booth right there next to the circle. Aye ... it's a rollicking good fiddle they play and once you hear 'em you'll be wanting to dance a Highland Fling. They'll show you. It's easy to learn."

Paul and Betsy walked over to the booth and began what turned out to be an afternoon filled with more fun than either of them had ever known. They spent the afternoon going from amphitheater to amphitheater, learning the different dances and then sampling the food that went with the areas where the dances had originated. There were Greek folk dances and gyros, Country and Western line dances and barbeque, Cajun zaidaco and shrimp etoufee, German polkas knockwurst, and the list went on. Only a few dances proved to be too hard to catch on to quickly. They would dance for a while and then go and sit for a while until someone would come up with a laugh and drag them back into the dance circle again.

They were sitting at a table eating Bavarian rouladen and resting from the Bavarian folk dances. "Want to go back and do that Highland Fling again?" Betsy asked.

"Yeah," Paul answered quickly. "We can get some more of that cider, too."

They were about to head back to where they had started when suddenly it got quiet at their venue. The dance floor emptied and a couple took the center, wearing masks. They proceeded to dance what could only be described as a combination of ballet and Bavarian folk dancing set to a fast beat rhythm.

"Have you ever seen anyone dance like that?" Betsy asked as the couple finished.

"No ... not ever," Paul answered honestly.

The couple removed their masks. It was Baralicia and Georaldon, and Paul's mouth fell open in astonishment.

They came over and Baralicia smiled at Paul as he introduced Betsy, "You didn't know did you?" she said as she shook hands with Betsy.

"Know what?" Paul asked.

"We are this year's Co-re-alis Dance Champions."

"No," Paul answered, "I didn't know."

"Yes," Georaldon grinned, "Dance is as big a sport for us as Palacrosse. All of these festivals have dance competitions, and points are awarded. Every year an annual winning couple is crowned at the Winter Festival."

"And we won last year," Baralicia concluded proudly.

"Why did you wear masks?" Betsy asked.

"Because it takes the personalities out of the judging," Georaldon answered, "The judges never know for sure who you are."

"Were you competing just then?" Paul asked.

"Oh, yes," Baralicia laughed. "We will dance a total of ten different competitive dances today. That one was number six. They are all judged."

"It was the most beautiful thing I ever saw," Betsy said, still in awe.

"By the way," Paul interjected, "What is going on with this Angus Mac Tavish?"

"You guys met Angus?" Georaldon asked with a chuckle.

"Yeah, he had the first refreshment stand coming in."

"He did? We haven't gotten that far yet," Baralicia said licking her lips. "His apple cider is the absolute best."

"His bangers aren't bad either," Georaldon added, "He didn't give you the hard stuff did he?"

"No," Paul answered. "He winked and said we couldn't have that until we got older."

"Good," Baralicia said with a nod, "We separate intoxicants into two categories. You are allowed to have beers, hard ciders and wines once you have graduated from high school. The harder stuff like whisky you are not allowed to have until you're twenty-one."

"He said he is ... or was ... a Scotsman," Paul said.

"Yes and proud of it too."

"How does that happen," Betsy asked.

"Over the years several thousand Earthantan people have come into contact with us in a ways where we could not disguise our identities. Honestly, most of them figured it out and came looking for us. Those who look hard enough usually find what they seek. When that happens we always give those people the opportunity to join us."

"Do any refuse?"

"Well, they could," Georaldon said, "All that would happen is that we would do a mind erase. It's painless. Angus would have woken up back on his farm after a long nap. But ... for the most part ... no ... I only know of one or two who have chosen not to join with us."

"He knows about the Stack," Betsy announced, "Angus Mac Tavish I mean."

"Of course he does," Georaldon answered, "The orderly that brought you out after Ornith's surgery is his wife. You don't have to worry about Angus. There is no such thing as a secret that is not safe with him."

"He's married to an Atlantan?"

"Yeah, for about a hundred and fifty years now," Georaldon answered.

"People from Earthantis and Atlantans can intermarry?" Betsy asked.

"Yes," Baralicia said simply but in a fashion that indicated that this was a long subject. Just then the elves at a nearby venue began playing Cajun zaidaco. "Come on," Baralicia said taking Paul's hand, as Georaldon grabbed Betsy's, "We'll show you guys how to really lay one down."

Baralicia and Georaldon worked with Paul and Betsy and showed them a number of steps that were more advanced than what was taught in the instruction booths. The elves caught on immediately and provided a more intricate beat, and the other dancers in the circle gave them plenty of room. When they were finished, both Betsy and Paul were breathless … thrilled … but breathless just the same. Neither Baralicia nor Georaldon were even breathing hard.

"Let's get a snack," Baralicia suggested, and the four of them went over to a refreshment booth nearby. A man there heaped up platters of Cajun shrimp for them.

"Umm … good stuff," Georaldon said with his mouth half full, "Well … we'll leave you with that for now. Do you want to catch up with us later?"

"Sure," Paul answered.

"How about at the Highland Fling at ten o'clock? We can get

some of Mac Tavish's cider."

"Great!" Paul agreed.

As Baralicia and Georaldon disappeared into the swirling crowd, Betsy spoke up, "I hope they show us more dance steps."

"Me too!" Paul said with a nod, "I had no idea that dancing like this could be so much fun."

Just then some of the dancers pulled them back into the zaidaco circle.

ψ

The four members of Q3 approached the Palacrosse field for the opening match of the Thanksgiving Palacrosse Tournament. They were beginning this set of matches in fourth place in the Quadro cup standings, but over the seven-day holiday, which included both a Palacrosse tournament, and a Chorda tournament, they hoped to move up.

They had drawn Q6, the first team they had ever played in Palacrosse and they were tied with them for fourth place. Whoever won would move in sole possession of fourth, and the other team would drop back to fifth. That was not the way Paul wanted to start the tournament and all three of his friends felt the same way.

The whistle sounded, and they all jumped into the field. The coach tossed in the Wobble, and the game was on.

The wobble passed near Jim who tried to pass it to Betsy, but it was intercepted by a Q6 member who hit it in the general direction of the Q3 goal, but it missed, and ricocheted off of the back wall. Jennifer intercepted it and tried to get it out past the attacking Q6'ers. Her shot passed too near another of the Q6'ers and she hit it straight at Q3's goal but it didn't have enough spin and curved off at the last second and missed. Jennifer had bounded back toward their goal and picked up the wobble as it caromed off of the back and managed to hit it out past the three Q6'ers who were clustered near Q3's goal. Betsy got it from there and passed it to Paul. The last Q6'er was maneuvering to intercept, and Paul knew that he only had an instant to get a shot off at their goal. He hit it well but missed. The wobble bounced off of the back and came out near the Q6'er. He hit it forward and got it to a team member. The Q6'er hit the wobble at Q3's goal again, and this time it went through.

Q6: 1, Q3: 0

Paul looked at his teammates. It was time to bear down. Jim bounded off of the wall, and managed to intercept the wobble as it ricocheted around the field. He hit it gently towards Betsy. A Q6'er bounded towards Betsy, but before he could get there, she passed the wobble over his head to Paul. Paul deadened the wobble. He saw that Jennifer was about to come open so he hit it to where she would be. Jennifer made a nice pass to Jim, who got the wobble to Paul. Paul got it to Betsy. Betsy hit the wobble to Jennifer, and she hit it to Paul, and he hit the wobble through the goal.

Q6: 1, Q3: 1

The game seesawed back and forth through the rest of the first period, and into the second. Each time one team got into a position for a shot, someone from the other team managed to block it. Neither team got a good shot on their opponent's goal for the remainder of the first period, but right after the break, Q3 got a score, followed almost immediately by another score from Q6 and that's how the second period ended.

Q6: 2, Q3: 2

The bell for the third period sounded, and Paul moved to the middle with Betsy, Jim moved back to protect their goal, and Jennifer moved towards Q6's goal. The coach threw in the wobble, and the Q6'ers got into position for the first hit. The girl took a shot on goal from the middle on the court. She hit a nice shot with plenty of spin so the wobble flew in a nice smooth trajectory, but her shot was way off the mark, and Jim was waiting. He intercepted it, deadened it, and passed it to Betsy, who did the same thing, passing the wobble to Paul. Paul also deadened it, allowing Jim time to move to the middle and Betsy time to move forward. Paul didn't have a clear pass to Betsy. A Q6'er was in the way, so he passed the wobble back to Jim. Jim deadened it, and then passed it to Betsy, just barely getting it past a bounding Q6'er, but she got the wobble and deadened it. There was a Q6'er bounding to intercept the shot where he thought she was going to hit it, so she took her time. Once the Q6'er had floated clear, she passed it to Jennifer. Jennifer also deadened it, took careful aim and hit it directly through the center of the goal.

Q6: 2, Q3: 3

The Q6 team tried hard to rally, but their play was not well organized. They hit a number of shots in the general direction of Q3's goal but none of them went through.

Finally a Q6'er got into a position to get off a good shot. He had deadened the wobble and was about fifteen feet from Q3's goal. Betsy bounded to intercept from behind and stole the wobble before he could hit

310

it. She had nowhere left to go, and was about to have to somersault to bound off of the wall. It was practically impossible to hit the wobble while you were trying to do that, let alone accurately, so she did the only thing she could. She didn't somersault and took the time to get off a good pass to Jim and then crashed headlong into the field wall.

Jim bounded off of the wall, and managed to reach Betsy's pass. He hit it towards Jennifer who had come back towards the middle. One of the Q6'ers bounded towards Jennifer, but before he could get there, she passed the wobble, below him to Paul. Paul deadened the wobble and saw that Betsy had recovered from crashing into the field. She was OK, and had moved forward. Paul passed it on to her, and began trying to move towards the other team's goal. Betsy deadened the wobble and played for time. She just sat there and floated with the wobble while Jennifer and Jim tried to get into a clear position. One of the Q6 girls bounded directly at Betsy, intending to break up the stall and make her do something and Betsy, passed the wobble to Jim before the Q6 girl got there. Jim saw that Paul was only one bound out of the range they had practiced. He hit the wobble to Jennifer, and Jennifer passed it to Paul who was actually closer than they had practiced. He hit the wobble hard so that there would be little arch to its travel, and it went through the goal.

Q3 4, Q6 2.

There was still two minutes remaining. Q6 tried as hard as they could, but the last shot they were able to get off went wide to the right as time expired. The match ended up 4 to 2. Q3 had won its first Palacrosse match of the Thanksgiving Tournament and had moved up in the standings.

As they were walking away from the court, Paul grinned at Betsy, "You're going to learn to hate playing Q6."

"Why's that?"

"Last time we played them you went crashing into the field wall too."

"Oh, yeah. I forgot," she said.

"I was glad to see you were OK." He looked at everyone and nodded. "That was the best Palacrosse game we've played yet," Paul commented. "I hope we do as well at Chorda."

ψ

Paul sat facing his first opponent in the Thanksgiving Chorda Tournament. He was playing Anne Chastain. So far, he had never beaten her, but things were looking up in this match. For one thing, Anne was a bit little gushy about Carl and the fun they'd had at the Fall Music Festival and that affected her concentration. Not only that, she was a little dizzy with all of her plans for the upcoming dance. The event would be in two days and she could think of little else, and Paul was ahead as a result. At the moment he had taken two more of her power pieces than she had of his and although there were many traps she could lay to even the score, the odds now favored him as long as he didn't screw up.

"Chorda," Paul said as he moved his colonel into a position to attack her general.

"Darn," she said. There was only one piece she could use to block

312

Paul's attack. She moved her 1ˢᵗ Lieutenant into a position to block Paul's colonel. Four moves later there was nothing she could do and Paul took her general.

"Nice game," she said with a gracious smile.

"Thanks," Paul replied.

"Are you guys planning to go out anywhere after the dance?" she asked.

Paul nodded. Freshmen and sophomores were not allowed to take dates into Hawk's Nest but they could go down to Co-re-alis. "Yes. Betsy doesn't know it yet, but we are going down to Co-re-alis … to a park for teenagers called Hangin' In.

"Are you really?" Anne said wistfully. "It isn't against the rules is it?"

"No." Paul explained, "Baralicia told me all about it. Hangin' In is a specific area of Co-re-alis that freshmen and sophomores are allowed to go without active adult supervision. It's on the Rules Card. It's an area just for teenagers. I'm taking her to one of the restaurants there. It's called Mader's. There is also another one but I don't know its name. They also have a teen club called Dazzle and a nice park. It is a well-lit park where we can go for a walk. Freshmen aren't allowed anywhere else. Sophomores have a part of the town directly surrounding Hangin' In that they can roam around in. It is all chaperoned by the Atlantans, but I understand that they are very unobtrusive about it. They sort of pay attention to what is going on without butting in."

"They have all of that just for us?" Anne asked.

"No, it's for their teenagers too," Paul answered.

313

"Oh," she replied, "How many of us are going down?"

"Jim and Jennifer, and Betsy and I for sure," Paul answered, "I'm not sure about anyone else.

Anne sighed, and then looked at Paul. "Would you say something to Carl?"

"Whoa … Let me get this straight," Paul said in mock shock, "You want me to tell your boyfriend where you want him to take you?"

"Please, Paul," she asked him sweetly, "There are still two days until the dance, and that should be enough time."

"Sure," Paul answered with a shrug and a smile, "Glad to help."

When the evening's points were tallied, only Betsy had lost. Q8, the team in third, had started three points ahead, but they had lost three out of four. Q3 was now only one point behind them. Q5 was still five points ahead.

The next two days resulted in a blur of activity. Q3 had lost its second Palacrosse match to Q5, although it had been pretty close, but Q8 had lost to Q6, so the standings had remained the same. The Chorda matches of the previous evening had resulted in Q3 going two for four, but so had Q8. Again no change in the standings.

Then had come the last Palacrosse match. Q3 and Q8 had drawn each other and it turned out to be a hard fought match, but Q3 won in the end. They were now tied with Q8 for third, but the tie was broken that evening in the Chorda matches. Q3 went four for four, while Q8 went two for four. The tournaments were over. Q3 had gained ground and was now is second place, a total of six behind Q5. It was now time for the Ball.

ψ

Jim and Paul sat waiting out in the common area. Both of the girls' women sponsors were in their suite helping them get ready.

"You'd think with all of that help they could be on time," Jim complained, and looked at his watch for the tenth time in five minutes. The Ball had begun ten minutes ago.

"Girls are never on time for this sort of thing," Paul said finally. "My mother isn't, and my sister certainly isn't."

"Yeah, but what would happen if her date didn't show up on time?"

"That's different."

"Why different?"

"I don't know," Paul answered, "It's a girl thing."

"Yeah ... well ... being on time is a guy thing."

"OK," Paul said with a laugh, "so next time ask a guy." Just then the door to the girls' suite opened, and the sponsors came out first. Next out was Betsy, and as she came into the Common Area Paul rose to his feet. It was not something he even though about, more of an involuntary reaction. The girl standing in front of him was stunning ... radiant ... and he found himself on his feet without even thinking about it. She was wearing a light pink satin gown, demurely bare shouldered except for a narrow braid. It flowed down to her feet and had Paul looked he would have seen that her shoes matched the dress perfectly, but he couldn't take his eyes off of Betsy's face to look at her feet.

Jim was also on his feet, but he had no eyes for Betsy. His were

315

rooted on Jennifer. Her dress was a light blue satin affair with dark blue trim. "Oh my," he said, "You look so lovely."

Jennifer smiled broadly.

Paul drew in a deep breath and tried to find something to say. Finally he just sighed and reached out and took Betsy's hand, "You … are … so … beautiful." The overwhelming sincerity of his words earned him the loveliest smile he had ever seen.

"Thank you, Paul," Betsy said and took his hand.

"Twitter patted," Jim had whispered to Paul as they offered the girls their arms to escort them to the dance. "I think we've been twitter patted."

Paul recognized Jim's reference to the Disney movie Bambi, "Yeah, something like that," he replied under his breath.

As they walked into the dining hall that had been converted into a ballroom, they all noticed that most of the tables had been removed. The only ones remaining were set up against the walls on two sides of the room. They contained del droids set up for beverages and snacks. The hall was already full of many students and the orchestra of elves that had come up from Co-re-alis was filing into the hall with their instruments and would start to play shortly.

Paul glanced at Jim and noticed that it was crowded over by the del droids. There weren't any girls over there though. Mostly what was happening was that the boys would leave the girls and go over and get the beverages and then return. The older girls did not seem to be accompanying the older boys over. That worked for him.

"Would you like some punch?" Paul asked Betsy.

"Yes, thank you," she answered.

A few minutes later Professor Barnard Nimrodel came in and strode to the podium. He tapped three times on it with a conductor's baton, and then began conducting a waltz.

"I love the waltzes," Betsy said casually.

Paul knew enough to understand that this was a signal. "Would you like to dance?" he asked.

"Oh, I'd love to," Betsy answered, and they made their way out to the area of the dining hall that had been set up for a dance floor. They were not alone. One of the characteristics that the Atlantans were looking for in their students was assertiveness, and the floor filled quickly with couples. He and Betsy joined them, and they soon found themselves having an excellent time.

"You know," he said as they were waiting for the elves to begin another piece, "We are getting pretty good at this."

"Yes," Betsy agreed, "We are."

They danced several more dances, and then took a break for refreshments. Then there was more dancing, followed by another break and so on.

Time flew by. Some of the older students were beginning to make their way towards the hallway. It would lead them back to Fellowship Hall and from there to the greenhouse.

Paul looked at his watch. "Three hours!" He looked at Betsy. "We've been dancing for three hours. Time is flying!"

Betsy broke into another of those radiant smiles, delighted that Paul had gotten so wrapped up that he had lost all track of time. "I'm having a good time too," was all she said.

"Are you ready to head down?" Paul asked.

"Yes," Betsy answered.

Paul looked over at Jim and Jennifer who had walked off of the dance floor and over to them. "How about you guys?"

"Yeah," Jim agreed, looking at his watch, "We've got plenty of time until our reservation, but it's a good idea to start."

They walked to the greenhouse. Jim and Jennifer followed and moments later they were down in the Civic Center of Co-re-alis. Baralicia had shown Paul the way to Hangin' In so he led the four of them. They walked past the hospital and several other civic buildings and came to the park. It consisted of an acre of grounds with well-manicured walking paths, several gazebos where a couple could sit and talk, as well as strategically located benches. On one side was one restaurant; on the other was the second.

"I made our reservation at the one that serves German food," Paul announced, "It's called Mader's."

"What does the other one serve?" Betsy asked.

"It's more Mediterranean," Paul answered. He looked at her and shrugged, "I thought we'd try the German stuff first."

The food was excellent. After dinner they went for a walk, hand in hand in a park. It was a perfect evening. One they would remember for the rest of their lives. When Paul and Jim finally made their way back to their room neither had a lot to say. The vision of a girl dressed up in an evening gown needed no amplification.

Chapter Sixteen
Show Time

John Moriarty took the bank bag from the courier and waited for him to leave. He looked quickly. The cash he had become accustomed to finding there was in its usual envelopes in its normal amounts. He removed half of the money in Ben's envelope and put it in his own. He placed Ben's in his suit coat and headed for the mill floor.

Ben Johnson watched Moriarty coming towards him. He was talking to two of his foremen. Moriarty would join the conversation for a few moments to be polite and when the foremen left, the real meeting would begin. It would start with the cash, and then proceed to the hydrazine disposal. Ben knew quite well that there could be no one around for that meeting. Lately John Moriarty had been acting a little funny, and Ben had begun thinking about carrying a tape recorder, but he hadn't decided to go that far. Not yet anyway. The truth was that the money was nice. The cash in the envelopes came to $60,000 dollars a year … extra … above and beyond his salary.

Had he known that this was half of what the company actually sent him, and that Moriarty was skimming the rest he would have been furious. He didn't know but even so, he had decided he wanted out. What they were doing gnawed at his conscience especially after they had switched from sodium hydroxide to hydrazine. It was becoming something he didn't want to do no matter how much money was involved. There were things in life more important than money. The problem was that he simply could not tell Moriarty that he was not going to play ball anymore. Moriarty held most of the cards. At least as long as he worked for Apex Paper, but he had begun circulating his resume and looking for another job. Once he found one, he would leave the dirty work to Moriarty and set about clearing his conscience.

ψ

The members of Q3 stood by the rocky outcropping where they had hidden their equipment. It was time to go back to retrieve the data. Ornith was perched on Paul's shoulder. Paul had tried to talk him out of it but Ornith was coming and that was that.

"OK," Jennifer began "Everyone knows how to disable the cloaking devices, right?"

"Right!" The other three answered in a chorus.

Paul looked around at his friends. "We all know what happened last time. Let's be extra careful. Is everyone ready? OK hoods up everyone. Everyone check the pixies."

There were nods all around as everyone's hoods came up. He and Ornith had fashioned a special shoulder seat. It looked more like a sock but appearances can be deceiving. There was an Atlantan material similar in function to Velcro on the bottom, and that firmly attached it to the uniform. It would not let a Pix or Pixie fall off. They had made four of them and all were in use. No one wanted a repeat of what had happened to Ornith. "OK. Jennifer and I will wait here until Betsy and Jim have

320

verified that there is no vessel in that stack."

Betsy nodded. "Once we check that out, we'll call you, and then retrieve the video cam."

"And we'll Jump to the top of the stack," Jennifer concluded, "And retrieve the Chromatograph and the computer."

"Right," Jim agreed with a nod, "After that we all meet at the edge of the meadow."

"OK," Paul acknowledged, "We're all ready, so let's go do this thing." Jim and Betsy disappeared. "You're sure you really want to go back up there," Paul asked Ornith one last time.

"I'm going Paul," Ornith answered, "You're ... going ... so ... I'm ... going."

Jim and Betsy had Jumped into the stack room in a "Cloaked" condition and it was a good thing. There were four men in there pulling a vessel out of the south stack. Over by the doorway leading back into the Mill itself were four more. The last time they had been in the stack room, there had been two of the vessels by the north stack and one by the south stack, plus the one inside.

"It looks like they only have four of those vessels," Jim said quietly.

"Yeah," Betsy agreed, "And they are pulling one out of the south stack now."

"Look," Jim pointed at the men removing the vessel; "Those guys aren't wearing masks like last time."

"That must mean that the vessels are empty."

"Right," Jim agreed, "But do we have any way to know how long

321

they have been empty?"

"Good question," Betsy answered looking around the room. "Well ... there are their masks over there." She pointed at the desk by the door. "So they brought them, but at some point they decided they didn't need them."

"So that vessel has been in there long enough so that they were sure it was empty," Jim concluded.

"So we're OK, but there could re residues left over in the stack for some time," she noted.

"True, but they probably never clean them out completely. It's been long enough that the main release is over. The masks should protect them."

Betsy nodded, "Georaldon said they would. He should know.""

"OK, I'll tell them," Jim said activating his comm unit, "But we can't turn off the Cloaking device on the video cam until these guys leave."

"Right," Betsy agreed. "We'll have to wait them out."

ψ

Paul looked at Jennifer after he had signed off with Jim. She nodded. Seconds later, when the colors stopped swirling, he was on the platform and moved quickly out of the way so Jennifer would have an unobstructed Jump. A couple more seconds and she was up on the platform too.

"I'll disconnect the comm cable," Paul said and got down on all fours and crawled over to the chromatograph. He unscrewed the cable coming out of the back.

"We've got good data," Jennifer announced. She had booted up the computer's recall function to be sure that they had the data. "I'm saving it to a disk and shutting down. How are you doing Paul?"

"I've got the sampling tube disconnected," Paul replied. "I'm starting on the chromatograph now. It will only take a second."

"OK," Jennifer said, "saving to disk is complete. I'm ready. How are you doing Renalee?"

"I'm fine," the Pixie answered.

"I'm about done here too," Paul said. "How are you doing Ornith?"

"I'm OK. I have my hood up and can't smell anything. I would remember that smell."

"I'll bet you would," Paul said as he finished. "OK. I'm done, Jennifer. Let's get to the meadow."

ψ

Betsy and Jim had waited almost ten minutes for the men in the stack room to push the four empty vessels out of the stack room and leave before they de-Cloaked the video camera. Once the men were gone, the de-Cloaking and retrieval was simple.

"Ready?" Jim asked.

"Ready, let's go," Betsy replied. Both of them knew that Paul and Jennifer had the more dangerous job and they were anxious to rejoin their friends. They both Jumped to the meadow and found that Paul and Jennifer had beaten them there.

"No problems, Ornith?" Jim asked.

"No," the little Pix answered with a thin smile, but that was all he said. It was clear that he had been worried and was relieved to be down.

ψ

"Look over there," one of the guards stationed with the dogs on the other side of the meadow said, "It's those kids."

The second guard looked in the direction the first guard pointed. "You're right," his partner replied, "Let the dogs out."

"You don't want to yell at 'em first? See if they go away?"

"No," the second guard answered, "Our instructions are clear. If we see them we say nothing. Just let the dogs out, and call the guard captain to help clean up the mess. Then we're supposed to go chasing after the dogs like they got out by accident."

"But they are just kids," protested the first guard.

"I know," answered the second guard with a cruel sneer, "And they are going to get chewed up or worse." He looked at his partner with a hard stare, "But I need this job. So do you, and we have our instructions."

There was nothing the first guard could say to that. "OK, let's go let them out," he said finally with resignation. The two guards went over to the kennel gate, and rattled it several times to get the dogs attention and get them riled up. Then they opened the gate. All eight dogs went running out of the kennel. They saw the Q3'ers and began charging across the

324

meadow.

$$\psi$$

"Doggies," Ornith called out, "Doggies are coming."

"Let's get out of here," Paul said and tried to Jump.

The same bong he had heard before went off. *"Warning,"* it said, *"You have exceeded the allowed energy draw. It will be fifteen minutes before the belt is sufficiently recharged for you to transport or cloak."*

"So that's what you meant last time?" Betsy said.

"Yeah," Paul said realizing she had heard the same warning as he spun around from the mill and looked back into the meadow behind them. He saw Rottweilers charging across the meadow towards them. "Darn," he exclaimed, "We can't Jump for fifteen minutes. None of us. Can you tell how many dogs, Ornith?"

"Eight," the Pix said.

"Do you have flashblasters?" Paul asked as a plan developed in his mind.

"Yep," Ornith answered.

"Wait a minute," Betsy said quickly. "He can't go after all eight of those dogs by himself."

"Of course not," Ornith answered as Aurileol, Gwenivere, and Renalee flew down.

"We have flashblasters too," Gwenivere announced.

"You do?" Betsy asked in surprise.

"Yep," all of the Pixies said.

325

"OK, then. Are you guys all right with this?" Paul asked.

"Yes," Gwenivere answered, "Ornith is the best at this game but we have all played it. As long as we stay in the woods we will be fine."

"Why do you need to stay in the woods?" Paul asked hurriedly.

"Because we need trees to dodge around," Ornith answered. "We can hold them off for a little while. Maybe nine or seven minutes. You need to find a place to hide."

Paul began looking around frantically as the dogs closed on their position.

"Over there," Jim yelled, "See those rocks. Over there those men won't be able to track us. We can get out of the dog's line of sight on the other side of those rocks and loose them."

"Right," Paul agreed, "Let's go. Ornith, we are heading for that outcropping of rocks. We'll see if we can find a place to hide over there."

"OK," Ornith answered, "We'll start chasing the doggies right here."

Paul headed for the outcroppings followed by the other three. Their path took them into the brush on the edge of the meadow and out of the direct line of sight of the guards who were now running across the meadow after the dogs. The members of Q3 picked their way quickly to the outcropping, and climbed up on it. "You guys go ahead and see if you can find a place to hide," Paul called, "I'll stay here and watch."

As Jim forged on with Jennifer and Betsy, looking for a good hiding place, Paul watched as four Pixies took on eight well-trained attack dogs ... dogs that had heard enough fireworks by that time not to be scared of the noise. Ornith waited until the dogs were out of the meadow and into the woods and then flew straight at the lead dog. Just like before, that tactic stopped the dog in his tracks. As Ornith got close to the dog's head he feinted to the right drawing the dog's attention in that direction, and then cut sharply around to the left, swatting the Rottweiler on the ear as he flew by. This maneuver startled the dog and he snapped at Ornith, but when the dog's massive muzzle snapped shut there was nothing there but air. The little Pix had moved out of the way and the tactic had produced exactly the result Ornith wanted. The dog had stopped and Ornith could toss the flashblaster so that it would go off in front of the dog's eyes.

BAMM!!! A silver slammer went off. Unknown to John Moriarty, you could train a dog to get used to the noise, but not the flash of light. That dog would be useless for a couple of minutes while his eyes recovered.

BAMM!!! An orange crusher tossed by Gwenivere went off followed immediately by a blue blaster tossed by Aurileol and a green weenie by Renalee.

Ornith spotted another dog and chased after him. In short order all eight of the dogs were blinded by the light, but one by one they recovered and took up the battle again, not with the kids of Q3 but with the Pixies who were tormenting them. Once again Paul watched as Ornith and the rest buzzed the dogs. Just like the first time, one by one, the dogs sat down on their haunches and began pawing at their eyes for the effects of the flashblasters.

It was working. The dogs were stopped, at least temporarily.

"Over here!" Paul heard Jim cry and looked around. He ran over to where Jim was standing. On the backside of the outcropping was a small natural cave. It looked like it might be hard to get down there, but that would actually work in their favor.

"Comm unit on ... Ornith," Paul said, activating his communicator and connecting with Ornith.

"Ornith here," came the reply.

"How are you doing?"

"Very well. We've chased the doggies three times now. They are all sitting down pawing at their eyes right now."

"Great!" Paul exclaimed.

"We only have two flashblasters left, and the guards are coming now."

"OK, why don't you come back with us?"

"OK," Ornith answered. "We will be there in a minute."

Paul looked at the other members of Q3. "The guards might leave once they get the dogs on leashes."

"And they might not," interjected Jennifer.

"Right," Betsy said. "It depends on whether they let those dogs loose on purpose or by accident."

"Who wants to bet on "accident?" Jim asked.

"Not me," Jennifer said.

"Me neither," Betsy announced.

"So," Paul concluded, "We're unanimous. Let's get down there into that cave."

"Paul," Ornith said as the Pixies joined up with them. He was a little out of breath and swinging his arms like he did for emphasis, "They ... did ... not ... go ... back ... they ... are ... searching."

328

"Did they find our tracks?"

"Yes," Ornith answered and plopped down onto his spot on Paul's shoulder.

"OK," Paul said. "You were great. All of you were."

They scrambled down the rocks above the entrance to the cave. It was difficult going, but after about two minutes they had gotten down to the opening.

"How far back do you think it goes?" Jim asked as they peered into the dark space.

"Don't know," Paul answered.

"What if there is some animal in there?" Jennifer asked.

"We can't wait out here," Betsy said, "We'll have to chance it."

"No we won't," Paul said as he remembered the conversation he'd had with Georaldon about the predators in the Outer Ring of Co-re-alis. He held out his Power Ring, "Light" he said, and a bright light jumped out from the ring and lit up the cave, "Come on," Paul said and started making his way into the cave. "We've got almost eight more minutes until we can Jump."

Paul moved the light back and forth as they maneuvered their way back into the cave. It was only slighter higher than six feet. After a few feet they came across the remains of a campfire.

"Someone's been in here before," Paul noted as he worked his way around the charred rocks.

Jim reached down and felt the remains of the wood. "Yeah, but it's been a while,"

They followed the cave back about fifteen feet and came to a small bend. Paul shined his light around the corner. The cave went back another ten feet and ended. The section containing the bend was narrow. They would have to walk single file through that choke point. Just on the other side, Paul noticed a big branch. It was about three feet long, and an inch thick. As his friends filed past him he looked the situation over. There was no way more than two of those dogs could get through that space at one time. If he had to, he could use the stick and hold the dogs back so he bent over and picked it up.

ψ

The guards, with the dogs on their leashes were totally baffled. "I don't get it," the second guard said to his partner, "How did them kids get away from the dogs?"

"We were pretty far away," the first one said, "Too far away to tell for sure, but when one of those firecrackers went off a dog would sit down and start pawing at his eyes. That's all I could see."

"It must have been the flashes blinding them"

"Probably."

"They'll need a minute to get their eyes back to normal. Then we can track 'em."

"How did those kids get close enough to use firecrackers like that?"

"I don't know," the first guard said, "But it don't make no difference. All we have to do is follow their tracks. Let's go."

The guards waited a minute until the dogs were ready and then followed the tracks; first to the brush, and then around to the outcropping of rocks. "These kids are smart," the second guard said. "We can't track 'em across the rocks."

"No. But we can pick up where they left on the other side,"

"Yeah, let's go."

The guards clamored quickly across the rock outcropping. More by accident than by skill, they happened directly on the spot above the cave.

"OK," the second guard said, "There ain't no tracks leading away."

"That means they are still around here somewhere," the first guard concluded. "Let's split up and look around some more."

One of the guards took four of the dogs and went in one direction, and the other one went the other way. The second guard happened upon the cave entrance quickly. "Hey! Look here," he shouted to his partner.

ψ

Paul's watch hands glowed in the dark. As his eyes adjusted to the darkness, he looked at his watch carefully and did the math in his head. "Four minutes," Paul whispered. They had a little less than four more minutes left before they could Jump.

Paul could hear the guard shout and looked at his watch again. "Three more minutes," he announced in a voice that was barely a whisper.

"What do we do if they let those dogs come in here?" Jennifer asked. There was urgency in her voice.

"We can chase them," Ornith suggested, "But we only have two flashblasters left."

"No," Paul decided quickly, "There are no trees to dodge around in here. I've watched them snap at you. It's too dangerous. If you couldn't get far enough away they would bite you in half. It's narrow up at that choke point and only one or two can get in there at a time. I've got this branch and in a tight space like that I can beat them back for as long as we need."

"Maybe they won't find us," Betsy hoped aloud.

"Shhh … " Jim said, "I hear something."

ψ

"Do you suppose them kids is back in there?" the second guard asked as he peered into the darkness of the cave.

"I don't know. Did you bring a flashlight?"

"No! Why would I do that? It's broad daylight."

"I was just hoping. I don't really want to go in there without a light. Do you?"

"Nope. Let's let the dogs in"

The first guard looked at the snarling dogs, teeth bared, straining at their leashes. "If those kids are in there, they won't have any chance at all."

"That's the general idea," the second guard said as he started taking off the leashes. He released the dogs and they went charging into the cave.

ψ

Paul could hear the dogs coming. "Glove … Hood," he said. The uniform quickly covered his hands, and completely hooded his head. He picked up the branch and moved to within three feet of the narrow bend with the branch held out in front of him. The first Rottweiler came charging into the narrow spot and Paul rushed forward straight at the dog. Dogs, even trained attack dogs, are not prepared for that. The lead dog dug in his heels to stop and snarled. Paul brought the branch down hard on his snout and the dog yelped in pain. The dogs coming up from behind were crashing into the first one. A second dog tried to get around the first one and Paul hit it on top of its head too. The first dog tried to move closer and Paul raised the branch and quickly hit the first dog again. He kept hitting at first one dog then the other. They were yelping and snarling, but they had stopped. The rest of the dogs were bottled up behind the first two.

"OK," Betsy said, "We can Jump now I think."

"You guys go on and make sure," Paul said urgently. "I'll hold them until we know.

"OK," Betsy said, "We're ready."

The three of them disappeared, but Paul was not watching them. He was continuing to hit the two dogs with the stick.

"We can go now," Ornith announced, "Everyone else has Jumped.

Paul visualized the rear gate to the school, dropped the stick and tapped his fingers. The kaleidoscope of colors was a welcome sight and when they stopped he was standing with his friends.

Paul sucked in a long breath and let it out slowly.

"That was a little close," Betsy said.

"Yes … Yes it was," Jim said as the four friends looked at each other, and then he smiled, "But we did it! We really did it."

"Sweet!" Betsy announced.

"Totally," they all responded

"Let's get up to the school library and get a look at our data," Jennifer suggested.

"OK," Paul said quietly and looked at Betsy, "But let's get the gas chromatograph back down to Co-re-alis first."

"That's a good idea, Paul," Betsy agreed and looked at Jennifer. "Have you gotten everything you need?"

"I've downloaded all of it onto a disk. Why don't you let me make three copies first?"

Jennifer sat down on the grass and booted up the laptop. In less than a minute she had the copies. "OK. I'm finished," she said getting to her feet.

Betsy looked at Paul, "Ready?"

"Yeah," Paul said and picked up the instrument while Betsy picked up the laptop, "We'll see you guys in the library."

Paul and Betsy materialized the main Library in Co-re-alis. In a matter of minutes they had returned the gas chromatograph. They Jumped to a place just outside of Fellowship Hall and joined Jim and Jennifer. The four of them sat down and began sifting through what they had.

"There," Jennifer said pointing to the computer screen. "There is the first release."

"Yep," Betsy said, "And look over here. It's a positive ID for hydrazine."

"It sure is," Paul agreed. "Let's see if that ties in with what we have on the video camera." They looked at their video records, and sure enough, fifteen minutes before the release; a vessel had been loaded into the south stack.

"OK," Betsy said with satisfaction, "We've got them. What's next?"

"We print out this data and get it to the right places," Jennifer answered.

"When?" Paul asked.

"Well. Today's Saturday," Jim said, "And it's getting late, "Why don't we do it tomorrow."

"Tomorrow!" everyone said in agreement.

Chapter Seventeen

Consequences

On Sunday afternoon they split up into two groups as before. Paul and Betsy had the EPA and the Washington Post. Jim and Jennifer had the local paper and the FBI. This time everyone knew exactly where they were going. They started after lunch. By the end of the day, they had left packages for all four groups, and they had left no trace.

Paul and Betsy were standing outside of the Washington Post. "We did it," Betsy said.

"Yes," Paul agreed, "But it's not over. Not until we find out how much trouble we're in."

"Right," Betsy agreed. They took one last look at the Washington Post and Jumped back to the school.

By noon on Monday, while the members of Q3 were sitting in their classes, things were moving. The Washington Post had called the EPA and the FBI for confirmation. Of course neither group would confirm anything, but the fact that the Post had the story got both groups working on what their next moves might be. In a fashion that was typical of Washington, both the FBI, and the EPA began checking the political connections of Apex Paper. Then the Hawk's Nest Examiner called. Still neither group would confirm, but the reporter from the Examiner let the FBI know that the EPA had the data too. That got the FBI into high gear. Action had to be taken. If two different papers had it, one large and one small, as well as another agency of the Federal government, the story was going to get out. The last thing the FBI, or the EPA for that matter, needed was for a story like this to break with them having taken no action. On the other hand, if the story broke along with details of action being taken, that would work out very well. Late Monday afternoon, the FBI, together with the EPA were in Federal Court seeking a search warrant.

It was granted. No one knew where the data came from, but since search warrants were granted on a routine basis as a result of anonymous tips, no one cared. The data was credible and that was more than sufficient to get warrants for legal searches to produce the evidence on which convictions could be based.

At 7:00 AM, the FBI and the EPA were in Hawk's Nest working out their game plan. The FBI would handle all of the criminal investigation matters but they wanted the EPA's Hazardous Materials experts on site. The EPA was only too happy to cooperate. At precisely fifteen minutes past eight, the authorities planned to move in.

ψ

John Moriarty sat at his desk reading the report from his Chief of Security. There had been an incident involving students from the school over the weekend. Against all odds, the dogs had not chewed those teenagers up.

That was hard to believe.

The dogs had not actually succeeded in biting one of them. No blood had been found, not anywhere. No blood – no bites, not from those dogs.

That was even harder to believe.

The guards had found footprints and had tracked them to a cave. They thought they had the students cornered in there. When a flashlight was finally found, the tracks that led into the cave were explored. They were footprints. The size that would be left by young teenagers, and they went into the cave. There was no way out, but the kids were not there, and could not possibly have snuck past the guards. It was a mystery and the only conclusion that his Chief of Security could come to was that the tracks were older ones, left on a previous visit. The man had no explanation as to how the students could have gotten away, so he concluded that they had not been in the cave at the time.

Moriarty thought about that for a minute.

So the students had gone in there. The tracks had to belong to someone, and they were the wrong size for adults. His Security chief had come to the only logical conclusion, but Moriarty smelled a rat. Something was wrong. Those kids had been there. He didn't know where they had gone, or how they had gotten away, but they had.

How they had done it was not important at the moment. Why had they come back at all? Even more important, why did they continue coming back? That was the question. He did not have a good answer, and that made him nervous. There was nothing special about that particular meadow … except that it was behind the mill. There were thousands of places to explore in the park if what they wanted was a nature walk … thousands … unless … the object of their interest was the mill itself.

Moriarty tapped his fingers as his mind continued to race.

338

That was it. Those kids were back there snooping on the mill.

He sat tapping his fingers on the table. Ben had released hydrazine over the weekend. Those kids were part of a science academy, were they not? An academy staffed by scientists who were also teachers. The worst possible combination. Teachers were idealists. Why else would anyone go into teaching? There wasn't any money in it. They went into teaching because they were Do Gooders. Scientists were notorious for their environmental sympathies, and they had the training to do something about it. The combination was dangerous.

"Do Gooders," he said with a sneer.

Whatever those students were doing, their teachers could be behind it somehow, and that made the problem worse. He remembered the woman in the ally. Kids by themselves were not going to be a problem. They would not have the recourses to collect any truly incriminating data. Not by themselves. But if those students had gotten a whiff of something wrong … if they had gone to their teachers … the teachers would have access to air sampling equipment. Getting nosey kids to take air samples behind the mill, as a science project was just the sort of thing that teachers like the one he had encountered would encourage.

"Blast all Do Gooders!" he exclaimed.

He reached over and booted up his computer. The only records he had ever kept were in some files on his private drive on the computer on his desk. He had some notes …. calculations concerning the profitability of switching over to hydrazine mostly, but there were at least two with costs of dumping vs. disposal. There was not much, but it didn't take much to connect him to what Ben was doing. If those files were found, he could not plead ignorance and that would be a disaster. He simply could not take the risk. Years ago he had installed a program that would scrub any trace of selected files from his computer. He accessed the program and selected the files and activated the program. When it was finished, it would erase itself without a trace. In ten minutes the only evidence connecting him to illegal disposal operations would be gone.

ψ

There were two teams. Each was composed of eight FBI agents, and two EPA experts. One team moved stealthily through the forest near the Mill around to the back of the plant itself and took up a position behind the brush line and waited. The other team drove to a position that was just out of sight of the guardhouse. Once everyone was in position the team leader gave a signal. The team in front moved rapidly to the guardhouse threw open the door and served their warrants on the two guards there. They were informed not to call the office, but one of the guards tried to anyway. He was restrained and then both were handcuffed and left on the floor of the guard shack.

The agent in charge of the front group keyed the microphone on his radio, "Guardhouse secure," he said.

That was the signal for the group in the rear to move. They cut down the fence, and broke down the door to the stack room. There were four workers preparing to place a hydrazine tank into the north stack. The mill employees were presented with copies of the search warrants. None of them put up a struggle and the area was secured. One of the EPA experts looked at the tank carefully and then nodded at the agent in charge of that group, "Red-handed," she said.

The front group had split into two groups. One went immediately into the plant to secure that area. The EPA people went with that group. The four FBI agents went into the office building itself.

An important portion of the evidence would be the company's own records. There would be little difficulty gaining the evidence that the company was releasing toxic waste but in order for criminal charges to be filed against specific individuals, evidence had to be secured proving who was responsible. Testimony of individual actions were required to charge individuals with a crime. Sometimes that testimony came from individuals, but more often that evidence would come from the company's records. There would be no paper shredding, or burning to impede this investigation. One agent remained at reception to prevent her from spreading an alert; one went to accounting to secure those records. Two went to Moriarty's office.

John Moriarty's secretary was busy typing a letter when two Federal Officers stepped briskly in.

She looked up. She was not used to people coming into her area without first having been announced by the receptionist at the front desk. "Who are you ... barging in here like this?' she demanded.

"FBI, Ma'am" the agent said showing the secretary her badge, "We have search warrants. Is that Moriarty's Office?" she asked pointing at the door behind the desk.

"You can't go in there," Moriarty's secretary insisted.

"Oh, yes we can," a different agent said and tapped the warrant.

The secretary reached over to push an intercom button to alert John Moriarty, but one of the FBI agents grabbed her hand. "Not a good idea, Ma'am," she said firmly.

The other agent walked over, drew his gun and threw open the door.

John Moriarty had a completely shocked look on his face as he looked up from the scrubbing program to find a man with a gun standing in his doorway. The gun was not pointed at him. It was pointed down and away, but it was in the man's hand none the less. In the man's other hand was a Badge.

At that moment as John Moriarty looked at a Federal Officer standing in his doorway with a gun in his hand he had never been so glad of a decision in his life. The scrubbing program had only a few seconds left to go and all he needed to do was stall.

"FBI," the agent announced, and moved to the side. All FBI agents had seen training films of a person behind a desk shooting through the front of the desk. That was almost impossible when the law enforcement officer was standing to one side. "Put your hands on the desk and then move away," he ordered.

"I don't understand," Moriarty said, but he did understand. All he needed was a few more seconds.

"Just do it," the agent said, "Do it now!"

The agent out with the secretary called in to her partner, "I can't shut the system down from in here. They are not networked."

"Get your hands out where I can see them and move away from that desk," the agent in with Moriarty demanded.

342

John Moriarty was no fool. All he had to do was stall for about five more seconds, and no one would be able to prove he knew anything. He eased away from his desk and brought his hands out slowly, "Of course officer," he said putting his hands on top of the desk as slowly as possible.

"Move away from the desk," the agent commanded, "Now."

Moriarty complied, but slowly, and then he saw his computer screen go blank. He got up calmly and moved out of the agent's way. By the time the agent slid into the chair, the notes were gone, the scrub program was gone ... not even a ghost in the machine remained.

He was clean.

His superiors were clean.

Ben Johnson was the only one who was not. That was a pity, but you couldn't make an omelet without breaking some eggs.

Moriarty counted the cost as the agent searched for evidence. There would be a fine. Probably a large one. Corporate would pay that and not even blink. It would be a pittance compared to the money they had saved.

There would be special monitoring installed that would prevent further dumping of waste acids through the stack. That was OK because he could find other ways. The mill might be shut down for a month ... two at the most. After that it would be allowed to re-open. The 287 jobs the mill provided were too important to the region.

All in all, this would not turn out to be too big a deal in John Moriarty's world. The same would not be said for Ben Johnson. Ben Johnson's life as he knew it was over.

The members of Q3 were leaving self-defense class. There was one more week of classes. The next week would be spent studying and the following week they would take their semester exams. Once their exams were complete they would be off for three weeks. Professor Glorfyndor was standing outside the class. "Would you four accompany me to my office?" he asked.

Paul looked at Betsy. There was no way out of this. "Sure," he said simply.

They followed the professor to his office, and as they entered, they noticed that four chairs had been set up in front of the professor's desk and two more, flanking his chair behind the desk. There was no question as to where they were to sit, so Paul walked over to one of the four chairs and sat down. His Quadromates followed silently.

Professor Glorfyndor walked around his desk and as he did so, Professors Galvyndor and Flyndor joined him. All three sat down as well. Professor Glorfyndor slid a newspaper over to each of the students. Paul picked up his. It was a copy of the Hawk's Nest Examiner.

"BUSTED !!! " screamed the headlines. It was followed by a story about the FBI / EPA raid on the Apex Paper Mill. There was a picture of the mill and a picture of John Moriarty standing by while another man, unidentified by the picture, was being led away in handcuffs. The mill had been shut down for thirty days for full testing by the EPA. The field agent in charge of the investigation said that no evidence had been developed to suggest that John Moriarty knew about the waste dumping but that Ben Johnson had been arrested in connection with the crime.

"Could this story possibly have any connection with the fact that a gas chromatograph was checked out of the Library at Co-re-alis a month ago and was checked back in yesterday?" he asked solemnly.

"Yes, sir," Paul answered slowly, "It is connected."

"Could this story possibly have any connection with the fact that Ornith was missing for almost three weeks?" he asked just as solemnly.

"You knew about that?" Paul said quickly.

"Of course, Paul," Professor Galvyndor answered in a voice as solemn as the one Professor Glorfyndor was using. "We really don't miss much."

"Yes, sir … er … ma'am," Paul answered, not knowing who to direct the answer towards. "There is a connection. He's OK though."

"We know that too, Paul." the professor said. "The Seniors here all run graded C-Ops. You know that. One thing you don't know is that we're set up to monitor all sorts of things. We do not eavesdrop on Atlantans, but we do monitor things in general. Another thing you don't know is that the safety and health of Atlantans always takes precedence over the success of those operations. That includes Pixies. While it is true that Ornith is doing fine now, it is also true that he was seriously injured."

"It's my fault," Betsy blurted out suddenly, "I was the one who pushed to do something in the beginning."

"No … it's not," Jim said firmly looking first Betsy and then back to the Professor, "We did this together, sir. All of us."

"That's right," Paul and Jenifer agreed in unison.

The three professors smiled. "Fault," Professor Flyndor explained, "is not exactly a word to use in this context. Fault denotes a mistake, and that has yet to be determined. It is certainly not a "Fault" to try and correct a wrong. Yes, Ornith was hurt, but in Atlantan Society we don't play blame games about things like that. Not with people who are willing to learn. Mistakes may well have been made, but in response to that, we of Atlantis … teach. You have conducted an unauthorized C-Op but that is not a rules violation. You're not in trouble for that. There is a debriefing after all C-Ops. It's how we learn from both our successes and our failures. We are here to talk about this particular operation. If mistakes were made, we want you to learn from them; so perhaps you should just explain exactly what happened."

The explanation took the better part of two hours. Dinnertime came and went and the professors had a Del droid sent in to serve dinner. It floated into their office in the middle of Paul telling about the Jump down to Co-re-alis with Ornith.

"Let me be sure I understand you correctly," Professor Galvyndor asked carefully, "You dove headfirst off of a three-hundred foot smoke stack to rescue Ornith?"

"That is exactly what he did, Ma'am," Betsy said. The pride in her voice was unmistakable.

"And you had figured out what to do in advance if there was a problem, so you knew you wouldn't be hurt?" Professor Glorfyndor asked.

"Yes, sir," was all Paul could think of to say.

"Remarkable," the professor said looking at his two colleagues. "Simply remarkable."

"How did you know to go to Co-re-alis?" Professor Galvyndor asked. "That was exactly the right thing to do, but you are not taught those procedures until your junior year."

"Georaldon told me what to do if there was ever a medical emergency," Paul answered.

"Did he know of your plans?"

"No," Paul answered, "Although we had to tell him once Ornith got hurt."

"What did he say?"

"He said that as a sponsor he was not required to inform you," Paul began.

"At what point did he say that," Professor Galvyndor asked abruptly.

Paul hesitated for a second. He could tell from her tone of voice that the answer could have consequences for Georaldon. Finally Paul realized that stalling was not going to help. "It was after the doctor told us they had Ornith stabilized," he answered slowly. "He asked if we intended to finish this C-Op."

"Gwenivere," Betsy interrupted, "told them that if we didn't then all of this was for nothing."

"For future reference, that is not exactly true," Professor Flyndor corrected, "As far into this as you were, we would have made arrangements for someone to take over." She looked back at Paul, "Please continue,"

"Georaldon made us promise we'd use our hoods when we went back up there," Paul explained, "and made sure that we all understood that if we'd been wearing them that none of this would have happened. He and Baralicia said that if we'd promise to wear them when we went back they wouldn't say anything. He said that this would all come out though. He said that all C-Ops had an inquiry afterwards, and that it would be better if the operation were successfully concluded before it happened. The last thing he said was to be careful. If we had any questions about safety to back off and get help."

"All true ... all true," Professor Glorfyndor said with a nod. "This is the inquiry he spoke of by the way."

"Oh," all four students said in unison.

"Go, on, Paul," the Professor urged, and Paul finished the story.

"Before we get into the specifics, I need to inquire as to your grades." He looked at two other professors.

"Their grades aren't great, but they are more than good enough," Professor Flyndor said as she referred to some notes. "They all received acceptable marks on their mid-terms and their homework is up to date. There is no reason to believe they will not pass their first semester final exams. As to the term ending exams before summer," she looked directly at all four students, "those are a lot harder, and they will need to pick things up a bit by then, but there is time enough for that."

"OK." Professor Glorflyndor began "So the time they spent on this C-Op hasn't harmed their academic standing?"

"Perhaps a little, but not overall," Professor Flyndor concluded.

"Good," the Headmaster agreed and looked at the members of Q3. "No outside activity, however well-conceived, can be good if it interferes with what we are trying to teach you. We eventually need you to run a hundred C-Ops not just one," stated Professor Glorfyndor as he stroked his beard in thought. "In hindsight, is there anything you would do differently?"

"Wear our hoods," both Paul and Jennifer said in unison.

"Make sure the Pixies had more of those flashblasters. We ran out," Betsy added.

"Well," Professor Glorflyndor said with a smile, "there are other things on your belts you could have used too. You'll learn more about that next year."

"Or sooner," Professor Galvyndor interjected, "Probably sooner for these four. They seem to be figuring a lot of this out on their own."

"I am junior here," Professor Flyndor stated, "So under the Rules of Atlantan Inquiry, I will state my findings first. These students should be instructed that in the event they are going into an area with potentially dangerous fumes, there are protective breathing devices that could be used, not just the hoods, and further that it is the responsibility of the humans to see to it that the pixies are using whatever protective equipment that has been selected. Other than that lapse, this is a satisfactory C-Op. Were they Seniors, they would have been instructed in the necessity to use hoods and other protective gear, and the failure to do so would have caused me to give them a grade of "C-". However, they are not Seniors and had not been instructed in such procedures. They learned a great deal on their own, and if they'd had a little more concern for their safety, they could have learned about those devices too. For that reason, I cannot give them an "A". I would grade this C - Op as "B-", and believe it should be so recorded in their permanent files."

Professors Galvyndor and Glorfyndor looked at each other for a moment and then nodded, "So ordered," the Headmaster said to the computer recording the session, "this inquiry is concluded." He looked at the four students. "Well done. Very well done indeed!"

"Do those grades count in the Quadro Bowl?" Jennifer asked.

"Yes they do," Professor Galvyndor answered with a smile, "they most certainly do. Your quadro picks up eight points altogether. That's what you get for a B- on a C-Op"

The four of them looked at each other. This they were not expecting. The extra eight points would put them into first place, two points ahead of Q5.

"Next time," Professor Glorfyndor concluded, "Pay more attention to your personnel safety. As brave as it was to dive off of that stack after Ornith, and being brave is certainly good, in fact nothing truly useful is ever accomplished without a measure of courage, but smarter is better than braver, wiser is better than both and combining all three is best of all. Next time try to be a little wiser."

Paul looked first at Betsy, and then at Jim and Jennifer. There would be a next time and all four of them knew it. They all nodded and Paul looked back at the Professor, "Thank you, Sir."

Author's Note

I hope you enjoyed reading this book as much as I enjoyed writing it. One of the hardest things to do as an author is not the actual writing. That can be daunting, but it is what we love to do. One really hard part is developing an audience. If you have the backing of a major publisher, that is relatively easy. But to get the backing you have to have an audience especially these days, so this turns into a Catch 22. You need the backing to get the audience; you need the audience to get the backing. Developing an audience is always a struggle. This is the same for all authors trying to become established, and you can help. If you like a book and want to help, please tell your friends. That is how audiences are built. If you liked this particular book, I hope you will tell your friends.

Thanks,

Keith Burnett

History of Chorda

Chorda was invented on Atlantis approximately 11,600 years ago. The original names for the pieces came from the military ranks of the nation of Algoras. They have been changed throughout history to reflect the military ranks of different Atlantan nations. In the year 600 AD, an abbreviated version of Chorda, called Chess, was given to the Indus civilization as a test of their intellectual development. In the year 1650 A.D the Atlantans decided to adopt English as their principal language and renamed the pieces after the ranks of English Army Units.

Rules of Chorda

1. Chorda is played on a board similar to a Chessboard except that it is eleven squares in each direction.
2. There are two sides: Green and Gold.
3. The Object of the game is to take your opponents General.
4. Each player has twenty-two pieces. General (1) – One wide strip topped by one medium stripe, Colonel (2) – Four medium stripes, Major (2) – Three medium stripes. Captain (2) – Two medium stripes, 1st Lieutenant (2) – One medium stripe topped by one thin stripe, 2nd Lieutenant (2) – One medium stripe, Sergeant (3) – three chevrons, Private (8) – one chevron.

5. Pieces set up as follows: On the back row beginning at the left, 2nd Lieutenant – 1st Lieutenant – Captain – Major –Colonel – General – Major –Colonel – Captain – 1st Lieutenant – 2nd Lieutenant. The row directly in front of the back row sets up as follows: Private – Private – Sergeant – Private – Private – Sergeant - Private – Private – Sergeant – Private – Private.

6. Pieces move as follows:

General: one space in any direction

Colonel: Unlimited in any direction. May not move through any piece.

Major: Unlimited Diagonally only. May not move through any piece.

Captain: Unlimited Right to Left and Forward and Back only. May not move through any piece.

1st Lieutenant: Two spaces in any direction, or three spaces forward or backward, right or left, followed immediately by two spaces at right angles. (Like a knight in Chess only three spaces by two spaces instead of two by one). May move over pieces, both friend and foe.

2nd Lieutenant: One space in any direction, or two spaces forward or backward, right or left, followed immediately by one space at right angles. (Like a knight in Chess). May move over pieces both friend and foe.

Sergeant: One space in any direction. Attacks only diagonally.

Private: One space forward only. Attacks only diagonally.

7. If the movement of your piece terminates on the space occupied by a piece of your opponents, you take that piece and remove it from the board.

8. Whatever rank piece moves onto a space occupied by the opponent's piece, the piece that was there first is removed regardless of rank.

9. Two pieces of the same side may not occupy the same space.

10. Each move has a time limit. For normal games that time limit is 60 seconds. There is no requirement that a player keep his hand on his game piece. Resetting the timer signifies that the player has completed his move. Failure to complete the move and reset the timer before time expires allows the opposing player to remove any one of the offending player's lowest ranking remaining pieces. Advanced players, by mutual consent, and before the game begins, may agree to different time limits either longer or shorter.

11. Any time a piece is moved into position to threaten the General, "Chorda" must be announced. Failure to announce "Chorda" before resetting the timer incapacitates that piece from making that move. (If you fail to announce "Chorda" you may not take your opponent's General.)

12. Except for Army Colonels, any piece reaching the back row of the opponent may be promoted to the next higher rank. Promoted pieces move according to the pattern of the rank they have been promoted to for the remainder of the game or until taken. Each player receives three rubber promotion rings. After they are used, that player may award no more promotions. Placing one of the rubber rings on the promoted piece signifies promotion. If the opponent takes a promoted piece, the promotion ring is lost with the piece.

The History and Rules of Palacrosse

History

Palacrosse was invented on Atlantis approximately 11,200 years ago. In its first form it was played on a grassy field. About 600 years after the introduction of Palacrosse, Enclosed Court Palacrosse was introduced. At that time the name of Palacrosse as played on a field was changed to Grass Court Palacrosse. The rules of Enclosed Court Palacrosse are similar but it is played inside a fully enclosed court. Doubles - Enclosed Court Palacrosse was, and in some circles, still is, played by two couples, a man and a woman, or a boy and a girl, on each team inside of a court similar to but larger than a racquetball court. Quad - Enclosed Court Palacrosse is played on a court like a racquetball court only larger still. When flying harnesses were developed 9,600 years ago, Palacrosse underwent another transformation, and Flying Palacrosse was developed. Today on Earthantis, as in other Atlantan communities scattered across the Galaxy, Flying Palacrosse is the most popular form of the game although Grass Court Palacrosse, and Enclosed Court Palacrosse still survive in Atlantan culture in their original form. In the year 820 AD, an abbreviated version of this sport was given to the Cherokee Indians. This sport became known as Lacrosse.

Rules

Rules common to all forms:

1. The Wobble is a rubber ball like a racquetball. It is 3" in diameter, with the center of gravity 4% off center. When dropped from a height of 36 inches onto a hard surface, the Wobble must rebound 24 inches. The Wobble weighs 4.5 ounces and is red in color. Beginners may substitute a Racquetball for a Wobble.

2. The true Wobble Paddle is constructed of Aluminum. It has a handle five inches long by 1.25 inches in diameter. It is wrapped by a smooth leather grip that is $1/16^{th}$ of an inch thick. The Paddle itself is also Aluminum. It is ¼ inch thick, circular, 10 inches in diameter, and the center of the circle is 15 inches from the end of the handle. There are $3/8^{th}$ inch diameter holes drilled ½ inch on center. Around the circumference is a ½ inch foam pad. Beginners or those who do not have access to a proper Wobble Paddle may substitute a Padded Racquetball racquet. The padding is essential to protect ones fellow players.

Rules for Grass Court Palacrosse

1. Palacrosse in all of its varieties is a Co-ed sport. It is never played any other way. A Grass Court Palacrosse team consists of two men or boys and two women or girls.

2. The Court Boundaries measure fifty feet by 100 feet.

3. Wobbles going out of bounds are retrieved and brought in bounds by the team that did not hit it out of bounds. The Player doing this stands just out of Bounds at a point not

closer to that team's goal. He must use the Paddle to hit the ball back into the court.

4. The goal is on the centerline of the court, fifteen feet from the end. It is constructed of 2" diameter tubing with an inside diameter of six feet. Its Center is five feet off of the court, and a tubular base holds it there.

5. There is a four-yard radius Exclusion Zone around each goal. Players are not allowed inside of that zone. Entering the Zone by accident is forgiven, however hitting the wobble from within the Zone results in a goal being awarded to the opposite team.

6. Inadvertent contact is a part of this sport. Intentional contact is not. Two players who are closing on the wobble for the purpose of hitting it and who contact each other results in no foul, however, contact is not allowed by players who do not have a legitimate shot at the wobble. If one player has a shot at the wobble and the other does not, no contact is allowed. Screening is a part of this game. Jostling by players where one is attempting to screen the other is not allowed. The player being screened must find a way around the screening player without resorting to contact. Intentional contact is penalized by awarding a goal to the opposing team.

7. There are four ten-minute periods with a five-minute break in-between. Substitutions are not allowed. All of the team's players play for the entire game. Sides are

changed after each period.

8.   A goal results either by penalty as outlined above, or when a player hits the Wobble through the opponent's goal, no matter which direction the Wobble passes through.

9.   Each team is allowed one two-minute time-out per period. They must be in possession of the wobble to call a time-out. After the time-out, they must bring the Wobble back in-Bounds at a point not closer to their opponent's goal as they were when they called the time-out.

10.   Palacrosse teams are either two, four, or six players per team. Protective Headgear similar to hockey helmets is required of all players. Padding is not worn. Spiked shoes are prohibited.

Rules for Enclosed Court Palacrosse

1.   Doubles Palacrosse is played on a racquetball court. The goal is Three feet on it's inside diameter.

2.   The Quad court is the same size as in grass court except that it is walled in. It has a ceiling that is twenty feet high. The Wobble may be played after it bounces off of the side or ceiling walls. There is no out of Bounds. The size of the goal is the same as in grass court.

3.   All other rules are the same.

Rules for Flying Palacrosse

1.   The Field is generated by a field generator. It is sixty yards long

and twenty yards in diameter. All other rules are the same as with Enclosed Court Palacrosse.

www.ingramcontent.com/pod-product-compliance
Lightning Source LLC
Chambersburg PA
CBHW050030030726
47506CB00001B/199

* 9 7 8 0 6 1 5 8 7 2 9 4 0 *